<u>*5.0 out of 5 stars* **Fantastic read!**</u>

Reviewed in the United States on June 22, 2024

Very well written, captivates you and keeps you drawn in. The author is a great writer and I can't wait to read the second book!

– Amazon customer

Responses to William R. DeHay

<u>*5.0 out of 5 stars* Excellent stories of redemption and great character development make this a must-read!</u>

Reviewed in the United States on May 30, 2024

William DeHay is a truly gifted storyteller! I found your first installment of this series hard to put down once I started reading it, and you left me wanting to read the next parts of the story! Your book was an excellent example of what leadership can do for people to lift them out of hopelessness, and how forgiveness, kindness and keeping an open mind about people (even your foes) can be transforming (and bring material and spiritual wealth your way!) My favorite statement by Jamie in the book: "Dreams are sacred. They give us a picture of what our lives could be like. No one should ever laugh at another man's dreams. As brethren, we should encourage each other to dream, and dream big."

What I really liked about the antagonists in the book: if you gave the bully, crook, and pessimist a chance to tell their story, or showed them kindness that they may not deserve, you ended up with a hero, an educated man who cared about the people that worked for him and the welfare of wounded warriors, and turned a pessimist/morale-killer into an optimist. So things aren't always so black and white. I highly recommend this book because it is an excellent story by itself, and leaves the reader anxious to read the next part of the series.

– Greg S.

5.0 out of 5 stars Great post-war story

Reviewed in the United States on June 20, 2024

Verified Purchase

This is a really well-written story about a side of war that is often overlooked, the soldiers who return home damaged or broken. Bill DeHay brilliantly captures their battles to overcome their disabilities, rebuild their lives, make sense of what they have endured and overcome the demons that haunt their minds. First of a series, I look forward to the next installment.

–Russ S.

5.0 out of 5 stars Absorbing

Reviewed in the United States on June 9, 2024

From where this story begins to where it ends is a journey that holds many surprises along its way. It is a unique story told by a great author. Remarkable, first novel.

– William W.

A Different War

The Collins Family Saga
Book 1

William R. DeHay

A Different War

A Different War

Copyright © 2024 by William R. DeHay

eBook ISBN: 978-1-963927-00-9

Paperback ISBN: 978-1-963927-01-6

Hardback ISBN: 978-1-963927-02-3

Audiobook ISBN: 978-1-963927-03-0

Cover and interior design by Gordon Saunders

To all who have served

Chapter 1

The Beast

November 1918

There's a beast in each of us. Most people never meet theirs. Captain Jamie Collins wasn't like most people. He met his outside the ruins of a once-idyllic French village. His infantry company had been ordered to take the German-occupied trench they were facing. The citation to Jamie's medal said he hadn't waited for the preparatory artillery barrage to lift before charging across no man's land by himself. Though wounded repeatedly by friendly fire, he still managed to disable four enemy machine guns and eliminate their crews. What that meant in human terms was that a score of German mothers would never see their boys again. Jamie felt no remorse. The gunners would have slaughtered his men without mercy.

Some say Jamie was incredibly brave. Others say he must have been insane. The truth lay somewhere in between. Amid the sound and fury of the artillery barrage, Jamie snapped. A corporal was moving down the line, passing out hand grenades from a bag slung over his shoulder. Jamie grabbed the bag, and without a thought of survival—without any thought at all—he climbed the assault ladder and went over the top alone. It wasn't a willful act. It was pure impulse. As though something wild, violent, unpredictable had taken control of him.

It was a miracle he survived.

Was he insane? Momentarily. Was he brave? Without a doubt.

With the enemy's rapid-fire MG08/15 heavy machine guns out of action, Jamie's platoons advanced across no man's land with only light casualties. Not surprisingly, the reprieve Jamie bought his men came at a high personal cost. Shrapnel from a field artillery piece can tear through a house, let alone through a man. First Sergeant Robert Nielsen found Jamie crumpled beside a smoking machine gun nest. Nielsen grasped Jamie's wrist and felt for a pulse. Nothing. He tried Jamie's carotid artery with the same dismal result.

Having too much respect for Jamie to leave his body for Graves Registration to retrieve later, Nielson picked up his fallen captain and carried what he believed was Jamie's corpse to the nearest battalion aid station. There, an over-wrought triage doctor formally pronounced Jamie dead—prematurely, Jamie liked to point out.

The doctor's mistake was discovered with no time to lose. Against all odds, the medical staff were able to stabilize Jamie. The following day, he was moved by rail ninety miles south of Verdun to American Expeditionary Force Base Hospital 15, Chaumont. There, in surgery after surgery, enough jagged metal was removed from Jamie's chest, abdomen, and legs to build a bridge across California's

Golden Gate. Sadly, he remained paralyzed from the waist down.

The Meuse-Argonne Offensive raged on. A dozen of Jamie's men, including Sergeant Nielsen, were carried off the battlefield to take up residence in one hospital or another ... or a morgue. The carnage finally ended on Armistice Day, 11 November 1918. Transatlantic troopships then began transporting American soldiers back to the States.

By the middle of December, Jamie was stable enough to travel. But his doctors were worried. Jamie hadn't spoken since being wounded, and there was no physical explanation for his silence.

Late Christmas Day, Jamie was startled out of a daydream by Doctor Stone, the physician in charge of his case. "Good news, Major Collins. You'll be on your way home before year's end."

Jamie spoke. One word.

* * *

Monday, 06 January 1919. Walter Reed Army Hospital, Washington, D.C.

The succession of wheelchairs, trains, ambulances, and ships had been exhausting. Jamie endured stoically. He would have happily passed through the gates of hell to be back in the States.

An ambulance took him from Union Station to Walter Reed. His orderly wheeled Jamie onto an orthopedic ward, where he was met by a smiling nurse. "Welcome to Walter Reed, Major Collins. I'm Nurse Rawlings, head nurse on your ward."

Jamie returned her smile. "Pleased to meet you, ma'am." He looked around. In appearance, his ward in France was much the same. But there was one enormous difference. His new ward was in America.

"Sir, your doctor will be here soon to greet you. In the meantime, is there anything I can do for you?"

"No, thank you, Nurse Rawlings. I'd just like to rest for a while."

Nurse Rawlings hadn't left Jamie's side before a distinguished gentleman in a white coat joined them.

"Good afternoon, Major Collins. I'm Doctor Lawrence. I'll be overseeing your care."

Jamie was immediately comforted by the competence Doctor Lawrence projected. "I'm sure I'll be in good hands," he said.

"It's good to hear you speak. I understand you weren't the most talkative patient in France."

"I was as puzzled as anyone by my silence." Jamie sat up a little straighter. "But I think I finally understand."

Doctor Lawrence folded his arms. "If you ever want to talk about it, people say I'm a good listener. And so is Nurse Rawlings."

Jamie looked from doctor to nurse. "Do either of you have a few minutes now? I'd like to get it off my mind and then let it go."

"I have all the time in the world," Nurse Rawlings said.

Doctor Lawrence shrugged. "That goes for me, too."

Jamie closed his eyes momentarily as he tried to think of the right words. "I lost a lot of men in France. Nothing I could say was going to bring them back. At the time I didn't know what was going on in my mind. But now I realize silence was way of mourning them."

Nurse Rawlings bowed her head, then slowly looked up. "That, Major Collins, was a beautiful tribute to those you lost."

"I agree," Doctor Lawrence said. He canted his head. "I'm curious. What brought you out of your silence?"

"Christmas Day was life-changing for me. In the afternoon, I was presented with the Medal of Honor and promoted to major. That evening, my doctor told me I'd be heading home by the end of the week. When I heard that, it was as though the men I lost were telling me I'd mourned them long and well enough, and it was time to get on with my life. Then, for the first time in two months, I spoke. One word."

Nurse Rawlings moved half a step closer. "I'd love to know what you said."

Jamie stared off into the distance. "Home."

Doctor Lawrence thrust his hands deep into the pockets of his white coat. "Major Collins, I promise I'll do everything I can to get you out of here and back home as quickly as possible."

So as not to appear ungrateful, Jamie waited until the end of the day before requesting a transfer.

Along with Walter Reed, Letterman Army Hospital had been designated an orthopedic center for amputation and paralysis cases from the American Expeditionary Force. Letterman was on the grounds of the Presidio of San Francisco, only a hundred miles up the coast from Jamie's hometown, and even closer to the university where he was determined to resume teaching once he was released from the Army. Letterman was where Jamie longed to be.

When his transfer request wasn't immediately granted,

Jamie resubmitted it the next day. And the next. He continued resubmitting it day after day.

* * *

Friday, 28 February 1919.

Doctor Lawrence, who had quickly become Jamie's favorite doctor, approached with a huge smile. "Good evening, Major Collins. After a good bit of backroom politicking, and without stretching the truth too much, I finally persuaded the higher-ups that you'd receive better treatment at Letterman. And lo and behold, they've finally granted your transfer request." Doctor Lawrence tapped the paperwork attached to the clipboard he was carrying. "By the middle of next week, you'll be heading to San Francisco." He lowered his clipboard. "Are you all right?"

It took Jamie a moment to gather himself. "I've been dreaming about returning to San Francisco ever since my division was activated."

"I wish I were going with you," Doctor Lawrence said. "I know Letterman well. I did my residency there. In those days, it was the army's best-equipped, best-staffed hospital, and by all accounts, it still is."

"I just wish I'd been sent there in the first place."

Doctor Lawrence glanced over his shoulder. "I try not to be cynical, but my guess is the brass wanted you here so visiting Congressmen and Senators could meet 'the hero who was raised from the dead' and then be more inclined to increase our funding."

Jamie nodded. "I try to think the best of people, too, but I wouldn't be surprised if you were right."

Doctor Lawrence got a far-off look. "Letterman was the first army general hospital staffed by women of the Army Nurse Corps—and the source of the best wife a man could hope for." He smiled at Jamie. "Maybe you'll find the woman of your dreams there too."

"In my condition, it wouldn't do me much good," Jamie said, then quickly added, "but that kind of thinking won't do me any good either."

"I'm sure it isn't easy for you to keep a positive outlook, so let me give you more good news. A friend I served with during the war is the head nurse on one of Letterman's orthopedic wards. I've arranged for you to be placed in her care. I think you'll find her to be a kindred spirit. Not only is she one of the most highly skilled and compassionate nurses I've ever worked with, she's also the bravest. She's one of only four women, all nurses, to be awarded the Distinguished Service Cross."

"The DSC? That's a combat award!"

"You're right. And there's only one higher, as you well know, being one of the few living recipients."

"Was she in combat?"

"You tell me. When her field hospital came under artillery fire, she used her body to shield an unconscious patient from flying shrapnel. And though she was seriously wounded, she carried on, refusing medical attention until she'd seen to all her patients."

"I'd say that was combat." Jamie tried to imagine a woman that brave. The image that came to mind was an older woman built like a football lineman.

Jamie sighed. Most who were aware of his combat record expected him to be a large, ape-like creature, and none too bright. He didn't like being stereotyped that way—no doubt this exceptional nurse wouldn't either. Besides, Jamie had learned that bravery had nothing to do with one's size and physical strength and everything to do with one's strength of character.

Jamie followed Doctor Lawrence's gaze around the ward full of broken men. "As far as I'm concerned," Lawrence said, "war is mass insanity—but I've seen more progress in the treatment of cases like yours during the last year than I saw during my first decade in practice. And Letterman's been the leader in many of those advances. I'm optimistic that they'll do wonders for you."

Jamie lowered his head and tried to blink back tears. Since being wounded, he'd become much more emotional. Worse, his emotions often crept up on him with no warning. He could be talking with someone and suddenly find himself laughing or crying for no reason.

Doctor Lawrence placed his hand on Jamie's shoulder. "There's always hope."

Jamie wiped his cheek with the back of his hand. "I haven't given up hope. What concerns me is that I'll hope for too much once I'm back in San Francisco. There's a girl, you see. Back in the trenches, when I dreamed of a future together ... I didn't picture myself in a wheelchair." With all his mental strength, he forced such thoughts from his mind and put on a smile. "Regardless, I can't wait to be back in California."

"I understand you're from the West Coast."

"That's right. And some of the happiest moments of my life took place in San Francisco."

Doctor Lawrence leaned in closer. "Better keep that to yourself. It's against army regulations to post a soldier somewhere he'd like to be."

Jamie smiled as he pushed down on the arms of his wheelchair and tried to find a more comfortable position.

Doctor Lawrence set his clipboard aside. He bent down and repositioned Jamie's feet on their rests. "Letterman's neurology department is outstanding. And they're pioneers in the field of physical therapy. It'll be the perfect place for you."

Jamie stared at his useless legs. "I just want to be closer to home. I'm not expecting a miracle."

"I'm not talking about a miracle. I'm talking about you fighting to make the most of your paralysis under the care of the best neurologists and physical therapists the army has to offer."

Jamie set his jaw. "A man can grow tired of fighting."

Doctor Lawrence stood up straight. "The medal Congress awarded you tells the world what kind of fighter you are. I'm willing to bet the day will come when you'll be able to stand eye to eye with me."

Chapter 2

Letterman Army Hospital

Sunday Afternoon, 09 March 1919

After a seemingly interminable rail journey, Jamie arrived in San Francisco. From his stretcher in the back of a Model T Ford ambulance, Jamie could see that the City by the Bay had grown in the last two years. Fewer horse-drawn vehicles roamed the streets. Gasoline-powered automobiles, buses, and trucks were everywhere. Electric signals controlled traffic at major intersections. A web of telephone and power lines crisscrossed overhead.

The jolt of the ambulance's wooden-spoked wheels as they passed over a set of cable car tracks triggered a flood of memories. He could picture the girl he'd met on a cable car shortly before he was shipped overseas. He hadn't heard from Rachel in two years. And though he tried, he never found the right words to write to her.

Jamie's ambulance drove west through the Presidio and onto the hospital grounds. After circumnavigating the rectangular central green, the driver hit the brakes in front of the main entrance. The ambulance came to a jarring halt. Jamie cried out in pain—though he had no feeling below his waist, his back gave him constant grief.

A medical corpsman dressed all in white, who looked like he could easily trounce Atlas in a wrestling match, appeared at the tailgate. He climbed into the ambulance and towered over Jamie.

The corpsman rendered a crisp salute. "Good evening, Major Collins."

Since Jamie wasn't in uniform, he was surprised to be saluted. Nevertheless, he smiled and returned the salute smartly. "And who might you be?"

"Sergeant Nick Hendricks, sir, senior corpsman on your ward."

"Pleased to meet you, Hendricks." Jamie glanced out the small side window of his ambulance. "Why have they brought me to the front of the hospital?"

"Sir, the CO wants to welcome you personally."

Jamie wished he could crawl under his stretcher. "I don't want any special treatment," he mumbled.

"Sir?"

"Never mind." The attention his Medal of Honor brought him was a minor form of torture for a man who shunned the spotlight.

Hendricks moved to the foot of Jamie's stretcher. The ambulance attendant took the head. Together, they moved Jamie out into the open air. With remarkable ease, Hendricks picked Jamie up like a toy soldier and placed him in a wheelchair. He began pushing Jamie up the steep incline toward the hospital's main entrance. Jamie clenched his teeth to keep from swearing. Before being wounded, he could have given a gazelle a run for its money in a foot race.

They reached level ground just shy of the door. "Stand by," Jamie said. He took control of the wheelchair and spun it around to face the bay. A fleet of brightly colored sailboats darted here and there. Jamie raised the collar of his hospital robe and wrapped it tighter around himself. "I wouldn't want to be out sailing on a day like this."

"Sir, they must be real diehards not to wait 'til spring."

"I've lost track of time with all the traveling. What day is it?"

"Sunday, sir. March 9th" Hendricks glanced at his wrist-watch. "Nearly 1630 hours."

The sound of waves gently lapping on the nearby sandy shore took Jamie back to before the war. He filled his lungs with crisp, salt air. Billowing white clouds were moving in from the open ocean, like the hand of God passing through the Golden Gate. "Brings back memories," Jamie said under his breath.

"What's that, sir?"

Jamie couldn't answer. All his strength was being spent trying to block out memories of the girl he'd met on the cable car.

Hendricks pointed across the bay. "There's talk, sir, of building a bridge from here to Lime Point on the Marin County side of the Golden Gate."

"That would be an engineering marvel," Jamie said, happy for the distraction. "Over two miles long. With enough clearance for ocean-going vessels to pass beneath. Two hundred feet tall, at least."

Hendricks whistled. "Sir, that's about the height of a twenty-story building. They couldn't pay me enough to work anywhere near that high up."

"Heights bother you?"

"Yes, sir. I'm not brave like you."

Jamie grasped the armrests of his wheelchair. "I'll tell you how brave I am." He pivoted his chair, putting his back to the bay. "I have to sleep with a light on in my room at night."

Sergeant Hendricks showed no surprise. "Lots of men who served at the front can't abide the dark, sir. Who knows what lurks in the shadows?"

Jamie did, and he wished to God he didn't. "Did you serve at the front?"

Hendricks nodded. "Yes, sir. I was a stretcher-bearer my first three months in France. After that, against my wishes, I was re-assigned to a base hospital."

"I've yet to meet a stretcher-bearer who isn't brave." Jamie pointed to Letterman's main entrance. "Let's get this over with."

As they approached the main entrance, a door opened seemingly of its own accord. A harried-looking junior officer barely managed to get his toes out of the way as Jamie's wheelchair rolled past.

A short, balding colonel approached the instant Jamie and Hendricks entered the hospital's foyer. "I'm Robert Thornburgh, commanding officer. It will be my honor to oversee your care while you're with us." He patted Jamie's shoulder. "Soldiers like you make me proud to be an army doctor."

Proud? What kind of soldier—what kind of *man*—was he? Yes, his actions in France saved American lives. But he'd killed dozens of the enemy—most just boys who undoubtedly didn't want to be fighting in the trenches any more than Jamie did.

"Major Collins?"

Jamie forced a smile. "Thank you, Colonel Thornburgh." He avoided eye contact. This wasn't the time or place to bare his soul.

Colonel Thornburgh signaled Hendricks to follow as he led the way through a maze of corridors. The CO's entourage dutifully trailed behind. Passersby stared. Jamie could imagine them wondering why people were fussing over this guy who couldn't even walk. Had they asked, Jamie would have said he was nobody special.

The layout of Letterman appealed to Jamie's love of symmetry. The buildings, exclusively wood-framed since the great earthquake, many three stories tall, formed three sides of a rectangle around a central green. The open side provided the surrounding buildings with an unobstructed view of the bay.

Covered walkways linked the buildings. Where San Francisco's hilly terrain was especially severe, one could leave the ground floor of one building, traverse an enclosed passageway, and, without changing elevation, end up on the second floor of an adjacent building. Such was the case as they entered Building Three.

The procession stopped in front of Ward 321. Two of the colonel's staff rushed forward and pulled open a set of double doors, revealing a cavernous, rectangular bay. The view toward the far end of the ward from where Jamie sat resembled a boulevard. In the "median" stood two large rectangular tables, one near, the other further along. Stout white columns marked the edges of the median. The boulevard's "traffic lanes" consisted of highly polished dark wood wide enough to accommodate wheelchairs. Bordering the lanes and placed perpendicular to the traffic flow were the patients' metal-frame beds, twelve to a side, twenty-four in all. A footlocker at the end of each bed served as a buffer between traffic and patients. Ceiling-to-floor windows flooded the ward with natural light and provided an abundance of fresh sea air.

"Wait out here," Colonel Thornburgh told his staff.

As Hendricks and Jamie followed Thornburgh through the ward's double doors, the nearest patient rose awkwardly, crutched his way to the end of his bed, steadied himself on his one foot, and held a salute.

American soldiers don't normally salute indoors unless they're in uniform, on duty, and carrying a weapon. Hendricks had pushed Jamie well past the man before Jamie even thought to return his salute.

At the next occupied bed, a man with no legs rolled his wheelchair to the end of his bed and sat at attention, saluting. Jamie looked to the end of the "boulevard" and saw all the patients lining up at the foot of their beds.

A patient whose right sleeve was empty rendered a salute with his left arm. Each man, whether missing a hand, foot, arm, or leg, or like Jamie, was "merely" unable to use a limb or two, rendered a salute as he was able. Jamie held his belated return salute as Hendricks pushed him toward the nurses' station at the end of the open bay.

"What have you gotten me into here?" Jamie whispered over his shoulder to Hendricks.

"Sir, this is an orthopedic ward where we treat only amputees and paralytics. A new man on a ward like this, where patients stay for weeks on end, is a big deal. And your Medal of Honor makes you something of a celebrity. The men want to welcome you with their best foot forward, so to speak."

Jamie would have preferred to slip by unnoticed.

Six nurses were lined up at attention in front of the nurses' station. Two stood together, a step forward from the others. The one on the right looked exactly like Jamie imagined a nurse who'd been awarded the Distinguished Service Cross would look: an older woman built like a football lineman. The one on the left was easily ten years younger. She was a strikingly beautiful woman with copper hair and green eyes. Jamie had never seen green eyes before.

"Nurse Eliot is the head nurse on your ward," Thornburgh said with notable respect. "Nurse Eliot, this is Major Collins."

"Pleased to meet you, sir. Welcome to Ward 321."

Jamie was shocked that it was the younger nurse who replied.

So she was the woman Doctor Lawrence referred to as one of the most highly skilled and compassionate nurses he'd ever worked with as well as the bravest.

Jamie had never felt such an immediate attraction to anyone. Not even to the girl he'd met on the cable car before the war. It wasn't just Nurse Eliot's beauty. This remarkable woman had put her life on the line to protect those under her care. She'd be able to understand him in ways no other woman ever could—and vice versa. A kindred spirit indeed.

"Doctor Lawrence sends his compliments from Walter Reed," Jamie said to her.

"That's nice to hear, sir," Nurse Eliot said. "Doctor Lawrence is an excellent physician, and a true gentleman."

"I know Art Lawrence," Thornburgh said to Jamie. "He's a great doctor." He turned to Nurse Eliot. "Please treat Major Collins as you would family."

Nurse Eliot stood a little taller. "As I do all my patients, sir."

"Which is why we're placing him on your ward." The colonel turned to Jamie. "I'll check in on you once you're settled."

Jamie had to force himself to look away from Nurse Eliot. "Thank you, sir. I'm sure I'll be in good hands."

The instant the colonel turned his back, Nurse Eliot took charge. She indicated the woman next to her. "Sir, this is Nurse Wolenski, assistant head nurse on our ward."

Jamie smiled at Wolenski. He wondered how it came about that she was reporting to the younger woman, and how that was working out. Presumably, it had to do with Nurse Eliot's DSC.

Jamie was curious about the four nurses lined up in the background. Eliot and Wolenski wore the standard nurses' hospital duty uniform: a light gray cotton dress that flowed to six inches above the floor and featured long sleeves with white cuffs and a low turned-down white collar. The front of the dress was covered by a white bib apron with deep pockets.

Jamie always looked at a person's left collar to determine their corps. Eliot and Wolenski wore identical pins: a gilded caduceus—two serpents intertwined around a herald's staff —with the letters ANC superimposed in white enamel. Theirs was the insignia of an Army Nurse Corps registered nurse.

The other four nurses wore a uniform Jamie had never seen before. The white bib apron they wore was the same as the RNs', but their dresses, although similar in style, were made from light blue chambray. The insignia pinned to their left collar was a bronze lamp superimposed on a caduceus. All four looked a little lost. Hendricks bent down a little closer to Jamie's ear. "One nice thing about Letterman is we're home to a unit of the brand-new Army School of Nursing."

Jamie hardly glanced at the student nurses. He was too captivated by Nurse Eliot. Her strong, round chin, high cheekbones, and wide-set eyes made him think of paintings of Helen of Troy, who legend had it was the most beautiful woman of her day. But the fables of Helen never mentioned a bearing as regal as Nurse Eliot's. Fittingly, her uniform was immaculate. The pleats in her skirt were so sharp Jamie imagined they could cut through metal.

Nurse Eliot inclined her head slightly. "And these are our 'bluebirds,' sir." With a sweep of her arm, she indicated the four blue-chambray-clad young women. "They're part of a group of nineteen student nurses who've recently joined us from Camp Kearney. They've just completed a four-month preliminary course where, along with a bit of medical training, they were treated to a good dose of strict military discipline, including daily drill under an experienced drill sergeant."

The bluebirds grimaced. Hendricks smiled.

"They'll be receiving the rest of their medical training here at Letterman," Nurse Eliot said.

"The same training they'd get in a civilian school?"

"Yes, sir. As specified by the National League for Nursing Education. Except our bluebirds will be under military control. For the next three months, these young ladies will split their time between ward duties with us and classwork with the rest of their group."

Jamie smiled at the students. "That should keep you busy," he said. They seemed nervous as they smiled back.

Jamie looked around the open bay. "I counted twenty-four beds," he said to Nurse Eliot. "Are they all occupied?"

"Sir, we're caring for seventeen enlisted men on the general ward."

As she spoke, Jamie was struck by Nurse Eliot's dignity and commanding presence, not to mention her intensely green eyes. Dark eyebrows and long, dark lashes accentuated their luminosity. The Stanford Art Gallery once had a display of emeralds. They looked dull by comparison.

"Six nurses for seventeen enlisted men?" Jamie interleaved his fingers and tapped his thumbs together. "I like the sound of that."

Nurse Eliot raised her chin. "Six on this shift, sir, which is barely enough. There's work enough for a dozen more nurses on this ward."

"If you ask me," Hendricks mumbled, "one nurse is worth a dozen doctors."

Nurse Eliot gave Hendricks a look Jamie couldn't interpret.

"Before the war," Nurse Eliot said, "there were only 500 RNs in the entire Nurse Corps. Now, there are almost 21,000 of us." She turned to the student nurses. "And if these fledglings fulfill their promise, we just might be adding four more in a little less than three years."

Jamie scanned the students' eager faces. "I'm sure you'll each be a credit to the Corps."

He was unable to stifle a yawn. He turned to Nurse Eliot. "It's been a long trip. Although it's early, if you'll deliver me to my bed, I'd like to sleep for a week or two."

"Certainly, sir. When was the last time you had anything to eat?"

"Early this morning. Real early. Still, I'd rather sleep than eat."

"That's good, sir. Doctor Crandall recommends that you not eat anything more before he sees you."

"Doctor Crandall?"

"Head of neurology, sir. He's currently reviewing the medical file that came with you from Walter Reed."

"This late on a Sunday?"

"Sir, all our patients are special. You're just a little more so."

Jamie knew it would be useless to protest.

"This way, sir." Nurse Eliot marched off with Hendricks and Jamie in her wake. Two bluebirds followed.

"Where are you taking me?" Jamie said.

"Sir, I understand that at Walter Reed and in your hospital in France, you were on a general ward with several dozen other officers. To give our officers as much peace and quiet as can be found on a busy ward, they're assigned private rooms."

Jamie grasped his armrests with a death grip. "I'll be in a private room? By myself?"

"Why, yes, sir. Is that a problem?"

Since being wounded, Jamie had never been alone. He had always been on a ward with dozens of patients, an exam room with at least a couple of nurses or orderlies, or an operating theater full of medical staff. Being in a private room would surely bring back terrifying memories of being declared dead and left alone on the cold, hard ground at a battalion aid station. Jamie wasn't sure he could deal with that.

Nurse Eliot was staring at him, waiting for an answer.

He wished he were brave enough to admit to his fears. He forced a smile. "It might feel like solitary confinement after being in the presence of so many others for so long."

"We'll check in on you often," Nurse Eliot said. She led the way to Jamie's private room at the far end of the ward.

The bluebird who brought up the rear of the procession carried a briefcase-sized wooden box. She placed it on Jamie's nightstand. From it, Nurse Eliot extracted a mechanical sphygmomanometer with a dial face. "May I take your blood pressure, sir?"

"Certainly." He'd be happy for her to do whatever she wanted with him.

She fit the cuff around his upper arm. "My, sir, you've been keeping fit."

A current of warmth flowed from the top of Jamie's head to his waist. "Maneuvering myself around in a wheelchair is good exercise."

She leaned down, placed his forearm between the side of her chest and her upper arm, pumped the bulb of the cuff, and placed the bell of her stethoscope in the crook of his arm. She was remarkably gentle. He would swear he could feel her heart beating in rhythm with his.

She slowly loosened the valve on the bulb as she listened to his pulse. "Very good," she said. She removed the cuff and stood. She handed the device to the nearest bluebird. "With your permission, sir, I'd like to listen to your chest."

"Be my guest." Jamie opened the top of his robe. Although Nurse Eliot was merely doing her job, he was honored to be the center of attention of such a capable woman.

After listening to his lungs and heart, Nurse Eliot meticulously folded her stethoscope and put it in her pocket. "Clear lungs, strong heart. Apparently, you don't smoke."

"No, ma'am. That's one nasty habit I haven't fallen prey to."

"You'll never be sorry for that, sir."

The big corpsman spoke up. "Nurse Eliot doesn't allow smoking on her ward, sir."

"Really. I'm amazed the men stand for that."

"Sir, Nurse Eliot and I believe fresh air is best for the men."

Nurse Eliot ignored Hendricks' comments. "You may return that to its case," she said to the bluebird holding the blood pressure device. The student nurse placed it haphazardly in its box. Nurse Eliot gave her a cold stare. The bluebird swallowed hard, rearranged the device, and stepped back.

Nurse Eliot patted it and closed the lid. She glanced out the window. "You have a lovely view of the bay from here, sir." She faced Jamie. "The Presidio's a beautiful place. I hope you'll take every opportunity to enjoy the scenery while you're with us."

Hendricks leaned a little closer to Jamie's ear. "Sir, the nurses are the only scenery the men are interested in."

Some might have considered Hendricks' comment a little too familiar, coming from a sergeant to a field-grade officer. Jamie let it go.

"There's harmless banter between men and nurses on every ward," Nurse Eliot said. She looked at Hendricks. "I make sure it remains harmless."

Hendricks shrugged. "Sir, the RNs have seen it all, so the men concentrate on the bluebirds. They still blush."

Jamie was confident that before long, the student nurses would be giving as good as they got. He smiled as he recalled how it had been for him in Officer Training School. Being one of the smaller men, he had endured an uneven measure of hazing from the training cadre's favorite cadets. Jamie turned the joke on them. No one ever figured out how he altered his main tormentors' personnel records so convincingly that they spent the next week after graduation laboring away as buck privates in the cavalry, assigned to a disciplinary platoon, where their primary duty was mucking out stables.

As for Jamie, he had no intention of making the student nurses blush. He would treat them as they deserved. With kindness and respect.

"Rest well, Major Collins," Nurse Eliot said. "And please, don't hesitate to let me or any other member of the staff know if there's anything we can do for you. With your leave." She backed out of the room.

Though she was gone, Jamie could still feel the warmth of her touch and picture her dazzling green eyes.

Chapter 3

A Ray of Hope

Sunday, Late Afternoon, 09 March 1919

Once Nurse Eliot was gone, the bluebirds stood aside and let Hendricks take over. He lifted Jamie from his wheelchair and placed him on his bed. Jamie felt so helpless. He wondered how a student nurse would manage to transfer him if Hendricks or one of the other corpsmen wasn't around.

"Sir," Hendricks said, "I'll leave you in the care of the bluebirds for now, but I'll be back to check on you later."

With military precision, the student nurses covered Jamie with a crisp sheet and topped it off with a warm blanket. The shorter, shy one fluffed his pillow. "DaSilva," her nametag read. The other nurse tucked him in as she might her little brother. He never got a clear look at her nametag.

"Is there anything else we can do for you, sir?" Nurse DaSilva said.

"No, thank you." Jamie appreciated the excellent care

they were giving him while resenting like hell that he couldn't do such simple things for himself.

The nameless nurse led the way toward the door. As the last in line, DaSilva reached for the light switch.

"Halt," Jamie said in his well-practiced command voice.

Both froze.

"Leave the lights on." His words came out harsher than he intended. "Please."

DaSilva jerked her hand away from the switch as though it might nip her fingers. The bluebirds exchanged glances. Neither said anything. During their preliminary training, it would have been drummed into them that it wasn't their place to question an officer.

"Rest well, sir," DaSilva said, parroting Nurse Eliot. She followed the other student nurse out the door.

Jamie was alone for the first time since mistakenly being declared dead. He had tried to prepare himself for this moment. His plan was to concentrate on completing the paper he started writing before his reserve unit was activated. He hadn't looked at *The Dual Nature of Light: Particle or Wave?* since the war interrupted his first year as an assistant professor of physics at Stanford University. Once finalized, he believed this paper would be a significant contribution to the field of quantum mechanics.

His plan didn't work. He began to panic.

Four months and fifty-five hundred miles removed, Jamie's fear of abandonment was overpowering. He reached for his call button and pushed it again and again until he was afraid it might shatter.

"Get ahold of yourself," he said out loud. He knew someone would be along any minute.

His "call button" at the battalion aid station in France

had been a prayer. Private Clarence Thurgood of Graves Registration was the man God sent in response. Thurgood was among the poor wretches assigned the gruesome task of retrieving, identifying, transporting, and burying American dead.

Jamie met Private Thurgood after being transferred to a field hospital. He learned from Thurgood that it was standard procedure for a corpsman to start a saline IV immediately upon the arrival of an unconscious patient at a battalion aid station. It was Thurgood's job to remove such extraneous items from their bodies when he came to collect them. When he ripped the IV from Jamie's arm and heard Jamie moan, Thurgood stumbled backward and fell on top of a soldier who really was dead.

"Did you hear that?" Thurgood said to the corporal in charge of his squad. "That one's still alive."

His squad leader gave him a pitying look. "If you want to survive this job with your mind intact, you need to stop listening to the dead."

Ignoring his leader's sage advice, Thurgood scrambled to his feet and ran from doctor to doctor, begging each in turn to take another look at Jamie. One after another refused.

Jamie could picture the scene. Even in the Twentieth Century, many weak-minded officers would have dismissed Thurgood's 'emergency' as the manifestation of the superstitious beliefs and overactive imaginations they attributed to 'colored troops.'

Had Thurgood not persisted until he found a doctor who was color blind, Jamie would not have survived. As for the term 'colored troops,' Jamie preferred the more exact expression, 'human beings.'

Despite the penetrating cold of a San Francisco March

evening, Jamie threw his blanket aside and tried to get out of bed. With a Herculean effort, he managed to prop himself up on his elbows. His paralysis stopped him there and ignited a rage in him. It burned white hot as he thought of how things used to be and what might never be again.

He caught a glimpse of himself in the mirror above the sink at the foot of his bed. What a pitiful creature he was, struggling just to sit up.

Still, if the army planned to warehouse him in this room until they could conveniently get rid of him, they would be in for a surprise. They said he fought valiantly in France. They were about to see what a real fight looked like if they thought he would accept being confined to this room—let alone to a wheelchair.

Jamie crashed back onto his pillow. The beast in him began to stir. He pounded his lifeless legs with his fists. Who was he kidding? What kind of fight could he mount when he couldn't even get out of bed?

He heard someone approaching. The student nurse who had tucked him in appeared at his bedside, vulnerable, eager to please. He wouldn't be able to live with himself if he unleashed his beast on her.

He forced himself to take several deep breaths, and his beast began to subside. "Cold," he managed to say through clenched teeth. She couldn't know he was not referring to the temperature of the room.

She radiated warmth as she retrieved his blanket, leaned in close, and tucked it under his chin. Her subtle scent reminded him of the girl he'd met on the cable car. Tears of longing clouded his vision as he searched the nurse's blouse for her nametag. "Hobbes," he read with some difficulty. His blurry eyes focused on her ample chest. The sight stirred only anger. His paralysis precluded any other arousal.

He looked into her face. She smiled, and his rage melted away. "Thank you," he said weakly.

Nurse Hobbes ran her hands briskly up and down her bare forearms. "This damp ocean air penetrates right to the bone, sir." She was a pleasant-looking young woman, pretty in her own way. Her open, friendly smile made her more attractive than women far prettier.

Jamie managed a smile of his own. "Somebody famous once said, 'The coldest winter I ever spent was a summer in San Francisco.'"

"That's generally attributed to Mark Twain, sir, although there's no evidence he ever actually said it."

Jamie's brow rose.

"I was an English major, sir."

"What made you switch to nursing?"

"My brother and my cousin were both wounded while fighting in France. Their letters home were full of praise for the nurses who cared for them."

"Have they been demobilized?"

"My cousin has. My brother's buried in a small cemetery somewhere near Le Havre."

Jamie's gut twisted into a knot. "I'm sorry."

"As should be the American artillery commander who placed his guns near my brother's hospital."

Jamie shook his head. "Assuming proximity would deter counterfire was a wicked gamble some artillery commanders took."

"In this case, his gamble didn't pay off. An enemy round —presumably falling short by accident—killed or wounded a doctor, three nurses, a corpsman, and five patients. My brother was one of those killed." She smoothed Jamie's already smooth blanket. "After Joey was killed, I couldn't sit at home and do nothing. Then, last May, the Secretary of War authorized the Army School of Nursing. I applied and was thrilled to be accepted. I hope that someday, someone else's brother will write home to tell his family how well I treated him."

"Last May? That was before the armistice. Surely, the army doesn't expect you to complete the program now that the war's over."

Nurse Hobbes straightened her back. "Sir, I volunteered to serve 'for the duration,' which to me means until every wounded American soldier is back in the States and released from the hospital."

Jamie looked upon her with added respect. "That's a big commitment."

"Nowhere near as big as my brother's, sir."

A middle-aged doctor entered Jamie's room. His insignia identified him as a Lieutenant Colonel. Nurse Hobbes snapped to attention and stood motionless, breathless.

"Relax." The doctor shifted the thick folder he was carrying from one hand to the other. "Too much formality stresses the patients."

"Sir, we were taught to—"

"Yes, I apologize. You were doing exactly as you were told. The truth is, too much formality stresses me." His smile came and went almost like a twitch. "Are you finished here?"

"Yes, sir."

"Thank you, nurse."

She smiled at Jamie and quickly left.

"Good evening, Major Collins. I'm Doctor Crandall,

head of neurology." His smile returned and stayed. "You can call me 'Bob.' "

Jamie nodded toward the door. "I think you scared her."

Doctor Crandall seemed surprised. "That wasn't my intention. I have nothing but respect for those young women." He kicked Jamie's guest chair closer and sat. He crossed one leg over the other and balanced his folder on his knee. "Nurse Hobbes, like the other bluebirds you've met, are members of the inaugural class of the Army School of Nursing."

"I'd heard the school was new," Jamie said. "I didn't realize it was that new. I'm an educator myself. I'd be interested in learning a little about the school."

Doctor Crandall gave Jamie a penetrating stare. "Wouldn't you rather hear what I concluded after reviewing your medical file?"

"Surely that can wait a minute or two." The truth was, Jamie was afraid to hear what Doctor Crandall concluded in case it was bad news.

"Well, if you really want to know." Doctor Crandall lifted the folder from his knee and set it on Jamie's nightstand. "Hobbes and her classmates are in a unique position. Although the Adjutant General authorized a military uniform and the insignia you've seen them wearing, the students in the ASN were 'sworn in' as civilian employees of the Medical Department of the Army. That means they can drop out and return to civilian life any time they please—as did about a third of Hobbes' class when the armistice was signed."

"I'm impressed by Nurse Hobbes, sir. She's in it for the long haul."

"I doubt she's motivated by the fifteen-dollar-a-month

allowance ASN students receive." Doctor Crandall smiled. "I've been watching all the bluebirds. Hobbes, and DaSilva, are particularly good. We're lucky to have them. I just hope the army doesn't stab them in the back."

"Sir?"

"The ASN was a wartime expediency meant to turn out RNs as fast as possible. Now that the war's over, the students' exact status—and the future of the school itself—are up in the air. I hope the Army has the foresight to continue the school because we might need a rash of RNs someday soon, considering the state of turmoil Europe's still in."

"If the school continues, and Hobbes and her classmates graduate, what will become of them?"

"If they pass a state licensing board, they can apply for admission to the Army Nurse Corps. If all goes to plan, they'll be accepted in the order of their class standing—assuming there are vacancies in the corps. Those who fail, or for some other reason don't meet ANC standards, will become ordinary civilians again."

"With all the ward duties they'll be required to perform," Jamie said, "it sounds like the Army's asking an awful lot of them in exchange for their fifteen dollars a month."

Doctor Crandall nodded. "They get room and board, such as it is, and the possibility of a degree in nursing. Otherwise, I agree. And it won't get much better if they're accepted into the Army Nurse Corps."

"You make it sound rather ominous."

"Not ominous, just damned unfair. Probably fewer than one soldier out of a hundred realizes that nurses have no rank—"

"No rank?" Jamie said. "I assumed—"

"That's the problem. People assume. The reality is the army considers female nurses a necessary evil and treats them as such. By tradition alone, their status falls somewhere between the enlisted ranks and officers—which can be awkward when telling corpsmen what to do, or even when giving assignments to subordinate nurses."

"An army needs a rigid command structure to function smoothly," Jamie said.

"Absolutely. That's why I'm happy to say there's light at the end of the tunnel. Along with other forward-thinking medical officers, we've finally gotten a bill before Congress that addresses the situation. If it passes, nurses will be granted 'relative rank' in the grades of Second Lieutenant to Major."

"Relative rank, sir? What's that?"

"They'll be entitled to wear the insignia of their rank, but they'll continue to be addressed as 'Miss' or 'Nurse.' And their pay will be approximately half that of a male officer of the same rank."

Jamie thought of his sister. Although she wasn't one to complain, a touch of bitterness occasionally crept into Ali's letters. Her medical degree was from a fine university, yet she had to prove her worth to nearly every male doctor she encountered.

"You're right, sir," Jamie said. "That's damned unfair."

"At least we're making some progress toward better treatment of our nurses. But I'm not here to talk about the wrongs of the world." Doctor Crandall stood and placed the folder he had brought with him on the bed next to Jamie's lifeless legs. "This ton of bricks is your medical file. I've been reviewing it, and I must say, you received excellent care at AEF Base Hospital 15, Chaumont."

He stared at Jamie, no doubt asking himself how Jamie could still be alive. "You had shrapnel throughout your body. One piece broke two ribs and lodged close to your heart. One millimeter this way or that, and you'd be dead. Your doctors worked miracles to get you through life-threatening wounds to your chest and abdomen. And the bullet that impacted your temple could easily have killed you. You were lucky to suffer only a concussion, a hairline skull fracture, and a scar."

Jamie felt the scar on his temple. "I'm truly grateful for the care I've received. I just wonder, was there anything more that could have been done about the injuries that left me paralyzed?"

"Not that I can see. Their primary concern was to keep you alive."

Jamie shrugged. "I guess it wouldn't have done me a whole lot of good to be able to walk if I were dead."

Doctor Crandall laughed. "I wouldn't put it quite that way, but you're right. And I'm glad you're not wallowing in self-pity as some men in your condition are."

"Self-pity? When I charged that battery of German machine guns, I didn't expect to survive. Every day since has been a gift from God." Jamie turned his head toward Doctor Crandall. "I can read, I can write, and I can teach from a wheelchair. That's what I'm trying to focus on, the things I can do, not the things I can't." Like being unable to father children.

Doctor Crandall put his hand on Jamie's shoulder. "I was told you were brave. Now I believe it."

"Don't get me wrong, sir. It's a constant battle." Jamie sighed. "One I don't always win."

Crandall set Jamie's medical file on the nightstand and roughly pulled back the blanket Nurse Hobbes had so carefully arranged. "Mind if I look at your legs?" He didn't wait for an answer before palpating Jamie's thighs, hinging his knees, and flexing his ankles. He cupped each foot in his delicate hands.

"Good circulation," Crandall said to himself. He leaned in closer. "This is very important, so before you answer, give it some serious thought. Your records indicate that you had feeling in your legs and could move them, however haltingly, for the first day or two after your injuries. Is that correct?"

Jamie thought for a few seconds. "I was sedated, slipping in and out of consciousness. But yes, as I recall, that's correct."

Crandall pulled an X-ray negative from Jamie's records and held it to the light. "The X-rays they took of you in France have about as much resolution as one would get from shining a flashlight on you from across the room. We can do much better here."

Doctor Crandall absentmindedly pulled the blanket up to Jamie's chest with his free hand, leaving the sheet hopelessly tangled at Jamie's feet. Had a bluebird done such a haphazard job, she'd have been reprimanded.

"Letterman has one of the most advanced X-ray machines in the US. I'm going to have Sergeant Hendricks take you to our radiology lab without delay. I want a complete spinal workup. We need to know the precise location of any shrapnel your doctors may have missed."

Jamie could feel his pulse begin to race. "What do you hope to find?"

"Your body was peppered with shrapnel. If one of those pieces had severed your spinal cord, you would have become paralyzed instantaneously, and permanently. The fact that your paralysis came on over a day or two rather than suddenly could mean a piece is impinging on your spinal cord, and the resulting swelling is causing your paralysis. If so, and we removed the piece without causing any further damage, the swelling may go down, and your paralysis may be temporary."

"But ..." Jamie raised his head from his pillow. "Why didn't they think of that at Walter Reed?"

"According to your records, they did. But they don't have our X-ray machine. Which Doctor ...." He glanced at Jamie's medical records again. "Doctor Lawrence used in his argument to get you transferred here."

Jamie was beginning to panic again. "But isn't it too late? It's already been four months since I was wounded."

Doctor Crandall rested his hand on Jamie's knee, which, of course, Jamie couldn't feel. "That's why I don't want to wait another minute."

Jamie stared at the ceiling. The thought that he might someday walk again was overwhelming. "Please don't give me false hope."

Doctor Crandall put his hands in his pockets. "Hope is never false."

Jamie's spirits soared. Since losing the use of his legs, he had refused to think about his future. With this small ray of hope, for the first time in weeks, he allowed himself to think about the girl he'd met on the cable car.

Chapter 4

Captivated

Tuesday, Noon, 10 April 1917

Deployment of his army reserve unit was only a matter of time. Having lived a near-monastic life while pursuing his bachelor's, master's, and doctoral degrees at a demanding university like Stanford, Jamie knew shockingly little about the real world. Here it was, 1917. He'd be 25 years old in another month, and to his profound regret, he'd never even kissed a girl. If an enemy bullet was going to find him, he wanted to live a little before he died.

San Francisco was only an hour by train north of campus. Jamie planned to visit the city, ride the cable cars, and see some sights. He'd saved a little money. Dinner in a nice restaurant also appealed to him. He just wished he could share it with someone.

Jamie walked from campus to the Palo Alto train station, where he ran into his friend Ainsley and three of Ainsley's fraternity brothers.

"Jamie!" Ainsley said. "What dragged you out of your cave and away from your books?"

"The war. I figured I should visit the city and live a little before we're called up." He looked over the group. "You guys look like you're off on a mission."

"It's Ainsley's 21st birthday," the frat boy, who was clearly the group's "Big Man," said.

Jamie clasped Ainsley's hand. "Congratulations."

"We're taking the birthday boy to the City by the Bay for a proper celebration," another brother said.

Big Man put his arm around Ainsley's shoulder. "We aim to get Ainsley drunk and help him fill the purse of a lady engaged in the world's oldest profession—our treat."

From the worry lines creasing Ainsley's forehead, Jamie got the impression Ainsley wasn't too keen on the idea. At his first opportunity, Jamie took his friend aside. "Do you want me to come along and make sure your 'brothers' don't get you into too much trouble?"

"Naw. I'm supposed to be an adult now. If I can't take care of myself here, how will I manage when we get to France, and I have to look after my entire platoon?" Ainsley glanced at his frat brothers. "But I'd welcome your company on the ride to Union Square."

Thick fog greeted Jamie, Ainsley, and the frat boys when their train pulled into San Francisco's 3rd and Townsend station. They crammed into a taxi. Big Man, whom Jamie found insufferably arrogant, gave their driver terse directions: "Geary Street, Union Square."

It was a tight fit in the taxi, resulting in a lot of elbowing and cursing. A thunderous fart from someone in the back seat about caused a riot—all standard fare for the frat boys and one reason Jamie was never tempted to join a fraternity.

The taxi rattled to a halt at Union Square as the sun broke through the fog. No end of shouting and shoving took place as everyone piled out. The thought that these *boys* might soon be leading men into battle was too much for Jamie. He approached Ainsley and stuck out his hand. "Happy birthday." He began to walk away.

"Hey," Ainsley said, "you sure you don't want *me* to come along and keep *you* out of trouble?"

"Aww, let him go," Big Man said. "He's no fun anyway."

Ainsley shrugged. "See you around campus."

Jamie didn't mind being on his own. Though he liked people, he was just as comfortable in his own company.

Union Square was surrounded by seven- and eight-story buildings—an impressive sight for a small-town boy like Jamie. He drifted toward the square's centerpiece. A plaque at its base identified the 97-foot-tall monument as a tribute to Admiral George Dewey's 1898 victory in the Battle of Manila Bay. At the top stood a nine-foot-tall statue of the Goddess Victory. Jamie's neck began to hurt from staring up at her. The model must have been quite a woman if the artist's depiction was accurate.

Jamie put aside fantasies of engaging with a nine-foot-tall woman and aimlessly circumnavigated the square. When he found himself back on Geary Street, he crossed over to look at the paintings on display in the windows of an art gallery. "Hutchins Fine Art, Established 1885," it said above the door.

One painting, in particular, captured Jamie's imagination. It depicted a cable car seen through the mist of a rainy day. It wasn't the scene that was striking. What caught his attention was the artist's startling use of color. The painting was signed "Rach L." in the lower right-hand corner. Whoever Rach was, he certainly had talent.

The ringing of a cable car bell drew Jamie like a Siren's song. He spotted the car as it was pulling away from its stop. It didn't matter to Jamie where it was headed. One never knows where adventure might be found.

He broke into a full sprint. It was no contest since he could almost hold his own in a footrace with a cheetah. He jumped aboard before the car had even reached top speed.

Several passengers were queued in front of the conductor. Jamie took his place at the end of the line. The posted fare schedule advertised an all-day "blue" pass for a nickel. Jamie watched as the conductor verified the date on the 7-day "red" pass of the girl in front of him. Her voice had an almost musical quality as she thanked the conductor. And her smile—one would think she was having the best day of her life.

The directory on the bulkhead between the front and rear compartments of the car said Jamie was on the Powell–Hyde Line. The sun's position told him they were headed north, toward the waterfront. That was fine with Jamie. He didn't want to have come all this way and not see the bay.

The enclosed rear compartment held no attraction for Jamie. He made his way to the open-sided front compartment where two outward-facing benches ran fore and aft, with the driver standing in a narrow gap between them. Jamie sat a few feet from the girl who had been in the ticket line ahead of him.

The driver was beside Jamie. To watch him work, Jamie turned sideways, facing the front of the car—and the girl he found so fascinating. He rested his arm on the back of the bench.

There was no need for the driver to steer since cable cars run on tracks. Still, the man was kept surprisingly busy as he worked the controls.

As Jamie studied the driver's movements, he couldn't help stealing surreptitious glances at the girl next to him. She would have stood out in any crowd. While waiting in the ticket line behind her, he could just barely see over her head. That meant she had to be only a few inches shorter than Jamie's five foot nine. True, she wasn't nine feet tall like the Goddess Victory, but she was lovely enough to have been the artist's model. Her perfectly symmetrical features were framed by curly blonde hair cut daringly short to shoulder length, as was the trend with modern girls. Her blue eyes sparkled in the sunlight. "Eve," Jamie thought her name should be, for she was the first woman to captivate him so completely.

Jamie had to force himself not to stare at her. He tried to focus his attention on the cable car driver, a burly man of medium height, early to mid-forties, who sported a full beard and mustache. His heavy coat, big leather gloves, and stocking cap contributed to his bearish appearance, although his quick smile would have suited a teddy bear more than a grizzly.

Jamie began peppering the driver with questions. Leonard was the man's name; *Gripman* was his title.

Eve, the girl next to Jamie, took an interest in the questioning and turned sideways toward the rear of the car so she was facing Leonard—and Jamie. As she rested her arm on the back of the bench, her hand was almost touching Jamie's.

"Yes," Leonard said, "the job does require a good bit of skill—and awareness." He rang the car's bell. Its insistent clamor had the most comical effect on a daydreaming pedestrian who had wandered too close to the tracks.

Eve laughed along with the pedestrian. "I believe you enjoyed that," she said to Leonard."

He smiled. "Best part of the job, ma'am."

"I'm sure quite a few men would be happy to trade jobs with you," she said.

Leonard smiled. "Maybe so, but I wouldn't want to trade with them."

Jamie was entranced by Eve's refined manner. Everything about her seemed so ... so feminine. He pointed to the controls Leonard was manhandling. "Would you mind telling us what all those levers and pedals do?" His use of the word "us" was intentional.

"I'd be happy to. You see this here lever?" Leonard indicated a long metal shaft that ran through a home plate-sized opening in the floor near his feet. "It's the main control. We call it the 'grip.' " He pushed forward on the shaft, and the car began to slow. "On the other end is what I think of as a giant pair of pliers. When I pull back on the grip, its jaws close on the cable. When I push forward, the jaws open. Closed jaws mean the car's moving at the same speed as the cable—a constant nine and a half miles per hour. Open jaws mean the car's either coasting or at rest."

"You make it look easy," Jamie said, "but I'm sure it's not."

Leonard flexed his massive biceps. "There's an art to driving a cable car. You have to grip the cable with the right amount of pressure at the right time. Too much pressure when the car's starting out, and the passengers will think they're riding a bucking bronco; too little, and the car will never make it up our steep hills." He stood, chest out, shoulders back. "It takes practice and strength to do it well."

It was taking all Jamie's strength not to stare at Eve. "I'm sure stopping the car is equally challenging," he said to Leonard.

"Right enough, sir. First, you have to let go of the cable. Then you step on the wheel brake pedal." He indicated a shingle-sized metal rectangle near where the grip passed through the floor. "A gripman needs good balance to brake smoothly." He did a little dance on the pedal, and the car gradually slowed. "If I need more braking power, I use this here track brake lever." He indicated a lever next to the grip. As he pulled back on it, the car slowed rapidly.

"I imagine a gripman's biggest challenge is anticipating what pedestrians and other vehicles are going to do," Eve said.

"For sure, young lady. Otherwise, with such a big, heavy car, someone could get crushed."

Jamie found himself staring at Eve unabashedly. She didn't seem to mind. Thank goodness the days of billowing petticoats covered by ankle-length skirts were gone. Eve's fashionably short black skirt revealed a pair of extraordinarily shapely calves. Her simple turquoise blouse peeking out from under a tweed coat complimented her perfect complexion. Jamie couldn't remember seeing a prettier girl, ever.

Jamie wasn't bad-looking himself, at least according to his mother, and she wouldn't lie. She said his square jaw, sandy brown hair, and blue eyes made him look pleasingly rugged, whatever that meant. He also kept himself remarkably fit. He glanced at his trousers. They weren't new, but they were clean and recently pressed. He unconsciously straightened his shirt collar, feeling slightly shabby next to a girl whose coat alone probably cost twice as much as his entire wardrobe.

Leonard offered a constant narrative on the fine art of cable car operations all the way to the end of the line near Beach Street. When the car trundled to a stop, passengers began getting off.

"Which do you find more challenging," Eve asked Leonard, "traveling downhill to Beach Street or back up to Powell?"

"Feel free to stay onboard," Leonard said to his star pupils. "If you've got time, I'll show you how hard a gripman has to work to climb back up to Union Square."

Eve smiled as she settled back onto the bench. Jamie was more than happy to stay. They watched the conductor help Leonard push the car onto the center of the Beach Street turntable, rotate the table almost 180 degrees, and push the car back onto a parallel set of tracks.

A handful of new passengers got on. In less than five minutes, the car was on its way up the hill to Union Square. Jamie was thankful none of the new passengers chose to sit in the front compartment.

The sights and sounds spellbound Leonard's eager pupils as they climbed Russian Hill, passed Union Square, and approached Market Street and the Powell Station turntable. They remained glued to their seats as Leonard and the conductor turned the car around. At four in the afternoon, not many passengers got on for the return trip to the Beach Street terminal.

Leonard's mastery of the grip was on full display as he shepherded the car toward the waterfront. He artfully used a combination of wheel and track brake to let riders off. Eventually, Jamie and Eve were the only passengers.

All their questioning must have befuddled Leonard because, against all the rules, he brought the car to a complete stop and offered to let Jamie try his hand at the controls.

Jamie was right. It wasn't as easy as Leonard made it look.

They came to a flat run with little traffic. "Want to take a turn at the controls?" Leonard asked Eve.

Her eyes opened wide. "Does the car have a good emergency brake?"

Leonard laughed. "Don't worry, young lady. Our emergency brake is so simple and effective only a genius could have thought it up."

She pointed to a red-handled lever near the grip. "I assume that's what activates it."

"Right you are, miss. If I pull that there lever, it will drive an 18-inch steel wedge into the slot the grip passes through and stop the car within a couple of feet. It works so well that on the rare occasion a gripman has to use it, more often than not, a mechanic has to come out from the maintenance shop and cut it free using a welding torch."

Leonard's answer must have been what Eve wanted to hear. She edged past Jamie into the gripman's compartment and took over the controls. Jamie remained standing just behind her.

Eve's smile soon eroded into a look of consternation as she struggled to apply enough pressure to the grip or operate the brake pedal without losing her balance.

"Come on," Leonard said to Jamie. "Give her a hand.

Wrap your arms around her and take hold of the grip together."

Jamie was more than slightly taken aback by Leonard's insistence. "May I?" he said to Eve.

Her nodded consent seemed to lack conviction.

While trying to be as unintrusive as possible, Jamie reached around her and placed his hands on the grip alongside hers.

The gripman's compartment was a tight fit to begin with. Though it wasn't Jamie's intention, with two people crammed so close together, he felt he was practically mauling Eve.

"Hard to keep your balance, isn't it?" Leonard said to Eve. "Lean into your friend. Let him support you."

Friend? Jamie wished. He expected Eve to correct Leonard's misconception. Instead, the contours of her body soon molded to his, and her spontaneous laughter filled the compartment like a Mozart violin concerto.

Jamie had never been so close to a girl. To his surprise, what stood out most was how good she smelled.

Their fun ended all too soon when the conductor stormed to the front of the car. "Are you trying to get us both fired?" he shouted at Leonard. "If management gets wind of you letting a couple of kids drive the car, we'll both be up the creek."

Jamie reluctantly took his hands off the grip and stepped back from Eve. He was surprised by how confidently she pushed forward on the grip and how easily she kept her balance as she applied the wheel brake. The car lumbered to a stop. Eve extended her hand to Jamie. "Rachel," she said.

Rachel. That was even more appropriate than Eve,

considering how completely Rachel of the Bible had capti-vated Jacob.

What's the proper etiquette for a gentleman when meeting a lady who's been pressing her body against his for the past five minutes? Jamie kept it simple. "I'm Jamie."

Leonard's face turned red. "I'm sorry. I thought you two were together."

"Don't be sorry," Rachel said. "I'd be surprised if I weren't the only girl ever to operate a cable car." She placed her hand on Jamie's forearm. "And I couldn't have done it without ... 'James,' was it?"

"Jamie," he replied.

She smiled. "I couldn't have done it without Jamie's help."

The conductor returned to the back of the car. Leonard reclaimed his rightful place. Jamie and Rachel sat together. The car soon reached the end of the line.

Rachel stood. "Thank you for a wonderful adventure," she said to Leonard.

After adding his thanks, Jamie stepped from the car and offered Rachel his hand to help her down. She took it without hesitation. They watched together as Leonard and his conductor rolled the car onto the Beach Street turntable. They waved as the car pulled away.

Jamie stood shoulder to shoulder with Rachel as they looked out over the bay. Brightly colored sails darted here and there. Waves lapped at the sandy shore. Crisp salt air filled his lungs. A storm was moving in from the open ocean, like the hand of God passing through the Golden Gate.

"San Francisco is a beautiful place," Jamie said. "I'm glad I finally got to see it."

"I guessed you weren't a local. What brings you here?"

"The war. I'm a graduate student at a university about thirty miles south of here. I thought it would be a good idea to see the city ... while there's still time."

"Thirty miles south? Would that be Stanford?"

"Yes. Down on the Farm, as they say."

"The Farm?"

"The campus is on land that had been Leland Stanford's Palo Alto Stock Farm. He used to raise racehorses there. Now they try to raise scholars."

Rachel smiled, but her smile quickly disappeared. "You said you wanted to see the city 'while there's still time.' Are you planning to enlist?"

"I'm a member of the Student Officer Training Corps, so I'm already committed."

Rachel looked concerned. "Then I hope you'll carry many happy memories of this visit with you to France."

"It's certainly been memorable so far." He stopped himself before adding, *because of you.* He didn't want to risk scaring her away.

With a hand on either side of her neck, she tossed her hair off her shoulders. "I never thought I'd get to operate a cable car." Her eyes sparkled. "I have a friend back home in San Diego who was born in the Bay Area. She's always going on about the cable cars. She'll be amazed when I tell her I've driven one."

"I hope the cable cars will be around for years to come," Jamie said. "But being confined to tracks, with their limitations and inefficiencies, I'm afraid the days of cable cars roaming the streets of San Francisco are numbered—unless the city fathers have the foresight to preserve some of the more scenic lines as tourist attractions."

Rachel gave Jamie a sideways glance. "That sounds like something my father would say."

The inflection in her voice left no doubt he'd been paid a high compliment.

A mischievous twinkle lit up Rachel's eyes. "Do you like chocolate?"

A big guilty grin was Jamie's answer.

Rachel pointed behind Jamie to an enormous sign towering over a block-long building. "That's Ghirardelli's chocolate factory. They have the most divine candy shop."

In no time, they were surrounded by more varieties of chocolate than Jamie knew existed. They became like children in a ... candy shop. Jamie would have exhausted the shop's inventory had Rachel not set such an impressive example of self-control. He splurged and bought each of them a chocolate bar.

They left Ghirardelli's and retraced their steps to the cable car turnaround, where they sat on a bench overlooking the bay. "Please tell me about yourself," Jamie said.

Rachel answered between nibbles from an almond chocolate bar. "I moved to San Francisco about a year ago, right after college. I'm studying painting at the California School of Fine Arts."

"Where'd you go to college?"

"Vassar."

Rich girls attend Vassar. Sure, there might be a few scholarship students. Rachel's clothes broadcast that she hadn't been one of them. What would she think if she knew that without the Thayer Scholarship, Jamie could only have dreamt of attending Stanford?

"You must be a good student to have graduated from Vassar."

"Valedictorian, Class of '16."

Jamie detected not a hint of conceit in her reply. "I'm impressed."

Rachel sat a little taller.

He appraised her like a fine work of art. "Were you an art major?"

"I did a double major in math and astronomy."

"Really. Is there a connection between math, astronomy, and fine art?"

She gazed up at the stars, which were only beginning to appear in the evening sky. "Astronomers began taking photographs of the sky almost as soon as photography was invented, but to this day, when we want to depict the colorful scenes we see through our telescopes, we can only resort to hand-coloring black and white photos." She folded her arms. "That takes a bit of training. So, at Vassar, the art and astronomy departments got together to offer a class they called Astro-graphics. When I took the course, I discovered I had an unexpected talent. A unique way of using color to bring out the nuances of nature."

"Due to your astronomer's understanding of the properties of light?"

Rachel canted her head. "I never thought of it that way. Maybe so."

Jamie put his arm over the back of the bench. "Why'd you decide to pursue art instead of astronomy?"

"It wasn't really up to me." She frowned. "Even with my grades, none of the graduate astronomy programs I applied to were eager to admit me."

"Because you're a woman," Jamie said. It was a statement, not a question.

Rachel clenched her jaw. "I can't think of any other reason."

"That's so unfair."

She turned to him abruptly. "Do you mean that, or are you just telling me what you think I want to hear?"

Jamie recoiled. "I mean it. I like women. My mother was a woman; my sister is a woman; someday, I hope to have a wife who's a woman."

Rachel laughed. "I'm sorry. I'm not used to having a man on my side."

"My sister had to fight a similar battle when she applied to medical school."

"Did she win?"

"She's now Alice Collins, MD, thanks to the University of Edinburgh, and no thanks to any medical school in the US."

"Maybe she's more determined than I was. Or maybe her alternatives weren't as attractive." Rachel raised her eyes to the sky. "I love astronomy, but that doesn't mean it has to be my life's work. Art offers much more freedom." She crossed her legs at the ankles. "Being the low 'man' on the totem pole at some obscure observatory probably wouldn't have been very satisfying anyway. And as a woman, advancement would have been slow at best. In art, I'm free to do as I please. For instance, lately, I've been having a great time illustrating stories about the solar system I've written for my cousin's children." She got a faraway look. "I dream of having my own gallery someday where I can display only works of art I admire."

"Including some of your own?"

"Possibly."

Jamie leaned forward and rested his elbows on his knees.

"I'm glad you're enjoying art, although it would have been nice if you'd had more choice in the matter." He looked at her out of the corner of his eye. "But who am I to talk?"

Rachel pushed a lock of luminescent blonde hair behind her ear. "Why not you?"

"Because I was the beneficiary of the kind of treatment you and my sister suffered."

Rachel's eyebrows pinched together. "You?"

Jamie sat up. "A while back, a man named Thomas Thayer established an annual scholarship to Stanford School of Engineering. It was supposed to go to the top graduate from my high school."

"Supposed to go?"

Jamie gazed out over the bay. "There was a clause in the scholarship charter few people were aware of. Mister Thayer was of the era when it was generally assumed only boys would want to be engineers. When the scholarship committee learned that the top graduate from my class was a girl, they belatedly disclosed that the Thayer Scholarship was only open to boys." Jamie looked at Rachel. "I was the top male graduate in my class, so I received the scholarship that, in all fairness, should have gone to ... Elaine, I believe her name was."

I believe? The name Elaine Stanton was seared into his brain. Would he ever forget the pain in her voice when she accused him of stealing her future? "Not a day goes by that I don't pray I've made good use of the opportunity her disappointment gave me."

Rachel looked at him with the most sympathetic expression. "It's sweet that you still care. But let me ask you this. If you had refused the scholarship out of protest, would it have gone to Elaine?"

"No. According to the terms of the scholarship, it would have been offered to the next most qualified boy."

Rachel put her hand on Jamie's forearm. "Then you shouldn't blame yourself."

Her gentle touch gave Jamie a longed-for measure of absolution. "You're right—but I still feel guilty."

Rachel folded her hands in her lap. "Do you know what became of Elaine?"

"I heard she got a scholarship to California State Normal School in San Jose, where she earned a math degree and a teaching credential."

I heard. He knew exactly what became of her. She was teaching math at their old high school.

"Let's hope she's found happiness in teaching," Rachel said.

Please let it be so. "What about you?" Jamie said. "Art's a tough way to make a living, isn't it?"

Rachel smiled. "Do you mean, how will I keep from starving?" She glanced across the bay. "I'm more worried about where my art studies will soon take me."

"Sounds like you're about to start a new adventure."

"I've satisfied the residency requirements for my Master of Fine Arts degree. All I have left to do before I can graduate is turn in a portfolio, which I can complete anywhere." She tracked a sailboat as it moved close to shore. "Jason Roach, one of the more progressive professors at CSFA, is leaving. Along with some of his creative friends, he's planning to start an artist's colony and art school in La Jolla. He's invited me to be among his first students."

"La Jolla. That's just north of San Diego, isn't it?"

"That's right."

Had Rachel heard the anxiety in Jamie's voice?

"Jason's ultimate goal is to turn his school into a fully accredited art institute."

Jamie considered it a dangerous sign that Rachel referred to this roach by his first name. He didn't give a damn about Professor Jason Roach's plans. What concerned him was that Rachel was going to be moving away. "I've never been as far south as La Jolla."

"Having been born and raised in San Diego," Rachel said, "it will be a homecoming of sorts." She knitted her brow. "I am a little worried, though. Rumor has it that Professor Roach resigned from CSFA rather than being fired for inappropriate behavior toward several female students. I can only imagine what his friends are like. Plus, I've heard stories about what goes on in artist colonies."

Jamie turned to her. "Stories?"

"I'm a good little Christian girl." Rachel crossed her arms. Was she hugging herself for protection? "I'm afraid I won't fit in with their bohemian lifestyle."

Jamie turned up his palms. "Then why go?"

"For my art. I might learn something I couldn't learn anywhere else."

"Will you be sorry to leave San Francisco?" What Jamie really wanted to know was whether she'd be sorry to be so far from him.

She turned toward the sprawling cityscape. "There's a lot I'll miss about the city. And I'll hate having to give up my apartment. It's a nice little studio at the top of an 1870s Victorian near the summit of Russian Hill. I have a lovely view of the bay from my windows."

Jamie began thinking about what kind of work he might find in San Diego. He then chided himself for making more of their "relationship" than there was. "When will you be leaving?"

"As soon as I deliver a batch of my paintings to Hutchins Fine Art."

"Hutchins—across Geary Street from Union Square?"

"That's the place. To support CSFA, they place a student's painting in their window each month. I'm the lucky student this time." She raised her chin. "And now they've agreed to display some of my paintings on consignment."

"That's great."

"I'd just left Hutchins when I got on Leonard's cable car."

No wonder she looked so happy when he first saw her. And thank goodness Hutchins is close to the Powell-Hyde cable car line. Otherwise, she and Jamie might never have met. "Have you sold many paintings?" He was trying to remain calm.

"Hmm. Let me think." Rachel began counting on her fingers. "I believe I've sold exactly ... zero." She laughed. "We all have to start somewhere."

Jamie liked that she didn't take herself too seriously.

She gave Jamie a penetrating look. "My father was an engineer. You remind me of him."

Another compliment. This one accompanied by a touch of sadness. " 'Was' an engineer?" Jamie said.

Her voice wavered. "He died in an industrial accident when I was fifteen."

Images of Jamie's own father's death flashed through his mind. "I'm sorry."

She stared at her stylish cross-strap shoes. "I miss him. His inquisitiveness, his laughter, his kindness—his unconditional love." Rachel wrapped herself tightly in her coat. "He was always thoughtful, always considerate." She looked at Jamie. "Which brings us back to how I expect to make a living as an artist when I haven't sold a single painting. The answer is I won't have to. My father left me a generous trust, which I gained control of last year when I turned twenty-one."

Jamie was surprised she would disclose something so personal to someone she'd just met. Surprised and honored. "Your father must have been very successful. The engineers I know would be hard-pressed to fund even a meager trust."

"He was very inventive." The pride in her voice came through loud and clear. "Father held dozens of patents, some astonishingly lucrative. They were the source of the bulk of my trust." She looked at Jamie for a moment. "It's funny that I'm comfortable telling you all this. Our shared adventure on the cable car and your openness about your scholarship tell me you're someone I can trust."

"I've been told I'm a good listener." He smiled at her. "So, your father. What kind of work did he do?"

"A little bit of everything. He particularly enjoyed anything having to do with transportation: trains, trucks, automobiles, even airplanes. I know he had something to do with the carburetor on the Model T Ford." Rachel glanced at an approaching cable car. "Do you remember me asking Leonard about the emergency brake on the cable car?" Jamie nodded. "My father held the patent on that, too."

Jamie's jaw fell. "And you kept that to yourself?"

"I didn't think anyone would be interested."

Jamie had a thought. "Might your trust enable you to open your own art gallery soon?"

"That's my dream." She faced Jamie. "Enough about me. What kind of engineer are you?"

"Actually, I'm a physicist."

"Oh?"

"After my first year at Stanford, I realized I'm more interested in theory than applications. I loved the physics courses that all mechanical engineering majors were required to take, so I petitioned the Thayer Scholarship Committee. They allowed me to change my major to physics."

"I don't know many students who, as undergraduates, didn't change their major at least once."

"Me either. Fortunately, the Committee granted my request." Jamie turned to her. "This is an exciting time to be a physicist, considering the recent startling developments in relativity and quantum mechanics." He could feel himself blush. "I'm sorry. I'm getting carried away."

"You needn't apologize. I admire your enthusiasm."

And he admired everything about her! Jamie set his jaw resolutely. "If I pass my orals next month, I'll have earned a Ph.D. in theoretical physics, and Stanford has practically guaranteed me an assistant professorship."

"Impressive for someone so young," Rachel said.

"I've been lucky. I've had a couple of original ideas that my thesis advisor and I developed into papers that were published in a leading scientific journal, *Physical Review*."

"I'm sure luck had nothing to do with it," Rachel said.

Jamie smiled. "Thanks for your vote of confidence." He sighed. "My orals worry me, though. I have a terrible memory. Without my reference books, I might struggle."

Rachel smiled. "Then I wish you the best of luck with your orals."

Though they hardly knew each other, he sensed that she was proud of him, which made Jamie proud of himself.

A nearby clock tower chimed the time. "Speaking of orals," Jamie said, "despite the chocolate we've just had, are you hungry?"

Her face brightened. "Famished."

"There's a nice-looking restaurant across the way." Jamie swallowed hard before asking, "Will you join me?"

There was no hesitation in her response. "It would be a pleasure. But it will have to be Dutch treat since it won't be a formal date."

Jamie suppressed a flash of irritation. Did she think he was a pauper? He could afford to treat her. He'd just have to go hungry for the next week if he did.

He stood and offered her his arm as he'd seen gentlemen do in the movies. She smiled and took it without hesitation.

Chapter 5

Encouragement

Sunday Evening, 09 March 1919

By 7:00 PM, Sergeant Hendricks was wheeling Jamie through the doors of Letterman's X-ray lab and into a room full of strange-looking equipment.

"Byron, this is Major Collins," Hendricks said to the X-ray engineer.

To Jamie, Byron looked even stranger than his equipment. He was tall and incredibly thin. Though he couldn't have been much older than Jamie, his long, disheveled, white hair made him look much older. His waistcoat with tails were, without a doubt, the most pretentious costume Jamie had ever seen a professional man wear.

Byron barely acknowledged Hendricks and completely ignored Jamie. Hendricks looked at Jamie and rolled his eyes. "I'll leave you to it, Byron. With your leave, sir." Hendricks headed for the door.

"Hold on, Hendricks," Byron said. "Will you help me get this gentleman onto the examination table?"

"Since when did the Mighty Byron need help lifting a patient?"

"Only recently."

Hendricks effortlessly lifted Jamie and placed him on what looked to Jamie like a mortuary slab.

"You seem more run-down every time I see you," Hendricks said to Byron. "Doesn't your wife feed you anymore?" He looked Byron up and down. "Maybe you should see a doctor."

"Naw, I'm fine. Just tired lately, that's all." He twisted Jamie this way and that.

"What's your wife think about your condition?"

"She says I should see a doctor."

"I rest my case," Hendricks said.

Byron worked Jamie into an awkward position and held him there. "What bothers me," Byron said to Hendricks, "is that I'm too tired to play with the boys when I get home, and now Barbara wants a girl. We keep trying, with no luck yet."

Hendricks' bulging biceps were on full display as he folded his arms. "You should keep trying. A girl would be a real blessing."

Jamie began to seethe. He would punch one of them if they didn't stop talking about fatherhood. With his injuries, even if he had feeling "down there," it was doubtful he'd ever be able to father a child.

"Gentlemen." There was an edge to Jamie's voice. "Do you think we can get on with the X-rays?"

"Sorry." It was the first time Byron acknowledged Jamie. "I'm working overtime. You're about the hundredth patient I've X-rayed today. I guess my bedside manner has suffered."

"Overtime?" Jamie said. "There's no such thing as overtime in the army."

"I'm not in the army. The manufacturer provides an engineer with each X-ray machine. I'm it."

"And they make you wear that outfit?"

Byron looked down at himself. "I sure wouldn't wear this getup if I didn't have to."

Hendricks chuckled. "Every time I see you, it makes me think the circus is in town." He turned to Jamie. "Sir, if I'm no longer needed, I'll wait outside."

"Fine," Jamie said.

Byron dismissed Hendricks with a halfhearted wave.

Jamie didn't say anything more until Hendricks was out of hearing range. Being an officer and Medal of Honor recipient set him apart from the men as it was. He didn't want it to become general knowledge that he'd also been a physics professor before the war. "I did a little work with X-rays in graduate school," he said to Byron.

"That's interesting." Byron's distracted tone indicated otherwise. He held Jamie in place with one hand. Using his free hand, he lowered what looked like a box camera hanging from the ceiling and placed it about six inches above Jamie's middle. With his shaky free hand, he pushed a button. A whirring sound emanated from deep within the guts of the machine and continued for about two seconds. When it stopped, Bryon rolled Jamie half a turn and repeated the process.

"This is supposed to be my day off," Byron said. "But I can hardly remember the last time I actually had a day off. One of us engineers is always calling in sick, and somebody has to cover for him. I shouldn't complain, though. The pay's good, and the overtime's great. I only wish I didn't feel like I'm working myself into an early grave."

If looks were any indication, that's precisely what Byron was doing.

"When I started this job a year ago, my hair was thick and dark. Now, look at me. And I'm always tired."

Jamie craned his head and looked directly at Byron. "How many patients do you X-ray in a day?"

Byron shrugged. "I don't know. Twenty, easy. Sometimes more."

"And you stand right next to your patient while the machine is radiating?"

"Sure. I have to make sure they don't move."

Jamie grabbed Byron by his wrist. "Don't you realize what that much radiation is doing to you?"

"You and that surgeon." Byron jerked his wrist free. "If it weren't safe, the company would have told us."

* * *

An hour later, Colonel Thornburgh and Doctor Crandall were standing on either side of Jamie's gurney in a pre-op room. A tall, gaunt doctor entered the room and stood at the foot of Jamie's gurney. Despite his inferior rank, Doctor Regenstein was introduced with deference.

Crandall held up an X-ray negative in each hand. "We've been comparing the previous X-rays they took of you with the ones we took here, and I've got to say, our man knows what he's doing. In France, they only managed to take a few images of you lying flat on your back or on your stomach." Crandall put one of the images aside. "Our man took high-resolution images of you from multiple angles, and they reveal over a dozen pieces of shrapnel in your back and upper legs."

Jamie could feel the blood drain from his face. "My God! You have to do something!"

"Relax," Doctor Crandall said. "Most will work their way out harmlessly over time. Others can be left where they are. The body has the ability to encapsulate metal fragments, rendering them harmless. One piece, though, does concern us. It's very close to your spinal column." He held the remaining image to the light. Jamie could barely make out a light patch next to what must have been vertebrae. "That piece could very well be the cause of your paralysis. Doctor Regenstein here is our best surgeon. I'd like him to remove it."

It felt like an elephant had sat on Jamie's chest. "Would … would that mean I could walk again?"

Colonel Thornburgh smiled. "There's no guarantee, but that's our hope."

This was the first evidence-based encouragement Jamie had received from the medical staff. "Then let's get on with it."

Colonel Thornburgh's expression became grave. "Before we do, you should know that removing that piece of metal will be risky. If something goes wrong, your condition could become even worse."

"And if we leave it where it is?"

Doctor Regenstein spoke for the first time. "There'd be no hope of your condition ever improving."

This guy wasn't one to sugarcoat things, which was fine with Jamie. He wanted to know exactly where he … stood?

"And remember," Crandall added, "even in the best case, it will take time before you notice any difference."

Jamie searched the face of each doctor in turn. Thornburgh and Crandall appeared optimistic. Regenstein remained stone-faced.

"I'd rather take the risk than live without hope," Jamie said.

Regenstein moved a little closer. "Nurse Eliot tells me you haven't eaten in quite some time, so I intend to operate immediately. Only the hand of God has kept that piece of metal from severing your spinal cord. If we wait another minute, even the slightest twist or turn could be catastrophic."

Jamie took a deep breath. "May the Lord guide your hand," he said to Doctor Regenstein while trying to keep every part of his body immobile except his mouth and vocal cords.

Doctor Regenstein left without another word.

It had been nerve-wracking waiting to be taken to the X-ray lab. The wait to be taken to the operating room was worse. Jamie took courage from Doctors Thornburgh and Crandall's optimism. He just wished Dr. Regenstein was as encouraging.

Chapter 6

Like Old Friends

Tuesday, Late Afternoon, 10 April 1917

The wind was freshening as Jamie and Rachel made their way the few hundred yards to the corner of Hyde and Beach Streets. Clouds were beginning to obscure the few early-riser stars. The maître d' at Nunzio's Italian Restaurant was kind enough to show them to a window table.

Rachel pointed. "That's Alcatraz Island, the site of the oldest lighthouse on the west coast."

Jamie looked north about a mile and a quarter. "And the site of a military prison ever since the Civil War." He felt a chill. "It sure is daunting. No wonder that's where the government plans to lock up conscientious objectors, draft dodgers, and deserters now that we're at war."

"Not a pleasant thought. Still, don't you agree the island accents a stunning view?"

To Jamie, it was nowhere near as stunning as the curves revealed when he helped Rachel out of her coat.

They sat across from each other. The maître d' handed each a menu.

"Remember, Dutch treat," Rachel said.

The idea still didn't sit well with Jamie, although it saved him from potentially having to hitchhike back to campus. He hoped it would be different someday. As a physics professor, he could live comfortably, although he'd never be rich. Unless, like Rachel's father, he invented something worth patenting—which for a theoretical physicist was unlikely.

Jamie watched as Rachel idly adjusted the delicate chain around her neck. The gold cross suspended from it pointed directly at her cleavage. She caught him staring.

"I like your cross," he said.

It was hard to tell whether she believed it was her cross he was staring at. She grasped the ancient symbol of atonement and forgiveness. "I wear it every day as a reminder."

"Of what?" Jamie said without thinking. When she didn't answer right away, he was afraid he'd gotten too personal.

She smiled. "That we don't have to be perfect to be loved by God."

As far as Jamie could tell, she was perfect.

Their waiter came shuffling out of nowhere. "Good evening. I'm Alessandro. It will be my pleasure to be your waiter this evening." From his accent, Jamie guessed he was brought up in a home where Italian was the dominant language. Alessandro picked up the multiple-page wine list Jamie had ignored and handed it to him. "Would you care for a pre-dinner drink or perhaps a fine bottle of wine to go with your dinner—while it's still legal."

Jamie looked at him. "You sound worried."

"I'm sorry. I shouldn't get political. I'm a little upset,

that's all. The Evening Chronicle's just arrived, and there's another front-page article about Wayne Wheeler and his Anti-Saloon League." Alessandro looked around the dining room with evident pride. "My grandfather opened this restaurant in 1889. It's been in our family ever since. It's taken us many years to develop the best wine list in the city. But if the 'drys' have their way, selling it will be a crime, and our entire cellar might as well have been destroyed in the '06 earthquake."

Jamie took the list with little enthusiasm. "Rachel?"

She held up her hand. "I'm sorry, Alessandro, I've never had a taste for alcohol."

Jamie's grin was so wide his face hurt. "We have that in common. Although," he quickly added, "I'd never vote to take away anyone else's right to imbibe."

Rachel looked up at Alessandro. "I don't think you have to worry about the drys. How likely is it they'll get enough states to vote to prohibit alcohol when it's been a staple for thousands of years?"

Jamie rested his hand on top of the table. "You might be surprised. Wheeler's putting a lot of pressure on politicians all across the nation."

Alessandro looked from Jamie to Rachel and back. "I probably shouldn't sell you any alcohol anyway. I believe you're already intoxicated with each other."

Jamie could feel blood rush to his cheeks. Rachel smiled and placed her hand on top of his.

If the roof had blown away and the walls collapsed, Jamie wouldn't have noticed. He was staring at Rachel's hand too intently. It was exquisite. Long, slender fingers, perfect nails—if one ignored the remnants of paint around her cuticles—and incredibly soft and warm. But it wasn't form or fitness that thoroughly captivated him. It was her decisiveness. It would have taken Jamie weeks to find the courage to hold her hand.

Alessandro smiled. "I'll leave you two alone for a few minutes. If you happen to think of it, take a look at the menu, and when you're ready, give me a wave. I'll come take your orders."

"Th, ..., thanks," Jamie stammered.

Rachel smiled at his joyous discomfort and gave his hand a little squeeze.

At the next table, a waiter, who was undoubtedly Alessandro's younger brother, was turning the presentation of a bottle of wine into a dramatic production.

Rachel leaned closer to Jamie. "All this fuss about alcohol," she said. "If Prohibition passes, I don't think it will stop people from drinking. My guess is people will get their alcohol from the black market, creating a new class of entrepreneurs who will become fabulously rich and powerful selling and distributing an inferior product at a higher price."

"All while operating completely outside government regulation and without paying taxes," Jamie said.

Rachel closed her menu. With his free hand, Jamie waved Alessandro over. They ordered. Alessandro bowed and backed away. To Jamie's amazement, Rachel never let go of his hand.

She glanced across the room to where Alessandro's brother and the maître d' were looking at the evening Chronicle together. "I suppose if I ran a business that involved the sale of alcohol, I'd be worried about Prohibition. But for me, the whole issue is trivial compared to the story dominating the news lately."

"America's entry into the European war?"

"Exactly." She searched his face. "From your look of concern, my guess is you're expecting to be called up soon."

"Most likely." His gaze was drawn to Alcatraz Island, which was where he'd end up if he gave in to the urge to run when his unit was mobilized. "The only reason I was willing to vote to reelect President Wilson was his promise to keep us out of the war."

"Politicians and their promises," Rachel scoffed. "Still, I would have voted for Wilson too, if women were allowed to vote."

"Considering where men voters have gotten us, if I had my way, *only* women would be allowed to vote. Then maybe we wouldn't get involved in senseless wars."

Her eyes bore into him. "Surely you don't mean that."

"No. You're right. What I'd really like to see are equal rights."

She leaned back in her chair. "How did a young man such as yourself come to hold such a ... progressive point of view?"

Jamie shrugged. "I haven't always been a progressive. Not that I've ever been against equal rights. I just never gave it any thought until my poli sci professor made me realize how unfair the current situation is."

"I can't imagine too many physics students lining up to take a poli sci class."

Jamie grinned. "I only took it because I had to. It satisfied a general education requirement for my BS degree. But I'm glad I did."

"Really?"

"Professor Beard was a visiting professor from Columbia University and a founding member of the National Men's League for Women's Suffrage. He was also an advocate for a woman's right to an education, as was Jane Stanford, Leland Stanford's wife. Professor Beard made me question why women such as my sister and you aren't allowed to vote. You're both smarter than most of the men I know. And my sister shouldn't have had to go all the way to Scotland to attend medical school. And then there's Elaine Stanton and her disappointment over the Thayer Scholarship. And, of course, yours when none of the graduate astronomy programs you applied to were eager to admit you."

Rachel smiled. "I wish more men felt the way you do."

"And I wish Woodrow Wilson had kept us out of the war."

Jamie watched a couple walk past the window hand-in-hand. If it weren't for the war, he could dream of strolling hand-in-hand with Rachel someday. The reality was that soon, he could be up to his knees in mud at the bottom of a trench in France. "On graduation day—assuming I pass my orals—along with my doctorate, I'll receive a commission as a captain in the US Army Reserve and be put in command of an infantry company."

"Infantry? With a Ph.D. in physics?"

"As desperate as the army is for infantry officers, that's where they've placed me."

Rachel tightened her grip on his hand. "I've read about the shocking number of casualties the British and French infantry suffered early in the war."

"You don't have to tell me. The life expectancy of their junior officers was about two weeks, with a one hundred percent turnover within six months." Jamie absentmindedly nudged his spoon over a fraction of an inch to align it perfectly with his knife. "As a company commander, it won't be my job to lead attacks. That will fall to my platoon leaders. My challenge will be to provide my men with the leadership they deserve." He stared at their tablecloth and went silent.

"Jamie?"

"I'm sorry. I was thinking, if I hadn't won the Thayer Scholarship, I couldn't have afforded to go to college." He combed his hair off his forehead with his fingers. "Odds are I'd be a private in some other captain's company. Then I'd really be in the thick of it."

Rachel's chin quivered. "I'll pray for you every day until I know you've returned safely to the States."

Jamie cocked his head as dogs sometimes do when they hear an unexpected sound. "You'd do that for a stranger?"

She tightened her grip on his hand. "I'll do that for you."

Jamie turned away and blinked several times. How was it possible that he could be sitting there holding hands with such a remarkable woman? She was beautiful, intelligent, talented, politically aware, compassionate—he could go on and on. And she was going to pray for him while he was away fighting a war that made no sense to him. "Maybe I should call you *Saint* Rachel."

"Trust me. I'm no saint."

The busboy chose that moment to bring them a small loaf of sourdough bread and several pats of butter. Jamie could have punched the guy because he had to free his hand to break the bread and offer half to Rachel.

She leaned back in her chair. "Do you have a girlfriend?"

The bread tumbled from Jamie's hand. "I believe that's what's called a non-sequitur."

A burst of laughter erupted from the couple at the next table. Jamie couldn't help envying them. "I've never had time for a girlfriend." He smiled. "Actually, that's only one reason

I don't have a girlfriend. Like most physics students, normally I'm afraid even to talk to a girl."

"You mean a handsome and debonair gentleman such as yourself hasn't left a trail of brokenhearted lovers in his wake?"

He looked at her. "Now you're teasing me."

"You're right, and I shouldn't. I went to an all-girls high school and then a women's college. My father and cousin are about the only men I've ever been brave enough to talk to—other than you."

Jamie looked around to make sure he wouldn't be overheard. "I've never even kissed a girl."

Rachel leaned in close. "And I've never even been kissed."

Had he been brave, Jamie would have climbed over the table and rectified that injustice there and then. "I've lived the life of a monk while at Stanford. One bad grade, and I could have lost my scholarship. I couldn't risk devoting even an hour to dating." He looked at Rachel, then quickly looked away. "That's no way to get close to a girl."

"This may sound terribly arrogant, but plenty of boys have asked me out. I say 'boys' because their approach has always been to try to impress me, either with their daddy's money, their athletic ability, or their supposed bravery. My answer has always been, 'no.' Perhaps I think too highly of myself, but I've been waiting for a real man to come along, a man who impresses me just by being himself. A man like you."

Jamie was so dumbfounded he could only stare at her with his mouth hanging open.

"There's a boy at CSFA who's been pestering me for months. When the US declared war on Germany, he told me he was going to enlist and win the war all by himself. Whereas you, who could be mobilized any day, haven't bragged about coming home with a chest full of medals. Your concern is whether you can provide your men the leadership they'll deserve." She took his hand again. "That's something a real man would say. That impresses me." She sighed deeply. "And now you could be off to war before we have a chance to really get to know each other."

Jamie's mouth had gone dry. He picked up his water glass. His hand was shaking so badly he sloshed half its contents down his wrist. "You're everything I've ever wanted in a woman," he said so quietly he wasn't sure she heard him.

Her tender smile removed all doubt. A soul-satisfying warmth swept over him. "How is it we're able to be so open with each other?"

"I thank our gripman," Rachel said. "When Leonard told you to put your arms around me, you looked as terrified as I felt. The only reason I didn't object was that you'd shown more interest in getting your hands on the controls of the cable car than on me. And didn't we laugh well together? Like old friends." She pushed a flow of golden hair behind her ear. "Or maybe it's because we learned it was safe to lean on each other before we even introduced ourselves."

Alessandro appeared with their dinners. Jamie watched Rachel savor the first bite of her Chef's Petrale Sole Special before digging into his Salmon Sicilian. It was no surprise that her table manners were impeccable.

After taking several leisurely bites, Rachel froze with her cutlery poised over her plate as though she was overwhelmed by a startling thought. After a moment, she seemed to resolve whatever weighty matter had possessed her. To his astonishment, she wolfed down several more bites and then pushed her plate aside.

"Is there something wrong with your dinner?"

Rachel smiled enigmatically. "It's delicious. I just don't want to be too full."

For what, Jamie didn't ask. Out of politeness, he also pushed his plate away.

Chapter 7

Tincture of Time

Sunday, Late, 09 March 1919

Jamie found himself bathed in brilliant white light. He wasn't sure whether he was dead or alive. A blurry face appeared above him. For a terrifying moment, he thought it was the triage doctor who had declared him dead. The face slowly came into focus. "N ... Nurse Hobbes?"

"Yes, sir."

"Where ... where am I?"

"Surgery recovery, sir."

Jamie frantically felt his legs. Nothing.

"Your surgeon wants to speak with you, sir." Nurse Hobbes ran off.

"Did they get that piece of shrapnel?" he called after her. Likely, she hadn't even heard his weakened voice.

He ran his hands across his hips. Still no response.

Nurse Hobbes soon returned with Doctor Regenstein.

The doctor's stone-cold expression did nothing to alleviate Jamie's fears.

A few seconds later, Doctors Crandall and then Thornburgh entered the room. Their expressions were 98.6 degrees warmer than Regenstein's. "The surgery couldn't have gone any better," Crandall said. "That piece of shrapnel we saw in your X-ray images *was* impinging on your spinal cord."

Doctor Regenstein came to life. "The thing was about the size of a dime with ragged edges sharp as a razor. After I removed it, we discovered there was one little place where the edge was curled over on itself. There and only there, the edge was as dull as the side of a coin." He thrust his hands into the pockets of his white coat. "That dull, curled-over bit is what was pressing against your spinal cord. Other than some swelling, I couldn't see any damage to the cord itself."

A wave of panic swept over Jamie. "But ..., but if you removed it, why don't I feel any different?" He frantically touched his legs. "I still don't feel a thing."

Doctor Thornburgh put his hand on Jamie's shoulder. "Remember, it's going to take time."

"How long?"

Crandall ran his fingers through his hair. "A week, a month, maybe more. We have to give the swelling time to go down before we can say anything definitive."

Nurse Hobbes absentmindedly smoothed Jamie's blanket. "Tincture of time, Major Collins. That's what my mother always used to prescribe."

Thornburgh chuckled. "Mothers often know best."

Regenstein put an icy hand on Jamie's forearm. He looked like he just might smile. "You should take it easy for a while. With the shrapnel gone, there's no more danger in twisting and turning. But the more active you are, the longer it will take for the swelling to go down, and the longer it will be before we know how much mobility, if any, you'll ultimately regain."

"Don't expect a big change overnight," Crandall said. "When feeling returns, which we all hope will be the case, it will come gradually. And though you'll be obsessed with trying to detect any little change, it will probably sneak up on you when you least expect it, starting as a sensation in your waist area." He smiled. "Any questions?"

"My mind is racing so fast I can't put any into words."

"No rush," Crandall said. "We'll be monitoring you closely, and the nursing staff will take good care of you."

"Thank you, doctors. Thank you very much."

"You're welcome," they said in unison.

Regenstein turned to Hobbes. "You may return the major to his room now, nurse."

Jamie held up his hand. "Stand by. I'm worried about something."

Doctor Crandall shrugged. "There's not much more we can tell you. We just have to wait and see how things progress."

"This isn't about me. I'm concerned about the engineer who took my X-rays. He doesn't look well." Jamie lowered his voice. "When I was a graduate student, I got to be part of a group using X-rays to see whether they could detect internal cracks in various metals. Their hope was that they'd be able to predict metal fatigue. But before we were allowed anywhere near the machine, we had to sit through a briefing on the signs of radiation poisoning. I suspect your X-ray engineer's sorry condition is a result of the radiation he's exposing himself to day after day."

Doctor Regenstein folded his arms. "You come out of surgery, and one of your first concerns is about the X-ray engineer?"

"I think I'm right to be concerned."

There was a noticeable thaw in Doctor Regenstein's icy exterior. "You *are* right. The man who took your X-rays is particularly reckless in exposing himself to radiation. Since he's a civilian, we can't order him to take precautions. But for almost a year now, I've been trying to get the manufacturer to require all their X-ray engineers to stand behind lead shielding while their machines radiate."

"Apparently, they haven't listened."

Defying all odds, Doctor Regenstein managed to look even more dour. "Not yet, they haven't. But I've collected volumes of solid data that support my demand. I was about to send them a copy, along with another petition to mandate shielding for their engineers. Would you be willing to add your name to that letter? If they refuse to listen to a mere physician, maybe they'll listen to a physics professor from a prestigious university like yours."

Nurse Hobbes did a double-take. "A physics professor?"

Jamie motioned for her to keep her voice down. "I'll thank you to keep that to yourself, Nurse Hobbes."

"Sir?"

"My rank will be a big enough obstacle to making friends on the ward. If the men find out I was a professor before the war, that will drive an even bigger wedge between us, and I'll spend my entire time here in friendless isolation."

Nurse Hobbes pantomimed sealing her lips. "Count on me, sir. I won't tell."

Doctors Crandall and Thornburgh swore to secrecy.

Regenstein grunted. "I'm not one to talk. Now, regarding shielding for our X-ray engineers, I think your endorsement of my petition will make a difference."

Jamie raised his head from the gurney. "I'll be happy to sign anything."

Doctor Regenstein really did smile. He patted Jamie on the shoulder and left the room without so much as a goodbye.

Crandall looked at Jamie. "Not the warmest individual, but I can tell you, he's an excellent surgeon, and his heart's in the right place." He turned to Hobbes. "Carry on, nurse,"

As Nurse Hobbes wheeled Jamie toward his ward, Jamie took the opportunity to get to know her better. "I believe Nurse Eliot said you've recently completed your preliminary course."

"Yes, sir, at Camp Kearney."

"Where's that?"

"Sir, Camp Kearney is about ten miles northeast of my hometown, San Diego."

Jamie's heart began to beat a little faster. "I know it's a long shot, but do you happen to know a girl named Rachel Lawson?"

Nurse Hobbes' face brightened. "Why, yes, sir. We're practically related. Her cousin, Carl Lawson, is married to my cousin, Caroline Simmons. I met Rachel at their wedding."

Jamie's pulse ratcheted up another notch. "Do you know her well?"

"No, sir. We only met that one time, but I liked her." Nurse Hobbes smiled. "She's very pretty, sir. Is she your girl?"

Jamie ran his hands over his thighs. "I don't know. She's never seen me in a wheelchair. It will be one thing if I'm able to walk again. If not, it would probably be best if we never saw each other again."

Nurse Hobbes brought Jamie's gurney to a stop. "Sir, if Rachel is anything like the person I think she is, it would be a mistake to shut her out of your life."

Chapter 8

The Point of No Return

Tuesday Evening, 10 April 1917

It was noticeably colder when Jamie and Rachel left the restaurant. He was surprised to find the courage to put his arm around her shoulder—just to keep her warm. They strolled west along the waterfront with her leaning into him as she had at the controls of the cable car. This time, it was Jamie who needed support. The warmth of Rachel's body against his was making his knees weak.

"Life's funny," he said. "If Leonard's cable car bell hadn't caught my attention when it did, I wouldn't have been able to chase his car down, and we'd never have met."

"I'm sure fate would have brought us together one way or another," Rachel said.

After a few more steps, she came to a dead stop. She turned toward Russian Hill. Her resolute stare gave Jamie the impression he was watching a pantomime of someone deciding to do something momentous and to hell with the consequences. "We're not far from my apartment. Would you like to see the paintings I plan to take to Hutchins in the morning?"

Jamie's heart practically tripped over itself. "I'd love to," he managed to say through a constricting throat.

A light rain had begun to fall. They hopped on a Powell-Hyde cable car for the short ride up Russian Hill. Soon, they were standing in front of a string of brightly painted three-story Victorian rowhouses variously known to the locals as the Painted Ladies or the Seven Sisters. They climbed the steps of one of the more colorful ones. Rachel led Jamie through a warm, softly lit entrance and up two flights of stairs. They reached the top breathing hard in unison.

Her studio apartment consisted of a large, open room with a stovetop and sink off to one side, a toilet in a small enclosure in one corner, and a bathtub nearby. A very inviting couch with a crocheted afghan folded over its back sat facing a window. Her bed lay perpendicular to the couch and opposite the front door. An easel stood near the gable-end window. The oddly intoxicating aroma of paint thinner and perfume permeated the room. Rain tapped lightly on the roof.

Rachel removed her coat and kicked off her shoes. "Give me your jacket." She laid it on top of her coat, which she had laid across a pile of cushions.

Jamie's imagination was running wild, as was his heart.

With a sweep of her hand, she indicated a group of paintings leaning against the far wall. "Take a look."

Jamie stopped halfway across the room and pointed to a distinctive "Rach L." in the lower right-hand corner of the closest painting. "I've seen that signature before." He sensed Rachel hovering just over his shoulder. He was struggling to keep his breathing under control. "And I thought Rach was a man."

"I think you'll find that's not the case," Rachel purred in his ear.

Jamie was so out of his depth he didn't know what to do. To give himself time to think, he began flipping through her canvases. They were of various scenes: skyscapes, landscapes, and cityscapes. One similar to but about half the size of the one he'd seen in the window of Hutchins grabbed his attention. It was an impression of a cable car emerging from a bank of fog.

All her paintings were done in an ethereal style that used color in a way Jamie could never have imagined. They gave the viewer the sense of seeing the world through the mist of a dream. Each was signed "Rach L.."

"What's the significance of the signature?" He still had his back to her.

"My cousin and his kids call me 'Cousin Rach,' and my last name's Lawson. I think it's cute that Rach L. and Rachel sound the same."

"A blind man would be able to see that you have an extraordinary talent."

She had moved even closer. Jamie turned to face her. "Thank you," she said bashfully.

The thought that leads to no action is only a dream—and Jamie was tired of dreaming. He pressed his lips to hers.

They laughed together at the ineptness of their first kiss. They soon got the hang of it, as they had with the controls of the cable car.

Rachel pointed to her couch. "Let's sit." She covered them both from knee to shoulder with her afghan. They snuggled so close Jamie would have sworn they had become one. His imagination had not done justice to how nice it was to be so close to a woman.

Between kisses, they shared more about themselves. As a child, Jamie had taken apart every toy he ever owned to see how it worked, and easily put them back together. Rachel had practically grown up on the back of a horse, often riding bareback. She even did a little showjumping in her early high school years.

Their kisses became more intense as they laughed, marveled, and sympathized with each other's histories. Jamie's hands, as though they had a will of their own, became more and more adventurous. When his hand "accidentally" found its way inside Rachel's blouse, he apologized.

Rachel made sure such an accident wouldn't happen again by undoing the top buttons of her blouse. "Are you shocked by my brazenness?"

Jamie's inability to speak served as his reply.

"So am I." She looked directly into his eyes. "Let's make love."

Jamie's heart was beating so hard he was afraid it might crack a rib. "Shouldn't we be in love if we're going to make love?"

"We don't have time to fall in love. You could soon be on your way to some distant battlefield. And I'll be in San Diego. Can we settle for affection rather than love?" She stared into his eyes. "You do like me, don't you?"

"More than I can possibly say."

"Time is not on our side," Rachel said. "You can bet every letch at Professor Roach's artist colony will try to seduce me the minute I arrive. I don't want to fall prey to one of them. I want to learn the ways between a man and a woman with you, someone who won't consider me a conquest. And not to be morbid, but you could soon be dying in the mud at the bottom of a trench somewhere in France, never knowing what it's like to lie with a woman."

Jamie's basic instinct was to jump at the chance to make love with her. Yet he hesitated. He'd been brought up to believe sex outside of marriage was a sin. But which was the greater sin, fornication or killing a man simply because he was wearing a different uniform than one's own? Regardless of the government's propaganda, Jamie was not convinced God had given Americans permission to kill Germans. And yet, that was the government's express purpose in sending Jamie overseas. If he did his country's bidding, he was afraid he'd be damned regardless of what he did with Rachel.

"If you're worried about unwanted consequences," Rachel said, "don't be. I've read every one of Margaret Sanger's 'What Every Girl Should Know' columns. Our timing couldn't be more perfect for a couple wanting to avoid conception."

Jamie sat as still as a statue.

"Please don't say no," Rachel said. "I can't handle rejection." She lowered her eyes bashfully. "Besides, I think I could love you."

She helped Jamie to his feet and led him toward her bed.

"I've...." Jamie was afraid to say it. He tried again. "I've heard it can be painful for a woman her first time. I couldn't take any pleasure in hurting you."

"You are sweet." Rachel placed her palm on his cheek. "You needn't worry. Not after all the horseback riding I did as a girl. If we're gentle and patient, we should be fine."

"I'm glad you said, 'if *we're* patient,' because I've also heard that a guy can have a problem too his first time if he's really nervous."

Rachel smiled. "I guarantee you're no more nervous than I am." She rested her forehead against his. "Let's take it slow and easy. And if either of us becomes overwhelmed, let's back off and start again."

Though Jamie had lost the will to resist, he hadn't lost the will to tease. He held her at arm's length. "I have a confession to make." He hung his head. "Some of the happiest times of my life were spent in the arms of another man's wife." He watched with pleasure as the color drained from Rachel's face.

"Are you shocked? Don't be. I was an infant, and that woman was my mother." With a mischievous grin, he began unbuttoning his shirt.

Once Rachel realized how completely Jamie had taken her in, she grabbed him by the belt and dragged him to her bed. She threw back the blanket and top sheet, pushed him down, and practically jumped on him.

"Is this what you call slow and easy?" Whatever she called it, he was thankful. He knew she was only being playful. How better to help him overcome his nervousness?

"That you can joke and tease at a time like this makes me want you even more," she said.

Chapter 9

A Wise Woman

Monday, 10 March 1919

Nurse Hobbes wheeled Jamie back to his private room and made him as comfortable as possible. She slipped out the door, leaving the overhead lights on.

Jamie sensed that it was past midnight, making it exactly two years since he met Rachel. He heard heavy footsteps as someone entered the room. "Still awake, sir?" Jamie turned his head. It was the big corpsman, Hendricks.

"Unfortunately." Jamie looked at his wrist to no avail. Someone had relieved him of his army-issued wristwatch while he was in the hospital in France. "I'm surprised you're still here. It's got to be what, 0300 ... 0400?"

Hendricks checked his watch. "Right you are, sir. It's near 0330, according to my watch."

"What shift are you on?"

"Sir, I volunteered to look after you until you're well settled."

Jamie craned his neck to look at Hendricks. "Why would you do that?"

"I'm the senior corpsman on this ward, sir. It's only right that I look after you myself."

Not only was Jamie more emotional since being wounded, he'd become unjustifiably suspicious of others. But what hidden motive could Hendricks have in looking after him? "Thanks. I appreciate that. And I admire your sense of duty."

Hendricks stared at Jamie momentarily—like he wasn't used to his efforts being recognized by an officer. "Kind of you to say so, sir." He smoothed Jamie's blanket at the foot of his bed. "Sir, I thought you'd be asleep after the day you've had."

"It's hard to sleep when all I can do is lie on my back and stare into the lights. And the foghorns! Do they ever stop?"

Hendricks glanced up into the glare of the overhead lights, then quickly looked away. "Have the lights been on all this time, sir?"

"I asked the nurses to leave them on."

Before Hendricks could ask, Jamie added, "You were at the front. You should understand. The instant I find myself in the dark, I'm right back in the trenches."

Hendricks' broad shoulders slumped. "Sir, you're not the only one who sleeps with a light on. Now that I'm back in the States, I'm getting better, but sometimes ...."

"If I had the use of my legs, I could at least roll onto my side."

"I could get you an eye mask, sir."

"I tried one at the hospital in France. It did a great job of plunging me into total darkness, which is exactly what I want to avoid."

Hendricks nodded. "I understand, sir." He drummed his fingers on Jamie's metal nightstand. "Let me see what I can do for you."

After emptying Jamie's catheter bag and attending to his other needs, Hendricks headed for the door. "I'm going to run a little errand, sir. I should be back before you have a chance to miss me."

Twenty minutes later, Hendricks returned with a gooseneck lamp in his massive hand. He placed the lamp on Jamie's nightstand and twisted it until the bulb pointed toward the wall.

"That's real considerate of you, Hendricks." Jamie angled his head. "Please tell me you didn't steal it off the colonel's desk."

Hendricks tapped the side of his nose. "No, sir. I *requisitioned* it from supply, like the good soldier I am."

"Come on, Hendricks. I doubt they carry items like that at supply. What's the story?"

Hendricks remained silent.

"I won't tell. I promise."

Hendricks moved a little closer. "Sir, I took a little walk over to Supply, which never closes, this being a hospital and all. When I walked in, the corporal behind the desk was studying a girly magazine—probably the only thing he's ever studied. He shoved it under a pile of requisition forms he should have been tending to. 'What's up, sarge?' he says, all innocent-like.

" 'Not much, Parker,' says I. 'You got a lamp I can have?'

"Lamps not being the usual kind of thing a corpsman asks for, Parker gets a little suspicious. 'What kind of lamp?'

" 'Something that will fit on a patient's nightstand,' says I.

"Parker decides to get cute. 'I never noticed the wards needing more light.'

"I keep my cool. 'That's the problem. One of my officers can't sleep without a light on in his room, but the overheads keep him awake.' "

Jamie squirmed inwardly. "I'd hate for everyone to know I'm afraid of the dark."

"Don't worry, sir. I didn't identify you, and Parker's too lazy to try to figure it out for himself."

"All right. What's this Parker character say next?"

"The little creep leans on the counter and grins. 'Sorry, sarge. The army doesn't issue nightlights—or teddy bears.' "

Jamie gritted his teeth. "The son of a bitch."

"I look at him, calm as you please. 'You know this is a hospital, right?'

" 'Yeah, I had noticed,' says he.

" 'And we treat soldiers who were wounded at the front?'

"Parker's grin disappears.

"I lean over and place my elbows on the counter, our faces less than a foot apart. 'Did you serve on the front lines?'

"Parker moves back an inch or two. 'No,' he says all meek-like, "but the supply depot I was assigned to wasn't far behind them.'

" 'How many enemy machine guns did you take out all by yourself?'

" 'That wasn't my job.'

"I look at him like he's something disgusting stuck to the bottom of my shoe. 'Were you awarded a bunch of medals for valor?'

"Parker starts to stand. I'm too quick for him. I grab the front of his shirt and about jerk the little squirt out of his shoes. 'Until you have a chest full of medals, you've got no room to make cracks about teddy bears.' I let go of Parker's shirt and give him a little shove."

Jamie couldn't keep from smiling.

" 'Now, about that lamp,' I says calmly.

" 'We ... we don't stock lamps,' says he.

"I point to the gooseneck lamp on the desk behind the counter. 'What about that one?'

"He's shook now. 'Th, ..., that's Supply Sergeant Kelly's lamp.'

"I smile sweetly. 'It'll do.'

" 'But ... but what will I tell Sergeant Kelly?'

" 'Play dumb,' says I. 'You can do that, can't you?' "

Jamie laughed hard—something he hadn't done in months. "I like it." He was referring to Hendricks' story and that he was laughing again. "And that's exactly why I sent my first sergeant whenever I needed something out of the ordinary from supply."

"Anything you want, sir, you let me know."

"I can think of three things off the top of my head."

"Name 'em, sir."

"The first two shouldn't cause you too much trouble. I could use a notebook and a pen."

"I'm sure I can manage that, sir. And the third?"

"Can you do something about the foghorns?"

Hendricks laughed. "I'll get right on that, sir." He switched off the overheads, then paused in the doorway. "The foghorns used to bother me, too, sir. Now when I hear them, it's like they're telling me how to navigate this crazy world of ours without crashing against the rocks." Hendricks shrugged. "Goodnight, sir." He stepped out of the room.

Jamie lay in the soothing dim glow of *his* lamp, thinking how lucky he was to have Hendricks on his side.

While waiting for sleep to claim him, Jamie made a game of trying to identify the various sounds that found their way into his room. Most were recognizable as activities he'd grown to expect in a busy hospital. Instrument trolleys rolling down hallways, men snoring, nurses and corpsmen talking quietly.

One sound, however, puzzled him—an occasional rhythmic crescendo and diminuendo of rushing air. The sound was associated with the piteous wheezing coming from the room directly across from his. Jamie's eyelids grew heavy as he theorized about it.

* * *

The first thing Jamie did when he woke was feel his legs to see whether they were "awake" too. Though Doctor Crandall said it could take a month, maybe longer, before he'd feel any difference, it was hard not to be disappointed.

The good news was he'd slept well in the dim light. His game of "identify the sound" had turned all the noises around him into an enjoyment rather than an irritant. And happily, he came to embrace the ghostly moan of the foghorns. As promised, Hendricks had done something about them: he'd changed Jamie's perspective.

Jamie pushed his call button. DaSilva, the shy bluebird who had fluffed his pillow on the day he arrived, quickly appeared by his bedside.

"Good morning, Nurse DaSilva. Will you please help me into a wheelchair?"

Nurse DaSilva referred to the paperwork hanging from the clipboard at the foot of Jamie's bed. "Sir, to protect your sutures, Doctor Regenstein doesn't want you to sit for an extended length of time so soon after your surgery."

Jamie didn't argue. Only a bully would try to pressure a bluebird into disobeying a doctor's orders. But she'd have to have been blind not to notice his disappointment. "The doctor's notes do say we can give you your sponge bath, sir."

Jamie's eyebrows shot up. "He doesn't want me to sit, yet he'll allow you to roll me from side to side?"

"Yes, sir. There's no more danger to your spinal cord. He's just concerned about the sutures he placed in your back." She smiled. "Please relax, Major Collins. I'll return in a flash with the things we'll need."

Jamie resigned himself. "Yes, nurse."

Relax. Not much chance of that. Jamie couldn't resist running his hands over his thighs again. Nothing. He clenched his teeth to keep from swearing.

A few minutes later, Nurse DaSilva returned, wheeling a trolley loaded with a basin of steaming water, a towel, a sponge, and a rubberized mat. She smiled. "Now, we'll give you a nice bath, sir."

Jamie looked toward the door to see who would be joining her. The answer was no one. DaSilva wasn't the first nurse to refer to herself in the plural. Must be an occupational hazard.

"With your permission, sir." She folded his sheet and blanket over, fold after fold, until they were neatly arranged at the foot of his bed. She then placed a thin, waterproof mat folded in thirds lengthwise flat on the bed next to Jamie's side.

"Now, sir, it's simply a matter of rolling you from side to side while I unfold your waterproof mat beneath you. In step one, I'll raise your knee and place the sole of your foot flat on the surface of the bed. Then, using your knee for leverage, in conjunction with your shoulder, I'll roll you a quarter turn so you're lying on your side." She did so and then wedged Jamie's pillow against his shoulders to keep him in place. She slid the mat as close to Jamie's back as possible and unfolded the third furthest from his back so only the nearest third was still folded over the middle.

Jamie struggled to keep a straight face. Didn't she realize he'd been through this process a hundred times? It was touching, though, that she put so much heart into the task.

"Now, sir, in step two, we roll you onto your back on top of the partially unfolded mat." She removed his pillow and rolled him flat on his back.

"Nurse DaSilva."

"Sir?"

"I appreciate you telling me what you're doing step by step, but you must realize I've been receiving daily sponge baths for the last several months."

Her face turned crimson. "Sir, Nurse Eliot taught us that an informed patient is a calm patient."

"A wise woman, your Nurse Eliot," Jamie said.

Nurse DaSilva smiled. "*Our* Nurse Eliot, sir."

He liked the sound of that. "Please, carry on. Nurse Eliot's right. It upsets me when someone comes in and starts manhandling me without any explanation."

"Right you are, sir. In step three, ..." Soon, Jamie was lying flat on his back on the unfolded mat. He couldn't say he'd enjoyed the process, which made him feel like a grilled cheese sandwich. He did, however, enjoy his interactions with such an eager student. "You're much gentler than the corpsmen. Well done."

Nurse DaSilva beamed with pride. "Now, we can give

you a good wash without worrying about getting your sheet and mattress wet." She unbuttoned Jamie's pajama top and froze at the sight of his scars.

"Not a pretty sight, am I? Makes you wonder how I survived—a question I've asked myself a thousand times."

Nurse DaSilva stood straight and blinked hard several times.

"The answer's simple," Jamie said. "Someone back in the States was praying for me."

The corners of her mouth twitched into a forced smile. "Sir, I'll start with your back." She gently lifted him into a sitting position. "The doctor says you can sit for a few minutes at a time." She worked his pajama top off his shoulders and down his back. "Oh, sir," she gasped.

He wasn't surprised by her reaction. He'd seen himself in a mirror. The scars on his chest were bad; those on his back were hideous.

He could feel her silently sob as she ran her sponge over his disfigured shoulders. His mind drifted to Rachel. How would she react if she ever saw him naked again?

"Oh, sir, I wish I could wash away all your scars."

"Don't be concerned about my scars. I'd suffer my wounds all over again to save my men."

Nurse DaSilva's tears only increased. "I'm not crying over your scars, sir. I'm just so moved by what the best of men will do for the sake of others."

Jamie was struck dumb by the depth of her emotion. His eyes misted over. He gave himself over to her gentle touch. No further words were needed. They communicated only through their eyes and smiles until she had him properly dressed and tucked under his covers. She stood. "May I do anything else for you, sir?"

Her question sounded like a plea. Such enthusiasm touched Jamie. In all the sponge baths he'd received, no one had shown as much respect as Nurse DaSilva. "Tell me, who will normally be administering my sponge baths?"

"Either myself or Nurse Hobbes, sir, whichever of us is on the day shift."

"If she shows half the care you have, I'm a lucky man."

"Thank you, sir. That's very encouraging."

The rest of Jamie's day passed quietly. Knowing someone would come running if he pressed his call button, he no longer panicked when left alone—so long as there was a light in his room. He slept nearly the whole day.

Chapter 10

A Dream or a Vision?

Tuesday, Late Evening, 10 April 1917

A chill had settled in Rachel's studio. The intensity of the rain had increased. Jamie wrestled the tangled blanket from the foot of the bed and tucked it around Rachel's shoulders. He listened to her breathe, slow and untroubled. She mumbled something incoherent. Odds were, she wasn't dreaming about being president of the faculty wives club any more than his dreams would be filled with happy times as a hanger-on at an artists' colony. He could only imagine a physicist being an embarrassment to her in such an environment, if not an outright impediment to her art. On the other hand, with her academic record, she could easily fit into his world. But would she want to?

Rachel began to stir. She opened her eyes and smiled at him. Then she began to cry.

"What's wrong?"

"It breaks my heart that the war is going to tear us apart."

Jamie held her tight. "I was afraid you were regretting what we've done."

"Never! I'm happier than I've ever been."

Jamie held her even tighter. "So am I."

"I do have some conflicted feelings, though. I keep asking myself why 'a good little Christian girl like me' doesn't feel guilty about us making love."

"And?"

"I've been too busy thanking God that we found each other. Still, it's hard to reconcile my complete lack of remorse with what I was taught in Sunday School."

Jamie shared her concern. Yet he was great at rationalizing. "Neither of us is married. We're mature, fully informed, consenting adults who were expressing affection for one another." He wasn't going to mention his fear that someday he might have to pay a price for giving in to temptation. At the moment, he didn't care. As Rachel said, if he had stood on principle, he could soon be dying in the mud at the bottom of a trench somewhere in France, never knowing what it's like to lie with a woman.

"That's all true, but what does it say about my morality that I coerced you into making love?"

"Coerced?" Jamie almost laughed. "You say you're no saint? Neither am I. When I first saw you, I didn't say to myself, 'There's someone I'd like to have a platonic relationship with.' My first thought was, 'I'd sure like to see what's under that expensive tweed coat.' And when Leonard told me to wrap my arms around you, I wasn't thinking, 'I hope we reach the end of the line soon so I can let go of her.' I was hoping we'd never reach the end of the line. Do those sound like the thoughts of someone who's been coerced into making love?"

Rachel did laugh. "It's a good thing I didn't know what you were thinking, or you would have scared me to death."

"On the other hand, after we'd spent a little time together, my main thought was, this is someone I'd really like to know better."

Rachel bowed her head in modesty.

Jamie gently lifted her chin. "As for *our* morality—ours since everything we did, we did together—if I were a lawyer, and we had to answer for having sex outside of marriage, I'd take our case to *the* highest court, plead guilty, and throw ourselves on the mercy of the court. The Judge knows what we've done. More importantly, He knows our hearts, our strengths, and our weaknesses. We must surrender to His judgment."

Rachel couldn't have looked more relieved if Sir Lancelot had rescued her from a dragon. "You're right. I surrender."

He looked into her eyes. "You are a remarkable woman. When I get to France, it will comfort me knowing you're back in the States praying for me." He closed his eyes for a moment. "If the war's anything like I expect, I'll need all the prayers I can get."

"We can all say that."

"We're not all going to be asked to lead an infantry company into battle." He stared off into the distance. "Nothing in my life so far indicates that I'm at all brave. And I'll have to be to lead my company in the manner my men will deserve."

"I'm sure you're braver than you realize."

"I appreciate your confidence in me, but ..." He pictured

himself back in high school. "Is it likely someone who used to run and hide from the school bully will suddenly find the courage to stand up to the whole German Army?"

Rachel sat up and looked him in the eye. "When you get to France, and the bullets and shells start flying, if that bully hasn't weaseled his way out of serving, I'm confident he'll be the one who runs, and you'll lead your company with distinction."

Her faith in him touched Jamie's heart. "You say you'll pray for me every day until you know I'm back in the States and safe? I'll pray for you every day until I've breathed my last breath."

Rachel tried to speak. No words came out. She tried again. Still no words. Instead, she cradled him in her arms and rocked him back and forth, which said more to Jamie than words ever could.

Soon, he was asleep in her warm, protective embrace.

He had no idea how much time had passed before he was awakened by Rachel thrashing around in her sleep. Her eyes suddenly opened. She sat up and looked around the room in a panic. She focused on Jamie. "Thank God you're alive." She threw her arms around his neck and held on tight.

Jamie could feel her heart racing. "Bad dream?"

"Yes, and it was terrifying." Rachel stopped squeezing the life out of him and curled into a fetal position with her cheek pressed against his chest. "It was about you."

"I hope you don't find me terrifying."

"No. I was frightened *for* you, not *of* you." She looked up at him. "May I tell you about it?"

"I don't put much stock in dreams."

"I do." She took a deep breath. "Usually, my dreams are a collection of disjointed images. This dream was different.

The images fit together and told a story. I'll spare you the details and just say I watched in horror as you were wounded so badly you were mistaken for dead."

Jamie's stomach churned. "Now you're scaring me."

She wiped a tear from her cheek and smiled. "Don't worry. In the end, you made a full recovery."

Chapter 11

A Heart of Gold

Tuesday, Early Morning, 11 March 1919

Jamie was already awake when the first rays of morning light crept through his window. Against his better judgment, he reached out and took hold of the trapeze bar suspended from the head of his bed. He was elated to discover he could lift himself into a sitting position. Unfortunately, having no control over his lower body, he crashed back down as soon as he let go.

A less optimistic person may not have considered that progress. A less determined person would have regarded it as reckless. Jamie was neither. The doctors said his spinal cord was no longer in danger, only his sutures. And sutures could be replaced. He knew he'd be a fool not to take it easy for a few days and give the swelling of his spinal cord a chance to go down, but he'd never been a patient man.

He pushed his call button. It was again Nurse DaSilva who came running. She gasped as Jamie rose from his bed—

or, more accurately, raised himself into a sitting position with only the aid of his trapeze bar.

"When Doctor Regenstein was in last night," Jamie said, "he cleared me to sit in my wheelchair starting this morning. Will you please help me into it?"

Nurse DaSilva edged toward the end of Jamie's bed as she might approach a sleeping tiger. She grabbed his clipboard and jumped back. She glanced at the paperwork and then quickly at Jamie as though she was afraid if she took her eyes off him for more than a second, he might take off and fly around the room. She patted Jamie's unfeeling foot. "I'll run and get an assistant. I'll be back in a jiffy."

"You don't need an assistant. I'll help."

He grasped his trapeze bar with both hands. "Bring the chair over next to the bed and guide my legs. I'll do the rest."

Nurse DaSilva couldn't have looked more astonished if Jamie had asked her to help him walk on the ceiling. "Major Collins, you've just had surgery. You mustn't even think of doing anything so strenuous."

Jamie lifted himself until only the dead weight of his heels rested on the bed. "As you can see, I'm not a weakling. I'm sure the two of us can manage." After Jamie lowered himself back down, Nurse DaSilva took it upon herself to straighten his legs.

She stood ramrod straight. "Major Collins, Nurse Eliot forbids us to transfer patients by ourselves, and I'd sooner disobey a direct order from General Pershing than deviate from one of Nurse Eliot's directives."

Jamie smiled. "She does have that effect on one, doesn't she?"

"Yes, sir."

"Before you run off in search of a helper, tell me, what do you think of Nurse Eliot?"

"Oh, sir, it's not my place to comment on my superiors."

"Come on, nurse. I won't tell."

She canted her head. "Well, sir, since it's all good, I guess it can't do any harm." She smiled. "I have the utmost respect for her. She's demanding but fair and encouraging if she sees we're trying." She laughed. "Did you know she leads her bluebirds in calisthenics, self-defense drills, and a run every morning—except Sundays?"

"I'm amazed. Self-defense drills?"

"Nurse Eliot says nurses operate in a man's world. She wants us to be able to protect ourselves—both from the enemy and from 'overly friendly' patients and staff. Especially the staff."

"That makes sense considering the number of doctors who think they're God's gift to women."

"Sir, she gave us a self-defense demonstration during our first session. She asked for a volunteer. Like a fool, I raised my hand. She had me try to grab her. The instant I touched her, I found myself on one knee with my wrist bent backward. She apologized for the rough treatment, but I had the feeling she was laughing beneath her look of concern."

"I'll have to remember to watch my step around her." Actually, he was already watching his step around her. She was one person he didn't want to embarrass himself in front of.

"I don't mind telling you, sir, it's a challenge trying to keep up with her. Which, to me, makes her a great motivator. We all try." Worry lines creased her forehead. "As for the calisthenics and the run, Nurse Eliot said it wasn't uncommon for nurses to work 48-hour shifts during the war when there was a big push on. She wants us to have the endurance to handle situations like that and the skills to defend ourselves if need be." Nurse DaSilva moved toward the door. "Now, lie back, sir, and I'll return in two shakes of a lamb's tail with someone to help me get you into your chair." She slipped out the door.

"I'm not going anywhere," Jamie said to her disappearing back. Calisthenics, self-defense drills, and a run? No wonder Nurse Eliot looked so incredibly fit.

Nurse DaSilva soon returned, accompanied by the head nurse herself. "Nurse Eliot. I'm honored you'd personally attend to such a trivial task as helping me into my wheelchair."

She stood next to his bed. "Sir, there are no trivial tasks when it comes to my patients."

At first, he thought she was kidding. Her expression said otherwise. He ran his hands down his legs. "My problem is I hate having to ask for help to do something *I* consider trivial."

Nurse Eliot moved closer. "Sir, our goal is to have you doing as much for yourself as possible," she placed her hand on his shoulder, "all in good time."

Her touch was electric. Something in her green eyes warmed him from head to waist. The deeper he looked into them, the more confident he was that her beauty was anything but skin deep.

"For now, sir, we'll use the sling lift to move you about."

"Sling lift?"

"It's an apparatus invented by the corpsman who makes our prosthetics. We use it to transfer patients safely without relying on physical strength."

At Nurse Eliot's direction, DaSilva trotted off to the hallway. She soon returned, towing a crane-like contraption that was on wheels and stood about seven feet tall.

"That looks like a cross between a bosun's chair and an engine hoist," Jamie said.

"Please, nurse, show Major Collins how it works."

"Yes, ma'am." DaSilva seemed thrilled to have an opportunity to show off her skills.

"This process, sir, is much like placing you in the middle of your bathmat. With your permission." She folded his sheet and blanket as she had for his bath. Instead of a mat, this time, she placed a sling, which looked like a small canvas sail folded lengthwise, on the bed next to him. "We use the same technique to place the sling beneath you as we do with the mat when we give you your sponge bath, sir."

Soon, Jamie was correctly positioned on top of the sling. "Well done," he said.

"Yes, very," Nurse Eliot said.

Had DaSilva been a feline, she would have purred.

Nurse Eliot maneuvered the lifting crane into position above Jamie's chest. She indicated the four hooks on the cradle suspended from the crane. "Proceed," she said to DaSilva.

DaSilva attached a hook to each corner of the sling. As she turned the crank on the side of the lift, the slack was taken up on the corners of the sling, and Jamie slowly rose above his bed. Simultaneously, as much as he tried to restrain it, the beast slumbering inside him began to stir. Their expertise in handling him brought to light how helpless he was. With his lifeless legs, he felt more like a sack of potatoes than a man. The beast raised its head.

DaSilva rolled the lift over to Jamie's wheelchair and gently lowered him onto its seat.

It was all done with the utmost care and efficiency. "Well done all around, Nurse DaSilva," Eliot said.

Although they were pleased with themselves, Jamie was seething. So much effort just to get him into his wheelchair. A man never likes to appear helpless in front of a woman—especially one he wants to impress.

No. I mustn't think like that. This isn't Rachel. This is a dedicated head nurse doing her job.

Nurse DaSilva knelt before him and carefully placed his feet on their rests.

With a tour de force of self-control, Jamie strong-armed his beast back into the darkest region of his soul. "You did well, nurse." And he meant it.

"Thank you, Nurse DaSilva," Eliot said. "You may continue your rounds. I'll take over from here."

DaSilva left.

"Thank you for being so kind to her, sir. Some patients aren't as considerate."

"I'm the one who should be thankful—and I am, for both of you. The trouble is I feel so ... so helpless."

"I can tell how much you dislike having to depend on others, sir."

"I've always taken pride in my independence."

"Sir, as soon as Doctor Regenstein gives his permission, I promise we'll work out a way for you to do more for yourself." She smiled, a warm, whimsical smile.

Jamie smiled back. "You look like a completely different person when you smile."

She lowered her eyes. "I'm not."

Jamie tilted his head. "You may have your bluebirds fooled—"

"Into thinking I have a heart of stone?"

Jamie smiled. "When I have no doubt it's a heart of gold."

The smile lines around her eyes deepened—then suddenly disappeared. "Sir, with all I saw during the war, sometimes I wish it were stone." Her smile returned but seemed forced. She leaned over and, with a bit of practiced tugging, smoothed the sling beneath him. "It's important that I not let the bluebirds know what a softie I am, at least not this early in their training."

She was so close he could smell the fresh starch in her uniform. He could smell the freshness of Nurse Eliot herself. Where her sleeve had risen, and her bare forearm touched his, it was like silk gliding across his skin. She was right. She was a softie. Her face was only a few inches from his. He could feel her warm, sweet breath on his cheek. The only other woman to get so close was Rachel.

He had to be careful not to let his imagination run wild. Nurse Eliot was merely doing her job. No doubt, she made all her patients feel special. And he had a promise to keep.

Chapter 12

A Promise to Keep

Wednesday, Dawn, 11 April 1917

Jamie was awake when Rachel began to stir. "When can I see you again?" he said.

She lifted her head from their shared pillow. "Are you asking me for a date?"

Jamie propped himself up on his elbow. "I suppose I am."

"I'll think about it."

It wasn't until Rachel laughed that Jamie was sure she was joking. She lowered her head demurely. "I was rather hoping you'd ask."

"So the answer's yes?"

She held up her hand as if to slow him down. "Yes—when the time is right."

"When will that be?"

"How about April 10th?"

Jamie smiled. "That was yesterday."

"I mean April 10th, 1920."

Jamie might have fallen over if he wasn't already reclining. "Are you serious? That's three years from now!"

"Even that might be too soon."

"I don't understand. Are you trying to get rid of me?"

Rachel shook her head. "Far from it. It's just that we have a few things we should attend to first."

"What things?"

"You have a war to fight. And we have our careers to consider. I need to establish myself in the art world. You need to begin working toward tenure. That would be difficult if we were trying to grow our relationship at the same time, with me in San Diego and you at Stanford. It would be best if we didn't see each other for a while or even write. And we should date other people."

It felt like she slapped him. "You want to date other men?"

"Not because I'd rather be with someone else. And you should date other women. We're so inexperienced at the dating game, if we don't date others, how will we know whether there's something special between us?"

As much as Jamie hated the thought of Rachel dating other men, she had a point. They were both complete novices at dating. Still, he was beginning to panic. "You could forget all about me in three years."

"Will you have forgotten me?"

"Never."

"And I'll never forget you." She took his hand and held it above her heart. "I swear I won't commit to anyone before we meet again."

"That's a huge promise."

"That's how much I want to see you again. We just need to be more worldly. If we're to make an informed decision about our future, we first need to know ourselves better. Then we can make a knowledgeable decision about what kind of relationship we want, be it none at all, clear across the relational spectrum to marriage, and death do us part."

Damn her logic. She was right.

"There's another reason I want to wait before our first date. I need time to convince myself of something."

"You're so full of surprises I'm not even going to guess what you have in mind."

Rachel leaned back on straight arms and locked her elbows. "When I left Hutchins yesterday, I was worried about how I would protect myself from Professor Roach and his friends. Now I'm worried about how I'll protect myself from a much closer threat.

"Me?" Jamie said.

"No, myself."

"What do you mean?"

"After Alessandro placed our dinners in front of us, it struck me that I might lose you to the war before we ever got to know each other properly." She canted her head. "I'm not blind to the way men look at me. In my wicked conceit, I believed I could have any man I wanted. And I wanted you. So I resolved right there in the middle of Nunzio's Restaurant that you and I would make love before the evening was over."

So that's the way it was. "I'm glad you did."

She sat up. "You may think that now, but next week, or next year, or the year after, a door could open, and you could find yourself face to face with some other woman who's perfect for you, a woman you'll want to spend the rest of your life with. A woman who might not appreciate me having seduced you."

Rachel turned and faced him. "I need to convince myself that I'm not going to seduce every man who appeals to me."

Jamie squinted at her. "How on earth are you going to do that?"

"With another promise: I swear I won't be intimate with another man from this day until our reunion three years from now."

Jamie unconsciously drew back from her.

She placed her palm on his cheek. "And since I practically forced you into our relationship, if you find that perfect woman, I'll understand."

Jamie captured her hand and held it tight above his heart. "I can't imagine meeting anyone as wonderful as you, but if the impossible were to happen, and I do find someone else, it wouldn't be because I was looking. And whoever she might be, she'll have to be patient because, like you, I promise I won't commit to anyone either before you and I meet again."

Rachel wiped a solitary tear from her cheek and smiled. "Then it's a date." She rolled over and retrieved Jamie's pants from the chair beside her bed. "If I'm to keep my vow of celibacy, I should start now."

Jamie didn't budge. "There's one more thing I'd like from you before I go."

Rachel looked at him as if to ask, what more can I give you?

"I may be asking too much."

She held her breath.

"I'd love to have one of your paintings."

She laughed. "I'd love for you to have one. Which would you like?"

"You shouldn't have to ask."

Rachel put on a cashmere robe. As Jamie gathered the rest of his clothes and dressed, she retrieved her 18- by 24-inch painting of a cable car emerging from a bank of fog—the one similar to the painting that captured his attention at Hutchins Fine Art—wrapped it in butcher paper and tied a string around it.

Jamie looked at the clock above her stove. He could be back on campus before lunchtime if he left right away.

With his hand on the doorknob, he turned to Rachel. "You were wrong, you know."

Rachel crossed her arms. "About?"

"You said we didn't have time to fall in love."

Rachel threw her arms around him. "I was right when I said I thought I could love you."

Jamie had never felt so invincible, like he could take on the entire German Army single-handedly.

"You'd better leave now," Rachel said as she stepped back and tightened the knot on her belt, "or my vow of celibacy won't last another minute."

Having too much respect for her to argue, Jamie gave her a chaste little kiss on the cheek and silently began to walk out the door.

"Wait!" Rachel shouted before he'd taken another step.

She ran across the room and grabbed his painting. "I hope you don't forget me as quickly as you forgot this."

"I'll never forget you," Jamie vowed.

* * *

Not more than twenty minutes after Jamie was back on campus, Ainsley was banging on his door.

"You're a mess," Jamie said. "When was the last time you slept?"

"It feels like a week ago." Ainsley flopped onto a chair. "That trip to the city was a total disaster. Start to finish. We got back just before midnight. I spent the rest of the night in the bathroom being sick. And my head! I swear I'll never drink another drop of alcohol the rest of my life."

Ainsley talked in circles and repeated himself several times before his account of his big night in the city made sense.

From what Jamie gathered, Ainsley and his fraternity brothers split up for a few hours and pursued their own adventures before reconvening to supervise Ainsley's "baptism" into the adult world.

On the last evening train back to Palo Alto, they swapped lies. One of the guys claimed he'd had the pleasure of being robbed at gunpoint. Another boasted that he'd met a young lady, and he only just managed to keep from going to jail when her parents showed up, and he learned how young she really was. Big Man said he'd entered a friendly poker game in the backroom of a classy restaurant and had to run for his life when the loser started a brawl.

Ainsley had been the worst of the lot with his pretensions of sexual prowess. Only now did he admit the truth. His friends hadn't broken the bank for him. The "pleasure palace" they'd taken him to was a shabby room in a boardinghouse above a cheap bar, where the primary activities were pounding mattresses and swindling customers. The pro whose company he'd ended up in was old enough to be his mother, and nowhere near as attractive. He'd been so wasted and couldn't remember what, if anything, he did with her—his best guess being that in his drunken stupor, he'd given her a half-hour paid vacation. When he got back to the frat house, he'd taken a shower. Then another, just in case.

Ainsley did credit his "sporting girl" with having a heart of gold. The frat boys had the foresight to leave their wallets at home and carry only disposable amounts of cash. Ainsley's stash was the princely sum of $15 he hid under the insert in his shoe: a tenner and five. When he reached the train station, he found in their place a one-dollar bill—enough for the train ride home. True customer care.

Even after admitting his gross exaggerations, Ainsley still put on an air of superiority. "I don't suppose you did anything exciting in the city."

"Actually, I did," Jamie said.

Ainsley crossed his arms and waited for Jamie's big reveal.

"I rode the cable cars."

Ainsley stared at Jamie for a moment and then shook his head. "A life-changing adventure, I'm sure."

Jamie glanced at Rachel's painting that was leaning against the wall just behind Ainsley and smiled. "You have no idea."

Chapter 13

Neighbors

Tuesday Morning, 11 March 1919

With the sling positioned beneath Jamie to her liking, Nurse Eliot stood. "Sir, the student nurses ...." She stopped herself.

"Yes?"

The color rose in her cheeks. She looked like a schoolgirl with a crush on the new boy in class. "Sir, the student nurses are in awe of you, and I must admit, so am I."

Her openness surprised Jamie. He hardly knew how to reply. "Don't be. What I did in France were the actions of a desperate man in an intolerable situation, not the Jamie Collins you see before you now."

"Sir, what you did in France may explain the student's awe. What impresses me is that you haven't let the war take the kindness out of you."

Jamie inhaled sharply. He stared at her for a moment, then covered his eyes and wept.

Nurse Eliot moved closer. "I'm sorry to have upset you, sir."

He looked up and smiled through his tears. "You haven't." He wiped his eyes and cleared his throat. "That was one of the nicest things anyone's ever said to me."

"Sir?"

He leaned back in his chair. "I've killed a lot of men. Men who, in most circumstances, might have been friends. That should bother me. It doesn't. I'd do again if I had to." He looked deep into her eyes. "Coming from you, someone who's dedicated her life to saving others, hearing that there's still some good in me goes a long way to dispelling one of my greatest fears."

Nurse Eliot canted her head. "Sir, I'd like to dispel it completely."

The compassion in her voice told him it would be safe to speak from his heart. "I'm afraid the war didn't turn me into a cold-blooded killer—it revealed me as one."

Her response was immediate. "No, sir," Nurse Eliot said. She sounded adamant. Inflexible. "You took the life of several to save many. That's not what a cold-blooded killer does. That's not who you are."

Her hands were on her hips. Her jaw set.

Another surprising response from an intriguing woman. Doctor Lawrence knew what he was doing when he had Jamie placed on her ward. If anyone could understand him, it would be Nurse Eliot. "The problem is, I don't know who I am." Jamie sighed. "I do know I'm not the man I was before the war."

"In what respect, sir?"

He looked into her eyes. "Not all my injuries are physical. I cry for no reason, laugh at inappropriate times, jump at sudden sounds, have an explosive temper, and I can't bear to be left alone in the dark. And worse, lately, I've become suspicious of everyone around me."

Nurse Eliot nodded. "Sir, those are common symptoms of shell shock—which we're here to help you overcome."

Jamie closed his eyes and massaged his forehead. "No man should have to see the things I've seen or do the things I've done."

Nurse Eliot moved even closer and placed her hand on his shoulder. "Sir, many patients experience inner turmoil after being seriously wounded. The best way to deal with it is to get your feelings out in the open. Talk to someone, as you're doing."

"And my suspicions?"

"I suggest looking at the world through a lens of healthy skepticism."

"Healthy ...? I don't understand."

"When your suspicions are based on reasonable evidence, accept them as a warning. When they're ground-less, ignore them."

Jamie was further intrigued. "Is that your approach to life?"

"Yes, sir. Follow the evidence. That's what I try to do."

Jamie smiled. "That's sound advice."

She crossed her arms. "Take it from your nurse, sir. With the proper care, all your injuries will heal, and you'll be your old self again."

Your nurse? Jamie loved the sound of that.

Nurse Eliot brushed an invisible speck off the front of her immaculate uniform. "Is there anything else I can do for you, sir?"

"I'd be grateful if you spare me a few more minutes of your time."

Nurse Eliot looked at the watch suspended from a ribbon attached to her blouse, a watch that was upside down to anyone facing her. "Sir, I'll be on duty for another seven hours. Will that be long enough?"

Jamie laughed. Nurse Eliot smiled again, an open smile that made Jamie feel as though she really liked him.

"Please, sit." Jamie gestured toward the guest chair by his bedside. "It's a pain in the neck always having to look up at people—literally."

Nurse Eliot dragged the chair nearer and sat, displaying a set of ankles that rivaled those of a certain girl Jamie hadn't thought of in the last five seconds. "I have a bunch of questions I hope you can answer."

"I'll certainly try, sir."

"First, why does the army have wards dedicated exclusively to paralytics and amputees?"

"Sir, there's a lot in common between the treatment and rehabilitation of amputees and paraplegics. Plus, our ortho wards are laid out with broad passageways to accommodate wheelchairs, as are our double-wide latrine stalls. It also helps that our beds are equipped with trapeze bars."

"That makes sense," Jamie said.

"Also, it's believed that putting amputees and paralytics on the same ward boosts their morale by reminding them that they're not alone in their disabilities."

Again, that made sense. "I wasn't on a ward like this in France or Walter Reed. What kind of treatment do you provide the men here?"

Nurse Eliot leaned back in her chair. "Our objective is to

help each of our patients realize the greatest degree of mobility and self-sufficiency their disabilities will allow."

Jamie suspected she was quoting from an informational pamphlet—one she probably wrote herself.

"We're proud of our success here," she said. "Our staff has developed some remarkable orthopedic devices, in particular the Letterman Leg, and we're pioneers in the field of physical therapy."

"Sounds encouraging."

Her voice wavered. "We do face some serious challenges."

"Such as?"

"Amputation-site infections are our biggest concern, followed by patients giving up on their rehabilitation."

"Giving up?"

"Sir, some of the men—far too many—have dismissed the idea that they'll ever be independent again. They view their physical therapy as torture and their artificial limbs as useless hindrances." A tinge of irritation crept into her voice. "Granted, some of our physical therapists think they're drill sergeants. And adapting to a new prosthetic can be challenging—and painful."

She leaned toward Jamie. "Sir, many of the men have withdrawn into their own world. That's led to depression and psychological isolation. I wish we could bring them together and get them to encourage one another. I just don't know how."

Jamie would have been very surprised if she wasn't going to keep trying.

"I've never been on a ward where patients stay longer than a week, two at most," she said. "I've had no training or experience in bringing soldiers together. And I haven't suffered the loss or use of a limb, so I'm just not one of them." Left unsaid was that Jamie fit the bill perfectly. "And I'm a woman," she added.

Jamie couldn't keep from smiling. In his opinion, being a woman was one of her more endearing attributes—along with being a caring person and a talented nurse.

"What about the senior non-commissioned officer on the ward? The senior NCO has always inspired me in every unit I've been part of."

Her mouth contorted as though she'd bitten into a lemon. "Sir, our senior NCO is Mess Sergeant First Class Reginald Binney—and it was a dark day when he crossed our threshold."

"Why? What's his problem?"

"Not only is he bitter and uncooperative, he seems to enjoy discouraging others."

If the senior NCO wasn't going to address the men's morale, it was up to the senior officer on the ward, and that was Jamie. But he was in no state to solve the problems of others. He needed to reestablish his own equilibrium. And he had a scientific paper to write.

Delegate. That's what they taught him in Officer Training School. "Since we can't count on the support of our senior NCO, is there another patient on the ward the men look to for leadership, someone they gravitate to naturally?"

Nurse Eliot perked up. "Yes, sir. That would be Sergeant Zanardi."

Voices—and laughter—from the room across the corridor drew Jamie's attention—unfamiliar voices of a man and a woman. Sadly, when the man laughed, he went into a coughing fit, followed by the sound Jamie had been puzzling over.

"What can you tell me about my neighbors?" he said.

"Sir, of the six private rooms for officers at this end of the ward currently—"

"Don't you think it's ironic that generals are placed in *private* rooms while privates are placed on the *general* ward?"

If Nurse Eliot looked like a different person when she smiled, she looked like a different species when she laughed —a higher species, of course. And what a captivating laugh it was. Gentle, ladylike, sounding as though it came from deep within a heart of gold.

"There was a cheerful young lieutenant from the Engineering Corps in the room kitty-corner from yours," Nurse Eliot said. "Sadly, he checked out last week to take up residence in the morgue."

Jamie had been around hospitals long enough not to be shocked by the staff's morbid humor, without which they'd surely go mad.

"I long for the day," there was a catch in her voice, "when some genius discovers a miracle drug we can use to fight the infections that can kill a man even months after an amputation."

Hearing the pain in her voice, Jamie wanted to get to his feet, take her in his arms, and comfort her—and wished he could. "I can only imagine what it's like to lose a man you've nursed for months."

"I'm sorry." Nurse Eliot self-consciously sat up a little taller. "I don't usually allow myself to get so emotional."

After all she must have seen during the war, Jamie was impressed that she still sympathized enough with her patients' struggles to get emotional. "I'm honored you feel comfortable enough with me that you let me see that side of you." Jamie leaned on his armrest. "Now, who's in the room next to me?"

Nurse Eliot smoothed her skirt. "That would be Captain Lucas Garnett."

"What can you tell me about him?"

"His story's particularly sad. During his first month in France, he was the victim of a harassment and interdiction round—"

"H and I, an artilleryman's idea of fun," Jamie said.

"Firing a single round at random locations behind our front lines was just another way for the enemy to make our lives miserable."

"We did the same to them," Jamie said.

Nurse Eliot sighed. "Captain Garnett suffered a traumatic amputation of his left arm below the elbow and severe injuries to his left leg. A few days later, the leg had to be surgically amputated above the knee."

Jamie glanced at his legs. A doctor in France told him they were useless baggage, and with all the damage they'd suffered, he'd be better off without them. Jamie wanted nothing more than to prove the callous bastard wrong.

"Last week," Nurse Eliot paused just long enough to check the doorway to make sure she wouldn't be overheard, "Captain Garnett received a 'Dear John' letter from his wife. Apparently, the foolish woman has a weak intellect. She claimed she couldn't imagine what good he could be to her now."

Foolish woman. What if Rachel rejected Jamie when she learned of his condition? What might Nurse Eliot call her?

"Captain Garnett had always been withdrawn. Since that letter, he's become a virtual hermit."

"Understandable," Jamie mumbled. He cleared his throat. "Who's in the room across from me?"

"First Lieutenant Tom Walberg—and a nicer man you'll never meet."

"What's his story?"

"He's the longest-tenured man on this ward."

"Another amputee?"

"Traumatic amputation of his foot by a land mine. And if that wasn't bad enough, his lungs were scorched by mustard gas as he lay on the battlefield awaiting evacuation."

"Why isn't he on a respiratory ward?"

"Sir, most respiratory cases are TB. They're sent to the General Hospital at Fort Bayard, New Mexico, for the dry, desert air. Lieutenant Walberg's at Letterman because the Presidio's cool, damp air is supposed to ease his suffering."

"Does it?"

"We believe so—that and his jet nebulizer."

"Jet *what?*"

"Nebulizer, sir."

"I'm not familiar with the term."

"It's a facemask connected by tubing to a compressor that forces oxygen at high velocity through a liquid medicine. The idea is to turn the medicine into an aerosol, which the patient inhales. It's a big, noisy machine that—"

"Noisy? That must be what I hear coming from his room at all hours."

"Probably. In Lieutenant Walberg's case, we're using it to administer epinephrine to relax the smooth muscles of his airways and saline to lubricate them."

"Does he use it all the time?"

"No, sir. Only as needed. I'm sure you've noticed that he struggles for every breath, and when he laughs, which I'm happy to say is often, he usually goes into a coughing fit." Nurse Eliot turned toward Lieutenant Walberg's room. "Between you and me, sir, I don't trust that machine. It malfunctioned the other day and started spraying pure epinephrine into Lieutenant Walberg's mask. If a bluebird hadn't heard it making a funny noise, it could have been fatal —an epinephrine overdose can accelerate or cause an irregular heart rate. Lieutenant Walberg's heart is already stressed."

"And yet you continue to use it?"

"I wish we had an alternative." Nurse Eliot cupped her hand next to her mouth. "I pray that it won't malfunction again, but if it does, I fear it will only hasten the inevitable."

"His condition is that bad?"

Nurse Eliot took a deep breath. "I'll just say it would be a miracle akin to Jesus raising Lazarus if Lieutenant Walberg leaves this ward alive."

A peel of female laughter wafted across the hall. "That's his sister in there with him now, sir. He's one of the luckier patients. A family member visits him every week."

"They must live close."

"No, sir. They come all the way from Chicago and stay in a hotel downtown while they're here."

"Must cost a mint."

"I don't think that matters to them, sir. His family owns one of the largest manufacturing companies in the Midwest."

"The war took him away from all that, and he can still laugh?"

"That's Lieutenant Walberg for you, sir. Always upbeat."

Walberg sounded like a man Jamie would enjoy meeting.

A bluebird appeared at Jamie's door with a question for

Nurse Eliot. The head nurse promised to return soon, excused herself, and left with the bluebird.

As Jamie watched Nurse Eliot disappear, he felt like a heel for not fighting his attraction to her. But Rachel said she'd understand if he found someone else. And maybe Rachel had found someone else herself.

It really didn't matter. Whatever attraction there was between himself and Nurse Eliot could only be one-sided. He couldn't imagine a vibrant young woman like her being attracted to someone in his condition.

He picked up the file folder Hendricks had placed on his nightstand. It had arrived in the mail the previous afternoon. Jamie placed it on his lap and rolled up to the movable tray table where he ate his meals. He flipped it open to the paper he intended to finish while in hospital, but his thoughts were too scattered to focus.

He set it aside, backed up his wheelchair, and headed toward Captain Garnett's room.

At the risk of being told to go to hell, Jamie rapped on the casing of Captain Garnett's open door. Garnett didn't stir. Either he was ignoring Jamie, or he was an exceptionally sound sleeper. Jamie was happy to put off meeting this man Nurse Eliot said had become a virtual hermit after receiving a dear John letter from his wife.

Jamie spun his wheelchair around and rolled the few yards to Lieutenant Walberg's room. The lieutenant's sister was nowhere to be seen. Jamie knocked. Walberg motioned for him to enter.

"Hi, I'm Jamie Collins."

"*The* Jamie Collins?"

Jamie wasn't sure how to respond—until Walberg's broad smile told him he was being teased.

"For some reason, people aren't overly impressed," Walberg took a ragged breath, "when I tell them I'm the one and only Tom Walberg."

Jamie grinned. "I imagine the difference is my handsome face and commanding presence."

Walberg laughed, which sent him into a coughing fit. He reached for a mask that was on the end of a hose. In his fit, he accidentally knocked it off its hook.

Jamie lunged for the mask and handed it to Walberg, who jammed it tight against his face and took a desperate breath. Jamie heard rushing air as Walberg breathed in. Mist shot from slits in the sides of the mask with every exhalation and every cough. Eventually, Walberg's breathing returned to the labored state Jamie was used to hearing. Walberg laid the mask aside. "Sorry about that, sir. Laughing's a bit hard on the old windpipes."

"Forget the 'sir' stuff. Call me Jamie."

"Yes, sir, Jamie, sir." Walberg grinned. "And I'd consider it a favor if you called me Tom."

Tom's cheerfulness almost broke Jamie's heart. His ashen complexion and the way he struggled for every breath made it abundantly clear that Nurse Eliot was right. Tom would never leave the hospital alive.

"You should have been here a few minutes ago." Tom put the mask to his face and took several breaths before lowering it. "You could have met my sister. She's a knockout and funny as the Keystone Cops."

Jamie glanced over his shoulder. "Will she be back soon?"

"Not until next Saturday. What about you? Will you be having any visitors?"

Jamie hesitated as he thought about Rachel. Maybe she'd visit if they hadn't made that silly promise not to see each other for a while. As it stood, she might not even know he was back in the States.

"Sorry. It's none of my business," Tom said.

"No, it's fine. My parents have passed away. All I have left is my sister, and she's in France. She won't be home for another nine months."

Tom reached over to his nightstand and picked up the white king from the chessboard Jamie noticed when he entered Tom's room. "What's she doing in France?"

"During the war, she was a contract physician for the British Army. Doctor Alice Collins—and I couldn't be prouder of her."

"She wasn't at the front, was she?"

"Of course. The Brits were desperate for physicians."

"The horrors she must have seen," Tom said.

"Officially, she was only supposed to deal with diseases and illnesses. That didn't last long. Out of necessity, she was soon putting her surgical skills to use treating battle wounds."

"Impressive. What's she doing now?"

"She's working for an organization called the American Women's Hospitals. They operate out of a chateau in Luzancy, treating French women and children displaced by the war."

"Sounds like you have every reason to be proud of her."

"She visited me in the hospital in France a couple of times." Jamie stared off into the distance. "That seems like a million years ago."

"That should make your reunion that much sweeter."

Jamie would have loved to introduce Ali to Tom. Regrettably, by the time her contract ended, Jamie had no doubt he'd only be able to show her Tom's grave.

In the meantime, Jamie was determined to become the best friend Tom ever had. Jamie pointed to Tom's chess set. "You any good?"

"I don't like to brag—" Tom stopped in mid-sentence. "At this stage of my life, I might as well. I was Intercollegiate Chess Champion my junior and senior years at the U of Washington."

"If you don't mind playing someone way below your skill level, how about a game?"

"What are we waiting for?"

Within fifteen minutes, Jamie had been convincingly thrashed. Tom didn't gloat. He merely reset the board and, from memory, began replaying their game move by move, critiquing each position and suggesting the best moves from each.

"How can you remember all those moves?"

Tom shrugged. "We remember the things we're passionate about."

They noticed Nurse DaSilva run past Tom's door toward the nurses' station. A moment later, she hurried the other way with Nurse Hobbes in her wake. Excited voices came from Captain Garnett's room. Soon, Nurse Eliot herself walked by with all the dignity that was her hallmark. The voices quieted. The bluebirds walked slowly toward the nurses' station. DaSilva was crying. Doctor Crandall brushed past them, heading toward Garnett's room.

Jamie and Tom looked at each other. "That can't be good," Jamie said.

One slight cough sent Tom into another fit. Without any prodding, Jamie handed Tom his mask. "Thanks," Tom managed to say between spasms.

"Do you want to rest?"

"Only if you promise to come back later for another game."

"That's a promise I'll be happy to keep." Jamie backed up and rolled to his room.

Chapter 14

An Officer's Duty

A few minutes after Jamie returned from Tom Walberg's room, Doctor Crandall burst in on him. Jamie grasped his armrests. "Garnett—is he dead?"

Doctor Crandall's jaw muscles looked like cables as he ground his teeth. "Cowardly bastard took his own life." Crandall pulled a piece of notepaper from his pocket. "At least he had the decency to leave a note. He'd been hoarding his pain and sleep meds for the last week. He fooled the bluebirds into thinking he was taking them on schedule by switching them out for pill-shaped candy he got from a too-helpful orderly. He took a week's worth of the real thing this morning. Never woke up."

Jamie felt a pang of guilt. "I thought he was only sleeping when I knocked on his door an hour ago. Could he still have been alive?"

"I doubt it. I'd say he's been dead a couple of hours."

"I assume there'll be an investigation," Jamie said.

"Certainly. That's why I'm here. Nurse Eliot called on

the intercom for a senior medical officer. I'll have to testify." Doctor Crandall sat heavily on Jamie's guest chair.

"Will Nurse Eliot get in trouble?" Jamie said.

"Wolenski's in charge of meds on this ward. Eliot doesn't have anything to worry about. Wolenski shouldn't either. This isn't a psych ward. The staff aren't here to protect the patients from themselves."

Jamie was relieved.

"The RNs have been around long enough to handle something like this," Crandall said. "The student nurses are the ones I'm worried about. They're going to think they should have seen through Garnett's ruse. If guilt and self-doubt cripple them, they'll never be any use to the patients— or themselves." Doctor Crandall ground his fist into his palm. "Sure, Garnett had it tough, but that's no excuse. So has every patient on this ward. What infuriates me is that Garnett was an officer, and officers are supposed to be leaders. What will the men on the ward think when they learn that an infantry captain took his own life? Hell of an example to set."

Doctor Crandall stood. "Sorry to dump all this on you. I had to talk to somebody, and you were my first target of opportunity." He left as suddenly as he appeared.

Jamie stared at the empty doorway. His mind was racing. Doctor Crandall was right. It is an officer's duty to lead. And hadn't Nurse Eliot pointed out a desperate need for leadership on their ward? Someone had to bring the men together and get them to support each other in their fight for independence.

Jamie pushed his call button. Ten seconds later, Hobbes, one of his favorite bluebirds, appeared in his doorway. At that pace, she would have crushed the field in any footrace.

"I'm sorry to bother you, Nurse Hobbes, especially after what you've just been through. Will you please tell Nurse Eliot I'd like to see her at her convenience?"

"Yes, sir." Nurse Hobbes stood eagerly awaiting further instruction. "Is that all, sir?"

Clearly, she wanted to do more. "There is." In France, Jamie had gotten used to men dying. Hobbes hadn't been there. He hoped to distract her from thoughts of Garnett's suicide.

Lately, it had occurred to Jamie that the intensity of his scientific studies had rendered him a bit too one-dimensional. He couldn't even remember the last time he read a book for pleasure. "You were an English major, right?" He didn't wait for an answer. "If you happen to be passing the base library, would you mind picking up one or two books you think I might enjoy?"

Her eyes sparkled. "Oh, sir, I love to share a good read." She checked her watch. "I go off duty in an hour. I can be over and back in no time."

"Whoa. Hold on. There's no need to rush."

In her excitement, she ran off like the devil himself was after her.

A few minutes later, Nurse Eliot was standing in Jamie's doorway. "Nurse Hobbes said you wanted to see me, sir."

Jamie would have stood at attention in the head nurse's presence—if only he could. "Yes. Please come in." He nodded toward the door. "She's good, you know."

"Hobbes?"

"Yes. And I should also mention DaSilva."

Nurse Eliot couldn't have looked prouder of her blue-birds. "Yes, sir. I agree"

"Why is it that when I push my call button, more often than not, it's one of those two who comes running?"

"Hobbes and DaSilva were the top graduates from their preliminary course, sir. I assigned them to be your primary caregivers."

First Hendricks and now Nurse Eliot—he could only hope these acts of kindness would eventually break down his suspicions. "That was nice of you."

"You deserve the best, sir. And so do they."

Jamie felt as though he might melt at receiving such a warm compliment. "You seem to enjoy having bluebirds on your ward."

"Yes, sir. They're enthusiastic and eager to learn. And I believe I have a lot I can teach them."

"I've done a bit of teaching myself," Jamie said. "It can be very rewarding."

"Yes, sir. And I hope to become more involved in their education."

"In what way?"

"Sir, after much soul searching, I've put the Army School of Nursing at the top of the list on my future assignment request form."

Jamie smiled. "In the infantry, we called those forms our 'dream sheets' since personnel seem to ignore them completely."

"That's what we call them in the Nurse Corps too, sir. But we can always hope."

"You say you put the school at the top of your list after much soul searching. Aren't you sure that's what you want?"

"Sir, I'm a nurse, first and foremost. That's what I do best. But I'd love to work for the school's next dean. Julia Stimson was the chief nurse at AEF Base Hospital 21, where

I served during the war. She's the most remarkable woman I've ever met."

Jamie closed his eyes momentarily and tried to imagine the most remarkable woman he'd ever met. To his surprise, it wasn't Rachel he pictured. It was the woman standing before him.

He had better sort out his feelings for Nurse Eliot before he or someone else got hurt. For now, best just to change the subject. "Base Hospital 21, where was that?"

"Rouen, sir, about 85 miles northwest of Paris."

"I was at Base Hospital 15, Chaumont, southeast of Paris."

"Yes, sir. I've seen your medical file." Nurse Eliot interlaced her fingers and waited. She obviously had other things to do. "Is there anything else, sir?"

Jamie looked past her toward the hallway to be sure no one was nearby. "Will you do me a favor?"

"Certainly, sir."

"Can you contrive to have Sergeant ... Zanardo, was it?"

"Zanardi, sir."

"Right. Can you contrive to have Sergeant Zanardi standing by the nurses' station at 0800 tomorrow—without letting on I put you up to it? I have a plan for bringing the men on our ward together, and it will have a better chance of working if only you and I know what I'm up to."

The corners of Nurse Eliot's mouth rose slightly. "Count on me, sir. I love a good conspiracy."

Chapter 15

Introductions

Wednesday, 12 March 1919

By 0800 hours, Jamie was in his wheelchair and ready to face the world. He rolled his way onto the general ward. Patients and staff stopped and stared.

"Good morning, Nurse Wolenski," Jamie said when he reached the nurse's station.

There were bags under Assistant Head Nurse Wolenski's eyes. Jamie guessed she had recently rotated off the graveyard shift—or rather, night shift, "grave" being an ill-advised term to use in a hospital setting.

She smiled. "Good morning, Major Collins. It's nice to see you up and about."

The one-armed man she had been conversing with snapped to attention as though he were spring-loaded.

"At ease, soldier." Jamie smiled. "Would you happen to be Sergeant Zanardi?"

Zanardi's mouth fell open. "Yes, sir. Company Supply Sergeant Carlo Zanardi, sir." The way he responded, one would have thought he was addressing the commanding officer of a division.

"I've heard nice things about you, Carlo." Jamie hoped that using the man's first name would help break down the barrier between officer and enlisted man. Jamie took out the notebook and fountain pen Hendricks got for him and made a quick note. *Zanardi, Carlo.* He underlined the name.

"*Carlo?*" Nurse Wolenski flipped through some paperwork on the duty nurses' desk. "It *does* say, Carlo. Funny, I never noticed."

"Everyone calls me 'Carl,' sir."

"Which do you prefer?"

He smiled broadly. "Carl, sir. And thanks for asking. My parents are the only ones who call me Carlo anymore."

Jamie wrote, *Goes by Carl* in his notebook. He put his pen in the breast pocket of his robe and stuck out his hand. "Pleased to meet you, Carl. I'm Jamie Collins."

Carl stared at Jamie's hand. Likely, he'd never shaken an officer's hand before.

"Don't worry. It's not porcelain."

Carl hesitated—then grasped Jamie's hand with a firm grip. "It's an honor to meet you, sir."

"Where you from, Carl?"

"Southern California, sir. Town called Redlands."

"They grow a lot of citrus around there, don't they?"

Carl's shoulders relaxed. "Yes, sir. My family's been growing oranges there for three generations."

Jamie raised an eyebrow. "I didn't realize oranges grew that slowly."

Nurse Wolenski giggled.

Carl nodded. "We grow 'em really big in Redlands, sir."

They both laughed.

"You have brothers and sisters, Carl?"

"Sir, I'm the youngest of seven kids."

"Almost enough to make up a full platoon." Jamie shifted his notebook from one thigh to the other. "How's your family managing while you're away?"

Carl brushed his shiny black hair off his forehead. "I doubt they miss me, sir. I've been away since before the war."

"Doing what?"

"Playing ball, sir. I was picked up by the Yankees when I was seventeen. I was pitching my way up through the minor leagues when the US went to war."

"I love baseball," Jamie said, "although I was never much good at it—except for running the bases."

Carl felt his empty left sleeve. "Sir, I was a lefty with a great fastball and a curve that backed batters right out of the box."

"Were you drafted?"

"No, sir." Carl held his head high. "Couple days after Congress declared war on Germany, a bunch of us players went down to the recruiter's and enlisted." Carl lowered his head slightly. "We thought we were being patriotic." He glanced at his empty sleeve. "Some didn't come home at all."

He didn't sound bitter. It was more like he wondered whether all the death and mayhem accomplished anything—something Jamie often asked himself.

"There were advantages to enlisting rather than waiting to get drafted," Jamie said, hoping to lighten the mood.

Carl perked up. "Yes, sir. It gave me a head start toward sergeant. And with a few stripes on my sleeve, it wasn't like at home. Being the youngest of seven always put me at the bottom of the heap."

Jamie looked around the ward. "I suppose these men are our family for now."

Carl followed Jamie's gaze. "Yes, sir. I suppose they are."

Jamie smiled. "You got any plans for when you get out of here, Carl?"

"Sir, all I ever wanted to do was play ball." Carl touched his empty sleeve. "I guess I better come up with a new dream."

"Players come and go. You ever think about coaching or managing?"

"I've only ever dreamt of pitching. It never occurred to me to try anything else."

"Might be worth thinking about."

Jamie retrieved his pen and jotted a few notes under Carl's name. *Company Supply Sergeant. From Redlands, southern California. Citrus grower. Youngest of seven kids. Enlisted. Had been a left-handed pitcher in minor leagues. Left arm amputated. No plans for when he's discharged from the army. Friendly. Natural leader???"* He capped his pen and closed his notebook.

Jamie turned to Nurse Wolenski. "Will you please direct me to the senior NCO on the ward?"

Nurse Wolenski shot a glance toward the nearest table in the median where three men were sitting. They had been staring at Jamie and whispering among themselves since he rolled onto the general ward. "Sir, that would be Sergeant First Class Binney. He's the one in the middle at that table over there." She busied herself with some paperwork on her desk.

Clearly, she wanted to keep her distance from Sergeant Binney. Fine. That fit right into Jamie's plan. "Carl, why don't you introduce me to him?"

Carl took a deep breath. "Sir, given a choice, I don't go anywhere near that man."

Jamie waited.

"I guess you're not giving me a choice." Carl squared his shoulders and led the way.

Sitting in a wheelchair at the head of the table was a little round man with a bulbous nose and round glasses on a round face. Two other patients sat in armchairs beside Binney and across from each other.

"Major Collins, this is Mess Sergeant First Class Binney."

Binney remained seated, which was no slight since he had no legs below his knees.

Carl started to leave.

"Stand by, Carl."

Carl dutifully obeyed.

Binney gave Carl a condescending smile, then turned his beady eyes on Jamie. "I've been looking forward to meeting you."

Jamie noted Binney's failure to call him "sir." "Likewise," Jamie said. He was indeed eager to meet the son of a bitch Nurse Eliot said made it his mission to destroy morale.

Carl introduced the other two men to Jamie. Unlike Binney, they responded respectfully.

"We were talkin' about our futures in the army," Binney said. "Which was a complete waste of time since none of us will have a future in the army."

Jamie took out his pen. Below Binney's name, he wrote, *Insubordinate. Arrogant little sod.*

"I understand you're the senior NCO on the ward."

Binney sat a little straighter. "That's right."

"I look forward to working with you, Sergeant Binney."

"Working with me?"

"As the senior NCO on this ward, I'm sure you're overseeing the men's rehabilitation with due diligence."

Jamie could feel the simmering bitterness behind Binney's poker face. "I do what I can."

"I'm sure you'd like to introduce me to the rest of the men," Jamie said, "but I can see you're busy working with these two. I suggest you delegate that to Sergeant Zanardi."

Binney looked Carl up and down. "That's a job Zanardi might be able to handle."

Carl held his tongue.

Insulting, Jamie added to his notes concerning Binney. *Couldn't lead his own rear end off a mountaintop.*

Jamie spun his wheelchair around, putting his back to Binney and his minions at what would henceforth be known as the "table of discontent."

Normally, the men would come to an officer for introductions. That didn't fit Jamie's plan. He pointed to the man in the bed closest to the nurses' station. "Let's go meet him," he said to Carl.

That unfortunate soldier looked like he was about to sit for a test he hadn't studied for.

"Sir, this is Sergeant Shipman."

Shipman snapped to attention. "Sergeant Harvey Shipman, sir."

"At ease, Harvey." Jamie introduced himself.

Like Carl, Shipman was surprised to have a major offer to shake hands—or perhaps Shipman's awkwardness had to do with the fact that he was missing his right arm, and Jamie was offering to shake with his left. In any case, Shipman's grip was warm and firm.

"Nice to meet you, Harvey."

"The pleasure's all mine, sir."

"I've never heard anyone call you Harvey before," Carl said.

"What do they call you?" Jamie said.

"Ship, sir."

"Is that what you prefer?"

"Yes, sir. I never liked the name Harvey.

Jamie centered his notebook on his thigh and wrote *Ship-man, Harvey* at the top of a fresh page. *Prefers Ship rather than Harvey.*

It would have been easier for Jamie to get to know the men if, by the end of the Great War, the army hadn't introduced so many ranks, branches, and specialties, each with its own insignia. Easier. Not easy. Even if the men were in uniform, with 128 insignia in all, Jamie still might not have been able to tell their Military Occupational Specialty.

"What's your MOS, Ship?"

"Eleven Bravo, sir."

"Infantry—the backbone of the army. Me too."

Ship puffed out his chest.

"How'd you come to be in this man's army, Ship?"

"I enlisted, sir."

"What kind of civilian life did the army take you away from?"

"Sir, I was a teller in my family's bank."

Carl perked up. "Your family owns a bank?"

"Relax, Zanardi. I'm not talking about the Bank of California. Ours is a little bank my granddaddy started. Morris County Community Bank, in the thriving metropolis of Council Grove, Kansas, population 3,000 people and 60,000 cows. We've served the farming community, wheat and livestock mainly, for three generations."

"Carl here comes from a multi-generational farming family."

"That right, Carl?"

Jamie looked at Shipman. "You didn't know that?"

Shipman shook his head.

Jamie looked from one to the other. "How long have you two been on this ward?"

"I believe it's been around four months for me, sir," Shipman said.

"You're not sure?"

"Yes, sir. Four months, sir."

Carl had been counting with his fingers. "About five for me, sir."

"What do you know about each other after living together for four months?"

They looked at each other.

"Zanardi's always got his head in a baseball magazine."

"And Shipman's always reading one of those paperback westerns," Carl said. "I also know neither of us has ever had a visitor."

Jamie pressed on the arms of his wheelchair and shifted his weight, something he often did when he was not pleased with a situation. "You got any brothers or sisters, Ship?"

"No, sir. It's only me and my parents—and an army of aunts, uncles, and cousins scattered across the county."

"Your parents, are they well?"

"My mother's taken my condition hard, sir." Shipman looked at his empty sleeve. "I guess we'll both have to get used to it."

"When's your discharge date, Ship?"

"I ... I don't know, sir."

"Have you asked?"

"No, sir."

"What do you plan to do once you're discharged?"

"Sir, I had dreams of expanding the bank. Opening a few more branches throughout the county. Becoming regional manager." He touched his empty sleeve. "Now, I'm not sure."

"Would customers trust you any less if you sealed a deal by shaking with your left hand?"

Shipman didn't answer.

After writing a few notes, Jamie capped his pen and returned it to his pocket. He glanced around the ward. Every man within earshot was straining to hear.

Jamie signaled Carl to move on to the man across from Shipman. There, he asked the same general questions and took notes. Nurse Eliot had appeared next to the nurses' station, where she was silently watching.

Jamie and Carl zigzagged down the rows of beds, interviewing each patient until only one was left. This last man was separated from the rest by several empty beds. "Who's that all by himself at the end of the ward?" Jamie asked Carl.

"Sir, that's Wilkins."

"What's his first name?"

"I'm sorry, sir, I don't know."

Jamie gave Carl a look. "Let's go find out."

Wilkins' bed was closest to the ward's entry doors and furthest from the nurses' station. He'd been the first to salute when Hendricks rolled Jamie onto the ward.

Wilkins must have gotten tired of watching Jamie interview the men. He was lying on his side, his back to the rest of the ward, a book in his hand. Jamie rolled up on him with Carl in his shadow. "Wilkins?" Jamie said.

Wilkins jumped. Jamie liked that about a wheelchair.

He could roll up on someone without them even noticing and scare the crap out of them. That, to Jamie's juvenile sense of humor, was great fun. "Why are you down here all by yourself, soldier?"

Wilkins slowly put down his book and removed his glasses. "Probably for the same reason you didn't return my salute when you first came onto the ward—sir."

Carl moved back a step. Jamie moved closer. "And why was that?"

"Look around," Wilkins replied in a deep, powerful voice. "You see any other colored faces?"

Jamie raised his chin. "What's your name and rank, soldier?"

Wilkins sat at attention. "Corporal Tobias Wilkins, sir."

"Well, Corporal Wilkins, let me set you straight." Jamie's tone was not unfriendly. "I didn't return your salute because neither of us was in uniform, you were not under arms, nor were you reporting to me. You shouldn't have been surprised that Hendricks pushed me well past you before it even occurred to me to return your salute. Actually, I'm the one who was surprised anyone would salute a man who was sitting in a wheelchair, wearing pajamas, a robe, and slippers."

"Sir, they told us in basic training that, as a matter of respect, we should always render a salute to a recipient of the Medal of Honor, no matter the circumstances."

"That's right, sir," Carl said in Wilkins' support.

Jamie looked at Carl. Carl stood his ground, a good sign for Jamie's purpose. He leaned back in his chair. "I don't think you should be down here by yourself. It's like you don't belong with the rest of the soldiers."

Wilkins looked at Jamie as he would someone who couldn't add two and two. "I'm not sure I do belong, sir."

"Really? I see you've lost a foot. Tell me, what color is your blood?"

"My ... my blood, sir?"

Jamie crossed his arms. "It's a simple enough question."

Wilkins and Carl looked at each other. Jamie could imagine them thinking, this guy's nuts.

"My blood's red, sir, just like everybody else's."

Jamie raised his voice so the men nearby would hear him clearly. "That settles it. As far as I'm concerned, when you put on a US Army uniform, you became khaki on the outside and red on the inside—just like every other soldier here. And that makes every soldier on this ward your brother in arms."

Jamie looked around at the patients who had crept close enough to eavesdrop. "If anyone here disagrees, I want to know right now." No one uttered a sound. "I'm going to be very disappointed if I find out later someone here isn't being straight with me." He grasped the arms of his wheelchair. "And believe me, I'm not someone you want to disappoint." No one dared speak up.

"Good." Jamie turned to Wilkins. "Now, let's start over." Jamie stuck out his hand and smiled. "I'm Jamie. It's a pleasure to meet you, Tobias."

Tobias took Jamie's hand as he would a live grenade. "I've ... I've never shaken hands with a white man before—let alone an officer."

"I'm honored to be the first." From Jamie's demeanor, one would never know there had been tension between them.

"Where you from, Tobias?"

He leaned back against the head of his bed. "St. Louis, sir."

"You got family there?"

"My mama and my sister."

"All I've got now is my sister." Jamie forced a smile. "How are they coping with you being in the hospital?"

"From their letters, sir, it sounds like their hearts are aching for me."

"When's your discharge date, Tobias?"

"They haven't told me, sir."

"Have you pressed them about it?"

"No, sir."

Jamie got out his pen. "What'd you do before the war, Tobias?"

"Sir, I was working on a Ph.D. in education at Howard University."

Jamie smiled. "An intellectual, huh?"

"I've been accused of worse, sir."

"Think of it more as a compliment than an accusation." He pointed to the book Tobias had been reading. "That looks like a textbook. You still planning to go into education?"

Tobias put his glasses back on and cradled his book. "I'd like to, sir. I just don't see how I can. I was working two jobs to pay my way." Tobias glanced toward the void where his foot should have been. "That's no longer an option."

Jamie made some quick notes, then put away his pen. "The enemy stole your foot. Don't let them steal your dreams."

Jamie backed up, pivoted, and rolled a few yards down the boulevard. Carl was right by his side. "Whose idea was it to isolate Tobias?"

"Not sure, sir. My bet would be Sergeant Binney."

Jamie draped his arms over the side of his wheelchair. "Let's find out for sure before we do anything about it." He looked at Carl. "By the way, when's your discharge date?"

Carl reached across his chest and touched his empty sleeve. "Don't have one, sir."

"Might not be a bad idea to find out. Eventually, the army's going to discharge all of us. We have work to do before any of us are ready to face the world again."

"Sir, I'll find out the discharge date of every man here, and I'll look into who's responsible for isolating Wilkins."

"Good. Then we can start shaking things up around here. We need to get the men to start supporting each other in their rehab. "Jamie grasped his armrests. "I can count on your help, can't I, sergeant?"

Carl looked like he'd just been promoted to sergeant major. "Yes, sir."

Jamie yawned. "I'm worn out. If you'll excuse me, I'm going to rest for a while."

He rolled toward his room. When he reached the nurses' station, he looked back and was gladdened to see Carl standing next to Tobias's bed. Though they appeared a bit awkward, they were at least talking. Jamie flipped back a few pages in his notebook to the entry concerning Carl. To his question, *Natural leader?* he appended, *Yes,* and underlined it twice.

He looked up and was rewarded by one of Nurse Eliot's heartwarming smiles.

* * *

It was almost time for lights out when Nurse Eliot entered Jamie's room. He sat up and straightened his collar. "Nurse Eliot. To what do I owe this honor?"

"Time for your vitals, sir."

"Isn't that a job for a bluebird?"

"They're all busy, sir."

She went through the routine of checking his temperature, blood pressure, pulse, and respiratory rate. She was good at what she did.

"You're a bit subdued this evening, sir."

Her voice drew Jamie back to the present. "Once we get the men to start supporting one another, I'm at a loss for what we're going to do to help them integrate back into society once they're discharged." The "we" was intentional.

Nurse Eliot canted her head. "Sir, isn't that what the Soldiers' Rehabilitation Act is supposed to do?"

The beast in Jamie raised its head. "It's supposed to provide job training tailored to the abilities of each disabled veteran. The way it was pitched to Congress, a farmer who lost a leg fighting in France might be trained in drafting. A factory worker whose lungs were burned by chlorine gas might be trained to be a pharmacist. Unfortunately, Congress didn't provide anywhere near enough money to pay for that kind of training. From what I've read in the newspapers, regardless of a man's specific abilities and interests, all the Act is doing is teaching disabled veterans how to do simple tasks like re-caning chairs and making rugs."

Nurse Eliot sighed. "Sir, that won't restore a man's sense of self-worth."

"My thoughts exactly. Which I suppose is one reason none of the men seem eager to leave this ward."

"Sir, in a brutal recession such as our country's currently experiencing, finding meaningful employment is a challenge even for the able-bodied. Here, the men have free room and board, caring nurses, and the companionship of others who know what it means to lose a part of themselves. A man who leaves here with no prospects for a good job will face unemployment—and possibly homelessness and starvation."

"But to stay means surrender," Jamie said.

Nurse Eliot looked at him for a long time, like she was taking a whole new set of vitals. "I wish there was something I could do to help."

Hearing those words, the beast in Jamie slithered into the darkest regions of his being.

Although Jamie was confident he could direct Sergeant Zanardi from off-stage as Zanardi broke down the barriers between the men and convinced them of the benefits of supporting their brothers in arms, some things should be dealt with personally.

Jamie had thought his warfighting days were over. Now, he had a different war to fight. He would make it his mission to form the patients on the ward into a fighting unit and lead them into battle against their isolation, depression, apathy, self-doubt, surrender, and every other psychologically crippling state of mind.

But would he be doing it for the men or Nurse Eliot? It wouldn't be the first time he restructured his life to please a woman he hardly knew.

"Let's do what we can here on the ward before the men are discharged," Jamie said, "but in the long run, I'm afraid it will take someone of means to establish a private charity to ensure their future."

Nurse Eliot smoothed her already smooth apron. "Sir, I'd give my full support to such a charity."

He looked into her eyes. She didn't look away. He sensed that she saw beyond his paralysis, that she was seeing a whole man ... capable of anything.

He'd always been good at wishful thinking.

Chapter 16

The Great Migration

Thursday, 13 March 1919

Jamie maneuvered himself from the toilet seat in one of the ward's double-wide latrine stalls and onto his wheelchair.

"Well done, sir," Hendricks said.

"I hope you haven't given me a preview of my future."

"Sir?"

"I'd hate to think the extent of my accomplishments for the rest of my life will be mastering the use of catheters and suppositories, and transferring myself between the toilet and my wheelchair."

"Don't short-change yourself, sir. Those are significant accomplishments for someone who's been through as much as you have."

Jamie wheeled himself out of the stall. "If you say so." He moved to the row of sinks and began washing his hands.

"I do, sir. And if I'm any judge of character, I'll wager you'll go on to accomplish great things in your time."

Jamie studied Hendricks' face as he took the towel being offered to him. "What a nice thing to say." And Hendricks had no reason to say it unless he meant it.

Maybe the world wasn't out to get Jamie. Hendricks had served at the front. He knew what Jamie was going through. They could understand each other. They could *trust* each other.

A warm feeling came over Jamie. As Nurse Eliot's DSC testified, they, too, should be able to understand and trust each other.

Hendricks held the door for Jamie and tried to keep his toes out of the way as Jamie rolled past. Once they were in the corridor, Hendricks took control of the chair. They headed toward Jamie's room.

Jamie glanced over his shoulder at Hendricks. "This is day four since my operation—and still no feeling. Is there any hope day five will be different?"

"I know it's asking a lot, sir, but please be patient."

Jamie knew that voice. He twisted around and looked up at Nurse Eliot. "Ah, the omnipresent Nurse Eliot. Good morning to you, ma'am."

"And to you, sir." She turned to Hendricks. Her smile disappeared. "Has Sergeant Hendricks been treating you well?"

"Very well, thank you."

An indecipherable look passed between the head nurse and her senior corpsman. What was going on between these two?

She pressed the clipboard she was carrying to her chest. "If there's anything I can do for you, sir, please let me know."

"I do have a question for you."

"Sir?"

Hendricks turned Jamie's wheelchair to face her. "Do you think it's right to stick Corporal Wilkins at the end of the ward by himself?"

Nurse Eliot tightened her grip on her clipboard. "No, sir, I don't. He arrived on the ward while I was on leave. I was not pleased when I returned and found he'd been isolated that way. He sacrificed for our county like every other soldier on this ward."

Jamie put his hands on his unfeeling knees and splayed his fingers. "Would I be correct in assuming our senior NCO is responsible for his isolation?"

"Yes, sir, Mess Sergeant First Class Binney." Her tone revealed her disgust. "The day I returned from my leave, I went to Corporal Wilkins and offered to move him to any bed on the ward."

"Then why's he still by himself?"

"Sir, he said it would cause more trouble than it would be worth if he were moved, so he'd rather stay where he is. And I wasn't going to force him to move."

She squared her shoulders. "Is there anything else, sir?"

"No, Nurse Eliot. But I want you to know I would have been very surprised if you had anything to do with his isolation."

She canted her head. "Thank you, sir." She walked away with her regal bearing on full display.

"She's a formidable woman," Jamie said. He looked at Hendricks. "You two seem to have a somewhat contentious relationship."

"Is that the way it looks? Sir, I'd lay down my life for that woman, and she'd do the same for me."

Jamie was stunned. "Then why—"

"It's a game we play, sir. When it comes to the quality of

care we give our patients, neither of us is willing to let the other get the upper hand."

"I'm sure there's a story behind that. I'd like to hear it."

Hendricks rolled Jamie into his room and parked his wheelchair near the window.

"Sir, Nurse Eliot and I met within a week or two of arriving in France. She was assigned to AEF Base Hospital 21, Rouen. Every month, nurses and corpsmen from her hospital did ten-day rotations through the field hospital I was attached to."

"Base hospitals were well behind the lines. Field hospitals were within two to four miles of our front," Jamie said. "Was yours?"

"Yes, sir. Well within the range of the enemy's artillery."

Jamie took out the pen Hendricks had gotten for him and began twirling it between his thumb, index, and middle fingers like a miniature baton. "You worked together before, and here you are together again. Is that a coincidence?"

"No, sir. She returned to the States a month or so before I did. I had a friend in personnel track her down. He told me that at her request, she'd been assigned to orthopedics at Letterman. When it was my turn to come home, the army offered me my choice of assignments. I asked to be sent to Letterman, only to find out she'd already requested that I be sent here and assigned to her ward."

A spark of jealousy shot through Jamie—which was crazy. Why should he care about her relationship with Hendricks?

Jamie cleared his throat. "I've been around the army long enough to know only exceptional soldiers are offered their choice of assignments. It's also a real compliment when a head nurse requests that someone she's worked with in the past be assigned to her ward."

Jamie's neck was sore from constantly looking up at Hendricks. He indicated his guest chair. "Please, take a seat."

Hendricks looked surprised. "Really, sir?"

"Really. It's a pain in the neck always looking up at people from this chair."

The big corpsman made Jamie's standard-size guest chair look like one of those little chairs Jamie remembered from kindergarten. "Sir, my first few months in France, I was a stretcher-bearer. Nurse Eliot and I would see each other now and then when she did her rotation through my field hospital. We were always friendly, but as busy as we were, we never really had a chance to talk or anything." Hendricks leaned forward. "Then, one day, she caught me helping myself to some antiseptic ointment from her supply cabinet."

Hendricks held his hands out, palms up, and examined them. "A stretcher-bearer's hands take a hell of a beating. Mine were so cracked and blistered I could barely lift an empty stretcher, let alone carry a man from where he fell all the way to a battalion aid station.

" 'What are you doing, soldier,' she said all formal-like—you know the way she does. I snapped to attention but kept my mouth shut. She must have seen what I was up to because she ordered me to show her my hands. I did, and she gasped, which kind of scared me, considering the gore and mayhem she dealt with every day. 'Sit down,' she ordered. I sat. Immediately." Hendricks smiled. "Only a fool would disobey Nurse Eliot."

Jamie chuckled. "I agree."

"She held my hands over a bowl, poured disinfectant over them, and began cleaning my wounds. I couldn't believe how gentle she was. Then she slathered more antiseptic ointment on my hands than I ever would have dreamt of stealing. She made me feel like I was her only patient. As she wrapped my hands in fresh bandages, I sat there like a lump, staring at her. It was as though I'd fallen into the lap of an angel.

" 'You are now on restricted duty,' she said.

"I wasn't sure I heard her right. 'Ma'am?'

" 'A stretcher-bearer needs to move fast if he's going to stay alive,' she said. 'Hands in this condition would surely slow you down. You are, therefore, specifically forbidden to carry another stretcher until I give you clearance. Is that understood?'

"The fact that nurses have no legal authority over corpsmen didn't stop me from instantly answering, 'Yes, ma'am.' Nurse Eliot's authority comes as a natural right."

"I know what you mean," Jamie said.

"Before my hands could heal, she pulled some strings and got me permanently reassigned to her ward at the base hospital." Hendricks went silent for a moment. "She said she needed someone strong to help her move non-ambulatory patients around her ward. At first, I resented her interference. Eventually, I realized she saved my life by having me reassigned. I was taking crazy chances retrieving casualties, like I was bulletproof or something." Hendricks stared at the floor. "I'm convinced she knew exactly what she was doing having me reassigned, and that's the only reason I'm alive today."

Jamie's respect for her kept growing and growing. "There are few things better in life than knowing your friends are looking out for you."

"And for them to trust you." Hendricks stood up and

walked to Jamie's window. "Can I tell you something that says everything you need to know about Nurse Eliot?"

"Please do."

"More than once, when enemy shells were falling near our field hospital, and shrapnel came whizzing through our tent, I looked up from cowering on the floor and saw Nurse Eliot still on her feet, caring for a patient."

Jamie shuddered. "Risky, to say the least."

"Sir, it wasn't just risky. She was hit. On more than one occasion."

"That's terrible! Bad?"

"Nothing life-threatening. Still, she bore some painful injuries like a real trooper." Hendricks paused.

"Please, go on."

"There was a time when Nurse Eliot and I were doing our rotation at a field hospital. We were swamped with casualties. That told us the enemy was up to something big. Their artillery had been working over our lines all day. Rounds were creeping closer and closer to us. We were ordered to get down on the floor. One man was unconscious, having recently come out of surgery. Obviously, he couldn't look out for himself. I looked up from the floor and saw Nurse Eliot beside his bed, shielding him with her body."

Hendricks faced Jamie. "I heard a dull thud followed by a heartbreaking moan. The back of Nurse Eliot's uniform was smoking. A streak of red began to trail down her back from the top of her right shoulder. She was gritting her teeth. Tears were streaming down her cheeks. And yet she stayed with her patient."

Hendricks sat again on the edge of Jamie's guest chair. "By the time the shelling stopped, several patients had suffered additional wounds, and the doctors were being run off their feet. Nurse Eliot ignored what was obviously a painful injury. Together, we made sure the patients on our ward were stabilized before I could corner her in the little area of our tent curtained off as our supply station. Blood had seeped clear down to her waist. 'Let me see to your back,' I said. She ignored me and tried to slip past. I stuck my arm out and blocked her way. 'Sit down on that camp stool,' I ordered her. Now, if nurses have no authority over corpsmen, corpsmen sure don't have authority over nurses. I was surprised that she obeyed.

"I stepped behind her and was shocked to see a jagged piece of shrapnel sticking out of a nasty gash just behind the top of her shoulder. I can only guess that her collarbone kept it from penetrating any further. Sir, for that piece of shrapnel to end up where it did, it must have come at her head-on. I can't bear to think what would have happened if it had come at her a little further to her left.

" 'Undo your top buttons,' I told her like I was in charge or something. She looked up at me, and that was the only time I'd ever seen her look vulnerable. I eased her top over the shrapnel and down to her shoulder blade. Though she was trying not to show it, from the way she was gripping the edge of the stool, she was obviously in a lot of pain. I was struggling to sound authoritative. 'You have a protruding piece of shrapnel that needs to be removed.'

"And you know what she said?"

Jamie shook his head.

" 'The doctors are all busy. Please extract it yourself.' "

Jamie sat up straight. "Had you ever done anything like that before?"

"No, sir. It's one thing to carry a wounded soldier on a

stretcher. It's something altogether different to poke and prod somebody's wounds. But what choice did I have?

" 'We're out of anesthetic,' I told her. 'I'll have to run next door to get some.'

"She raised her chin. 'No. We barely have enough for our patients. Just work quickly.'

"It would have been senseless to argue with her. I rolled up a towel and handed it to her. 'Bite down on this,' I said. I grabbed a pair of forceps. I can tell you my knees were shaking. Still, somehow, I managed to pull a jagged piece of metal the size of a quarter from the top of her shoulder. Her muffled cries told me how bad it must have hurt. With the shrapnel out, I dowsed the wound with antiseptic, which could only have added to her agony. 'You're going to need a few stitches.' I told her."

Hendricks wiped his forehead. Damned if she didn't say, 'Proceed.'

"Sewing someone up was way beyond my expertise—and I told her so.

" 'Nonsense,' she said. 'You've sown insignia onto your uniform, haven't you?'

"Sure, but—.

" 'It's no different. You'll do fine.' "

"Amazing," Jamie said. "She's the one bleeding—and she's encouraging you?"

"That's the way she is. And I'm sure glad. Her trust gave me courage. Still, it broke my heart having to stick a needle in her satiny-smooth skin. You can imagine how my hands were shaking. I did it, though, three stitches. How she managed to remain so still, I'll never know. She's a real soldier, our Nurse Eliot."

Jamie gripped his armrests. "Our Nurse Eliot isn't just any nurse. She's an ARMY nurse!"

"Exactly, sir." Hendricks wiped his forehead. "I placed a self-adhesive sterile dressing on the site. She then stood and, with her back to me, re-buttoned her top. She turned around and, as casual as you please, said, 'Thank you, Hendricks.'

"I didn't let on that I damn near passed out as I drew the suture through her skin. 'You're welcome, Nurse Eliot,' I said, trying to sound like it was nothing. As she started to walk away, I called out to her. 'When you get a chance, you should change your uniform top. The patients might be a little put off by all the blood on your back.' "

"Her 'red badge of courage,' " Jamie said.

Hendricks nodded. "After that, I took it upon myself to be her 'big brother' and protector."

"Was that necessary?"

Hendricks shrugged. "She's more than capable of taking care of herself—but she shouldn't have to. She was there to do a job. An important job." Hendricks shook his head. "Sir, I'm sure you've noticed she's rather good-looking."

Jamie almost laughed. "That's an understatement."

Hendricks gave him a penetrating look. "Some men seemed to think that was an invitation to pester her for a date every time they saw her. One doctor in particular just wouldn't leave her alone. Winters was his name. After about the hundredth time she told him no thank you, he grabbed her by her wrist. 'You must think you're too good for me,' he said with his face only inches from hers. I was nearby, which was good for Nurse Eliot and bad for Doctor Winters. I picked him up and dumped him headfirst into a half-full fifty-five-gallon drum of freshly washed bed linen that was waiting to he hung out to dry."

"Seriously? You could have been charged with battery."

"I probably would have had it been anyone other than Winters. Everyone knew him as an excellent physician, but you'd have been hard-pressed to find anyone who didn't think he had it coming. When Winters reported me to our CO, the colonel was totally unsympathetic. He told Winters if he ever touched another nurse, he'd be the one facing a court-martial."

"I'm glad you stood up for her," Jamie said.

"Sir, I'm sure you'd have done the same."

Jamie felt highly complimented.

"And you may get a chance. A friend in personnel told me Doctor Winters will be reporting for duty here at Letterman in late May."

"I appreciate your confidence in me," Jamie said, "but I'll probably have been discharged from the hospital by then."

"I hope so, sir. I'd hate for anyone to get in trouble because of a man like Winters."

Jamie vowed to himself that he'd come to Nurse Eliot's aid without hesitation if the need ever arose. "Did Nurse Eliot get the recognition she deserved for her bravery?" Jamie already knew the answer, but he wanted to hear the story from Hendricks' point of view.

"Yes, sir. And I'm proud to say I helped."

"How so?"

"The day she was wounded, I wrote a statement detailing her courage. When the medical officer in charge read it, he was duly impressed. With the help of several officers who'd witnessed her bravery on that and other occasions, he prepared a recommendation for a medal, and I'm happy to say our Nurse Eliot is one of only four women, all nurses, to be awarded the Distinguished Service Cross."

"Impressive," Jamie said. "There's only one gallantry award higher than the Distinguished Service Cross."

"You would know, sir, being one of the few living recipients."

"I'm glad Nurse Eliot got the recognition she deserved. Not all women are treated that fairly." Like Jamie's sister when she tried to get into medical school. And Elaine Stanton's heartbreak over the Thayer Scholarship. And Rachel's disappointment when she applied to graduate astronomy programs.

Hendricks glanced toward Jamie's door. In his mind's eye, he probably saw Nurse Eliot standing there. "Sir, she's the bravest person I've ever met—present company excepted."

There was a knock on the door. Hendricks jumped to his feet and stood at attention as Colonel Thornburgh entered the room. Thornburgh looked Hendricks up and down and scowled.

"Sir, I asked him to sit," Jamie said. "It's hard on my neck always having to look up at people."

Colonel Thornburgh's scowl disappeared. "At ease, Hendricks," the CO said. He turned to Jamie. "How are you getting along, Major Collins?"

"Sergeant Hendricks and the rest of the staff are treating me like royalty, sir."

Colonel Thornburgh looked at Hendricks. "Well done." His usual smile had returned.

"Thank you, sir. We're all just following Nurse Eliot's example." Hendricks and Jamie exchanged knowing looks.

"Keep it up."

"Yes, sir." Hendricks turned to Jamie. "Major Collins, please ring if you need anything." He moved toward the door. "With your leave, sirs." He deferentially stepped into the corridor and disappeared.

"Good man," Jamie said as soon as Hendricks was gone.

"I agree." Thornburgh faced the door. "He was one of the more legendary stretcher-bearers. Did you know he was awarded the Silver Star Medal?"

"No, sir, but I'm not surprised."

"With all the chances he took, he's lucky to be alive."

"Sir, people tell me I'm lucky to be alive. I don't think luck had anything to do with it. Call me crazy, but I believe I was spared—as was Hendricks—for a purpose."

Thornburgh studied Jamie's face for a moment. "In my medical practice, I've seen men die when their injuries were only slight, and others live when nobody thought they had a chance. I cling to the hope that each was taken or spared for a purpose." He squeezed his eyes shut like he was trying to rid his mind of unhappy memories. "But I didn't come here to praise Hendricks or discuss the mysteries of the universe." He smiled. "I came to ask if there's anything I can do for you."

"Thank you, sir." Jamie rested his palms on his thighs. "I do have an unusual request."

"Fire away."

"Would it be possible for me to move out onto the general ward alongside the rest of the men?"

Colonel Thornburgh put his hands in the pockets of his white coat. "Lonely?"

That wasn't it at all. Living among the men would be necessary if Jamie was going to draw *all* the patients together. Jamie blinked hard several times. "Sir, previously, I was on a ward with dozens of men."

"All officers, though, weren't they?"

"Yes, sir," Jamie lowered his head. He'd use the line he'd fed Nurse Eliot when she "threatened" to place him in a private room before Jamie was sure he could handle being alone. "It feels like solitary confinement in this room all by myself."

"I don't think I'd want to be alone either if I'd been left for dead." He took his hands out of his pockets. "Since you're asking for less than you're entitled to rather than more, I'll grant your request." Colonel Thornburgh took a step closer to Jamie. "You haven't been in the army as long as I have. Before the war, the divide between officers and enlisted personnel was as wide and deep as the Grand Canyon. That gap shrank considerably after living in the trenches and fighting together, but it's still significant. Keep in mind that you'll be invading enlisted territory. It will be up to you to ensure your presence doesn't make the men uncomfortable. If I hear any complaints, I'll insist you return to your private room."

"Thank you, sir. I'll do my best to fit in." If anyone were going to feel uncomfortable, it would be Jamie. He could live with that. If what he had in mind worked, a little discomfort would be a small price to pay.

* * *

Like a conjurer's act, Hendricks reappeared as soon as Colonel Thornburgh left.

"Hendricks, the CO has given me permission to move out onto the general ward with the rest of the men."

Hendricks looked around Jamie's featureless room. "Sir, I'm shocked you'd even consider leaving these palatial accommodations."

"Hard to believe, I know. Trust me. I have my reasons."

"Sir, the general ward isn't known for its peace and quiet."

Jamie turned toward the door. "At least I won't have to listen to Lieutenant Walberg's jet nebulizer night and day." He immediately regretted having said it. That machine was keeping Tom alive. "I just hope the men won't object to me invading their territory."

"Sir, the men got used to living elbow to elbow with their officers in the trenches. I don't think they'll mind."

"I hope you're right. And now I need to tell Lieutenant Walberg I won't be going far. I don't want him to think he'll be deprived of the pleasure of thrashing me in chess every day."

* * *

News of Jamie's impending move spread quickly throughout the ward. Nurse DaSilva and another bluebird were preparing a bed for Jamie next to the nurses' station. Normally, that would have been a preferential location. Not for what Jamie had in mind. "Excuse me, Nurse Eliot. Before they get any further, will you give me a moment to make some inquiries?"

"Inquiries, sir?"

"Don't worry. I don't have anything sinister in mind."

Jamie wheeled his way to the far end of the ward. Tobias Wilkins was reading a book and hadn't seen him coming. "Corporal Wilkins," Jamie said. Tobias was jolted out of whatever world his book had taken him. "The CO has given me permission to move out of solitary confinement and onto the general ward."

From Tobias's body language, Jamie could see he was expecting some kind of harassment.

"This is enlisted territory," Jamie said. "I know I'll be trespassing, but I'm hoping you'll be kind enough to allow me to bunk next to you."

Tobias slowly removed his glasses and stared at Jamie.

"Rest assured. I won't expect to be treated any differently than any other patient. There'll be no 'yes, sir,' 'no, sir.' You can call me Jamie, and I hope you'll allow me to call you Tobias."

Wilkins didn't answer right away. He looked around the ward. "I suspect there are men here who won't like you bunking next to a colored man."

Jamie looked at several men whose curiosity had drawn them near. "I suspect others will soon want to join us at this end of the ward. So, what do you say? May I bunk next to you?"

A sly smile crept across Tobias's face. "Yes, sir—Jamie. On two conditions."

Jamie had expected a simple yes or no. "Sure. Let's hear them."

"First, that you don't snore."

Jamie shrugged. "I've never heard me snore. And the second condition?"

"I'm only called Tobias when I'm in trouble. I ask that you call me 'Toby.'"

Jamie smiled. "You got it, Toby."

Toby put his glasses back on. "Then I guess I'll take a chance on you."

The rest of the men drifted off. DaSilva and the other bluebird carried Jamie's few belongings to his new bed.

* * *

The next day, Carl approached Wilkins. Jamie was close enough to eavesdrop.

"Corporal Wilkins, I have a request."

Wilkins reached over to his nightstand and picked up his well-used military-issue Gideon Bible. He held it against his chest as one would a shield. "What do you have in mind, sergeant?"

"Would it be okay with you if I took up the bed across from you?"

Toby set his Bible aside and glanced in Jamie's direction for an instant. "I'd like that, Sergeant Zanardi."

"Forget the sergeant stuff. Call me Carl."

"Only if you'll call me Toby."

Chapter 17

Unification

Monday, 17 March 1919

Over the weekend, Jamie was happy to discover that the general ward wasn't much noisier or busier than his private room. That began to change Monday morning.

An hour after breakfast, a short, thickset corpsman Jamie had never seen before pushed open the ward's double doors and strode in like he was the Colossus of Rhodes.

Carl shrank down into his bed. "My torturer," he mumbled.

The corpsman's voice boomed throughout the ward, "Let's go, Zanardi." He spun on his heels and left. Carl trailed behind with his head down.

Jamie waited until they were gone. "What was that all about?"

"That was Albright, Carl's physical therapist," Toby said. "The guy's been working Toby like a government mule."

An hour later, Carl dragged himself back unaccompanied. His glossy black hair was plastered to his forehead. His ordinarily dark complexion was pale as a cirrus cloud. Jamie envisioned a fox who had barely escaped a hunt. "Tough session?"

"They want me to learn to do things right-handed, and it ain't easy after a lifetime as a lefty." Carl looked at his hand as though it was a strange, foreign object. "They've got me doing something called manual dexterity exercises. They don't take much strength, just a lot of concentration. They've also got me doing all kinds of weightlifting and stretches."

Sometime later, a corpsman almost as big as Hendricks meekly entered through the double doors. Toby shrank at the sight of him. "Come on, Toby, we got work to do," he said with a slow, melodic Southern drawl. He sounded almost apologetic. Toby showed little enthusiasm as they left together.

Jamie looked at Carl. "Was that Toby's physical therapist?"

"Naw. That's the guy who makes prosthetics. He's been working on an artificial foot for Toby."

The sun was high in the sky when Toby hobbled back onto the ward. He clenched his teeth and tried to exercise some control over an artificial foot. He collapsed onto his bed, unbuckled the contraption, and threw it against the wall. He hunched over, massaged his stump, and used his shoulders to wipe his cheeks, no doubt hoping no one noticed his tears. "Hurts like hell," he said to no one in particular.

Jamie maneuvered his wheelchair to where Toby's prosthetic lay and picked it up by one of its straps. The device resembled a high-top boot, with the ankle simulated by a hinge with springs to return it to a neutral position after each step. It wasn't much heavier than a stout hiking boot. Jamie felt the padded socket Toby's stump was supposed to fit into. He worked the simulated ankle joint back and forth and was surprised by its suppleness. "Nice workmanship," he said. He didn't look up. "If I were you, I wouldn't be tossing it around like so much junk. It's your key to independence. And if I know the army, it's the only one you'll ever get."

Binney was watching from his usual spot at the table of discontent, smirking, apparently finding Toby's struggles fine entertainment.

* * *

Thursday, 20 March 1919

Jamie had been staring at the same page of a battered old copy of *Scientific American* for half an eternity. Eleven days since his operation, and still no sensation. Equally worrisome was the probability that if he didn't stop counting the days, he'd go crazy.

The doors to the ward burst open, and Albright, Carl's Mini-Colossus, came striding in.

"Every stinkin' day," Carl said.

"Come on, Zanardi. This will do you good."

"Yeah, yeah." Carl dutifully fell in step like a lamb to the slaughter.

Jamie rolled his wheelchair next to Carl. "I'm coming with you."

The corpsman held up his hand like a traffic cop. "Hold on, soldier. You'll get your turn."

Jamie spoke in a tone he'd developed only after weeks in Officer Training School. "What's your name, corpsman?"

The man snapped to attention. "Donald Albright, sir."

"Well, Albright, I'm Major Jamie Collins, and I say I'm coming with Carl."

Albright wilted. "Yes, sir."

Having found his backbone, Carl led the way down the central corridor to the end of Building Three. They entered a room that reminded Jamie of the gym at Stanford. Weights, cords, pulleys, and tables of various shapes and sizes were positioned around the room in an orderly fashion, as one would expect in a military hospital. Therapists Jamie had never seen before were working with other patients.

Albright tossed Carl a postcard-sized beanbag and had him throw it in the air and catch it a dozen times—with his right hand, of course. Carl looked thoroughly bored and a little peeved. He tossed it poorly and even failed to catch it one time. Albright showed little patience as he scolded Carl for every miss—or near-miss.

It was incomprehensible to Jamie that Carl would fail to catch it. Lefties grow up catching a baseball right-handed.

"Toss it to me," Jamie said. Being a righty, he easily caught the beanbag with his left hand. Jamie placed his right hand behind his back. His toss back to Carl using his left hand was so feeble it made Carl look like Cy Young. "It's not easy throwing with your non-dominant hand," Jamie said. He held up his left hand. "Toss it back."

Carl obliged, showing some enthusiasm. Jamie turned his wheelchair so he could throw across his body and generate more power. Ignoring the risk to his sutures, he fired it as best he could *at* Carl. With no effort, Carl caught it and fired it right back. With the added velocity, Jamie muffed the catch. It smacked him on the head to the accompaniment of much laughter from Jamie, Carl—and Albright.

Jamie grabbed the beanbag and winged it at Albright's head. Albright got his non-dominant hand up just in time to prevent it from landing square on the tip of his nose. He tossed it to Carl using his dominant hand.

"That's cheating," Carl shouted. He tossed it back. "Play by the rules. Throw using your off-hand."

Albright gamely tucked his right thumb in his back belt loop and "threw" the beanbag back to Carl.

"It's not a shotput," Carl said. "Get your weight behind it. Use your legs." He demonstrated with a lightning throw at Jamie.

Luckily, Jamie caught it this time. Otherwise, it would have stung. "Even without my legs, I can still throw better than Albright," Jamie said. He fired it at Albright's head.

It then became a free-for-all. No one knew who was going to be the next target. The speed and intensity picked up. Albright laughed openly whenever Jamie got nailed. Carl's competitive athleticism kicked in. Jamie and Albright both cheered him on. Jamie was sure the "game" gave Albright a better appreciation for the difficulty of the task he was demanding Carl perform. More importantly, Carl made progress—and he was excited about it.

"All right, Zanardi," Albright said, "now that we know what you're capable of, let's see how you do with the pulleys." Jamie also found a way to turn pulley exercises into a game. Albright, living up to his name, joined Jamie in making sure Carl, to the accompaniment of much rowdy cheering, also excelled at this new game. Other patients and their therapists watched. Jamie was sure they were envious.

By the time Carl and Jamie returned to Ward 321, Carl's

glossy black hair was again plastered to his forehead. This time, his dark complexion was flush with a glow of accomplishment. Jamie was exhausted.

"How'd it go?" Toby said.

Carl sat on his bed and smiled. "It's a lot easier when you got somebody in your corner cheering you on."

"From this day forward," Jamie said, "we're each going to have somebody in our corner cheering us on."

Nurse Eliot was nearby. She was a master at not letting her expression reveal her thoughts. But she couldn't hide the smile lines around her eyes.

* * *

Friday, 21 March 1919

Toby was sitting on his bed, holding his artificial foot, working the ankle joint. "The problem with this thing," he said to no one in particular, "is it only wants to hinge one way."

Jamie pointed to the ward's double doors. "I'll bet the next person to walk through those doors will be the corpsman who made it for you."

"I'll take that bet," Carl said from across the boulevard.

"Five to one on a nickel?" Jamie proposed.

"Who gets the five?"

Jamie laughed. "Me, of course. How likely is it that I can predict who will be the next person to walk through a door?"

"You must know something we don't," Carl said. "Make it three to one, and you're on."

"I'll buy into those odds," Toby said.

Jamie smiled. "You're both on."

No sooner were the words out of Jamie's mouth than Toby's corpsman came through the double doors. Jamie rubbed his hands together. "Three to one on a nickel, times two, equals thirty cents if my math's correct."

"There's no natural way you could have known who would come through those doors," Carl said.

Toby held up his artificial foot and worked the hinge another time or two. "It just doesn't feel right."

"You is supposed to wear the thing, not play with it," his corpsman said. He took it from Toby and held it like it was a baby bird. "I told you it would take some adjustment as you broke it in." The corpsman inspected it. "Let's go see if we can make it better."

Toby levered himself onto his crutches.

Jamie rolled to the foot of his bed. "I'm coming with you."

"Whoa, partner," the corpsman said. "Three's a crowd."

Toby crutched his way between the hulking corpsman and Jamie. "Charlie Gowan, meet Major Jamie Collins."

Gowan looked a bit wobbly, like he could use a pair of crutches himself. His eye began to twitch. "Major Collins, sir, I've heard so much about you. It's a real honor to meet you, sir. I'm, uh. I'm—"

"Nice to meet you too, Charlie. Now, let's see what we can do to make Toby's foot feel more like his own."

Jamie followed Gowan and Toby down the hall to the door across from the physical therapy room. They entered the prosthetics workshop. Jamie froze at the sight of the rows of tools laid out in precise order. "I could fall in love with this place," Jamie said. It was a bit creepy, though, with all the prosthetics here and there that were in various states of completion.

"You like to work with your hands, sir?"

"There are few things I enjoy more." Jamie picked up a wood chisel and felt its cutting edge. "When I was a kid, I used to build model sailing ships. My neighbor back home had turned his garage into a workshop. He used to let me use his tools, but he didn't have a tenth of the number you have here. And I could only dream of having a lathe or drill press."

"You ain't seen nothin' yet, sir." Gowan opened a six-foot-tall, double-door metal cabinet. "Check out these beauties."

Jamie practically salivated. "Are those what I think they are?"

"They is if you is thinkin' they's power hand tools."

Jamie rolled closer and touched the gun grip of a drill. "These are so new to the market I've never seen one before."

"Amazin', ain't it, that the army would supply me with the latest tools."

"They're as shiny as museum pieces. Haven't you used them yet?"

"Sir, I put 'em to the test the minute they arrived. I just believe in takin' care of my tools. Look around. You never gonna find a cleaner shop."

"I'm guessing you make everything from scratch to the exact requirements of each patient. Am I right?"

Charlie smiled. "Yes, sir. Metal, wood, leather—I work with 'em all. Anythin' the orthopedists dream up, I can make."

"I understand you invented the sling lift the nurses use to transfer patients between their beds and wheelchairs."

Charlie's eyes widened. "I'm surprised you knows about that, sir."

"I keep my eyes and ears open," Jamie said. "Did you also make Toby's foot?"

"Yes, sir. One of my better pieces."

Toby looked like he was about to say something. Out of fear it might sound negative, Jamie preempted him. "I'm impressed." He took the foot from Gowan and turned it over in his hands. "Damned fine workmanship." Jamie worked the hinge. "Did the orthopedist specify what kind of hinge to use?"

"No, sir. He give me a sketch, that's all. If my final product looks like his sketch, I can do as I please. It's only when I gets too creative that they come down on me."

"*Too* creative?"

"Some orthopedists get real touchy if they suspect me of thinkin' for myself. It's like, the whole thing has to be their idea, or they ain't happy."

"Do you think they'd notice if you swapped out this hinge for a double-acting spring hinge—you know, like what they have on saloon doors in Western movies?"

Gowan's brow furrowed. "Let me see that, sir." He mumbled to himself as he worked the single-action hinge. "Why didn't I think of that?" He set it on his workbench and began rummaging around in a large wooden box stowed below the bench.

Toby leaned against a storage cabinet, taking some weight off his real foot.

"I scrounge bits and pieces from all over the base," Gowan said over his shoulder. "I's sure I picked up one of dem hinges when dey replaced the swingin' doors between the kitchen and the mess hall."

Gowan shoved that box aside and began looking through another. "Here it is." Jamie handed him Toby's artificial foot.

Gowan held the hinge up to it. "If I cuts this here bit down, it just might fit."

Gowan slapped the hinge into a vise and started sawing away. Toby and Jamie exchanged looks. Gowan was in another world, completely caught up in his work. He held the cut-down hinge next to the old one. "Close."

He put the hinge back in the vise and took a file to it. After a good bit of grunting, he loosened the vise and held the hinge to the light. "Here," he said, handing it and Toby's foot to Jamie. "That look like it'll fit—sir?

"Forget the "sir" stuff. Call me Jamie."

"Yes, sir, Jamie, sir." Gowan picked up the file he had been using and held it at the ready. "Whatta you think?"

"Looks good to me. Let's try it."

Gowan dropped his file with a clunk, took the foot from Jamie, and unscrewed the old hinge. The double-action spring hinge filled the void perfectly. "Sit down, Wilkins. Strap this on and tell us how it feels."

Toby bent down, buckled the straps, and, with the help of his crutches, stood. After a tentative step, he leaned his crutches against the workbench and took several more steps. To Jamie, he looked like a man falling off an inclined roof. He expected Toby to unstrap the thing and throw it across the room again. Instead, Toby awkwardly walked the length of the workshop. "Look at me. I'm walking again!" With some effort, he turned around and walked back.

"Charlie Gowen—you're an artist," Toby said. "It feels almost life-like." He grabbed the corpsman's hand and pumped it. "I can't thank you enough!"

"Thank the major. It were his idea to change out the hinge."

"I merely asked whether the orthopedist would notice if you changed it." Jamie shrugged. "You did the rest."

From his appreciative look, Jamie guessed that Charlie wasn't used to being given credit for his work.

"Let's go show Carl," Jamie said. "Come on, Charlie."

Jamie rolled, Toby crutched, and Charlie fell in step like an old comrade as they moved down the central corridor to Ward 321. Jamie stopped two paces from the door and turned to Toby. "Do you think you can make it the rest of the way without your crutches?"

Toby handed them to Charlie. "Try to stop me."

One could have mistaken them for the three musketeers as they entered the ward.

"Look at me." Toby walked, however haltingly, up to Carl. "Charlie made a little change, and now you'd think my foot was real."

Carl looked dubious. He made eye contact with Jamie. Jamie pantomimed putting on a happy face. "That's great," Carl said with a convincing smile. "I can't wait to see what Charlie can do for me."

Charlie took Jamie aside. "Feel free to use my workshop any time, night or day, Jamie, sir."

"Thanks, Charlie. I'll take you up on that."

After Charlie left, Carl handed Jamie fifteen cents. "Okay, how'd you know it would be Gowan walking through those doors?"

"I never bet money unless I have an edge. In this case, I'd just heard Nurse Eliot tell one of the bluebirds that Gowan was on his way."

"That's hardly fair," Carl said.

Jamie laughed. "You're not going to find me risking my money on a bet unless the odds are stacked in my favor."

* * *

Saturday, 22 March 1919

A game of chess with Tom Walberg usually helped get Jamie's mind off how many days it had been since his surgery. As he passed the nurses' station heading toward Tom's room, he heard female laughter. Tom's sister was due to return.

"Jamie!" Tom shouted when Jamie appeared at his door. "Come in. Meet Laura."

Tom said his sister was a knockout. She was pretty, all right—slim, trim, and with a lovely face—but rather than being a knockout, she was more like a solid jab to the solar plexus. Rachel was a knockout ... and Nurse Eliot. Laura did, however, have a fabulous smile that made Jamie feel she was about to share the ultimate humor of the universe with him. Jamie rolled up to her. "Please excuse me for not standing."

She put her hands on her hips. "And Tom said you were a gentleman."

Most people seemed to think Jamie's paralysis defined him. Laura was different. She had that wide-eyed, open look that said it would be a pleasure to get to know him.

Tom could barely contain his excitement. "Laura's engaged!"

Jamie gave Laura a broad smile. "Congratulations. I'm sure your fiancé's a lucky man."

She smiled back at him modestly. "That's kind of you to say. Tom's been telling me the most complimentary things about you."

"And some are even true—or almost anyway," Tom said.

Laura slid her chair a few inches closer to Tom. "Please,

sit beside me where Tom can see us both." Jamie rolled his chair closer.

Tom worked his shoulders into his pillow and smiled. "Laura was telling me about one of the more eccentric professors she had at Vassar—"

Jamie grasped his armrests. "You went to Vassar?"

"Class of '15."

Jamie had to ask. "Did you happen to know a girl named Rachel Lawson?"

Laura sat up straight. "Yes, I did. Not well since I was a year ahead of her. But I certainly knew *of* her."

Jamie would never have bet that both Nurse Hobbes and Laura knew Rachel. "You knew *of* her?"

"Everybody knew her as the smartest girl in the school. And the kindest. And the prettiest."

Tom raised himself up on his elbows. "Who's this Rachel? Is she your girl?"

Jamie ran his hands down his thighs. "Once upon a time, I might have said, 'yes.' Now? I don't know. She's never seen me in a wheelchair."

A tense silence followed. Tom never mentioned a girl, and Jamie had been careful not to bring up the subject. If Jamie's chances of attracting a girl were bad, Tom's were dire.

"I admired Rachel," Laura said. "If she's the kind of person I think she is, she won't let a wheelchair come between you."

Jamie stared at his lifeless legs. "I might."

Tom's feelings aside, Jamie desperately wanted a woman's perspective. And Laura at least knew who Rachel was. He looked into her eyes. "Like Rachel, you're young. Attractive. You have your whole life ahead of you. A world to explore. If I were your fiancé, would you think twice about marrying me? In the state I'm in, I couldn't give Rachel children."

Laura stared back at him. "Love can overcome anything."

"What if she were to marry me out of pity rather than love?"

Tom sat up. "Isn't it for her to decide?"

Laura stood, leaned over, and kissed the top of Jamie's head. "You are a thoughtful man." She smiled warmly. "If Rachel doesn't want you, I do."

Jamie felt flush from the top of his head to his waist. "What about your fiancé?"

Laura smiled. "We could introduce him to Rachel."

* * *

Sunday, 23 March 1919

Jamie slept in and missed church services again. He rolled up on Toby. "How come the chaplain never visits our ward?"

"That's a sad story." Toby closed the book he'd been reading and pinched the bridge of his nose.

"Well, don't keep me in suspense."

"About a month before you arrived, the chaplain was in an accident. The taxi he was riding in got hit head-on by a municipal bus." Toby set his book aside. "Broke a few bones. Worse, he suffered a severe concussion. Word is that his bones are healing nicely. The problem is, every time the doctors think he's ready to return to duty, another complication arises from his concussion." Toby sighed. "A real shame."

"That is a sad story."

"He's a good man, the chaplain. Everybody likes him—except Sergeant Binney, of course."

"That doesn't surprise me about Binney. What about Sunday services?"

"Since they expect the chaplain to return to duty any day, he hasn't been replaced. Nor has a temporary replacement been appointed."

"So there aren't any Sunday services?"

"Not the usual kind. But some of us meet in the chapel Sunday mornings, read a few Bible verses, sing a hymn or two, and pray together."

"Would it be okay if I joined you?"

Toby hesitated. "You should know, most of us are colored —or rather all of us."

Jamie picked up his Soldier's Edition of the Gideon Bible and fanned the pages. "I've never noticed anything in here that says people have to be the same color to worship together."

"I just don't want you to feel out of place," Toby said.

Carl called out from his bed on the other side of the boulevard. "How about me? Would you welcome a white Roman Catholic?"

Toby steepled his fingers, which struck Jamie as appropriate. "If you proclaim Jesus Christ to be your Lord and Savior, I don't care if you're green and a member of the First Church of Mars, I'll welcome you."

"Then count me in," Carl said. He went back to reading a baseball magazine.

Toby lowered his voice. "Jamie, may I ask you a personal question?"

Jamie shrugged. "Ask away. If it's too personal, I just won't answer."

Jamie had no idea how Toby lost his foot, or Carl his arm, or how any of the other patients landed on Ward 321. It was an unwritten rule that no one ever asked. Patients only talked about such things when they were alone with their best friends, and they brought up the subject themselves, not because they were asked. Jamie was expecting something like that from Toby. He was surprised when Toby asked, "Were you a believer before you were wounded?"

After giving it some thought, Jamie decided it might do them both some good to answer. "Like most Americans of our generation," Jamie said, "I was raised as a Christian."

"What I'd like to know is—" Toby looked at the stump where his foot used to be, "how can you hold onto your faith when you've ended up in a wheelchair?"

This *was* getting personal, but Jamie sensed Toby's question was really about his own faith and the loss of his foot. "First of all," Jamie said, "I haven't ended up anywhere— yet." He leaned back in his chair. "If you promise to keep it to yourself, I'll answer your question."

Toby moved a little closer. "I promise."

"You might think I'm crazy."

Toby grinned. "Maybe I already think you're crazy."

Jamie took a deep breath. "My First Sergeant was convinced I was dead when he carried my body off the battlefield. Not knowing what else to do with me, he deposited what he thought was my corpse at the nearest battalion aid station. Since a doctor hadn't yet pronounced me dead, per standard procedure, a medical corpsman immediately inserted an IV in my arm. When the harried triage doctor finally took a look at me, he formally pronounced me dead and moved on." Jamie looked into Toby's eyes. "Everybody thinks that doctor made a mistake—everybody but me. I believe I really was dead."

Toby stared at Jamie like he was seeing a founding member of the First Church of Mars.

"I know this because my spirit, or my soul, or whatever you want to call it, had left my body and was hovering over the scene, watching it unfold."

Toby put a little more distance between himself and Jamie.

"I said you might think I'm crazy. Wait until you hear the rest." Jamie took a deep breath. "When a soldier from Graves Registration showed up and ripped the IV from my arm, I remembered someone back in the States was praying for me. In that instant, my spirit returned to my body, and I was able to moan. That one weak sound was enough to tell Graves Registration I was alive." Jamie closed his eyes briefly and tried to erase the scene from his memory. "You ask if I'm still a believer? Who wouldn't be after an experience like that?"

Toby was slow to respond. "But look at us. Our lives have been turned upside down."

"True. But here's the saving grace." Jamie ran his hands over his lifeless thighs. "When I arrived in France, I was worried that if I killed someone simply because he was wearing a different uniform than mine, I'd end up in hell. Then, I was confronted with a choice. If I didn't kill those I did, they would have killed my men. But isn't that the same choice men of conscience on both sides faced?" Jamie sighed. "I figure there's only one reason I'm not currently roasting in the lake of fire."

"And that is?"

"I was raised for a purpose."

Toby sat up straight. "What purpose?"

"I'm still trying to figure that out. But I'm convinced that someday, a situation will arise where only a man who has died and been raised from the dead can come to the rescue—a role I'm uniquely qualified to fill. And here's something even crazier. I believe that until I accomplish that purpose, I'll live on no matter what."

Toby sat speechless, staring at Jamie.

"As for you," Jamie said, "I can think of a reason you survived the battlefield despite all you suffered."

"Yeah? What's that?"

"When your future students see how much you've overcome in becoming a great teacher, it will inspire them to pursue their dreams despite anything life throws at them."

Toby shook his head. "You *are* crazy." He grinned. "But a good kind of crazy. The kind that makes me want to keep chasing my dreams."

* * *

There were faint streaks of red in the sky left over from an impressive sunset when Nurse Hobbes walked through the ward's double doors. She was carrying half a dozen books under her arm. "Good evening, Major Collins. I got these books for you from the base library." She set the books on Jamie's nightstand—then stepped in front of them. He tried to look past her. She moved a little to the side to block his view.

"Don't worry," Jamie said. "I'm not one to judge a book by its cover."

"I'm more worried that you'll judge the one on top by its author. Please give it a chance, sir. I'm sure you'll find it captivating." Nurse Hobbes glanced at the watch suspended from her uniform top. "I'm sorry, sir, I must run, or I'll be late for my shift." She trotted off, looking more than a little pleased with herself.

Jamie eagerly turned over the book on top. He chuckled to himself: *Pride and Prejudice,* by Jane Austen. Did Nurse Hobbes really think a hardened combat soldier would enjoy the work of a genteel nineteenth-century woman?

"What is it?" Carl said.

"*Pride and Prejudice.*"

Toby laughed. "My sister loves that book."

Carl was incredulous. "And Nurse Hobbes thinks *you're* going to like it?"

Nurse Hobbes' stack of books included works by Mark Twain, Jack London, Sir Arthur Conan Doyle, Miguel De Cervantes, and Thomas Hardy. Austen's book was the least appealing to Jamie. But Nurse Hobbes would be disappointed if he didn't at least give *Pride and Prejudice* a chance. He set it on his lap and rolled closer to the window at the head of his bed where there was better light. With low expectations, Jamie opened to Chapter One.

It is a truth universal, that a single man in possession of a good fortune, must be in want of a wife.

How long he stared at the opening sentence, he didn't know. Though his fortune was meager, he longed for a wife. Would Rachel even consider wedding herself to a man in a wheelchair? Would a woman like Nurse Eliot?

You mustn't think such thoughts, he said to himself. *They can only lead to pain.*

Hoping to bury himself in Austen's story, he read on. And on. And on.

"Amazing," he said aloud when he finished the first chapter.

Toby and Carl looked at him. "Nurse Hobbes was right. This is great stuff." He settled back in his wheelchair and let Austen take him to times—and customs—past.

Although the following few chapters were a delight, Jamie had never been one to sit and read for long without dozing off. *Pride and Prejudice* tumbled to the floor, jolting Jamie from a dream. He tried to pick it up. With no control of his lower body, it remained out of reach from the confines of his wheelchair.

He turned his chair and tried from a different angle. Same result.

"I'll get that for you, Jamie." Carl swung his legs over the side of his bed.

Jamie was struggling to restrain his beast. "No," he said. The word came out harsher than he intended. "I need to do things for myself."

He spun his wheelchair to the right. This got him no closer to retrieving Austen's masterpiece. His heart began to race. Others began to stare. Jamie didn't care. As he spun his chair hard to the left, his footrest struck his nightstand. The last bit of his self-control evaporated in an instant, and his beast arose. He began slamming his footrest into the leg of his nightstand again and again. Nurse Hobbes's entire stack of books tumbled to the floor, accompanied by a climbing arpeggio of expletives.

Carl ran over and stopped Jamie's wheelchair assault. "Easy, Jamie. Easy."

When Jamie looked at him, he didn't see Carl. In his mind's eye, he saw a terrified German machine gunner trying to levitate as a grenade rolled around at his feet. Jamie blinked several times. The beast in him slowly withdrew. He closed his eyes. "I can't even pick up a damned book without help."

Carl picked up the Austen novel with a trembling hand and offered it to Jamie. Rather than touch it, Jamie spun his wheelchair around and buried his face in his hands. He heard Carl restack the books and slip away.

The beast had won—again. And it would keep winning if Jamie didn't learn how to control it. He stole a glance between his fingers toward the nurse's station. The ashen look on Nurse Eliot's face told him she had seen it all.

Even before his assault on his nightstand, the men were a little ... cautious around him. Having caught a glimpse of the beast that lurked in him, they had a reason to be afraid.

And they weren't the only ones who were afraid of Jamie. One man on the ward was terrified of him. That was Jamie himself.

An hour later, Jamie was on his bed doing modified pull-ups using his trapeze bar—heels resting on top of his bed, legs and hips dead weight. Nurse Eliot was suddenly by his bedside. "Sir, you mustn't do anything so strenuous."

"I'm going stir-crazy. Exercise helps."

"Doctor Regenstein hasn't yet given you clearance to exercise." Nurse Eliot retrieved the clipboard from the end of Jamie's bed and tucked it under her arm without looking at it. "Tomorrow, it will be two weeks since your surgery. The doctor will be around to see you in the morning. If he's satisfied with your progress, he'll have your physical therapist start you on a gradual exercise program."

As conscientious as she was, it didn't surprise Jamie that Nurse Eliot knew how long it had been since his operation without looking at his chart. He rested his head on his pillow. "All right. I can wait a day."

"I suspect Corpsman Albright will give you as much of a workout as you can handle." She placed her hand on his shoulder and smiled.

To Jamie, a knighting by King George V of England wouldn't have been as big an honor as Nurse Eliot's touch.

* * *

Monday, 24 March 1919

First thing that morning, Doctor Regenstein visited Jamie—just like Nurse Eliot said he would. After a quick examination, Regenstein was nearly ecstatic—that is, he almost smiled. "You're a quick healer. It's time for you to start physical therapy."

Jamie *was* ecstatic—that is, he *did* smile. Toby and Carl were together, watching. They weren't smiling. They had been very cautious around him since his wheelchair assault on his nightstand. Jamie couldn't blame them. They were aware of Jamie's combat record. They knew Jamie was an exceptionally dangerous man. If something as simple as being unable to pick up a book off the floor could send him into such a rage, what else might trigger him?

An hour later, Corpsman Don Albright bulldozed his way onto the ward. Having devoured *Pride and Prejudice,* Jamie looked up from Mark Twain's chronicle of his time in the old west, *Roughing It,* another of the books Nurse Hobbes acquired for him from the base library.

Carl practically jumped to his feet. "I'm ready."

"Relax, Zanardi." Albright looked around the ward until his eyes met Jamie's. "I came for Major Collins."

Jamie dropped his book. "It feels like two years since my operation. Let's not waste another second." When he reached the door, he looked back. Neither Carl nor Toby had budged. "You're not going to make me endure Albright's torture chamber all by myself, are you? Don't worry. If I lose control, I won't take it out on you. I'll take it out on Albright's exercise machines."

"I'll come," they said in unison.

Albright wheeled Jamie into the corridor outside the ward, with Toby and Carl right behind. "Did you see how the rest of the men looked at us as we left together?" Jamie said. "What do you want to bet that before long, they'll be begging to join us at our end of the ward?"

"You told us you never bet unless the odds are in your favor," Carl said. "What is it this time?"

"Human nature. All men have an urge to band together with those of their kind."

Toby scratched his head. "Of their kind? The three of us couldn't be more different."

"We've each lost something of ourselves," Jamie said. "That makes us more alike than different. And we're all fighting the same enemy. A body that can't respond the way it used to. Our odds will be a lot better if we band together and fight that battle as a unit."

Carl smiled. "I like our chances."

* * *

Tuesday, 25 March 1919

190

Jamie wasn't surprised when Harvey Shipman showed up at the foot of Carl's bed. "What's up, Ship?" Carl said.

"I was wondering, uh, would you guys mind if I move down here next to you?"

Carl gave Jamie a look that said, *you were right again.* "It's not my call," Carl said. "I vote yes." He looked across the boulevard at Jamie and Toby. "How do you guys vote?"

Jamie shifted his weight in his wheelchair. "I vote yes."

Everyone looked at Toby. "It's unanimous," he said.

Carl offered Shipman his hand. "Welcome to the brotherhood."

Shipman grinned like a kid who had been handed the answers to an upcoming math test.

"Brotherhood," Jamie said, trying the word on for size. "I like that. The enemy robbed each of us of our wholeness. Instead of feeling diminished, let's be proud that our losses qualify us to be part of an exclusive club. Let's tell the world we're not ashamed of who we are. Let's call ourselves 'The Brotherhood of Loss.' "

Chapter 18

The Brotherhood of Loss

Wednesday, 26 March 1919

The day dawned sunny and clear. By noon, heavy clouds had moved in—nimbostratus for those like Jamie who found such things interesting. The ensuing rain put the men in a somber mood. As always, Jamie was the exception. He was having a fine time sitting in front of one of the floor-to-ceiling windows that usually admitted a flood of cheery light onto the ward.

Toby came up behind him. "Whatcha doin'?"

Jamie gave him a big, goofy grin. "It doesn't take much to amuse me. I've been sitting here enjoying the races."

"What races?"

The wind blew a scattering of raindrops under the roof overhang, where they impacted the window near eye level. Jamie pointed to two drops that had landed close together. "Which drop do you think will reach the sill first?"

"I don't know. The one on the left?"

"I'll take the one on the right." They watched as Jamie's

pick slid down the pane in fits and starts. Toby's drop followed its own intermittent path until it coalesced with a slower mover and took off like a shot. Jamie's was only halfway down the pane when Toby's crossed the finish line.

"I seem to have an unexpected talent," Toby said. He indicated two other drops that were prime candidates for another race. "I bet this time the one on the right wins."

"You're on."

It was a close race, run to the accompaniment of much shouted encouragement. Toby won again.

Carl wandered over. "Looks like you guys are having fun. Mind if I join in?"

Jamie waved him on. "The more, the merrier."

"You got some kind of game going?"

"Raindrop races," Toby said.

Jamie pointed out two likely contestants. He and Toby chose the same drop. Carl was happy to take the underdog, which promptly won by a mile as Jamie and Toby's pick stalled.

Shipman joined the party, and the cheering grew louder. Soon, most of the men on the ward were pushing and elbowing for a better view. Nurses and orderlies smiled as they watched from the sidelines. Anyone walking past Ward 321's double doors could easily have heard their shouts.

Cheers mixed with jeers as individual drops combined and raced for the finish line while others stalled and hung immobile. Soon, money was being wagered. Odds were offered and haggled over. All transactions had to be finalized in a few seconds in case a drop reached the finish line before agreement was reached. Toby called individual races like the announcer at the Kentucky Derby. Jamie naturally became the referee. Some races ended so quickly Jamie couldn't determine the winner. Player's whoops and hollers settled the issue.

Now and then, opposing drops would collide and become one. Jamie ruled such contests a tie, and all bets were canceled. Shouts reached an ear-piercing level when both drops happened to come to a momentary standstill, and the betting went wild. Occasionally, a gust of wind would deliver a new sheet of rain, wiping out the entire playing field. In such cases, all bets were declared null and void. A new race would begin. This went on for a good 45 minutes until the rain petered out.

The men wandered off, the big-money winners slapping each other on the back—and there at the table of discontent sat Binney, glaring at Jamie.

It had been the first time the men freely interacted with either Jamie or Toby. Jamie hoped it would be the beginning of things to come.

Nurse Eliot was smiling at him from across the room.

The next several days passed quickly as an ever-expanding electorate cast unanimous votes to welcome new members into the Brotherhood of Loss. Men whose backgrounds were as diverse as their names banded together as one unit—like one of Jamie's old platoons. Nurse Eliot was happy to have her bluebirds move Billy Lajoie, Doug Jankowski, Marty Churchill, Davy Leibowitz, Joe Vargas, and Bryan Peters to Toby's end of the ward.

All the beds were taken by the end of the week, completing the great migration. When relocation was no longer an option, a simple pledge to provide unqualified support to fellow brethren became the requirement for admission into the brotherhood.

Men who had lived within a few feet of each other as

strangers now considered themselves a single entity. The ward became their community. As senior officer, by a straw vote, Jamie was elected de facto Mayor of Ward 321—had Binney been asked, he would undoubtedly have voted for someone else. Himself, most likely. Jamie's primary mayoral duties were refereeing wheelchair races and apologizing to the bluebirds for the men's behavior.

As the brotherhood solidified, it became common for the brethren to gather at the table at Toby's end of the boulevard. This became known as "the brotherhood table." Many happy hours were spent there swapping outrageous tales about home, women, anything but the war. The consensus was that the truth of a story was much less important than its entertainment value. Unfortunately, in telling their tales, men who lacked the talent to lie convincingly had no choice but to fall back on the truth.

Such was Carl's plight one afternoon when Jamie and Toby returned from PT to find Carl sitting at the brotherhood table with his face buried in a magazine. Jamie silently rolled up on Carl. "What you readin'?"

Carl jumped about a foot. He held up his magazine for Jamie to see. "It's my April issue of *Baseball Magazine*."

"Anything interesting?"

"There's a story about an amazing play that took place back in '09."

Toby removed his glasses and gave them a quick wipe with the hem of his robe. "It must have been amazing if they're still writing about it a decade later."

Carl closed his magazine, pushed back from the table, and closed his eyes. "I can see it now—July 19th. A steamy Monday afternoon at Cleveland's League Park. Game one of a doubleheader between the Boston Red Sox and the team now called the Cleveland Indians."

Jamie rolled his wheelchair to the head of the brotherhood table—as a courtesy, the head of the table was reserved for Ward 321's de facto mayor. Listening to Carl show off his encyclopedic knowledge of baseball was always a treat. "You've got us hooked," Jamie said. "What's the story?"

Hendricks and Hobbes were changing Jamie's bedding. Nurse Eliot was also nearby. All were drawn to the table, like planets to the sun.

Carl took a deep breath. "It's the top of the second inning. The score's nothing to nothing. Cy Young is on the mound for the Indians. He's still a potent defensive weapon, even though his best years are behind him. Shortstop Heinie Wagner is set to lead off the inning for the Red Sox. Wagner is an average hitter but an excellent base runner. He's faced Young dozens of times during his career, the advantage usually going to Young. This at-bat goes Wagner's way. He leads off with a single. The Red Sox first baseman, Jake Stahl, then beats out a bunt that moves Wagner to second—a notable feat for Stahl, who holds the record for the most strikeouts in a season.

Carl skootched forward and rested his elbow on the table. "This is where it gets interesting. Red Sox's second baseman Amby McConnel comes to the plate and works the count to two balls and one strike. Everybody knows Young doesn't have the stuff he did earlier in his career. With an exceptional runner on second and a guy slowed by age on first, Red's manager, Fred Lake, decides to take a chance. He calls for a hit-and-run."

"Please pardon me for asking," Nurse Hobbes said. "What's a hit-and-run?"

It was Shipman who answered. "That's where a guy on base runs as soon as the ball leaves the pitcher's hand, and the batter's supposed to protect him by hitting the ball even if the pitch is outside the strike zone."

"That's right," Carl said. "Normally, a manager only calls for a hit-and-run when the count's in the batter's favor and the pitcher needs to throw a strike to avoid walking the batter."

"A risky call with Cy Young on the mound," Billy Lajoie, one of the earliest brethren, said. "Even late in his career, Young could still fire the ball past a batter more often than most pitchers."

"Yeah," Ship chimed in. "And on a hit-and-run, if the batter doesn't make contact with the ball, the runners are hung out to dry."

Carl nodded. "And that's the setup when Young leans in, gets his sign, winds up, and delivers." Carl sat back and looked around the room at his captivated audience. "As soon as the ball leaves Young's hand, Stahl and Wagner take off for second and third. McConnel connects, and Young barely manages to duck under a line drive. Indians' shortstop, Neal Ball, a utility player subbing for the Indians' injured first-stringer, makes an Olympian leap and snags the ball in the tip of his glove. By then, the speedy Wagner is almost to third. Ball runs to second base and lets his momentum carry him to where Stahl, who's been trundling toward second, runs into his outstretched glove.

"The entire play takes only a few seconds. The crowd of 11,000 applauds politely. The Indians' players remain on the field. Cy Young holds up his glove, expecting his shortstop to toss him the ball. The next batter leaves the on-deck circle and heads toward the batter's box.

"Instead of tossing Young the ball, the Indians shortstop rolls it to the mound and starts jogging toward the dugout.

" 'Where you goin'?' Young yells at him.

" 'That's three,' Ball says as though it was a routine play.

"In a chain reaction, first Young, then the rest of the players, and finally the fans, realize they've just witnessed the only unassisted triple play in major league history. It takes the grounds crew twenty minutes to pick up all the hats the crowd throws onto the field."

Ship spoke up again. "Let me see if I've got this straight. The shortstop catches the fly ball for the first out. He steps on second before the runner can get back. That's out number two. He tags the runner coming from first for the third out. Right?"

"That's it." Carl looked around the table. "And it gets even better. The crowd cheers wildly at the bottom of the inning when Ball comes to the plate. Two strikes later, Neil Ball sends them into a frenzy by lining a ball over the center fielder's head and circling the bases for an inside-the-park home run, the only home run he hits all season!"

Joe Vargas had been leaning on his crutches just behind Jamie. "Damn, I wish I'd been there."

"Listening to Carl," Jamie said, "I felt like I was there."

From the smile on Carl's face, you'd think he had hit a home run. He tilted his chair back on its hind legs and rested it against one of the columns that defined the boulevard.

"I bet that within a year or two," Jamie said, "radio stations nationwide will be broadcasting games live." He looked over the brethren. "Don't you think Carl would be a natural play-by-play radio announcer?" There was an enthusiastic chorus of agreement.

Carl rocked forward and let the front legs of his chair hit the floor with an echoing thud. "I'd love that."

"Why don't you get a head start by writing sports stories for the hospital newspaper?" Jamie said.

Carl frowned. "Don't you remember? I was a lefty?" He held up the stump of his left arm. "No matter how careful I am, no one can read my handwriting these days."

"You're a supply sergeant," Jamie said. "Don't you know how to type?"

"Sure, but not one-handed."

"Adapt," Jamie said.

Carl slowly stood. "Any idea where I might be able to scrounge me a typewriter?"

"Leave that to me," Hendricks said from the periphery.

Billy Lajoie rose to his feet—his real foot and the artificial one Charlie Gowen made for him, complete with a double-action spring hinge, like Toby's. "You make me want to get off my butt and start chasing my dream."

Marty Churchill, whose bed was now next to Carl's, turned his wheelchair toward Billy. "What dream is that?"

"How does 'Doctor" William Lajoie sound to you?"

"I like it," Marty said.

Billy smiled. "Before the war, I was a pre-med student at the University of Southern California. My dream was to go into ..." he rapped on his artificial lower leg, "orthopedics."

"Seriously?" Joe Vargas, who had suffered the loss of a foot, said.

"Having lost a leg yourself," Jamie said to Billy, "your first-hand knowledge of living without a limb should give you 'a leg up' on other orthopedists."

Billy groaned. "What a 'lame' pun." He turned to Carl. "I hope you master one-handed typing soon."

"Why's that?"

"I'd like you to type a letter telling USC I'll be re-enrolling as soon as the army sets me free."

"I admire your spirit," Marty said.

Billy smiled broadly. "What about you, Marty? What's your dream?"

Marty lowered his head. "If I said, you guys would only laugh."

Jamie grabbed the edge of the table with both hands and leaned forward. "Dreams are sacred. They give us a picture of what our lives could be like. No one should ever laugh at another man's dreams. As brethren, we should encourage each other to dream, and dream big."

A tense silence followed, eventually broken by Toby. "Go ahead, Marty. I promise I won't laugh."

"Jamie's right," Carl said. "We're a brotherhood. That means we all want to see each other's dreams come true."

Jamie remained stone-faced as every man at the table agreed with Carl. Inside, Jamie was shooting up flares and banging drums. When he arrived on the ward, Toby was treated as a pariah, and the men who did talk with each other were little more than strangers. Their universal agreement that they were a brotherhood was one of the greatest victories of Jamie's life.

He became aware of Nurse Eliot staring at him. They made and held eye contact. Her dark lashes amplified the intense green of her irises. She projected such tenderness Jamie was warmed to his core. Though no words passed between them, he would swear Nurse Eliot was inwardly celebrating with him.

Marty sat up straight. "This will probably come as a

surprise to you guys." He looked at Jamie as though for support. "I want to be an accountant."

No one laughed, although there were a few perplexed looks around the table. "The way I struggle with numbers," Davy Leibowitz said, "if my dream of owning my own grocery store comes true, I'm going to have to hire an accountant, especially come tax season."

Marty smiled. "I enjoy working with numbers." He looked around the table. "I come from the little town of Bonner about six miles outside of Missoula, Montana—"

"Missoula," Jamie said. "Isn't that the home of the University of Montana?"

"That's right." Marty was all smiles. "My family owns the general store in Bonner. I used to help my sister with the bookkeeping. When she got married and moved to her husband's ranch, even though I was still in high school, the job fell to me."

Bryan Peters pulled a chair out from the brotherhood table and sat, taking the weight off his artificial leg. "Sounds like a lot of responsibility for a kid in high school."

"I was proud of myself for being able to handle it. And I was good." Marty held his head high. "I did such a good job some of the other businesses in town asked me to keep their books. By the time I graduated from high school, I had a nice little bookkeeping business all my own."

"That's nothing to laugh at," Jamie said. "Accountants make good money." He smiled at Marty. "If that's what you want to do, I say press on."

Toby had been staring at Jamie. "What about you? You know all about us. We know practically nothing about you."

That was true. For some reason, none of the newspaper

accounts about Jamie's medal even alluded to the fact that he had a life before joining the army. "Peaches," he said.

The men stared at him. "Peaches?"

"When I was a little boy, my dad managed a big peach orchard near the mouth of Carmel Valley."

Doug Jankowski, whose bed was now next to Jamie's, rested his elbows on the table. "Where's Carmel Valley?"

"About 125 miles down the coast from here."

"Is your dad still at it?"

"Naw. The owners sold the land to some Eastern developers who'd never seen the place. They started selling it off acre by acre. Nearly broke Dad's heart. I don't know if there are any peach trees left anymore.

"We moved on, though—literally. Mom talked Dad into taking over a bakery in the little town of Pacific Grove about five miles north of the valley." Jamie smiled. "You can imagine the benefits of that for a boy with a sweet tooth. And Pacific Grove is right on the ocean."

"Did you spend your days on the beach soaking up the sun?"

"Hardly. The climate there is pretty much like it is here at the Presidio: cold and damp. The shore is mostly rocky, and the water is way too cold for swimming. I wouldn't have had much time for sunbathing anyway. I was up at four in the morning every day before school and even on Saturdays to help out in our bakery."

"When did you ever sleep?"

"I was in bed as soon as the sun set. In the summer, even before."

"Are your parents still running the bakery?"

"No. Dad died a few weeks after I graduated from high

school. Mom passed just before I was wounded. My sister's all the family I've got now—other than you guys."

"What became of their bakery?" Carl said.

"It was sold off as part of the settlement of Mom's estate."

"Being an officer," Toby said, "I suppose you weren't a baker before the war. What kind of business were you in?"

That was the question Jamie had been dreading. The men were just beginning to treat him as one of their own. The barrier between officers and enlisted had been large. He didn't want to add to that barrier by letting them know he'd been an assistant professor of physics at a prestigious university before his division shipped out for France. "I never was the brightest student," Jamie said. The pained face of Elaine Stanton, the girl who was the best student in his high school, flashed before him. "I got this far only because I made sure nobody ever outworked me. That won me a scholarship and made it possible for me to attend college. I became a teacher."

"You plan to go back to teaching?" Billy said.

Jamie hesitated.

Davy, who was in a wheelchair himself, spoke up. "You're not going to let your paralysis stand in your way, are you?"

"No," Jamie said. "My dream is to be the best teacher any student could ever hope for." Jamie sat back and folded his arms. "I know that's an almost impossibly high standard to meet, but I'm sure going to try."

All true. But not the whole truth and nothing but the truth. Once he and the men were more comfortable with each other, he'd be more open with them if he were ever asked what or where he taught. He glanced at Nurses

Hobbes and Eliot. They knew the truth. Thankfully, they kept it to themselves.

* * *

At mail call, Jamie received a letter from his sister and a thick 9 x 12 manila envelope. He quickly covered the return address on the envelope with his palm. He hoped no one other than Hendricks had seen that it was from Professor Ron Larson, Department of Physics, Stanford University. Inside was a recent issue of the European scientific journal *Physics Letters*. Jamie extracted it and quickly folded the cover over to conceal its title. The journal had been sent by Jamie's former thesis advisor, now colleague. It contained a paper written by the renowned Danish physicist Neils Bohr, one of the fathers of quantum mechanics.

The value of any scientific paper can be judged by how often it's cited by other authors. More importantly, by whom. In this issue of *Physics Letters*, Bohr cited a paper Jamie and Ron Larson had written before Jamie's reserve infantry unit had been activated—a huge career boost for Jamie and Ron!

Jamie would have to read Bohr's paper four or five times before he could be sure he understood it all.

Toby looked over from his bunk. "What ya' hiding there, Jamie? A girly magazine?"

Jamie could feel himself blush. He cared about what Toby thought of him. He held open the journal long enough for Toby to read its title. "Someone I knew at school wanted me to see it. His name's mentioned."

Again, all true, but not the whole truth.

Toby seemed suspicious but didn't press the issue.

* * *

Later that evening, Jamie was sitting by himself at the head of the brotherhood table, reading a short story from *North American Review*, an old magazine someone had left lying around. He happened to look up. Doug Jankowski was staring at him from across the room. Jamie tried to make eye contact. Doug looked away. That wasn't like Doug. Although he was missing an arm, he was as bold as any patient on the ward. "Doug," Jamie called out to him. "What's up?"

Doug slowly approached the brotherhood table, looking very unsure of himself. Jamie motioned for him to sit. Doug pulled out the chair next to Jamie and slouched down on it.

"I have a problem," Doug said. "I didn't want to mention it in front of the rest of the men. You being a teacher, I hope you'll help."

"I'll certainly try. What is it?"

"It's kind of embarrassing."

"It can't be any more embarrassing than some of the things I've gotten myself into over the years," Jamie said.

Doug smiled. "I come from Logan County, West Virginia," he said. "That's coal country. As many generations back as I know, the men of my family have been coal miners. That's what they did in Poland. That's what they do here in the US."

"An honorable occupation," Jamie said.

"For sure. The country would come to a standstill without coal." Doug rested his elbow on the table. "I grew up in a company town. The general store, workers' houses, schools, meeting halls, churches—all are owned by the coal company. Until I joined the army, I'd never met a man who didn't work for the company one way or another."

He reached across his chest and felt his empty sleeve. "Since mining was all we knew of the world, kids like me expected to follow in our fathers' and their fathers' footsteps and become miners ourselves. None of us thought we had any choice but to spend the better part of our lives deep underground covered in sweat and coal dust."

Doug looked lost in thought. Jamie pictured him imagining himself back in the mine and wishing he was somewhere, anywhere else. Jamie resisted the urge to fill the silence.

"Then I got drafted and got to see something of the world," Doug said.

"Drafted? I thought mining was a reserved occupation. Weren't you exempt from the draft?"

"The mines were overrun with guys trying to avoid military duty. Guys who were willing to work for practically nothing. I wasn't. And the union couldn't protect us from being underbid because of the wartime emergency regulations. I was laid off. A week later, I got a draft notice."

"The army was desperate for manpower early in the war," Jamie said.

"The Island Creek Coal Mine was closing in on me. I was happy to get the call. And happier still to meet guys from all over the country and from all walks of life. I realized I didn't have to go back to the mines—and now, with only one arm, I couldn't anyway."

"Have you decided what you want to do instead?"

"That's what I want your help with. Since miners don't need much classroom schooling, I dropped out early. Real early." Doug stared at the tabletop with his head down.

"Go on," Jamie said.

"The problem is," Doug checked over both shoulders, "I can barely read—which means I'm pretty much going to be out of luck when it comes to finding any kind of decent job." He grasped his armrest. "I'd give anything to be able to read like the rest of the guys." He looked at Jamie with pleading eyes. "You were a teacher. Will you help me learn to read, proper-like?"

"Certainly." Jamie thought for a moment. "I consider myself a pretty good math teacher, but Toby's much better qualified to teach reading. Let's ask him to help."

Doug scrunched his head down into his shoulders. "It's bad enough you know how dumb I am. You're an officer. You're supposed to be smarter than me. Toby's a corporal, just like me. We're supposed to be equals."

Jamie thought it obvious that Toby was well-educated. How could Doug not have noticed? "Toby has a degree in education from Howard University," Jamie said.

Doug's eyes opened wide. "Then why isn't he an officer?"

Doug must have spent a lot of time deep underground if he had to ask. "Because the army doesn't think colored men can handle the job."

Jamie followed Doug's gaze to where Toby was talking with several brethren. "That's crazy," Doug said. "I'd follow Toby anywhere."

Jamie was as proud of Doug as he'd ever been of one of his men. "You're a good man, Doug. Smart and brave."

"Sir?"

"It takes brains to realize what a disadvantage it is not to be able to read well and courage to do something about it. I promise, between Toby and me, we'll have you reading up a storm in no time."

"Thank you, Jamie, sir. Thank you very much."

"Don't mention it." And Jamie meant it. The last thing he wanted was for the men to start asking more questions about what he actually taught before the war, and where.

Jamie backed his wheelchair up and rolled toward the nurses' station. He intended to thank Nurses Hobbes and Eliot for not giving away what he really did before the war. As he drew closer, Nurse Eliot looked up from her clipboard and smiled.

Binney spoke from the table of discontent the moment Jamie's back was to him. "You're not doing these men any favor by giving them false hope."

Jamie spun around and stared at Binney.

"We both know none of these cripples will ever amount to anything."

The man knew just how to summon Jamie's beast. It wasn't necessarily his words. It was his smugness and his tone. Jamie knew he should ignore Binney and roll on to the nurses' station. His beast had other ideas. Jamie fought to keep it from taking over. He had to learn to control it. He had to.

He hadn't yet.

Jamie rolled closer to Binney—real close, eye to eye. He sensed everyone on the ward was watching. Jamie didn't care.

Binney gave a self-satisfied glance around the room. "What chance do these cripples have in this world?" He raised his coffee cup to take a sip.

Jamie swatted Binney's cup across the room, grabbed the front of Binney's robe, and drew him in until their noses were almost touching. "If you continue to poison the morale of these men, I will wring your short, pudgy neck." Jamie shoved Binney deep into the seat of his wheelchair.

Binney was indignant. "An officer can't strike an NCO. That's battery. That's a court-martial offense."

Carl stepped forward. "I didn't see an officer strike an NCO. What I saw was Major Collins warn you about poison. You should thank him for stopping you from drinking from your cup." He turned to Toby. "How about you? What'd you see?"

"Pretty much the same as you." Toby nudged Shipman. "How about you, Ship?"

"The coffee *did* taste like poison today. What about you, Nurse Eliot? Did you see anything like what Sergeant Binney is claiming?"

A cold hand squeezed Jamie's heart. Nurse Eliot had to have seen the whole ugly scene. Saw him strike a subordinate. What would she think of him now? And if she chose to, the by-the-book head nurse could get him in real trouble.

She marched up to the table of discontent. "I saw Sergeant First Class Binney fail to address Major Collins with the proper military courtesy—for which Sergeant Binney could be subject to disciplinary action."

Every word of support the men offered had shoved Jamie's beast further into its cage. Nurse Eliot slammed the cage shut. She remained stoic, except there were smile lines around her sparkling green eyes.

Binney turned to one of his minions. "How about you, Finlay? Are you blind, too?"

"Na, I ain't blind, and I didn't see nothin' neither."

Jamie and Nurse Eliot shared a conspiratorial smile. What was it about her? How could she, with just a few words, cage a beast that previously broke free at the slightest provocation—a beast that had killed a score of German soldiers?

A random question popped into Jamie's mind. Why didn't he think of Rachel every other minute the way he used to?

* * *

Saturday, 29 March 1919

Soon after breakfast, Hendricks showed up on the ward with a beat-up typewriter under one massive arm and a thick manila envelope under the other. He set the typewriter on the table in front of Carl.

Jamie wasn't surprised by Hendricks' resourcefulness. "Where'd you find that?"

"Admin set it out as surplus, sir. A note attached to it says it's stuck in upper case."

Carl reached out and pecked at a couple of keys. "That doesn't matter. With only one arm, I couldn't use a shift key anyway. I'll type everything in capitals."

"If you're going to do it," Jamie said, "you should do it right. I guarantee the minute we leave this ward, people will want to pity us—while at the same time trying to shut us out of their world."

"I don't want pity," Carl said. "It doesn't take two arms to be a complete man."

Jamie's pride in "his" men kept growing and growing. "I agree. But we should be aware that our disabilities will remind people of the suffering everyone experienced during the war—something they'll all be trying to forget. We'll have

210

to do things even better than those who aren't disabled to receive the respect we deserve." Jamie looked around the room. "Let's show the world how strong we are. After all, we took on the best the Kaiser had to offer, and they couldn't kill us."

Nurse Eliot was nearby, overseeing her bluebirds as they took patients' vitals. Jamie was rewarded with one of her heart-warming smiles.

He placed Carl's typewriter on his lap and turned toward the ward's double doors.

"Where you goin'? Carl said.

"Charlie's workshop. A few modifications, and you'll be typing upper and lower case like you were born to it."

"Hang on," Davy said. "I see a money-making opportunity here. I'll bet Carl is typing 20 words a minute within a month. Any takers?"

Shipman jumped at the challenge. "I think my man Carl can do better than that. I'll bet he can top 20 within three weeks."

Carl stood tall. "I was a supply sergeant during the war. I used to be able to type 40 words a minute, no sweat. I'll bet the whole world I'll be typing at least 20 words a minute within two weeks."

"Major Collins?" Hendricks held up the envelope he was carrying.

"Oh, yes. I don't want to forget this." Jamie took the envelope from Hendricks and passed it to Marty Churchill.

Marty turned the envelope over in his hands. "What is it?"

"Open it."

Marty pulled out a printed form. "It's an application for admission to the University of Montana." He pulled out a thick booklet. "*Basic Accounting, Volume 1*," he read aloud from its cover.

Jamie tapped the application. "You'll need a degree if you want to be a CPA." He looked around the table. "The base training office has applications to just about any school you can think of, plus enough correspondence courses to keep a man busy for a lifetime."

Marty stared at Jamie. "I ... I don't know what to say."

"I figured you might want to start earning college credit now through a correspondence course."

Marty flipped through the book. "Great idea."

"And you can let your former clients know you'll be home soon and ready to handle all their bookkeeping needs."

Marty tried to speak. It came out garbled. He tried again. "No one's ...." He cleared his throat. "No one's ever taken any interest in my future before."

Jamie looked around the brotherhood table. "There's not a man here who wouldn't be happy to see you succeed."

Except maybe Binney. If he had a heart, it was encased in concrete.

As Jamie was about to head out the door, he heard angry voices coming from the table of discontent. Larry Krauss rose abruptly and approached Jamie. "Sir, you should know all Binney can talk about is getting even with you." Krauss glanced toward Binney. "But I don't think he's got the guts to try anything."

Jamie wasn't surprised. "Thank you, Krauss. I appreciate the warning." Jamie looked across the room to find Binney staring at him through menacing half-shut eyes. "Aren't you worried about him seeing you talking to me?"

"Screw Binney. I'm sick of all his bitchin' and tired of

sitting around feeling sorry for myself." Krauss indicated a chair next to Jamie's wheelchair. "May I sit, sir?"

"Please do."

"Sir, I want something to look forward to when I get out of here. Will you help me figure out what that might be?"

Jamie could feel Binney's eyes boring into him. There was no way Krauss would ever return to the table of discontent.

* * *

Charlie Gowan wasn't in his workshop when Jamie arrived. It didn't take long to diagnose and correct the problem of upper and lower case on Carl's typewriter. Modifying the shift key so Carl could comfortably operate it with the stump of his forearm was a little more challenging. Charlie came in as Jamie was putting the finishing touches on his modifications.

"What you workin' on, Jamie?"

Jamie explained.

"Let me have a look." Charlie gave the typewriter a quick inspection. "Not bad. We might be able to make it even better if we tweak this here piece." Charlie showed Jamie what he meant.

"That's brilliant, Charlie. When you leave the army, you should open your own business making and repairing anything clients need."

Charlie smiled broadly. "I'm plannin' to. My term of enlistment is almost up. I'll be a civilian in about a month, and I've got big plans."

"Mind sharing them?"

"Mind? I'm bustin' to tell you."

Jamie settled back in his chair. "Fire away."

"I'm the first in my family to graduate from high school." Charlie couldn't hide his pride. "Still, I'm not gonna put on airs. I'm gonna carry on my family's tradition of makin' hand-crafted fine furniture."

"Really? What about prosthetics? You excel at that."

"I plan to do both—plus one or two other things that might surprise you."

The man was brimming with enthusiasm. "That's great, but we'll sure miss you here."

"I won't be goin' far. I've worked out a deal to buy a shop here in California—building, land, and tools all thrown in. And you'll never guess where it is."

"Where?"

"Your hometown!"

Jamie sat up straight. "Pacific Grove?"

"That's right. The deal's been in the works for over a month. When I mentioned it to Toby, he told me that's where you is from. What are the odds of that?"

"Aren't you from South Carolina? Pacific Grove's clear across the county."

"That's hardly far enough to suit me."

"Why? What's the problem?"

Charlie leaned against his workbench. "You ever been to South Carolina?"

" 'Fraid not."

"It's hot as hell in the summer, and the humidity can suck the life right out of you. My folks have passed. I don't have no brothers or sisters. There's nothin' to hold me back."

"No young lady waiting for you?"

"The guy I thought was my best friend married her last fall. I don't want to go back and have to see them together."

"Sounds like Pacific Grove's a better place for you all around. It never gets too hot, never too cold. And I'll lay odds that you'll find the woman of your dreams waiting for you there."

Charlie brightened. "Maybe I already have. The deal I've worked out is with a doctor and his sister. They inherited the shop from their dad. He was a master furniture maker. And the tools he had! My workshop here hardly compares."

"I can't imagine a shop better equipped than this one," Jamie said.

"Neither could I 'til I saw their place. The father wanted his son to take over the business. His son let him down and became a doctor instead."

Jamie couldn't keep from smiling. He doubted many fathers would feel let down if their son became a doctor rather than a carpenter. Then he thought of The Father and The Son.

Charlie got a faraway look. "Miss Lanie, the daughter, she's somethin' else. She wanted her dad to take her in as a partner. Her old man wouldn't hear of it. Even though she'd been workin' with him since she was a little girl and proved she was as good as any man, her father said carpentry wasn't suitable for a girl. Instead, he wanted her to become a teacher." Charlie smiled. "I guess Miss Lanie's an obedient daughter, seein' as how she's honored her father's wishes and has become a teacher."

Charlie leaned his hip against his workbench where Jamie had spilled a little machine oil he hadn't gotten around to cleaning up. "They could probably sell the land alone for what I's gonna pay. They don't want to. They want things to carry on just how they was as a tribute to their dad. The only down payment they want is a promise that I'll try to make a go of the business—a promise, mind you. Nothin' else. And here's a crazy twist." Charlie stood up straight. Jamie was too embarrassed to say anything about the oil stain on Charlie's pants. He surreptitiously wiped up the little bit of oil left on the bench. Charlie didn't notice.

Charlie held his arms out straight and put his hands together like he was aiming a pistol. "My first job in the army was as an armorer." Charlie let his arms fall. "Along with bein' a furniture maker, the old man was a gunsmith—he made some of the most beautiful stocks and grips you'll ever see. The sellers think the Lord Himself must have sent me to them because, with my background, I can also carry on the gunsmithin' side of their father's business—I mean, have I stumbled into a deal made in heaven, or what?"

"It sure sounds like it."

"I know more than a fair bit about gunsmithin', thanks to Uncle Sam, but I think there's a trick or two I've yet to learn. So get this. Miss Lanie promised to teach me all she knows about smithin', which I'd say is quite a lot judgin' from the prizes she's won for craftmanship and marksmanship. And you know what that means?"

Jamie had no idea.

"It means I can spend more time around her. And you should see her. She's a big woman—I don't mean fat. I mean tall and strong. Just the size for a man like me. She's also the kind of pretty that appeals to me. Not flashy, just solid good looks. And she's brimmin' with confidence, which I like in a woman. What really sets her apart, though, is she's awful sweet."

"She obviously made quite an impression on you." Jamie grinned. "She just might be the woman of your dreams."

"I wish. I'm just scared she's way too classy for the likes of me. She'd more likely be the woman of your dreams."

Jamie laughed. "I've got other plans. But hey, how'd you end up making prosthetics if you were an armorer?"

Charlie chuckled. "You knows the army. I had a friend from back home who was a corpsman. He told me the Medical Corps was looking for someone with the right skills to make artificial arms and the like. So I volunteered. I guess the Corps figured an armorer with a background in carpentry could fill the bill."

Jamie had to laugh. "That's the army for you." With Carl's typewriter on his lap, he backed up his wheelchair and headed for the door. "I wish you the best of luck with your new business, and I'll make a point of dropping in on you whenever I'm in Pacific Grove."

Charlie rose to his full height. "I'd like that."

* * *

Sunday, 30 March 1919

Jamie and Carl followed Toby through a maze of corridors to Letterman's chapel. From the outside, its double doors looked like any of the many wards. Inside looked much like any church building. A central aisle with a dozen pews on either side, narrow side aisles, a chancel consisting of a raised platform with an altar, and a pulpit offset to one side. One element of architectural flair gave the chapel a degree of distinction. The far end featured a large stained-glass depiction of Jesus standing before a flock of sheep. Morning light shining through the glass cast mesmerizing pools of colored light on and around the altar.

The men who had already arrived stared at Jamie and Carl. "These are my friends," Toby said. "Please give them a Christian welcome." The men greeted them from a cautious distance.

Toby sat in the front pew. Carl joined him. Jamie parked his wheelchair close by. He was ashamed to feel uncomfortable being one of only two white men among the worshipers. It shouldn't have mattered. Jamie hated to think Toby had pegged him correctly in their first encounter. And worse, his motivation for striking up his friendship with Toby could have had less to do with Toby and more with Private Clarance Thurgood of Graves Registration.

No, Jamie realized. He wasn't subconsciously trying to repay Thurgood for not giving up on him. Toby was a true friend.

On the hour, Toby stepped forward—which, thanks to Charlie, he could do. He opened the gathering with a prayer and then scanned the congregation. "Anyone who feels the calling, please share a passage from Scripture you found particularly moving during the week and tell us why it touched you."

A young man who didn't look old enough to be a boy scout, let alone a soldier, stood and read the story of the Good Samaritan from the Gospel of Luke. His enthusiasm was contagious. The congregation responded with shouts of "Amen," etc.

"Nice story, isn't it?" the young man said. "You might ask, does it speak to us today?" He looked from man to man. "I'll give you an example of how it does. A new orderly reported for duty on my ward. By his accent, I could tell he was from the Deep South. I was afraid of how this southern white man might treat me." The young soldier appeared to be swallowing down his emotion. Jamie braced himself for another example of bigotry, or worse. He'd seen enough of it overseas.

The boy soldier smiled. "It turns out this new orderly is as kind as any man I've ever met. Which reminded me that my neighbor isn't someone who looks like me or talks like me. My neighbor is anyone who shows me mercy." The young man sat to much praise from the congregation. Their passion moved Jamie.

Several others read passages from their Bibles and shared what they believed the Lord was telling them through their selected verses. Their openness and sincerity touched Jamie. Despite their outward differences, he was now perfectly at ease in their company.

"Thank you, brothers." Toby scanned the room. "Does anyone have any praises or prayer requests?"

The young soldier who had read the story of the Good Samaritan stood. "I thank the Lord for the Christian fellowship we're enjoying here today."

"Anyone else?"

Jamie had more requests than it would be fair to dump on these men all at once. He needed help conquering the beast that seemed determined to conquer him. His fears that the operation on his back had been a failure were beginning to overwhelm him. He had to resolve his conflicted feelings about Nurse Eliot and Rachel. And he needed help to keep the men on the ward focused on achieving their maximum degree of independence.

"Let's hear from one more," Toby said.

That was all the prompting Jamie needed. He raised his hand.

"The floor's all yours."

To be heard, Jamie rolled his chair to the front of the church. He happened to park it where he was illuminated by a shaft of colored light shining through the stained glass at the head of the chancel. He bowed his head. "Lord, you know how much I need Your help to fight the demons of doubt and anger in me. I'll save that for another time. Now I raise up to You the men on my ward. They have suffered greatly. Almighty God, please help me be like the Good Samaritan we heard about earlier. Help me inspire the men on my ward to dream big when they look to their futures. And if I can be of service in making their dreams come true, please show me the way. I ask these things in the precious name of Jesus."

"Amen, brother," the boy-soldier shouted.

Jamie's heart swelled with pride to be called 'brother.'"

"Anyone else?" Since no one raised their hand, Toby led the men in singing "Amazing Grace" and closed the service with another prayer.

The men filed out smiling, talking, laughing. Jamie lingered.

Toby approached Jamie's wheelchair. He motioned toward the door. "After you," he said.

"I need a minute."

"Okay. Carl and I will wait outside. Take your time." Toby ushered the stragglers out the door.

Jamie had asked God to use him as an instrument in making the dreams of the men on his ward come true. Since he was asking in the name of Jesus, his request had to include all the men—even Binney.

"Heavenly Father," Jamie's words echoed throughout the now-empty chapel, "please help me purge my soul of my loathing for Reginald Binney. Let me be of service in helping him pursue a dream that will bring him peace while honoring You. I ask these things in Jesus' name."

* * *

Monday, 31 March 1919

When Jamie awoke, Doctor Crandall was standing next to his bed. "Good morning, Major Collins. I hope I didn't wake you."

Jamie ran his hands down his legs. Doctor Crandall would have been blind not to see Jamie's disappointment. "I've been sleeping pretty well lately. It's exhausting trying to be alert to even the slightest return of feeling in my legs."

"I know it's easy for me to say, but we just have to wait for Nurse Hobbes' tincture of time to work its magic."

"I've never been a patient man. But waiting here on the general ward surrounded by others is easier than it would have been in my private room."

"I'm glad it's working out for you." He glanced at his watch. "I'm heading off to Colonel Thornburgh's senior staff meeting. Is there anything I can do for you before I go?"

"Yes, sir, and thanks for asking. Is there any place nearby where I can make some private telephone calls?"

"You can use my office. And take your time. The CO's staff meetings can last for hours." He turned to a blank page on his clipboard. "I'll draw a diagram to show you how to get there." He drew some lines and handed the paper to Jamie. "Building 100. Two buildings north of here. It's not far."

"Thank you, sir. I appreciate it."

Jamie was soon in Doctor Crandall's office. He'd used field telephones during the war. They were much more primitive than permanent landlines. Jamie was pleasantly surprised by the clarity of the voices he heard over Doctor Crandall's telephone.

Jamie's intent was to make some arrangements before being discharged from the hospital. His first call was to Stanford. He was heartened to hear that they were anxiously awaiting his return. Granted, his Medal of Honor wasn't a Nobel Prize, but it would lend the university a measure of distinction. If there was ever a time to use it as leverage, this was it. His next call was to the San Francisco Chronicle. He spoke with a senior manager who happened to be the father of a friend Jamie had known since their undergraduate days.

As Jamie worked through his list of calls, his excitement grew. The men wouldn't see any of this coming.

He smiled as he thought of how far he'd come since wanting to hole up in his private room and write a paper about the dual nature of light.

Chapter 19

A Prayer Granted

April Fools' Day, Tuesday, 01 April 1919

Jamie awoke to find Toby, Carl, Ship, and Nurse DaSilva surrounding his bed. "What is this, a death watch?"

"We were worried about you," Toby said. "You slept straight through Tuesday, and here it is Wednesday already."

Jamie turned to Nurse DaSilva. "You wouldn't lie to me. Did I sleep through the entire day?"

"Sir, you showed no sign of a fever, so we thought it best not to wake you, although we were beginning to worry."

They all nodded in agreement.

Jamie was still trying to make sense of DaSilva's evasive answer when everyone burst out laughing.

"April Fools," Carl shouted.

Jamie pretended to laugh along with them. Inside, he was crying. Before their prank, by sheer force of will, he had stopped counting the days since his operation. Their April

Fools' Day windup forced him to face the fact that it had been exactly five months since he was wounded and 23 days since his surgery. And still, he had no feeling in his legs. He reached under his sheet and rubbed his hips.

Nurse DaSilva fluffed his pillow. "Sir, I hope you don't mind that I joined in on the men's little joke."

"Not at all. I like to think I can take a joke as well as the next guy. The four of you working together were pretty convincing. And I did sleep well last night. For a change, Toby's talking in his sleep, Carl's snoring, and Ship's nightmares didn't wake me."

Toby grinned. "If we're such a nuisance, I believe your private room is still available."

"No thanks," Jamie said. "I'd sooner put up with you guys than go back into solitary confinement. But I give you fair warning: April Fools' Day isn't over."

The men drifted off, looking rather pleased with themselves. Jamie looked at Nurse DaSilva. "And that warning applies to you too, nurse."

He shifted his weight to one side as best he could, reached under his covers, and massaged his hips again.

"Are you uncomfortable, sir?"

"A tad. I always hurt somewhere. This is different. It feels like I've got a prickly belt wrapped around my waist. Hot one minute, pins and needles the next."

Nurse DaSilva took in a startled breath. "Sir, this isn't your idea of an April Fools' Day joke, is it?"

"What? No. I just have this strange sensation around—"

"Oh, sir, that's wonderful!" She ran off in the direction of the nurses' station. Soon, Nurse Eliot was standing at Jamie's bedside, with DaSilva in her shadow. "Sir, your bluebird tells me you have feeling around your waist."

Every synapse in Jamie's brain fired simultaneously as a million dreams, prayers, wishes, and desires exploded into the light of day. "I am the happiest of fools!" he shouted. "I have feeling around my waist for the first time in five months, and I was completely oblivious." Jamie laughed until he wept.

Nurse Eliot put her hand on his shoulder and smiled as she wiped a tear from the corner of her eye. Jamie was elated to have shared this moment with her. He was sure she wasn't just a dedicated nurse doing her duty.

She put her hands on either side of his waist. "Do you feel this?"

Jamie nodded.

She moved her hands further down his torso. "And now?"

"Yes!"

Her smile was heartwarming. "That's wonderful progress."

Jamie imagined her fully embracing him—but that wasn't right. If he were going to be embraced by a woman again, it *had* to be Rachel. She was the one whose prayers got him through the war.

"Does this mean he'll be able to walk again?" Toby said from one bed over.

Nurse Eliot assumed her regal pose. "Let's not get too far ahead of ourselves."

* * *

Within the hour, Colonel Thornburgh was shaking Jamie's hand and slapping Doctor Regenstein on the back. "Didn't I tell you Regenstein was our best surgeon?"

"I only held the scalpel," Regenstein said. "The Great Physician guided my hand."

"I thank all three of you." Jamie ran his hands up and down his legs and smiled wistfully. "Now, my prayer is that this tingling sensation won't be the extent of my recovery."

Doctor Regenstein managed one of his rare smiles. "We'll have to let Nurse Hobbes' tincture of time continue to work its magic."

Throughout the rest of the day and into the night, Jamie alternated between thanking God for giving him a second chance, thinking about how radically different his life would be if he could walk again, and poking and prodding himself to see how far down his legs his sense of feeling might have progressed. Perhaps he was asking too much, too soon, because his explorations yielded only disappointment.

As for his intention to get even with the April Fools' Day pranksters, this was a day to celebrate, not to get revenge.

* * *

Wednesday, 02 April 1919

The next morning, after sitting up with the aid of his trapeze bar, Jamie discovered that when he let go, he could remain sitting for a few seconds. It was as though overnight, dormant nerves woke up for the first time in months.

Doctor Crandall came by to examine Jamie. He pricked the soles of Jamie's feet with a needle. Jamie smiled at the pain. Crandall was almost as excited as Jamie.

The doctor worked Jamie's ankle joints. "You feel that?"

In his excitement, Jamie could barely breathe, let alone speak. He nodded.

"Close your eyes." Crandall tapped on Jamie's knee. "How many taps?"

"Two," Jamie managed to say.

He tapped on the other knee. "And now?"

"Three."

"Well done." He kneaded Jamie's calves.

"I can feel it! I can feel it all!"

Doctor Crandall patted Jamie's knee—which this time Jamie felt. "Now it's Corpsman Albright's turn to work on your muscle tone." He smiled broadly. "I'm so optimistic I predict you'll soon be on your feet again and standing tall."

Doctor Lawrence, who oversaw Jamie's care at Walter Reed Army Hospital, had said almost the same thing.

Rather than wait for his physical therapist to put him to work, Jamie immediately embarked on a punishing regimen of self-designed exercises intended to strengthen muscles he hadn't used in five months.

The brethren watched from a distance. Always watching. If their encouragement was tinged with jealousy, Jamie could understand. A man who lost an arm or a leg could never recover. But come on, guys, be happier for a brother.

Within a few days, Jamie regained the ability to push down on his footrests. "Look at this," he said to Hendricks. He began alternating between pushing with his left foot and then his right: left, right, left, right. "It's as though I'm walking."

Initially, he couldn't exert enough pressure to break an egg. Soon, he was making his wheelchair shudder under the force of his feet.

In no time, he developed the ability to raise his feet one at a time, half an inch off their rests. He added knee lifts to his exercise regimen: lift with the left, press with the right, lift with the right, press with the left, over and over, until he was drenched in sweat.

"Please, sir," Nurse Eliot said one day after watching him torture himself, "don't demand too much of yourself this early in your recovery."

Her concern warmed Jamie. "Thank you, Nurse Eliot. I'm sure that's good advice." He promptly ignored it and continued to push, push, push, all the while thanking God for every little sign of progress.

* * *

Easter Sunday, 20 April 1919

Since he'd been awarded the Medal of Honor, people seemed to think courage pulsed through Jamie's veins. It wasn't true. Though Albright, his physical therapist, was working him hard, Jamie had yet to find the courage to try to stand. Deep down, he didn't believe he had the strength—and probably wouldn't until he tried and failed countless times. But the thought of failure rattled the cage of his beast. If he tried—and failed—he was afraid it would break loose. There was no way of knowing what it might do. Yet he could feel the beast goading him. Taunting him. Jamie should have known better than to take the bait. But it was Easter Sunday, the day the Lord rose from the dead. There would never be a better day to try.

Jamie slid his feet off their rests and placed them flat on the floor. He motioned Hendricks over. "Please remove my footrests. I'm going to try to stand."

Hendricks bent down and took hold of one rest. "Are you sure you're ready for this, sir?"

"Not in the least. Stay close, will you?"

"Right behind you, sir. All the way." Hendricks removed both rests.

Jamie locked the wheels of his chair, gripped the armrests, and pushed himself up until his elbows locked. So far, so good. Now for the hard part. He strained to straighten his knees, willing his thighs to do the work. His legs began to shake uncontrollably.

Hendricks reached out to steady him.

"No." Jamie had forced the word out through clenched teeth. "I have to do this on my own." The shaking grew worse. Suddenly, his knees collapsed. He crashed back onto his seat, panting.

The beast now had the keys to its cage, working the lock. There was only one way to stop it. He had to stand. He had to.

Nurse Eliot rushed to his side and stood opposite Hendricks. "You're doing great, Major Collins. Why not try once more and then call it a day?"

Jamie tried again with the same dismal result. He wiped his sweaty palms on his pant legs. Nurse Eliot might be ready to call it a day. Jamie wasn't. Nor was the beast.

He could barely push himself up again. He collapsed even quicker this time.

His beast erupted like a volcano. "Get up," he ordered his legs. He slammed his fists into his quivering thighs when they refused to comply. "Get up," he bellowed. "Get up."

He tried again, giving it his maximum effort. He hovered for a second or two before crashing back down. He pounded his insubordinate thighs again.

Nurse Eliot jumped forward and grabbed Jamie's upper arm. "We're going to give you a little boost." She nodded to

Hendricks, who took Jamie's other arm. "On the count of three." Together, they lifted Jamie to his feet.

Nurse Eliot moved to Jamie's front and steadied him. "I've got him, Hendricks." Jamie didn't know whether to thank her or curse her for interfering.

"Now I'm going to let go, and you're going to stand on your own," she whispered. "You can do it, sir. We both know you can." Her lips were so close to his ear he could feel the softness of her breath.

Jamie stood for several seconds before starting to collapse. Nurse Eliot caught him and held him tight against herself. "You're doing great, sir."

She helped him regain his balance, loosened her grip, and let go altogether. Jamie stood for 15 or 20 glorious seconds. "You're on your feet again, sir, just like we knew you'd be."

"Yes!!!" He stood tall—and the beast withered and crawled back into its cage.

His legs began to tremble.

Nurse Eliot wrapped her arms around him again. "Let's not overdo it." With Hendricks' assistance, she lowered him to the seat of his wheelchair. She caressed his cheek. "Well done, sir."

Jamie took her hand and kissed her open palm.

She blushed. Took a step back. "Sir, I—"

Hendricks smiled. "I hope you're not thinking of kissing my hand too." They all laughed.

Two of Jamie's most improbable dreams had come true. He stood for the first time in almost six months, and Nurse Eliot had engulfed him in her arms.

* * *

Jamie was massaging his thighs between bites as he was having dinner. Hendricks was nearby. "A tad sore, sir?"

"More from the pounding I gave myself than from standing." Jamie looked up at Hendricks. "I'll tell you what, it scares me when I lose control like that."

"Is that what happened in France, sir?"

Jamie nodded. "You're getting to know me well." In France, his beast had saved lives—almost at the cost of his own. Back in the States, it had no mortal enemy to fight. Which meant it could strike anyone.

"Nurse Eliot was brave to step in the way she did and stop me from punishing myself," Jamie said. "I'm thankful I didn't strike her." He looked at Hendricks. "I'd never forgive myself if I hurt her."

"She'd have understood, sir."

Jamie nodded. "You know, I think you're right." He was silent for a moment. "The army's lucky to have such a dedicated nurse. We're lucky. She's everywhere at once, making every soldier feel special. It worries me, though, that she looks so tired lately. Do you think she's pushing herself too hard?"

"Sir. I believe it's her nightmares that are getting her down."

"Nightmares? Her too?"

"I'm sorry, sir. I probably shouldn't have mentioned them."

"Too late. What's the story?"

"Well, sir, she usually keeps her feelings bottled up tight, so I was surprised the other day when she let slip that her nightmares are coming more often and becoming more intense."

"I'm sorry to hear that." Sorrier than he cared to admit—

even to himself. "So many of us who served at the front are tormented by nightmares."

"You, sir?"

"After I took out the last of those machine guns, a German officer appeared seemingly out of nowhere. He leveled his pistol at my head and fired. Miraculously, he only grazed my temple. That German officer visits me in my sleep now and then, and I can tell you, he scares the hell out of me."

"Nurse Eliot is haunted by the ghosts of the men she couldn't save."

* * *

Wednesday, 23 April 1919

Over the next three days, Jamie mastered rising to his feet without help. This rapid progress astounded everyone: doctors, other staff, patients, even himself. The next "step" toward full recovery would be to walk. With cane in hand, Jamie stood. He didn't object when Hendricks positioned himself directly behind him. "Thanks, Hendricks. I wouldn't want to fall and hurt myself." He grinned.

For the first time in nearly six months, Jamie put one foot in front of the other and moved forward a step. Nurse Eliot was on the other side of the ward, holding her clasped hands below her chin like she was willing him on. Her lips were moving. He was sure she was silently mouthing, *you can do it, you can do it.*

Jamie put his other foot forward and moved closer to the brotherhood table where a handful of brethren were watching. Nurse Eliot's silent encouragement gave him strength.

He amazed himself by making it ten or twelve feet to the table. Carl stood and offered him his chair. Jamie collapsed onto it.

He expected the brethren to go wild with their congratulations. To his dismay, they were surprisingly restrained. Jamie was baffled and a little hurt by their reticence.

Nurse Eliot rushed to Jamie's side. "Well done, sir," she said, showing all the enthusiasm he expected from the men.

Jamie vowed never to sit in a wheelchair again and to hell with anyone who wasn't happy for him.

Other incidents made Jamie wonder whether the brethren were still heading in the right direction. Despite the support the men gave each other, their physical therapy and prosthetic fittings were still challenging. Bryan Peters was having a particularly difficult time adjusting to his artificial leg. No matter how Charlie Gowan adjusted it, the thing caused Bryan pain. Joe Vargas was in a similar situation with respect to his artificial foot. The orthopedist said the problem had to do with how their amputations healed and for Charlie to keep trying. Peters and Vargas didn't care where the problem lay. Together, they decided the benefits their devices might someday provide were too meager to justify the pain they caused. Their prosthetics sat unused—as dead as the limbs they left on the battlefield.

Jamie saw their decision as a disappointing setback for the brotherhood. He would have ordered them to tough it out if he weren't still concerned about the barrier between officers and men. But what are officers, if not leaders? And Jamie preferred to lead by example.

* * *

Friday, 25 April 1919

The opportunity to set an example arose as a side effect of Jamie's physical therapy. Stretching and flexing had caused a mass migration of the remaining pieces of shrapnel in his back and legs. Several pieces had already worked their way through his flesh and appeared as bumps under his skin. Without too much pain, a doctor removed them like pins from a pin cushion.

One piece, however, was not cooperating. It was about the size of a postage stamp. The thing was lodged beneath the skin on top of his right thigh near his knee. It would take more than a bit of coaxing to remove it. A doctor could easily have done the job. Jamie had other plans.

While the nurses were busy distributing evening medications, Jamie furtively liberated a bottle of alcohol, a wad of cotton, a pair of tweezers, and a self-adhesive bandage from the nurses' station. Once the ward quieted down for the night, he sat on his bed, pulled up the leg of his pajama bottoms, and swabbed the area above his knee with alcohol. He got out his razor and gave it an alcohol bath.

Vargas and Peters, along with several others, were watching from the brotherhood table. "Jamie, what the hell are you doing?" Vargas said.

"A little surgery. I've carried this piece of shrapnel around in my leg far too long." Jamie hoped he sounded more confident than he felt.

Peters turned his wheelchair in Jamie's direction. "Shouldn't a doctor do that?"

"No need. I can do it myself."

"Yeah, but why?"

"I want to be independent, don't you?

"Sure. We all do."

"I figure independence is a choice. If I'm going to get there, it will be because I got off my butt and made it happen, not because I sat around feeling sorry for myself. Besides, we've all been through worse and lived to tell about it. If it sets me free, I'm willing to shed a little blood, sweat, and tears. Aren't you?"

No one answered. Nor did they make eye contact with Jamie or each other. That didn't stop them from watching.

Jamie clenched his teeth, hoping that would keep him from crying out when he incised the lump on his thigh. As soon as the razor cut into his skin, he wished he hadn't recovered full feeling in that part of his leg yet because it hurt like hell, and he couldn't let the men think he was weak. He was surprised and, therefore, ill-prepared for the astonishing flow of blood.

Vargas half-covered his eyes. "I can't watch this."

Jamie pulled a clump of cotton from the wad he had "borrowed" from the nurses' station and used it to apply pressure to the incision. The bleeding stopped long enough for him to grab his stolen tweezers and dig for the shrapnel—another adventure in pain. With a tug, he extracted the jagged piece of steel and dropped it with a resounding clunk onto an empty plate on his nightstand. How he managed not to cry out, he'd never know. He used the rest of the cotton to soak up the remaining blood, then quickly slapped the self-adhesive bandage on the site. Joe Vargas threw up in the nearest wastebasket.

* * *

Monday, 28 April 1919

235

Jamie was sitting on his bed when Nurse Eliot came onto the ward carrying a tray loaded with supplies. "You look deep in thought, sir."

He never minded when Nurse Eliot interrupted his thoughts. Lately, most were about her. "You've proven to be remarkably perceptive, Nurse Eliot. Maybe you can help me figure something out."

"I'll certainly try, sir." She put her tray down on the foot of his bed.

"Why aren't the men happier about my recovery?"

Nurse Eliot thought for a moment. "They are happy, sir, but it means you're no longer one of them."

"But I was paralyzed for five months. I know what they're going through."

Nurse Eliot canted her head. "Not really, sir. You've had reason to hope from the day you arrived here. A man who's lost a limb has no hope of ever being whole again."

Jamie closed his eyes and rubbed his forehead. "You're right. I wasn't looking at it from their perspective."

She waited in silence for a moment. "Is there anything else, sir?"

"No, Nurse Eliot, and thank you for opening my eyes."

She smiled. "Any time, sir." She retrieved her tray and headed toward the nurses' station.

Chapter 20

A Life Taken

Saturday, 03 May 1919

The morning issue of the San Francisco Chronicle had just been delivered to the ward. MUNICH FALLS, the headline blared, further evidence of the turmoil Germany was still experiencing. Armed revolts had broken out across the country. Council Republics were proclaimed. The Munich Soviet Republic was perhaps the most prominent, though short-lived. Clearly, winning a war was more straightforward than securing the peace.

Nurse Eliot happened to be passing by the brotherhood table where Jamie was sitting. She looked lost in thought. "Excuse me, Nurse Eliot. I haven't seen either of my favorite bluebirds in a day or two."

Worry lines transformed her usually neutral expression. She glanced around and then spoke softly. "Sir, I've confined Nurse DaSilva to her bed. She's contracted the Spanish Flu."

Jamie set the Chronicle aside. "That's terrible. The men on the ward ... have they been exposed?"

"It's too early to know, sir. Nurse DaSilva was off duty a full day before she had any symptoms."

The flu had taken an exceedingly heavy toll in 1918. Now, there was a resurgence. If the flu hit the ward, it could take out the men as effectively as a machine gun. "Nurse Hobbes ... does she have it too?"

Nurse Eliot flashed a quick smile. "Our brave Nurse Hobbes volunteered to care for her classmate."

Brave was an understatement. "I hope they're going to be all right." He pointed at his newspaper. "It says here the Spanish Flu's already killed more than ten million people worldwide. A shocking number. A quarter of what the Great War claimed."

"Ten million and counting, sir." Nurse Eliot looked around the ward. "We can't let it get the upper hand here." She gestured toward the ward's double doors. "A doctor will be in shortly to brief the men on symptoms to watch out for. We'll need to isolate any of our patients who become infected." She hurried off.

Within a few minutes, a young doctor Jamie had never seen before entered the ward. Jamie liked to think he could spot a man who'd served at the front. This man, Jamie was sure, hadn't. It wasn't his youth that gave him away. He simply didn't have the vacant eyes or trampled look of a combat veteran.

"Gather around, men," the doctor called out. The men gravitated to the center of the boulevard. He stood on a chair so everyone could see him. "All right, listen up."

Since it was uncommon for a doctor to brief the men, they gave him their full attention—except Binney.

"Sergeant Binney," Jamie called out in his command voice, "this applies to you too."

Binney grudgingly rolled his wheelchair closer.

"Please proceed," Jamie said to the doctor.

"As you all know, a respiratory disease called Spanish Influenza has already killed a lot of people worldwide, including here in the US. It was bad in 1918. Now, it seems to be making a comeback."

The men looked at each other.

"Begging your pardon, sir?" Toby said. "All the patients here have been pretty much confined to this ward since they arrived. We're safe, aren't we?"

The doctor hesitated. "Well, uh ..." A low murmur rumbled down the boulevard. "It's impossible to isolate you completely," the doctor said. "At the very least, staff have to come and go."

"Men," Jamie said. "It's only fair to tell you that one of our bluebirds has contracted the illness."

"Who ... sir?" Toby said.

"Nurse DeSilva."

"What!" Binney erupted. "She was hovering over me like a mother hen just the day before yesterday. Does that mean I'm in for it?"

The room became deathly silent.

"Not necessarily," the doctor said. "We just don't know enough about how the Spanish Influenza spreads to say who will get it and who won't."

"That's far from reassuring," Toby mumbled.

"Our best defense is to detect this illness early," the doctor said. "The most common sign of infection is fever." The doctor looked around the ward. Did he think he could detect a fever just by looking?

"What else should we be looking for?" Jamie said.

The doctor smoothed his hair back. "Body aches, muscle and joint pain, headache, a sore throat, and an unproductive cough with occasional harsh breathing."

At that moment, Harvey Shipman happened to cough. The men around him moved back a step.

"Men," the doctor said, "the onset of the Spanish Flu is very sudden, striking people with almost no warning. It then rapidly evolves into the symptoms I mentioned a minute ago." He put his hands in the pockets of his white coat. "The danger of this influenza is its tendency to progress into pneumonia. That's what makes it so deadly."

"Yeah," Binney spoke up. "The papers say it kills kids and healthy adults just as easily as the weak and old. Some die as soon as forty-eight hours after getting sick. I'm not the only one that bluebird was flying around. Everybody here has as much chance of getting it as me."

Thank you, Sergeant Binney, you demoralizing little twit. Jamie said a silent, desperate prayer for Nurse DaSilva.

"If any of you start to experience even one of the symptoms I've mentioned," the doctor said, "you are to notify a nurse or orderly immediately." He looked around the ward. "Is that understood?"

A buzz of many conversations immediately filled the ward.

"Attention," Jamie shouted.

The men immediately came to order.

"The doctor asked if you understood."

"Yes, sir," the men answered in unison.

"Good," the doctor said. "Any questions?"

"Yes, sir." Toby squinted behind his army-issue glasses. "What's the treatment for those who do become infected."

The doctor clearly wasn't comfortable with that question. "I'm afraid the standard treatment is largely symptomatic and is intended merely to reduce the fever and pain." The doctor took his hands out of his pockets. "We use aspirin, cold compresses to the forehead, warm packs around the torso and lower extremities, and intravenous administration of isotonic glucose and sodium bicarbonate."

Toby's chin fell to his chest. "Lord help us," he mumbled.

"Any other questions?"

The men remained silent.

"Thank you, doctor," Jamie said on behalf of all present.

* * *

Sunday, 04 May 1919

Letterman's patients and staff were as susceptible to the Spanish flu as anyone. By the grace of God, Nurse DaSilva and, the day after the doctor's briefing, Mess Sergeant First Class Binney were the only ones on Ward 321 to become infected. Since DaSilva was being cared for in her quarters, Jamie couldn't follow the progression of her condition. Proximity allowed him to see that Binney had been hit particularly hard. Fever ravaged him within a few hours of the first signs of contracting the virus. Delirium set in.

It would have been hard to find a patient who felt sorry for Binney. Because of his constant complaining, the men—including his former minions, Krauss and Finlay—had already moved as far away from him as possible. The medical staff further isolated Binney by placing him in Captain Garnett's old private room.

Jamie stood in the doorway and watched Nurse Eliot swab Binney's sweaty forehead with a cold cloth. She was wearing a surgical mask, which accentuated her hypnotic green eyes. *Dear God ... what if she gets sick?* "Excuse me, Nurse Eliot. Shouldn't one of your bluebirds be doing that?"

She laid her damp cloth on the edge of a bowl of cold water. "With a sickness this contagious, the staff is overwhelmed. We all have to pitch in where we can—and I'd never ask one of my nurses to do something I'm unwilling to do myself. Still, we'll be hard-pressed to give Sergeant Binney the twenty-four-hour care he'll need."

She looked tired. Rundown. Each breath she took in Binney's presence put her further at risk. Was she strong enough to resist the deadly virus? She had risked her life to care for her patients in France. Now, she was facing an equally deadly enemy.

A random thought popped into Jamie's head. Why was he so concerned about Nurse Eliot with only a passing thought about Rachel's safety?

"Please, let me do that," Jamie said.

Nurse Eliot looked at Jamie wide-eyed. "Sir?"

"A real leader looks after all his men, not just the ones he likes." And a real man doesn't stand by and watch an exceptional woman risk her life for one of his men when he knows he can help.

"Sir. This disease is highly contagious. I respectfully ask that you not come any closer."

Jamie boldly stepped into the room.

Nurse Eliot's eyes showed her alarm. "Please ... I beg you."

"Are you immune?"

"Well ... no, sir, but it's my job."

"You are essential to the functioning of this ward. I'm not." And you're essential to me, he wanted to say, but this was neither the time nor place. "I'm the senior officer on this ward. Like it or not, that makes Sergeant Binney one of my men. And that makes me as responsible for his care as you."

"But sir—"

Every second she spent at Binney's side multiplied her risk. "Don't make me pull rank on you, Nurse."

She looked deep into his eyes. "I can't talk you out of this, can I, sir?" The answer was clear. "I'll get you a mask. But please, sir, don't expose yourself any more than necessary. No more pushing your body to the limit. Get the rest you need. Eat well. Sit close to the window and breathe fresh air as much as possible."

"Yes, Nurse." He forced a smile.

The look in her eyes said she wasn't buying it. "Sir," her voice shook slightly, "we're under orders not to alarm the men, but I warn you, increased exposure could kill you."

"Need I remind you? I'm not easy to kill."

She stared at him for a long moment. "Sir, if you get this, I swear you'll wish you were dead by the time I get through with you."

That was about the last thing he expected to hear from her. He smiled. "Duly noted. Now, please get me that mask."

After taking his post by Binney's side, Jamie's mindset began to change. Something about Binney in such a helpless condition got to Jamie like none of the mess sergeant's barbs ever had. The man's scowl was gone. He looked like a scared kid. Scared—and helpless. Like he was in the trenches, unarmed, without a friend in the world.

To Jamie's surprise, his heart went out to Binney. He

wasn't sure what turned Binney into such a malcontent, but right now, he just looked lost.

There was something so perversely wrong about surviving the war—only to lose his life here on friendly soil.

Jamie continued to sit by Binney's side with only momentary breaks, swabbing his sweaty forehead with a cold, damp cloth and speaking to him in low, comforting tones.

Binney was only semi-conscious. In case he understood what was being said, Jamie kept his talk upbeat. He told stories of courage and fortitude that inspired him when he was young. He told personal stories about growing up by the sea. He even told the dour sergeant a joke or two. Not surprisingly, Binney didn't laugh. That was fine with Jamie. He just wanted Binney to know he wasn't alone.

Nurse Eliot showed up all too often. So frequently, Jamie scarcely dared leave his post, fearing she would take over again.

"Major Collins," she said. "You need some rest. Let me do that."

Jamie waved her off. "I'll leave soon. You go take care of someone who really needs your help." Jamie hoped he wouldn't soon be the one.

Tuesday, 06 May 1919

By the morning of the second day, Binney was losing the battle. His breathing sounded like a baby's rattle. He was drenched in sweat. His labored words were incoherent. Still,

Jamie kept up his monologue. Nurse Eliot appeared in the doorway.

"Not a step closer," Jamie said. "I've got this under control."

She didn't come any closer. Nor did she leave.

Jamie gave her a sideways glance. "How is Nurse DaSilva?"

"No improvement, I'm sorry to say, sir."

"And Nurse Hobbes?"

"She's giving her classmate the best care possible." Nurse Eliot bit her lip. "But it doesn't seem to be helping."

Binney moaned.

"Never surrender," Jamie said to him softly. "Show the men why you're a Sergeant First Class. Get up from that bed and be the kind of leader the men on our ward deserve. Don't let them down. Don't let me down."

The short, rotund mess sergeant slowly opened his eyes and struggled to sit up. Jamie gently restrained him. "Easy. Just lie still and relax."

Before Jamie could stop her, Nurse Eliot rushed to Binney's bedside and laid her hand on his forehead. "His fever has broken," she said.

Binney began to panic. "I dreamt I died, and the devil was reaching for me. But someone pulled me back. That was you, wasn't it? Wasn't it, sir?"

Jamie was surprised to hear Binney call him "sir" for the first time.

"Your voice was like an anchor that kept me from drifting away—and here you are, sir."

"Major Collins has been by your side the past two days, Sergeant Binney. Without his care ... well ...."

Binney looked directly at Jamie. "Why, sir? Why would you reach out to me when all I've ever done is oppose you?"

Jamie was silent for a moment, then he shrugged. "Because that's what the Lord would have me do."

Nurse Eliot choked back a sob. She leaned down, kissed the top of Jamie's head, and then hurried off without another word.

Jamie could feel her kiss from the top of his head down to his newly revived toes. He watched her disappear through the door. "I shouldn't read too much into that," he mumbled.

This time, Jamie didn't mind Binney contradicting him. "Sir, it's clear that she thinks as much of you as you do of her."

Did Jamie dare believe it?

He was exhausted. With some effort, he stood.

Binney raised his head from his pillow. "Major Collins?"

Sir. Major. Jamie still couldn't get over the change that had come over Binney. "Yes."

"The other day, I heard you talking with a couple of men about their dreams for the future."

Jamie had heard that tone from men at the front when they had something heavy on their minds. "Go on," Jamie said.

"I've been a mess sergeant for more than twenty years. I bet I've baked going on half a million cakes and decorated thousands. I've won all kinds of awards for my decorating." He took a deep breath. "When I get out of here, I dream of working in a bakery and being their master cake decorator."

Jamie's mother had been a fair hand at cake decorating. Some of her cakes were true works of art. Could the round little sergeant be that accomplished? One never knew what talents others have. "Cake decorating—that's something you can do sitting in a wheelchair, isn't it?

It was one of the few times Jamie saw Reg Binney smile.

* * *

Doug Jankowski intercepted Jamie as Jamie was about to lay down and get some much-needed rest.

"Jamie, sir, I just want to thank you for pointing me in Toby's direction for help with my reading."

"Toby's the one to thank. And he's happy to help."

"I thank him every time we pick up a book together, which I'm happy to say is often. It hasn't been easy, but I've made more progress in the past few weeks than I thought possible. And now I have big plans."

"Mind sharing them?"

"You told the brethren we should dream big, so I'm going to shoot for the stars. I'm going to earn a college degree and a teaching credential and then wrangle a job teaching in the company school I went to as a kid. Having worked in the mines myself, I know they'll listen to me like they would no outsider. I'm going to teach others like me that working in the mines is fine if that's what they truly want to do. But that there's a big wide world outside Logan County, and education is their passport to explore it."

Doug's plan just about took Jamie's breath away. "I admire your ambitions," he said. "And I have no doubt you're going to light a fire in the minds of those lucky kids."

Doug walked away with the look of a man who knew exactly what he was going to do, and no one could stop him.

* * *

Wednesday, 07 May 1919

Nurse Hobbes was back on the ward. Her eyes were red. Her head was down. A knot of dread twisted Jamie's gut. When she drew close enough, Jamie grasped her wrist. "Nurse DaSilva ... is she ...?"

Nurse Hobbes closed her eyes and began to sob quietly. "Abigail DaSilva is dead, sir."

Jamie rose to his feet, wrapped his arms around Nurse Hobbes, and held her tight.

Nurse Eliot had been nearby. She rushed up to them and put a comforting hand on Hobbes' forearm. "We're all mourning Nurse DaSilva's passing," she said with notable tenderness. "But we're nurses. We must discipline ourselves to shed tears only in private. Otherwise, we could dishearten our patients."

Nurse Hobbes composed herself and stammered out an apology for her unprofessionalism.

Jamie would have none of it. "You can come to me anytime your heart's breaking. And that applies to you too, Nurse Eliot."

Nurse Eliot's chin quivered as though she, too, might cry.

Nurse Hobbes stepped back and stared at Jamie. "Sir, you jumped to your feet and supported me while I cried on your shoulder!"

Jamie looked at his legs. It was true. Without a thought, he had stood and supported Nurse Hobbes. He was amazed. "Time after time, I've been given strength when others needed me."

Nurse Eliot gave him such a warm smile he was afraid he might melt. "Your mere presence on this ward gives others strength," she said. She seemed embarrassed, as though she'd said too much. She cleared her throat. "Our Nurse DaSilva was an accomplished young lady. Did you know she was studying to be a concert pianist before voluntarily becoming a bluebird?"

DaSilva had established herself so firmly in Jamie's mind as a caring nurse that he could only imagine her in her bluebird uniform caring for patients. "She took her nursing duties so seriously I didn't even know her first name. Abigail, was it?"

"She went by Gail, sir."

"I'd like to get her parents' address. I'm going to write and tell them how much her patients appreciated her."

Nurse Hobbes looked like she was about to cry again. Jamie put his hand on her shoulder. "Would I be correct in assuming your first name isn't *Nurse?*"

Despite the situation, Nurse Hobbes smiled. "In our preliminary course, sir, they drummed into us that while on duty, 'Nurse' *would* be our first name. No exceptions."

Nurse Eliot smiled. "Then I temporarily relieve you from duty, Sarah Hobbes."

"Sarah," Jamie said. "That's a lovely name."

Nurse Hobbes lowered her eyes.

"Right, Sarah," Nurse Eliot said in the most gentle and caring tone, "you are now back on duty, and we have a ward full of patients to care for. Let's get on with it, shall we? We can both have a good cry later."

Jamie's respect for Nurse Eliot took another step toward the infinite. Real soldiers carry on, even when their hearts are breaking.

* * *

As the flu scare began to subside, life on the ward fell into a routine. The brotherhood grew stronger. Having seen how far Jamie would go to be independent, the men worked hard toward their rehabilitation, especially Vargas and Peters. Any man who tried to make a bluebird blush was likely to end up blushing himself. Syndicates were formed to cover all bets with favorable odds in a fruitless effort to dominate the raindrop races. Jamie could hold his own through the first fifteen or twenty moves in his daily chess games with Tom. Obstacle courses were set up for wheelchair races. The men grew stronger, more competitive. New track records were set daily for both the long and short wheelchair courses. Elaborate pranks made even Nurse Eliot blush. And Jamie's efforts to walk began to look less like a series of controlled falls and more like determined walking.

The men began pressing the staff about their discharge dates as they looked toward the future. Jamie hoped no one would ask him about his discharge date. He'd hate to admit that he was entertaining thoughts of staying on the ward forever—if that's what it would take to be near a certain green-eyed nurse.

Chapter 21

Butch

Thursday, 08 May 1919

This day marked a milestone for Ward 321. It was the day Private Anthony Lightner took up residence in Jamie's old room. Like Jamie, Lightner's reputation preceded him. Unlike Jamie, Lightner's reputation doomed him. The men on the ward suffered their losses through hostile enemy action. Even Binney—who was sitting on the throne in the latrine, reading a magazine, when an artillery shell came crashing down on him. Lightner took a different route to Ward 321. He shot himself in the foot to get out of combat—and ended up losing his leg to gangrene.

As if Lightner's mere presence on the ward wasn't enough to enrage the brethren, the fact that Private Lightner was placed in officer's country further infuriated them. They were near mutiny.

Carl marched to the middle of the boulevard and stood at the foot of his bed. "Somebody's got to do something about this." He turned to Jamie.

Clearly, Carl expected that somebody to be Jamie. Fine. Jamie had been giving the situation a lot of thought. He beckoned Hendricks to join him.

"What can I do for you, sir?"

"I still have trouble keeping my balance when I bend over." Jamie pointed to the footlocker at the end of his bed. "Will you please get my Class A uniform out of my footlocker and lay it out on my bed?"

"Your Class A's, sir?"

Hendricks' surprise was understandable. Since being carried off the battlefield in France, Jamie hadn't worn anything more formal than hospital pajamas and a robe. The Army's Class A uniform was comparable to a business suit.

Jamie stood unsteadily. "I'm going to pay someone an unexpected visit, and I want to make the proper impression."

Hendricks opened Jamie's footlocker. Just inside was a beat-up cardboard shoebox. Hendricks set it aside. He took out Jamie's uniform and laid it flat. He smoothed it here and there.

"The box, please." Jamie extended his hand.

Hendricks handed it over. Jamie removed the lid with a mixture of reverence and dread. Hendricks gasped when he saw it contained the dozen or so presentation cases Jamie's medals came in. Jamie extracted the cases and laid them out next to his uniform. "These haven't been out of this box since the day they were presented to me."

"Sir, if those were mine, I'd keep them in something nicer than an old shoebox." He pointed. "Especially that one."

Jamie picked up the blue case with the ornate gold strip along its left edge and *United States of America* printed in gold type on the lower right. *Medal of Honor* was emblazoned across the middle. Jamie opened the lid.

There lay a gold five-pointed star. In its center was the image of Minerva's head, encircled by the words *United States of America*. Each point of the star was tipped with a trefoil. The star was surrounded by a green laurel wreath suspended from a gold bar inscribed *Valor*. The assemblage was surmounted by an eagle suspended from a light blue ribbon bearing 13 white stars.

Hendricks whistled softly. "I've never seen one in person."

Jamie lifted it from its case. "Impressive, I'll admit." He ran his finger over the ribbon. "There were times back in France when my future looked so bleak, I wished it had been presented posthumously."

Hendricks inhaled sharply.

"Sorry," Jamie said. "I didn't mean to make you uncomfortable. It's a blessing we don't always get what we wish for."

"Sir, it amazes me that you and the other patients are as positive as you are. It's only natural that Old Man Negativity creeps in on you now and then." He was quiet for a moment. "Sir, may I ask what you intend to do?"

Toby and Carl had crept closer. Jamie squared his shoulders. "I'm going to have words with that man in my old room, and I'm not going to do it wearing pajamas."

Toby nudged Carl. "Jamie's on a mission. Let's give him some space." They crossed the boulevard and sat on Carl's bed.

Hendricks obviously wanted to know more.

"The last time Colonel Thornburgh paid me a visit," Jamie said, "he mentioned that Lightner was being transferred to Letterman. I told him I hoped the coward would be placed as far away from me as possible. Thornburgh just about floored me when he said he wasn't sure Lightner was a coward."

"What? Everybody knows Lightner shot himself to get out of combat."

"Colonel Thornburgh says Lightner was in the grips of shell shock and didn't know what he was doing."

Hendricks crossed his arms. "Do you believe that—sir?"

"Thornburgh's an expert on shell shock. He should know. Still, I have my doubts." Jamie smiled. "Then it was my turn to floor Thornburgh. I told him Lightner and I knew each other when we were kids."

Hendricks was equally surprised. "Were you friends, sir?"

"Good friends—way back in grade school. By the time we graduated from high school, I hated Lightner as much as I've ever hated anyone."

"Why? What happened—if you don't mind me asking, sir."

Jamie thought about it for a moment. "I don't mind. I might be able to put it in a better perspective if I talk about it." Jamie picked up his medal. "Just before we entered high school, Lightner's father died, his mother went away, and Lightner went to live with his grandmother. I don't know the details. I only know it was quite a scandal. Lightner changed after that. He'd always been a big kid—by the time we graduated from high school, he was almost as big as you. He became the school bully, and I was his favorite target." And I still harbor the humiliation, Jamie didn't say—and probably didn't need to.

"And here you are on the same ward a decade later," Hendricks said.

"That's not completely coincidental. Any amputee has a good chance of ending up at Letterman."

"Yes, sir, but they don't all end up on *our* ward."

"Colonel Thornburgh and I had a long discussion about my old 'friend.' The colonel is a wise man. He helped me see that the hatred I'd held onto for so long had contaminated my soul. I asked him to put Lightner with us so I could confront him and hopefully find a way to let go of the past. As Colonel Thornburgh said, true healing included body, mind, and soul."

Hendricks didn't look happy. "Sir, the men aren't going to like it if they find out you're responsible for Lightner being on their ward."

Jamie shrugged off Hendricks' concern. "It was either our ward or the ortho ward across the hall. No matter where Colonel Thornburgh put him, the men there wouldn't be happy about it."

"You're right, sir. But Lightner's in a private room in officer's country."

"I asked Colonel Thornburgh to put him in my old room —where he won't be a constant irritant to the men. And where I can hopefully resolve my issues with him."

"Sir, I'm not sure the men will understand your reasoning."

Hendricks was right. Jamie would be fighting an uphill battle. "Then please let me tell them in my own way."

"As you wish, sir." It was clear that Hendricks wasn't ready to let it go. "Do you know why Lightner has only now been transferred to Letterman?"

"Lightner was being held in a detention ward at Walter

Reed Army Hospital in DC. They were waiting for him to get well enough to face a court-martial. Nature intervened. His amputation wasn't healing well. The doctors decided they needed to amputate again further up his leg. If they operated at Walter Reed, no one knew how long he'd be there. That didn't sit well with the army brass. They couldn't wait to get him out of their showcase hospital where Senators and Congressmen on goodwill visits might see him."

"Sir, what about his court-martial?"

"Lightner's JAG lawyer was able to drag out his legal proceedings for months. Now that the war's over, the army just wants to get rid of him. They offered him a plea agreement, which Lightner accepted in a quick pro forma court-martial. In exchange for a guilty plea to the charge of damaging government property, Lightner will receive a dishonorable discharge when he's strong enough to be released from the hospital."

"The son of a bitch," Hendricks muttered.

"The court's finding still has to go through an automatic appellate process. Who knows, he might end up with an even lighter judgment. His story's a lot more complex than most people realize."

"Sir?"

"Lightner's records indicate that he was an exemplary soldier before he shot himself. He'd even been recommended for a Silver Star Medal."

Hendricks rubbed his chin. "Maybe I've been too quick to judge him, sir."

"Everybody deserves a fair hearing," Jamie said. "In Lightner's case, he believes people would be more understanding if they knew what led to him shooting himself."

Jamie glanced toward his old room. "If he wants to talk, I'll listen."

Jamie put his medal down. "I haven't seen Lightner in ten years. He might not even recognize me."

Jamie's mind drifted to days long past. "I don't need to wear my uniform and medals when I confront Lightner. But I'm only human. I deserve some revenge for all his bullying. This way, he'll see what his country thinks of the skinny little kid he used to torment."

"And this time, sir, you can intimidate him."

Good God. That's precisely what Jamie would be doing. But damn it, Jamie had endured Lightner's bullying throughout high school. Lightner deserved a little of his own medicine.

"Well, whatever you have in mind, sir, I'm behind you all the way. Even if it means Lightner gets a private room in officer's country."

Jamie looked at Hendricks, whom he'd come to think of as a friend. "You're a good man, Hendricks. I want you to know that the rest of the patients and I appreciate all you do for us."

Hendricks' eyes opened wide. "Thank you, sir. That's nice to hear."

"Tell me, are you planning to remain in the army now that the war's over?"

"Sir, I would if the army hadn't phased out all their male nurses."

Jamie wasn't sure he heard Hendricks correctly. "You want to be a nurse?"

"Yes, sir. I've given it a lot of thought and prayer. My wife is fully on board with me going to nursing school."

Jamie's mouth fell open. "You have a wife?"

"And two boys, ages six and eight."

Jamie felt about two inches tall. "I apologize for not having asked earlier. Is your family here at the Presidio?"

"Yes, sir. NCO housing's a few hundred yards down the street." Hendricks pointed at Jamie's medal. "My oldest will be thrilled when I tell him I've seen a real Medal of Honor."

"Bring your boys in sometime; they can see it for themselves." And I'll tell them what a hero their dad is in my eyes.

"Really, sir? You wouldn't mind?"

"Mind?" Jamie laughed. "I'd almost pay to have a visitor. And I like kids." He just wished someday he'd be able to have kids of his own.

Jamie opened the lids of each of his presentation cases. "These have an order of precedence." He placed them in their proper order on his bed. He looked at Hendricks. "Tell me ... why a nurse?"

"Sir, nurses are the medical professionals who provide the actual care for patients."

Jamie gave that a little thought. "You're right. I see a doctor maybe once a week, and only for a few minutes. I see the nurses every day for the duration of their shifts."

"It would be easier for me if I could enroll in the Army School of Nursing."

Jamie tried not to laugh. "I can't imagine you as a bluebird."

Hendricks frowned. "Uniform aside, sir, there are times when the men would prefer a male nurse."

"I know what you mean. I would have burst long ago if it weren't for you corpsmen. I wasn't about to ask a bluebird to help me use the latrine."

"I wish the army would recognize that and let men into the ASN."

Jamie didn't want to discourage Hendricks, but that was highly unlikely now that the army was no longer desperate for nurses. "Do you have an alternate plan?

"Yes, sir. I've been accepted into the Pennsylvania Hospital School of Nursing for Men. I start classes in the fall."

Jamie looked around the ward. Carl had left for physical therapy. Toby was in Charlie's prosthetics workshop. The rest of the men were also otherwise occupied. No one was clamoring for an orderly's attention. Good. That would give them time to talk. "What does Nurse Eliot think of you becoming a nurse?"

"Sir, with Nurse Eliot's reputation, Saint Peter would throw open the pearly gates, no questions asked, if I showed up with a recommendation as good as what she wrote for me."

"I'm not surprised." Jamie massaged his triceps. "I have a world of respect for that woman."

"Me, too," Hendricks said.

"I often wondered whether there was anything more than a professional relationship between you two. Now that I know you're married with kids, I hope not."

Hendricks stood tall. "Sir, she's far too honorable to mess around with a married man." He hesitated before adding, "I admit, though, if it weren't for the wife and kiddies, I would be interested in having more than a professional relationship with her."

"Can you keep a secret, Hendricks?"

Hendricks put his hand over his heart. "Sir, if you tell me a secret, I'll take it to my grave."

Again, Jamie looked around the ward. This time, to make

sure Nurse Eliot wasn't within earshot. He lowered his voice. "I *am* interested."

Hendricks looked Jamie up and down as might a father when a boy shows up on his doorstep wanting to take his daughter out on her first date. Apparently, Hendricks was serious when he said he'd taken it upon himself to be Nurse Eliot's protector. "May I ask, sir, do you have a girlfriend?"

Jamie felt like he was on trial. "I wish. There's only a girl I knew briefly before the war. I haven't seen or heard from her since, although we plan to meet again next April." All true, but far from a full disclosure. "She is special, though. If it hadn't been for her, I'd probably be dead."

"Dead, sir?"

"She promised to pray for me every day until she knew I was back in the States and safe. And here's something you'll find hard to believe: Before I shipped out for France, she dreamt I was so badly wounded I was declared dead, but I made a full recovery!"

Hendricks looked startled. "Sir, that sounds more like a vision than a dream."

"Whatever it was, it gave me the courage to keep fighting for my life when Graves Registration came to claim my body. Of course, I don't know that she kept her promise, but in my darkest hour, I believed Rachel ...." The name he hadn't said out loud in ages rolled off his tongue like a song. He had to start over. "I believed Rachel really was praying for me, and it made a difference." Jamie's throat tightened. "I don't know how I can ever repay her."

Hendricks canted his head. "Repay her, sir? What do the people you pray for owe you? Or those you put your life on the line for when you charged that battery of German machine guns?"

Jamie smiled. "I see your point. I've never asked for anything in return. Never would."

"Then don't you think a simple thank you would be enough to repay Rachel?"

Hendricks' sound logic gave Jamie a sense of freedom he never thought possible. "Thank you, Hendricks. You've removed a heavy weight from my conscience. If Rachel is who I think she is, she won't expect anything in return."

"Who you think she is, sir?"

Jamie averted his eyes. "The truth is, I hardly know her."

"Then how ...?"

"I was about to go to war. She was facing an uncertain future herself. Everything happened so fast. I found her fascinating. She flattered me. I cared about her. I believed she cared about me. And now ... and now that I've met Nurse Eliot ... I wish none of it had ever happened."

Hendricks stared off into the distance. "Sir, the past made us who we are today. Wishing it had been different is like wishing we were someone else."

Jamie was momentarily speechless. "Maybe you should forget about nursing and become a philosopher."

"Sir?"

"That's one of the most profound things I've ever heard."

"I don't know about that, sir." Hendricks absentmindedly smoothed the lapels of Jamie's jacket. "I'm curious, sir. I handle all the mail for this ward. Why haven't I seen any letters for you from someone named Rachel?"

In retrospect, the reason was so weak Jamie was embarrassed to answer. But Nurse Eliot's protector deserved to know. "We both needed time and independence to establish ourselves in our careers. We agreed to take an extended break from each other—with no contact at all. We settled on three years. Next April, to be exact."

Jamie felt like a fool when he saw how Hendricks looked at him. "Three years without any contact? Not many relationships could survive that."

"She promised not to commit to anyone before our reunion. And since she believed she practically forced me into our relationship, she urged me to carry on with my life as though we'd never met. And to date other women. That way, if we decided we wanted a future together, it would be an informed decision. And get this. She said if I found someone else, she'd understand."

Hendricks folded his arms across his chest. "Really, sir. With all due respect, that's a bit hard to believe."

Jamie couldn't blame Hendricks for being skeptical. "She's unlike any woman I've ever met."

"Supremely confident, I'd say."

"If you met her, you'd understand." Jamie sighed. "I didn't think I'd ever find another woman as fascinating as Rachel. So I promised in return that I wouldn't commit to anyone until after our reunion—a promise that would be much easier to keep if I hadn't met Nurse Eliot." Who was irresistible—and becoming more so with each passing day.

Hendricks met Jamie's eyes, like he was trying to read his mind. "I hope your intentions toward Nurse Eliot are honorable—sir."

The beast in Jamie began to stir. For Hendricks to think otherwise would be an insult. But Jamie knew Hendricks was just being protective of his "little sister." Jamie's beast lay back down. "Nurse Eliot fascinates me. And at the same time, she scares the hell out of me. I know I'm not good enough for her—but I'd be no good without her." That was a whole lot more than he intended to say.

"Sir, that's pretty much what I was hoping to hear."

Jamie could breathe again.

Hendricks smiled. "Sir, you're a man of honor—in more ways than one. You should tell Nurse Eliot how you feel about her."

"Tell her I find her irresistible, but if we got together, I wouldn't be free to commit to her until I clear it with some other woman next April? She'd think I was crazy."

"Sir, you might find that her life's just as complicated as yours."

Now that was intriguing. "How so?"

"It will take a special man to tear down the wall she's built around her heart. A wall she's put up to protect herself as well as anyone who might get close to her."

Jamie picked up his medal. "Too many lives have been shaped by tragedy. I hate to think Nurse Eliot's has."

Hendricks assumed a conspiratorial tone. "Sir, may I tell you a little about my friend?"

My friend—that was nice. "I'd love to know more about her. Just don't tell me anything she wouldn't want me to know."

Hendricks smiled. "That, sir, is why I think you're the one who should hear what I have to say."

"I'm all ears."

"Through no fault of her own, Nurse Eliot's heart has been broken. *Twice*."

Jamie stared at Hendricks. How could a man live with himself if he broke such a fine woman's heart?

"She believes she's cursed when it comes to marriage."

That opened Jamie's eyes. "Cursed?"

"A year or two after she joined the Army Nurse Corps, she became engaged to an army doctor. He died from malaria a month before they were to marry. A year later, she became engaged to a pilot in the Air Corps. He died in a flying accident a few weeks before their wedding day."

"No wonder she thinks she's cursed."

"Sir, Nurse Eliot is a wonderful person. She deserves to be loved by someone as tenderhearted and kind as her." He got a faraway look. "The problem is, not many men are self-confident enough to court a woman as brave and accomplished as she is. I've been hoping a special man would come along and sweep her off her feet. Someone not only as brave and accomplished as her, someone as tenderhearted and kind."

Jamie stared at the floor between his feet. "I wish I were such a man."

"Sir, I believe you are."

Jamie took in a startled breath. He'd love for that to be true.

After an awkward silence, Hendricks held up Jamie's uniform jacket. "Would you like me to have this pressed before you wear it, sir?"

"That won't be necessary. It will make the intended statement as is." Jamie smiled at Hendricks. "You know, if I were a gambling man, I'd put money on you becoming a nurse to rival Nurse Eliot herself."

"Thank you, sir. That's a real compliment."

Jamie was afraid he might have revealed too much about his feelings for Nurse Eliot. He touched his Medal of Honor. "This was presented to me in France by President Wilson himself."

"Really, sir?"

"It was a matter of me being in the right place at the right time rather than anything deliberate. The president was in France for the opening of treaty negotiations. On Christmas Day, he came to Chaumont to visit General Pershing's headquarters, review troops of the 26th Infantry Division, and have dinner at the division's mess hall. My hospital just happened to be in Chaumont. His staff shoehorned my medal presentation into his schedule."

Hendricks' eyes opened wide. "It must have been something getting to meet the president."

Jamie was silent for a moment. "I desperately wanted to ask him whether we accomplished anything with all our killing and destruction."

Hendricks was dumbstruck.

"I'm sorry. I've made you uncomfortable again."

Hendricks found his voice. "I'd like to have heard the President's answer."

Jamie was sure he and Hendricks were thinking alike.

They spent the next fifteen- or twenty minutes pinning Jamie's medals in their proper order on his uniform jacket. Hendricks showed no surprise to discover that Jamie had also received the French Republic's Croix de Guerre with Palms and been made a Chevalier of the Legion of Honor. Or that Jamie had been awarded the Silver Star for actions during his first month in combat.

To bring Jamie's uniform up to date, they replaced his captain's bars with the glistening gold oakleaf clusters of a major. "Christmas has always been special for me," Jamie said. "Last year, even more so. In addition to President Wilson pinning the Medal of Honor to my hospital robe, my division commander presented these to me. And the President was there adding his congratulations."

When they were finished with Jamie's jacket, Jamie put on a shirt and trousers for the first time in nearly six months. Since he still couldn't bend his knees fully, he needed help putting on shoes and socks. The socks were warm and comfortable. His shoes felt like lead weights after wearing only slippers for so long.

With Hendricks acting as valet, Jamie slipped his arms into the sleeves of his uniform jacket. Hendricks tucked and smoothed here and there and then stepped back and held a salute. Jamie smiled and returned it smartly.

When Jamie caught sight of his reflection in a window, his smile disappeared. After so many months of eating only hospital food, he looked like a stick figure wearing a uniform tailored for a man Hendricks' size. Still, the medals on his chest made a powerful statement.

With a cane in each hand, Jamie took several halting steps. When he reached the boulevard, he looked at the cane in his left hand as though its mere existence was an affront. He handed it to Hendricks. "Get rid of this thing for me, will you?"

Toby, Carl, and others picked that moment to return. They came in loud and laughing. All that stopped the second they laid eyes on Jamie.

Toby seemed alarmed. "You haven't been discharged from the hospital already, have you?"

"No. Nothing like that. I'm going to visit that man in my old room, and I want to make an impression on him."

With legs contorting every which way—the image that came to Jamie's mind was that of an octopus falling out of a tree—Jamie lurched to the doorway of his old room.

He stood there scrutinizing the big man lying in bed, staring at the ceiling. Lightner's sheet lay flat where his lower right leg should have been. A semi-cylindrical metal lattice cage held the sheet away from Lightner's fresh mid-thigh stump.

Broken. That was the thought that came to Jamie's mind. Like so many others Jamie had seen on the battlefield and in hospitals. For an instant, Jamie saw this remainder of a man not as the person he hated so much but as the boy who had once been a friend.

Jamie's beast began to stir—a friend who turned on him.

"Butch," the kids called Lightner when he and Jamie were in grammar school. Once they reached high school, it had better be "Anthony" if a kid didn't want a fat lip.

Jamie hobbled to Anthony's bedside. The big man slowly turned his head toward Jamie. His eyes were dull. Lifeless—until recognition opened them wide. "Jamie?"

"It's Major Collins to you, private."

Anthony's head sank into his pillow. "Have you come to gloat?"

"Gloat?" Jamie would be a liar if he denied it. But seeing Lightner there? Helpless? Friendless? Gloating seemed cheap, shallow.

"I read about you in *Stars and Stripes* while I was in the hospital in France," Lightner said. "They said you knocked out a battery of German machine guns all by yourself and earned a fist full of medals, includin' the Big One." He looked at Jamie with shame written across his face. "I hated to think what it would be like if we ever met again, you a hero and me charged with cowardice."

A hero? Not exactly how Jamie felt at the moment. "And?"

Anthony turned toward the wall. "I feel as low as a snake's belly."

Jamie thought it would feel good to put Anthony in his place. Instead, seeing any soldier in such a state made him sad. What if Colonel Thornburgh was right? What if Anthony hadn't been in his right mind when he shot himself? How many times had Jamie been pushed to the edge when the bullets and shells were flying all around him?

"The doctors say there's no fight left in you, that you've lost the will to live." Jamie was speaking more softly now. Less like an officer. More like an old friend.

Anthony looked at Jamie defiantly. "Why do you care?"

It was a good question. One Jamie wasn't sure he could answer. Maybe it wasn't Anthony he saw lying helpless before him, but Butch. Or perhaps it was because he saw a little of himself when he was in such bad shape in the hospital in France. "It doesn't matter why. What matters is that you not let what happened in France be the end of you."

Anthony sat up as best he could. "The army says I'm a coward. That's the end of the story for most people."

"Unless a court-martial finds you guilty of cowardice, it's only an accusation."

"Four men in the trench with me that day signed affidavits swearin' I put the muzzle of a rifle to my foot and pulled the trigger. Men I served with. Men I fought with. Men I have no reason to doubt."

"Your lawyer says you were in the grips of shell shock and didn't know what you were doing."

"It's the truth. My mind had gone blank."

Jamie searched Anthony's face for any sign of deceit. He found none. "I served at the front. I know what it was like. I'd believe you if you told me you were pushed over the edge."

"Then you're one in a thousand." Anthony's face contorted in anger. "Most people think my defense is a bunch of lawyerly bullshit. That I'm a cowardly son of a bitch who deserves a firin' squad."

"Who cares what most people think? Letterman's CO says there's nothing fake about shell shock. And he should know. During the war, he was the chief medical officer at a front-line hospital in France. He witnessed what shell shock can do to a man."

Anthony stared at Jamie. "Why are you defendin' me? I gave you hell back in high school."

It took a moment for Jamie to answer. "Because we used to be friends."

"Yeah, a long time ago."

Jamie took a deep breath. "There's a fine line between friends and enemies. A line that's a lot easier to cross than most people realize." A line Jamie felt he'd just put one foot over. He left the room without another word.

* * *

A handful of men had gathered near the nurses' station, Shipman among them. Jamie wondered how much they'd overheard.

"Sir, that man's got no right to be on this ward," Shipman said, "let alone in officer's quarters."

"You're right, Ship. And I'm the one to blame. I asked the colonel to put him here."

Ship couldn't have looked more startled if Jamie had hit with a two-by-four.

"I'll explain later," Jamie said.

The men stared in stunned disbelief. Jamie worked hard to walk with dignity as he limped back to his bed.

* * *

Saturday, 10 May 1919

Technically, Jamie and the other patients on Ward 321 were still on active duty. That meant that while admitted to the hospital, they had to wear standard-issue army clothing, usually pajamas, a robe, and slippers, or a tee shirt and shorts when undergoing physical therapy. Or they could wear their uniform.

Jamie hated wearing hospital garb. Although he was still a patient, he didn't want to feel like one. As he'd explained to Nurse Eliot early on, he'd always prided himself on his independence. He knew wearing his uniform would set him apart from the rest of the men. But nobody's perfect. Certainly not Jamie. Letting his pride overrule his logic, he vowed never again to revert to pajamas and a robe during duty hours.

The only uniform Jamie had available was his Class A. If an officer wears any part of his Class A uniform, he must wear the complete uniform, including all appropriate insignia and his medals or their representative ribbons. Jamie would wear his ribbons. Those he dutifully placed in their order of precedence in rows of four above his left breast pocket. The ribbon representing his Medal of Honor occupied the right end of the top row.

He paid Anthony another visit.

A nurse or orderly had propped Anthony up into an almost-sitting position. "I was afraid you'd be back," he said.

"You don't sound happy to see me." Nor did he look happy.

"Should I be?"

"Mine might be the only sympathetic face you'll see on this ward."

"Why are you even here?" Anthony stared at him. "You don't look like you need to be in a hospital."

"I'm still in rehab. I'll probably be discharged by the end of the month."

"Rehab? In your uniform?"

"I feel more like my old self when I'm in uniform."

Thankfully, an officer may remove his jacket while working in an office. As far as Jamie was concerned, visiting a patient in a private hospital room was enough like working in an office that he felt comfortable in removing his jacket. He draped it over the back of Anthony's guest chair. On his first visit, his valor awards had made a strong enough statement—perhaps too strong. Jamie sat.

"Look at us," Anthony said. "It's crazy where life's taken us. I was so eager for a fight when I got out of basic trainin', I thought I'd be the one with all the medals. Then I got to France and found out what it was like to be shot at." He looked at Jamie. "*Stars and Stripes* said it was a miracle you were alive." He stared at Jamie's legs. "They also said you were paralyzed from the waist down."

"They were right on the first count, wrong on the second."

"Doctors!" Anthony looked to where his leg should have been, his face a study in self-pity. "They weren't content to take my foot. Now they've cut off my leg. I can only wonder when they'll get around to choppin' off my head."

Anthony took a deep breath and let it out slowly. "I was proud of you when I read about what you did. Damned proud."

"Proud? Of a kid who used to run and hide from you back in high school?"

"You used to hide from me?" Anthony smiled the cruel smile Jamie remembered from earlier days. "That was smart. When we graduated, I was six-foot-two and weighed two hundred ten pounds. You were what? Maybe five-ten and a hundred and thirty?"

"Five-nine."

"Real smart." Anthony seemed to drift off, like his mind had taken him someplace he didn't want to go. "After my father was killed and my mother was sent to prison—"

"Wait a minute. Killed? Prison?"

"Where'd you think she was? On an extended vacation in the Caribbean?"

"I had no idea." Why hadn't anyone told Jamie this? Did they think he was too young to handle it?

"My mom stood trial, but we were both sentenced. Her to San Quentin, me to live with my grandma."

Jamie was in a state of semi-shock. "Your father was killed, and your mother went to prison? No wonder you changed."

"Changed? It turned me mean as a badger."

Jamie had mixed feelings. Though he was still resentful about the bullying, he felt slighted. "We were friends. You could have confided in me."

"No, I couldn't. I made a promise. A stupid promise that cost me more than I can tell you."

"If you want to talk about it now, I'll listen."

Anthony froze. He held up his hand for silence. "Later. There's that damned hissin' noise again. I think it's comin' from the room across the hall. Are they keepin' a giant lizard in there or somethin'?"

Jamie grinned. Some things never change. Since they were kids, Anthony chopped the "g" off every word that ended in "ing." "That's Lieutenant Walberg's jet nebulizer."

"His what?"

"A machine that helps him breathe. Not only did he lose a foot, he was gassed."

"Poor bastard."

"If you ever hear that machine start to sound funny, press your call button and tell someone to look in on him. If it malfunctions, it could kill him."

"Press my call button," Anthony scoffed. "Are you forgettin'? Everyone thinks I'm a coward. When I press my call button, the staff goes on break. I'm lucky if someone wanders by anytime within the next hour."

Jamie wasn't altogether surprised. There would have been worse in store for Anthony if he'd been placed on the general ward with the men. But for the staff to ignore his call button? Jamie was sure Nurse Eliot would put a quick end to that if she found out. "I'll check into that."

He dragged Anthony's guest chair closer and sat. "Colonel Thornburgh said your platoon leader recommended you for the Silver Star Medal just a week before you shot yourself."

Anthony picked up a glass from his nightstand. He gestured toward his water pitcher. Jamie stood and filled Anthony's glass. "Thanks," Anthony mumbled. He took a sip. "We relieved another platoon that had been at the front for weeks. It was a rush job. The trench map they gave my lieutenant was way outta date."

"That could be a problem," Jamie said. "Those maps were supposed to show the German positioning based on the latest aerial reconnaissance and photos. 'Latest' being the operative word. The battlefield was far from static."

"For sure," Anthony said. "That's why my lieutenant asked for a volunteer to lead a nighttime patrol into no man's land and scout out what we were facin'. My platoon sergeant volunteered me." Anthony put his arm over his eyes. "They thought I did a fine job. I thought the mission was a complete disaster."

Jamie sat again. "Mind telling me about it?"

"Mind? I'm dyin' to know whether a man with your history thinks my actions durin' that mission squares with me bein' a coward." Anthony laid back and settled himself. "With as much moonlight as there was, only a fool would have entered no man's land that night. I guess a fool is what Sergeant Southern thought I was after hearin' me brag about how I was gonna win the war all by myself. Toner and Garrapata, two other guys from my platoon, really did volunteer to go along."

Assigning men to dangerous missions was one of the worst parts of Jamie's job as a company commander. "I've been responsible for volunteering a few men myself."

"Yeah? Well, I can tell you, I didn't like it one little bit. Those Krauts weren't playin' around. They really wanted to kill us."

"No kidding?"

"Hey, that might have been obvious to you. To me, it didn't make a lick of sense. The stinkin' Kaiser decides he should rule the world, and suddenly a bunch of kids are tryin' to kill each other? For what?"

"I've asked myself that question a million times."

"And?"

"I'm as much in the dark as you."

Anthony took a sip of water. "My little suicide patrol hadn't gone more than a hundred yards before we stumbled across a shell crater the enemy was usin' as a listenin' post. The three of them opened up on us before we knew they were there. Garrapata was closest to me. He was torn to shreds, dead before he hit the ground. Somehow me and Toner managed to kill two of the bastards and wound the third. As you might guess, our little firefight seemed to wake the whole German Army. Every weapon in their trench line began rakin' us. I hit the dirt. Toner wasn't fast enough. He was hit, hit bad. By some miracle, I hadn't received a scratch."

Anthony's hand began to shake so violently half the water in his glass sloshed onto his bed. "Before you suggest I call someone to help sop that up, remember what I told you. When I press my call button, the staff goes on break."

Jamie recalled Nurse Eliot's advice concerning his suspicions: don't accept or reject anything as true without reasonable evidence. Jamie reached over and pushed Anthony's call button himself to see whether it was being ignored.

Anthony smirked. "You'll see."

"In the meantime, don't leave me stranded in no man's land. What happened next?"

"There I was, face-to-face with an armed enemy soldier." Anthony stared into his glass. "I tell you, I was so scared, I damn near pissed myself." He looked at Jamie. "What does a man who received our country's highest award for valor think of that?"

"If being piss-scared was a crime," Jamie said, "we'd all be up on charges."

"You?!"

"Me."

Anthony seemed to settle down a bit. "I had my rifle aimed at the last German's heart. It's one thing to shoot at the enemy from a distance. Another to shoot a man point-blank when he's starin' you in the face."

Something Jamie knew all too well. "Sometimes you have no choice," he said.

"Yeah? Well, I was damn glad this guy's hands shot up in surrender before I pulled the trigger. And there I was in the middle of no man's land with a prisoner on my hands and no idea what to do with him. He'd been shot in the chest. It was obvious he couldn't put up much of a fight. I took hold of his web gear and dragged his sorry self out of his hole. We belly-crawled back toward the American line while I held my rifle in his ear with one hand and dragged Toner with my other. When we got to within shoutin' distance, I let our guys know I was comin' in with a wounded American and a prisoner."

Anthony stared into the bottom of his glass. "It was pure luck we made it to an American trench without gettin' shot by either side."

"Do you know what became of your wounded man?"

"All I know is he was alive when the stretcher-bearers carried him away."

"That was one of the worst things about being at the front," Jamie said. "One day, you're fighting alongside a man. The next day, he's carried off, never to be heard from again."

Anthony got a far-away look. "Don't you figure that's the way the brass wanted it? If the troops knew how many of our wounded died, you officers would have had a hard time keepin' us expendables in the trenches."

Jamie wished he could say that wasn't true. "I think you showed true courage bringing in your wounded man."

"Comin' from you, that's a real compliment." Anthony

looked directly at Jamie. "Do you think my actions really were worthy of a Silver Star?"

"If I were your company commander, I'd have no trouble endorsing your recommendation."

"I don't know. I lost Garrapata in the process."

"You could have taken the easy way out. You could have shot your prisoner, left Toner to die alone, and crawled back to your lines by yourself. You didn't. Not only did you get the enemy to reveal his strength and position, you did everything you could to save Toner's life, and you brought in a prisoner for intel to interrogate. Despite losing Garrapata, which wouldn't have been unexpected in your situation, I'd say you completed your mission with distinction."

Anthony was silent for a moment. "Then why haven't I received that medal?"

To Jamie, the answer was obvious. The army wasn't going to award a man accused of cowardice a medal for valor. Which, to Jamie's way of thinking, was completely wrong. The actions that led Anthony's lieutenant to recommend him for a Silver Star Medal took place well before Anthony shot himself. "That's another thing I promise I'll look into."

Anthony smiled. "It sure would be somethin' if the army gave me a medal for bravery with one hand—and a dishonorable discharge with the other."

"Stranger things have happened. Such as a guy shooting himself in the foot and ending up losing his leg."

Anthony snorted. "There's no mystery in that. A guy who shoots himself is automatically labeled a coward, and cowards get the worst of everythin' in the army, includin' medical care." Anthony put his hand on his upper thigh and inched it toward his fresh amputation site.

Unsurprisingly, the medicos hadn't gone out of the way

to treat Anthony. Jamie probably wouldn't have treated a man with a self-inflicted wound any better.

Anthony exhaled loudly. "With the second-rate care I received, gangrene set in. They had to amputate my entire foot." He winced and jerked his hand away when he touched the end of his stump. "It didn't heal well. Infection began creepin' up my leg and past my knee, which led to them amputating again day before yesterday. And here I am."

Jamie sat staring at the floor. Anthony had exhibited real courage in the actions that led to his being recommended for the Silver Star Medal. That didn't square with shooting himself. "Will you tell me how it came about that you shot yourself?"

"Damn right, I will. Someone with an open mind should know the whole story." Anthony closed his eyes for a moment. Jamie could imagine him seeing the scene in his mind.

"Before we shipped overseas, I was promoted to corporal and put in charge of a four-man fire team. I'd never been in charge of anythin' before. I kinda liked it—until we came under fire, and I found out what it was like havin' men look to me for leadership when I didn't have a clue what I was doin' myself."

Jamie nodded. "A fire team's small enough for you to get to know each of your men. In a way, being in charge of several hundred men is easier. I didn't know them all personally."

"Three men were more than enough challenge for me." Anthony shifted his weight. "Anyway, about a month after I brought in that prisoner, the enemy was havin' a great time shellin' the hell out of us." He ran his hand across his eyes. "It was bad. I knew I'd lose my mind if it didn't let up soon. I didn't think it could get any worse. I was wrong. A shell landed in our trench just around the bend from us, takin' out half a dozen guys we'd shipped over with."

Anthony turned to Jamie. "Joe Ludecke, one of the men on my fire team, he was goin' crazy. I was near losin' it myself, but like a good team leader, I sat him down and tried to calm him."

"I tried to do that myself on occasion." More occasions than Jamie cared to remember. "It never worked."

"Joey was just a kid. He didn't belong on a battlefield. He should have been back in the States finishin' high school. Goin' out on his first date."

Jamie could relate to that. "Some of my men looked so young sometimes it felt like I was leading a Boy Scout troop."

Anthony's face clouded over. "The shellin' really got to Joey. I'd never seen him like that before. His eyes ... they were filled with terror. He started ravin' about how he was gonna shoot himself, so they'd have to send him to the rear. And just like that, he had the muzzle of his rifle jammed against his boot. I grabbed his weapon just as he pulled the trigger. His round couldn't have missed his foot by more than an inch."

Anthony turned to Jamie. "Joey went berserk. He scrambled to his feet and started up the assault ladder toward the top of our trench. I was still holdin' his rifle in one hand, but I managed to catch the hem of his coat with the other and tried to pull him back. You know how alert German snipers were. A shot rang out, and his head exploded. His blood and brains rained down on me."

Anthony stared at his hands as though he expected to see blood and tissue there.

"Anthony?"

"Maybe I should have let him shoot himself. Then at least he'd still be alive—but then he'd be goin' through the hell I'm goin' through." Anthony looked at Jamie.

"The other guys on my fire team testified that in an instant, I had the muzzle of Joey's rifle pressed against my foot, and I pulled the trigger."

Anthony grabbed Jamie by the wrist. "I swear I have no recollection of shooting myself." Jamie jerked his wrist free. "The doctors say I'd entered a catatonic state. It took a month of electric shock therapy to bring me back to my senses."

Anthony's pleading eyes locked onto Jamie. "Instead of blowin' off a toe, I mangled my whole foot. Right in front of the rest of my team. Would I have done somethin' that crazy if I'd been in my right mind? It was a reflex reaction. The enemy was shellin' the hell out of us, my man tried to shoot himself, I grabbed his rifle, his head exploded, and the next thing I knew, it was a month later, and I was minus one foot."

Jamie had no doubt Anthony was telling the truth—which meant he didn't deserve all the harassment he was getting—or the coward label. "Diminished capacity due to shell shock—that's what your JAG lawyer argued."

"Yeah. And it's a good thing he was convincin'. Otherwise, I might have spent the rest of my life in a military prison. My lawyer worked out a deal where I pled guilty to damagin' government property in exchange for a dishonorable discharge."

"I heard about that. What government property had you damaged?"

Anthony pointed to where his foot should have been. "Me."

Jamie could only shake his head. "That's the army for you."

"With the reduced charge, the army could get rid of me as fast and cheap as possible." Anthony looked toward the door of his room with what Jamie read as deep-seated fear. "Now, as far as the army's concerned, when I've recovered sufficiently, I can 'walk' out of here a free man."

Jamie was puzzled. It seemed as though Anthony was afraid to leave the hospital. "You don't seem thrilled by the prospect of being a free man."

Anthony's eyes opened wide. "A man who knows what I know can never be free." He turned away from Jamie. "Now, leave me alone, will you? I need to rest."

Neither of them was going anywhere soon. Jamie could take his time finding out what could make Anthony want to stay in a place where he was universally despised—and figuring out what to do about it.

As Jamie returned to his bed, it occurred to him that no one had responded to Anthony's call button. He couldn't imagine Nurse Eliot being part of such a conspiracy.

Chapter 22

Horror Stories

Tuesday, 13 May 1919

Jamie was standing beside his bed when Doctor Regenstein came rushing through the ward's double doors. "Good news, Professor Collins," he said loud enough for anyone at Jamie's end of the ward to hear.

Professor. Jamie cringed inside. He had worked hard to tear down the wall between officer and men. Except for Toby and Billy Lajoie, few brethren had any education beyond high school. They wouldn't think of Jamie as one of their own if they knew he had a Ph.D. and was an associate professor of physics at a prestigious university. As for Toby, he'd probably feel slighted that Jamie hadn't shared that with him. After bringing Anthony onto the ward, the wall between himself and the men was being erected again. The last thing Jamie wanted was to build it even higher.

Toby and Carl were not ten feet away. From their startled expressions, there was no doubt they heard Doctor Regenstein loud and clear.

Doctor Regenstein was bubbling with excitement—that is, he was smiling openly. "The manufacturer of our X-ray machine has finally mandated lead shielding for their engineers."

That was good news. It was a shame they hadn't done it earlier. "They'd open themselves up to all kinds of liability if they ignored another request," Jamie said, "especially now that it's backed up with your meticulous data."

"And your endorsement," Dr. Regenstein said. "They'd be fools to disregard the considered opinion of a physics professor from Stanford University."

Jamie stole a glance at Toby and Carl. They were staring at him as though he were Benedict Arnold. He could sense another brick being placed in the wall.

"And get this," Regenstein said. "They've offered to put us on a retainer if we'll serve as consultants!"

Jamie was stunned. "You're kidding."

"It's all true. I'm going to take them up on it, and I hope you will too, partner."

It was nice to know Regenstein was capable of genuine emotion. Jamie only wished he'd shown it in private. "Great work, doctor. Your perseverance will undoubtedly save lives."

Doctor Regenstein looked at his watch. "I couldn't wait to tell you. Now I must run." He dashed out the ward's double doors.

"You said you were a *teacher*." There was no mistaking the sense of betrayal in Toby's voice.

Jamie shrugged. "That's right. A professor's job is to teach. And that's what I did before the war, teach."

"There's a big difference between a run-of-the-mill teacher and a professor at a major university."

"You're right, Toby. Most teachers are required to earn a teaching credential. But you know how it is. You were working toward a Ph.D. in education when you were drafted. For no good reason, it's assumed that those with a Ph.D. know how to teach without having received any training." Jamie sat on the edge of his bed. "And it's Associate Professor. I have a long way to go before they make me a full professor."

"Would I be correct in assuming Stanford's holding your position for you?" Toby said.

"You would."

After a short, uncomfortable silence, Toby said, "Having seen the way you were trying to hide the journal you were reading the other day, I suspected you weren't being straight with us about what you did before the war." He forced a smile. "But I'm happy for you." Carl nodded his agreement. Neither showed much conviction.

All that work tearing down the wall between officer and men only for this to happen. Jamie foresaw an even greater wall being erected between professor and men.

Soon, everyone on the ward knew Jamie had been a physics professor before the war and that his old job would be waiting for him when he was ready to return. Though it was a relief that his secret was out, it was as he feared. The men became noticeably less comfortable around him. They stood or sat, as they were able, a little straighter in his presence. Their interactions with him became less frequent and more formal. "Sir" crept back into their vocabularies.

On top of that, everyone could see that Jamie's rehabilitation was progressing rapidly. He could walk reasonably well without the aid of the cane he carried only out of habit. Every step he took put more distance between himself and the men. Every inch of ground he gained in the battle for full mobility proclaimed that he was no longer eligible for membership in "their" brotherhood.

Jamie dreaded what was sure to follow: Quiet conversations among the brethren that would stop when he came near, looks of betrayal from amputees who could never be whole again, the sense of isolation that comes with being an outsider.

Tension also mounted as Jamie's visits to Anthony became as regular as his chess games with Tom Walberg. Jamie tried to explain to the men that Anthony's story was more complicated than they assumed. "Let me ask you this," he said one day to a group of men sitting at the brotherhood table. "None of you broke under the stress of combat. That tells me how strong you are. Rather than condemn Lightner, wouldn't it be more honorable for you to show compassion to someone who doesn't have your strength?"

The men were unmoved. Jamie understood. Making Anthony an object of universal hatred drew them closer together. Unfortunately, it also put another brick in the wall between them and himself.

Loyalty to an old "friend." That was Jamie's reason for defending Lightner. But was he being loyal to a fault?

* * *

The first thing Jamie did on his next visit to Anthony was push his call button to see how long it took for someone to respond.

Anthony smiled. "Still don't believe me?"

"I just want to be sure." Jamie draped his uniform jacket over the back of Anthony's guest chair and sat. "Mind telling me what's outside the hospital doors that makes you not want to leave here?"

Anthony sighed. "I'll tell you if you really want to know, but I warn you, you aren't gonna like it."

"Why don't you let me decide that?"

"Okay." Anthony took a deep breath. "Ever heard of a man named Matt Kavanaugh?"

"Sure, if we're talking about the founder of Kavanaugh Enterprises."

"He's the one. But he's not just the founder. He's the sole owner."

"Is that right?" Jamie leaned back in his chair. "The San Francisco Chronicle ran a story about him just last week. It said he's one of the most successful businessmen in the Western States."

Anthony nodded. "I saw that article. It also said he gives away lots of his money to various charities."

Jamie hadn't paid much attention to the article, but one thing stuck in his mind. "The Chronicle implied that he can afford to give away so much money only because he's the most consummate racketeer on the West Coast."

"The West Coast? I know for a fact that he's the most successful racketeer in the Western States."

Jamie canted his head. "How come you know so much about Matt Kavanaugh?"

Anthony exhaled loudly. "When I leave here, I'll either spend the rest of my life workin' for him—or runnin' from him."

Jamie was stunned. "Are you telling me you're mixed up with Matt Kavanaugh?"

"I said you weren't gonna like it."

"You were right." Now it made sense that Anthony was afraid to leave the hospital. "I'd be interested in hearing how that came about."

"Don't you remember me runnin' around with Sonny Kavanaugh our senior year of high school?"

"Now that you mention it." Sonny was one guy Jamie worked harder to avoid than he did Anthony. Sonny's arrogance and violent, aggressive nature made it clear he had a screw loose. "Is Sonny related to Matt?"

"Mister Kavanaugh is Sonny's uncle."

Not the best credentials for someone Anthony chose to run around with. "No wonder Sonny seemed to think everyone should bow down to him."

"You say you used to run from me back in high school? Sonny's the one I would have run from—if I hadn't been lookin' for a way into Kavanaugh Enterprises. Plain and simple: Sonny's nuts. Just look at him wrong, and you got a fight on your hands."

"I remember hearing stories about him fighting two kids at once."

"That's how nuts he is. But the thing is, he always came out on top."

"Tell me he was never dumb enough to pick a fight with you. He's not all that big. Someone your size could squash him like a bug."

"He did pick a fight with me—once."

"And?"

"Sonny can fight, that's for sure. But he was no match for

me. I knocked him around a bit, but I let him get in a few licks himself. Then we called it a draw."

"Are you serious? Why would you do that?"

"Because if I beat him, I knew I'd have to fight him again every time I saw him 'til he finally won—by any dirty trick he could dream up, no matter how insane it might be. When he figured we were an even match, we started hangin' around together."

Jamie's beast stirred at the thought that Anthony would drop their friendship and take up with a brute like Sonny.

Anthony held up his empty glass. Jamie obliged and then sat again.

"I wouldn't say I'm any greedier than the next guy," Anthony said, "but I'll go a lot further to keep from bein' poor. I was about to graduate from high school and was desperate to set out on my own. Problem was, I had no chance of findin' a decent job. Then Sonny introduced me to his dad, Robert—RK, everyone called him. RK ran Mister Kavanaugh's rackets on the Monterey Peninsula. RK gave me and Sonny each a job runnin' numbers for him."

"What do you mean, running numbers?"

Anthony looked surprised. "You're not familiar with the numbers game?"

" 'fraid not."

Anthony shook his head. "You must have led a sheltered life at that university of yours. The numbers game is a lottery where players try to guess a number from zero to 999."

"Is it legal?"

"Are you kiddin'? Hell, no, it's not legal."

Though this was a sidetrack, anything involving numbers interested Jamie. "What did players get for a match?"

"The Golden Gate game's the one me and Sonny worked. It's still goin'. It pays 600 to one."

"Six hundred to one? That gives the house a big edge. The odds against matching a randomly chosen three-digit number are a thousand to one."

"Sure. Mister Kavanaugh wouldn't bother if the odds weren't stacked in his favor. Or if the game didn't draw in so many players. Say a workin' man puts in a dime, and he gets a match. He walks away with $60 in his pocket. With that kind of money, he could go on a drunk for a week and still have enough money left to buy his wife a tweed coat to get back in her good graces for the rest of the year."

"Or forgo the drunk and buy his kids something nice, too," Jamie said.

Anthony shrugged. "Most people can afford to lose a dime. So, when you start talkin' about a return of 600 to one, they never stop to think how unlikely it is that they're gonna get a match. They keep puttin' in dime after dime, hopin' for a miracle."

Jamie put his arm over the back of his chair. "Not everyone can afford to lose dime after dime. What about some poor wretch who can't stop himself even while his family goes hungry? A dime can buy a loaf of bread or a can of Campbell's condensed soup."

"Mister Kavanaugh puts a cap on how much players can lose."

That was a surprise. "You mean he has a heart?"

"Hardly. It would be bad for business to bankrupt a customer if you want him and his friends in the game for the long run."

Kavanaugh wasn't a saint, but at least he capped players'

losses. "You say you were a runner. What part do they play in the game?"

"Runners are the ones who go around to all the taverns, barbershops, grocery stores, and the like to pick up players' bettin' slips and their buy-in cash. From there, they take the slips and the cash they've collected to the 'house,' that bein' RK in the game me and Sonny worked. After the winnin' number is chosen, runners retrace their steps and give any winners their earnin's."

"What's in it for the runners?"

"Runners get to keep ten percent of the face value of each bettin' slip."

"Isn't it dangerous for runners to carry a bunch of cash?"

Anthony looked at Jamie as he would a child. "Only a fool would hit a runner. RK was workin' on behalf of Mister Kavanaugh, and everybody knows Mister Kavanaugh has all kinds of informers—and enforcers. A busted-up fool would send a strong message."

"Would send? You mean Kavanaugh's bark is worse than his bite?

"No. I mean he's so intimidatin' no one's ever dared hit one of his runners."

Jamie still wouldn't want to chance it. "Does anybody care that the game's illegal?"

"The police don't waste their time tryin' to break up a numbers game—unless they're pressured by some politician out to get the anti-gamblin' vote. They know the game's gonna be up and runnin' again as soon as they turn their backs."

Sad, but undoubtedly true. "Were you a runner for long?"

"Naw. RK heard about how I would commit players'

names and bets to memory, so in the unlikely event the police stopped me, I couldn't be busted for carryin' bettin' slips. He was so impressed he sent me up to San Francisco to see Mister Kavanaugh—exactly what I was hopin' he'd do."

"I was always amazed that you could remember so many things, like the details of every newspaper article you ever read about your favorite baseball team, the Boston Red Sox."

"Hyperthymesia. That's the fancy word for a memory like mine. And I can tell you, it's more often a curse than a blessin'."

"How so?"

"You name a date anytime in the past, and I can tell you what day of the week it was, what was happenin' in the world that day, what the weather was like, and just about anythin' else you might wanna know."

"How's that a curse?"

"Except for the month I was in a catatonic state, I remember every little detail of anythin' bad that's ever happened to me throughout my life."

"That *would* be a curse."

"The army found out about my memory and wanted to put me through a bunch of tests to figure out how people like me do it. I refused—which, considerin' how I made out in the infantry, was a big mistake."

"Why'd you refuse?"

"I didn't want them messin' around with me like I was a laboratory rat."

"So, how do you do it?"

"I have no idea. All I know is that if I focus on one little item, like a date, I remember everythin' I ever knew havin' to do with that day. Like, three years ago today, 13 May 1916, Mister Kavanaugh called me into his office and told me one of his associates owed him \$5,293.27. Not only do I remember his associate's name and the exact amount he owed, I remember it was a Saturday, the day The New Zealand Division moved into front-line trenches at Armentières, France; the day American thoroughbred racehorse George Smith with jockey Johnny Loftus won the 42nd runnin' of the Kentucky Derby with a time of 2:04.00. I can also tell you what the weather was like in San Francisco that day, what was on Mister Kavanaugh's desk when we were talkin', where I was standin', his exact words and tone of voice—and a bunch of other stuff, includin' things Mister Kavanaugh wouldn't want written down." Anthony took a deep breath. "Worse, there doesn't seem to be any limit to the amount of stuff I remember or for how long."

"That's incredible," Jamie said.

"Like I said, it can be a curse. It's what got me shackled to Mister Kavanaugh."

"How so?"

"You remember my dad owned an investment brokerage company, right?"

Jamie nodded.

"He was real successful—at first. That didn't last. By the time me and you reached junior high, my family would have been out on the street if my grandma hadn't bailed him out. I promised myself early on I'd do whatever it took not to end up as a charity case. That's why I took the job runnin' numbers for RK. I figured I'd be set for life if I could weasel my way into Kavanaugh Enterprises. Once I met Mister Kavanaugh, and he started givin' me stuff to remember, I wasn't *set* for life. I was trapped. There was no way he was ever gonna let me go knowin' what I know."

"Maybe you'd have been better off being a charity case."

"I don't know. I admit, at the time, workin' for Mister Kavanaugh seemed like the perfect gig for a young punk from a small town with a chip on his shoulder the size of the Titanic: money, women, booze." Anthony's dreamy look evaporated. "Of course, I had to bury my conscience to work for a man who got rich off people's weaknesses."

"Yet you still call him *Mister* Kavanaugh?"

Anthony cringed. "Hell, yes. You disrespect Mister Kavanaugh, you end up floatin' face-down in the bay."

Jamie shrugged. "This is an army hospital. You don't have to worry about him here."

"Oh, yeah? I've still got Mister Kavanaugh's numbers in my head. Mark my words. Before long, he'll be in here, escorted by a senior officer from the base, askin' when I'll be back workin' for him."

"What? You mean Kavanagh's got his hooks into the base administration?"

Anthony gave Jamie that look again. "He's been providin' services and supplies to the base for years."

"Hang on. If Kavanaugh is such a wheeler-dealer, couldn't he have kept you out of the army?"

Anthony took a long drink of water and wiped his mouth on his sleeve. "I was framed for an extortion rap by one of Mister Kavanaugh's chief competitors—a thug named Danny Morelli. And wouldn't you know it? I had to appear before a judge Mister Kavanaugh hadn't gotten to yet. I was given a choice: prison or the army."

"Considering the outcome, prison may have been your better choice."

"Mister Kavanaugh made the choice for me. He figured there'd be less interest in his numbers on the battlefield than in prison. And that's how I got enlisted."

A bluebird appeared at the door.

"You took your time answering Private Lightner's call button," Jamie said.

She gave Jamie a blank look. "Call button? I don't know anything about a call button, sir."

"Then why are you here?"

"It's time to change Private Lightner's dressing, sir."

After mumbling a few colorful expletives, Anthony threw back his covers to expose his bandaged stump.

"I'm sorry I spoke harshly to you, nurse," Jamie said. "Please forgive me." Her smile said no offense had been taken.

Jamie stood to leave. His head was swimming as he tried to process all Anthony had revealed. "I'll see you later," he said to Anthony. He hesitated in the doorway and looked back.

He wished he hadn't. The bluebird had Anthony's bandages half off his stump. The sight turned Jamie's stomach. The bluebird's expression showed her alarm.

"I don't like the looks of this," she said.

* * *

When Jamie returned to Anthony's room later that day, Anthony looked like he had just been sentenced by a hanging judge. "You look terrible," Jamie said. "What's the matter?"

"A doctor was just in. My leg isn't healin' well. They've scheduled another surgery for tomorrow mornin'. Once they get a closer look, they might decide to do a little more sawin' on me."

Some people just can't get a break. "I'm sure you'll be

fine," Jamie lied. "If you want, I'll be here when they come to get you."

Anthony frowned. "No thanks. I'd feel like a condemned prisoner waitin' with the chaplain before bein' taken to the gallows. I don't even want to think about my operation. I've been lyin' here tryin' to block it out by daydreamin' about runnin' along a warm, sunny beach."

"Is it working?"

"Not in the least."

"If you want a diversion, I've got a question for you," Jamie said.

"Let's hear it."

"You say you became mean only after your mother went to prison." Jamie inclined his head slightly. "How'd she feel about that?"

"Damn," Anthony said. "I wanted a diversion, not to be hit over the head with a sledgehammer."

Jamie leaned his cane against Anthony's nightstand and sat. "Sorry. We can talk about something else if you'd rather."

"No. That's okay. It's time I open up to someone." Anthony took a deep breath. "Mom had no idea what kind of person I was becomin'. They wouldn't let a fourteen-year-old visit her in prison."

"I hadn't thought of that."

Anthony laid back, stared at the ceiling, and went silent.

Jamie watched silently as Anthony twisted his sheet around his hand like he was taping his knuckles before a fight. "I didn't do well with the anesthesia my last surgery," Anthony said. "I'm scared I might not wake up this time. In case there is a God, I have a confession to make."

Jamie leaned back in his chair. "You should talk to a chaplain, not me."

"I don't want to talk to a chaplain. I want to talk to you, someone who's been to hell and back. Someone who might understand." He looked toward the hallway. "Close the door, will you?"

After seeing to the door, Jamie eased himself back onto Anthony's chair.

"When my father's investment brokerage company began to fail, Dad started drinkin' like a fish. By the time me and you entered high school, he was a hopeless drunk. Some people can handle alcohol. Some can't. Dad was one of those weaklings who liked to start a fight when he was drunk."

Jamie had seen plenty of men turn into animals after a few drinks.

"He'd come home and start rantin' and ragin' at me and Mom, but he never hit us—not at first, anyway. That changed. And Mom got the worst of it." Anthony looked at Jamie with fire in his eyes. "There came a day when I couldn't take it anymore. He was roughin' Mom up. I jumped on his back like a wild man with arms and legs flailin'. 'Leave her alone, you bully,' I was screamin'. He pulled me off like a dirty shirt and tossed me aside. I ended up in a heap on the floor. Mom knelt by my side to protect me. Dad must have had some sense of decency. He left us alone—for the time bein'."

Anthony set his jaw. "I swore the next time he got rough with Mom would be the last."

That was chilling. "I remember your dad being a large man," Jamie said. "Even as big a kid as you were, it wouldn't have been an even match."

"Which made it even more cowardly for him to be beatin' up on Mom."

That was a bit ironic. By Anthony's standard, his bullying of Jamie back in high school made him a coward.

"I see how you're lookin' at me," Anthony said. "You're askin' yourself, who am I to call somebody a bully? I know it's no excuse, but we learn how to be from our parents. Those are powerful lessons that last a lifetime. Any bit of good that's in me, I learned from my mom. The rest, like it or not, I learned from my dad."

It was surprising that Anthony was that introspective. Apparently, he'd grown up a bit in the last ten years. "I'd say your mom had every right to defend herself—and you—by any means necessary."

"What if that meant she had to kill him?"

Jamie wasn't thinking about anything that drastic.

"Murder," Anthony said. "That's what the DA accused her of."

Jamie about choked. "That's not right. A woman has a right to defend herself. A mother has a duty to defend her child."

"Hell, yes." Anthony gave Jamie a long, hard stare. "The problem is, she didn't kill him. I did."

It felt to Jamie like the roof had caved in.

"Don't look at me like that," Anthony said.

"I wasn't." Jamie's reply, which, of course, made no sense.

"Then don't. It wasn't deliberate." Anthony sat up as best he could. "I was only tryin' to stop him from hurtin' Mom."

Jamie got up and moved to the window. "I'm confused. If you killed your father, why was your mom the one who was sent to prison?"

"She took the blame to protect me. She was afraid they'd

send me away. She'd heard stories about kids who were sent away and came back changed—not for the better. She figured she could handle a year or two in prison better than her kid could stand reform school."

"But he was attacking her. Even if she had been the one who killed him, it was self-defense."

"Sure. And she might have gotten off with no prison time at all if she'd taken the stand and defended herself. She refused. She was afraid the prosecutor would get the truth out of her. Then word would spread that I was the guilty one. She wasn't gonna let me grow up havin' people pointin' and sayin', 'There goes the kid who killed his father.' How would I ever get a decent job? What father would ever let me date his daughter?"

Jamie massaged his forehead. "Only a brave and loving mother would make the choice she did."

Anthony wiped the corner of his eye. "She was the best, my mom."

"I can't imagine how hard it's been for you to live with this secret all this time."

"With my memory, it's like the whole thing just happened. It was our cook's day off. Mom was in the kitchen cuttin' up a chicken for our dinner. I was tellin' her about my day at school. We heard the front door open. Dad came in. He staggered into the kitchen smellin' like a distillery and began yellin' at me for no reason. Mom stepped between us, and he hit her, hard."

Jamie moved back to the guest chair and sat wearily. What would he have done had he been in Anthony's shoes?

"Mom fell against the stovetop and burned her arm. She screamed from the pain. Instead of apologizin' and tryin' to comfort her, he ordered her to shut up. When she couldn't stop cryin', he raised his hand to hit her again."

Jamie got the feeling Anthony could see the scene playing out right before him.

"I grabbed the saltshaker off the counter and threw it at him as hard as I could." Anthony's eyes bore into Jamie. "Nailed him good. Right between his shoulder blades. He spun around and came at me with rage in his eyes. He landed a fist just below my eye."

Jamie couldn't imagine the terror a kid must have felt.

"What would you have done?" Anthony didn't wait for an answer. "I picked up the knife Mom had been usin'. All I wanted to do was stop him from hurtin' us. He lunged at me. I didn't mean to stab him. It just happened."

Jamie felt sick to his stomach.

"With the handle of the knife covered with chicken fat, I hadn't gripped it tight enough to kill him outright." Anthony looked at his hand. "The shock of bein' stabbed by his son must have brought him to his senses. 'What's happened to us?' he managed to say before collapsin' to his knees. He pawed at the knife, took a sharp breath, and pitched forward, drivin' the point into his heart."

Jamie gasped. Even memories of the battlefield didn't disturb him as much as his mental image of Anthony killing his own father.

"When the police asked what happened, Mom pretty much told them the truth, 'cept she reversed our roles. She said Dad had come home drunk and angry and started knockin' her around, that I had tried to stop him, and he struck me. She was desperate to protect me, and the knife fell to hand."

"A mother protecting her child? They don't teach much

criminal law in the physics department at Stanford, but surely a decent lawyer should have been able to get her off without any prison time at all."

"Like I said, she refused to testify." Anthony rubbed his thighs above the level of his fresh stump. "She swore if I ever told the truth, it would break her heart."

Anthony hammered his mattress with the side of his fist. "Five years the judge gave her. Five stinkin' years! For somethin' I did."

This was almost more than Jamie could take in. As a fourteen-year-old, how had Anthony managed as well as he had? No wonder he became mean as a badger. He had to have been in agony. Tortured. Angry at himself. Angry at his dad. Angry at the world.

"Mom told my grandma the real story. They agreed it would be best for Mom to take the rap and that I should go live with Grandma." Anthony turned his face toward the wall. "Grandma was a good person. She did everythin' she could to make Mom's stay in prison as tolerable as possible." His voice cracked. "There was nothin' she could do to protect Mom from TB."

"Tuberculosis?"

Anthony's neck turned red. "The women's floor at San Quentin was a tuberculosis incubator. It took her life in the second year of her sentence."

Dear God. The town had done a great job of keeping all this quiet. Jamie had been entirely in the dark. "I'm so sorry. I didn't know she was dead."

Anthony lowered his head. "If I'd spoken up, she'd still be alive. But it would have broken her heart. I don't know whether she'd ever have forgiven me."

Jamie was thankful he never had to make such a tough choice.

"The next time I saw Mom was at her funeral." The big man wiped a tear off his cheek.

If Jamie had known any of this, might things have been different? "Why'd you wait until now to tell someone what really happened? We were friends. Best friends. I could have helped—or tried anyway."

Anthony stared at the ceiling. "I promised Mom I'd keep it a secret so long as she or Grandma were alive. After all she did for me, keepin' that promise was the least I could do for her."

"Your grandmother, she's dead too?"

"She passed about six weeks ago while I was at Walter Reed. I'm all alone now."

Except for me, Jamie thought. But after enduring so many years of bullying, he still wasn't ready to come out and say so.

"She treated me good, my grandma. I should have shown more appreciation. Still, she left me her entire estate. Which means I'm now a rich man." He turned his face away from Jamie. "I guess me bein' her only livin' relative kind of limited her choices."

Jamie was at a complete loss for what to say or do. Needing time to process all Lightner had revealed, Jamie decided to take a sidetrack. He'd met Anthony's grandmother once while she was tending her garden, and he and Anthony—before Anthony changed—were heading to the beach together. Jamie could picture her. A tall, husky woman with white hair and a formal manner. But what he remembered most about her was her house. "Did your grandmother still own that big house by the beach?"

Anthony seemed relieved to be sidetracked. "Yeah. *BayView,* they called it. I love that house, 'though it can get downright spooky at night, especially when the wind blows, and it starts creakin' and moanin'." He stared at the ceiling. "It's mine now."

"It's a fantastic house from the outside. I'm sorry I never got to see the inside."

"Grandma was a very private person and good at keepin' secrets. Not many people got to see the inside of her house." Anthony's frown returned. "I can't imagine how she felt livin' in that mansion with a murderer."

Jamie winced. "Surely she didn't think of you as a murderer, not when she knew you were protecting your mom."

"You're right. She was glad I came to Mom's defense. The problem was I thought of myself as a murderer. Which is why I believed I belonged in Mister Kavanaugh's world and not hers."

Anthony ran the back of his hand across his eyes. "Mom made a huge sacrifice for me, and look how I repaid her. I became a two-bit hoodlum who disgraced himself in combat."

"Forget all that. When you get out of here, go home and make a fresh start."

"That would be good advice—if Mister Kavanaugh would let me."

"Is he someone you can reason with?"

"Yeah, unlike anyone else in his family. He understands people: what they think, why they do what they do. That's how he got to where he is today." Anthony shrugged. "But he's not reckless. I know things that could hurt him if they got into the wrong hands. What could I say to convince him his secrets are safe with me?"

"Tell him the war changed you. Not only did it cost you your leg, it scrambled your memory. Tell him all you want to do now is retire to a quiet place and live a life of solitude."

Anthony remained silent.

Jamie had to get through to him. "Think of the life you'll be able to live once you leave here. You'll be living in that big house by the bay, able to buy anything you want."

"Anythin' 'cept a new leg and a measure of self-respect. But even if Mister Kavanaugh bought the scrambled memory lie, he'd worry that someday things might come back to me. He'd still see me as a risk."

"Then you need to convince him you'd be a fool to betray him and jeopardize a life of privilege.

"That won't be easy. Besides, even if he let me go, I can't picture myself hobblin' around that big old house on one leg. Plus, my dishonorable discharge will be a matter of public record. It won't be long before everybody in town knows about it."

"That could be true no matter where you live."

"What a depressin' thought." A faraway look clouded Anthony's face. "Sometimes I wonder what our lives would be like today if Mom had been bakin' a pie instead of cuttin' up a chicken, and I had used her rollin' pin to knock Dad on the head instead of stabbin' him."

"If this, if that. You can drive yourself crazy asking questions like that. Considering which, I'd say you're remarkably sane for someone who's been through all you have."

Anthony covered his eyes with his palms. "As big and tough as I pretended to be, all I wanted was a happy family.

And that's what's crazy about me bullyin' you." He looked at Jamie. "Your parents treated me like a son. You and your sister treated me like a brother. Yet the kinder you all were, the more resentful I became. Like a fool, I took it out on you."

Jamie retrieved his cane and tapped it against the side of his foot several times. "Forget it. I forgive you."

Anthony couldn't have looked more thankful if Christ Himself had forgiven him. "That's the Jamie I remember. A guy I wasn't surprised to learn had charged a battery of German machine guns all by himself. And I know why you did it."

"You can't." Jamie placed the rubber tip of his cane between his feet and rested both hands on top of its handle. "I've never told anyone."

"We've known each other since grammar school. You're no mystery to me. An infantry company is the tip of the spear in combat. A lot of men died carryin' out their company commander's orders. For a man with a heart as big as yours, my bet is you'd reached your limit. Tell me you weren't gonna do everythin' in your power to keep another man under your command from dyin'.'"

Jamie's cane slipped from his hands. Someone finally understood! "You're right." He sheepishly picked up his cane. "I was already having a hard time living with myself after sending so many men to their deaths."

Anthony had told Jamie his horror story. It might do them both good if Jamie unburdened himself by telling Anthony his.

"I've never told anyone the whole story of what happened that day in France. I didn't think anyone would understand. I think you might."

Anthony seemed to take that as a high compliment, which, in a way, it was. "I'm listenin'."

Jamie took a deep breath. "We're not all that different, you and me."

Anthony's eyes narrowed. "How do you figure?"

"We both broke under the stress of combat. As a result, our lives were changed forever. As were the lives of others."

"What others?"

"The army had to send someone to the front to take our place. Which means we sentenced our replacements to the same hell we were desperate to escape."

"Thanks a lot," Anthony said. "You've given me somethin' else to feel guilty about."

"Every decision we make has consequences, some totally unforeseen. The captain who took over my company was among the last men killed before the armistice. If I hadn't staged my one-man assault, he wouldn't have had to take my place, and he might still be alive. On the other hand, who knows how many of my men would have been killed if I hadn't knocked out those machine guns?"

"Life's full of tradeoffs," Anthony said.

"You're right. I made my choice, and now I have to live with it."

"What were you doin' commandin' an infantry company in the first place? I thought you were a scientist."

"The army needed infantry officers." Jamie began dropping his cane straight down from a height of a few inches and bouncing it off its rubber tip. "My company was part of a division of reservists mainly from the Western States. My officers and I were all graduates of the Student Officer Training Corps. We were commissioned as Second or First Lieutenants, depending on our military training and civilian accomplishments. I was an exception. Because I did well in training, I was a little older than the others, and I had a Ph.D., I was commissioned a Captain. That made me eligible to command an infantry company."

"I should be glad I'm not as smart as you," Anthony said. "I only made corporal. And look how that turned out."

Jamie waved his hand dismissively. "That's a bunch of bull, and you know it. You're smart enough to have accomplished anything if you'd set your mind to it. Me, I'm more of a hard worker than smart. One of my platoon leaders, Ainsley Townsend, he was smart like you. He would have gone places ...."

"I take it he was killed."

Jamie couldn't bring himself to answer directly. "Ainsley and I were in the physics department at Stanford. He was an undergraduate. I was finishing my Ph.D. Though I was four years older than him, that didn't stop us from becoming the best of friends. He'd shown great potential throughout his military training. They made him a First Lieutenant. By the luck of the draw, he was assigned to my company. I made him my senior platoon leader." Jamie ran his hand over his eyes. "How naïve we were. We thought it was great that we'd be serving in the same unit." Jamie stood and walked to the window.

"What happened to him?"

Jamie spoke with his back to Anthony. "We were ordered to take the trench we were facing. I chose Ainsley's platoon to lead the attack. He and a dozen of his men were killed."

Jamie heard Anthony choke on a mouthful of water. "Do you feel guilty about it?"

Jamie turned to face Anthony. "No. I did what any

responsible company commander should have done. If I'd given Ainsley preferential treatment, he would have thought I didn't respect him. And if our battalion commander found out, I'd have been relieved in a minute, and some other captain would have taken my place. He might have ordered Ainsley to lead that attack—and you can bet whoever my replacement might have been, he wouldn't mourn Ainsley the way I do."

"At least your friend had someone to mourn him, unlike a lot of guys who fell."

"True, but none of that means I don't still have nightmares about Ainsley's death."

"Don't get me started about nightmares," Anthony said.

"With the loss of Ainsley and so many of his men and the casualties in my other platoons, my company was seriously understrength. I was sure we'd be withdrawn from the front and given replacements and time to train them." Jamie shook his head in disgust. "Not only were we not withdrawn, we didn't receive *any* replacements. Instead, we were ordered to relieve what remained of a sister company from our battalion that a few hours earlier had been decimated trying to take the enemy trench they were facing."

Anthony grunted. "That sounds like the army."

"It gets worse. No sooner were we in place than I was given the stupidest order I've ever received. We were ordered to attack the trench the full-strength company we replaced failed to take a few hours earlier!"

"A suicide mission for sure," Anthony said.

"Exactly." After all these months, the thought still ignited a rage in Jamie. His beast began to stir. Jamie impulsively whacked Anthony's metal wastebasket with his cane.

It sounded like a cannon's report as the sound reverberated throughout the room. Hendricks appeared in the doorway.

"No worries, Hendricks. I bumped Lightner's wastebasket, that's all."

"Right, sir." Hendricks had to know there was more to the story. He was smart enough to withdraw without comment.

Anthony wiped his forehead with the back of his hand. "Do that again, and that big orderly will have to change my beddin'."

Jamie smiled at the mental image that inspired. "Being the obedient soldier I am, I couldn't ignore the asinine order I'd been given. I passed it on to my platoon leaders, who unquestioningly went about preparing their men to be slaughtered."

Jamie was tempted to give the wastebasket another whack. "We were supposed to attack immediately following a short artillery barrage—as if a short barrage would do any good. Our artillery had pounded that German trench for over an hour before the previous company attacked. A battery of four well-dug-in heavy machine guns survived intact."

"Each capable of firin' 450 to 500 rounds a minute," Anthony said.

Jamie sat on the edge of his chair. "The shelling began on schedule. As I waited for it to end, I became more and more agitated. The noise was deafening. Debris was raining down all around us."

"Sounds like the scene when my man went crazy and threatened to shoot himself."

"That's why I hoped you'd understand." Jamie ran his forearm across his brow. "A corporal was moving down our line, passing out grenades from a bag slung over his shoulder. Without a thought, I grabbed the bag, and while our barrage was at its full fury, I went over the top by myself." Jamie shook his head. "It wasn't a deliberate act. Like you when your man's head exploded, I just reacted."

Anthony nodded. "I figured the only reason you believed my story was you'd been through a similar hell."

"Different trench. Same hell." Jamie took a deep breath. "With the bag of grenades over my shoulder, I charged across no man's land, leaping over barbed wire, zigzagging around shell craters, oblivious to our artillery as it exploded practically in my face. Subsequent POW interrogations revealed that the Germans reasonably assumed we wouldn't be so stupid as to attack a position we had so spectacularly failed to take a few hours earlier. Accordingly, they had withdrawn the bulk of their infantry to fill a breach in a trench further along their line. That left their machine guns with minimal close-in support."

"You were lucky."

"I don't believe in luck," Jamie said dismissively. "With our shells falling all around them, the machine gunners were keeping their heads down and didn't see me coming."

"Only a fool would stick his head up durin' an artillery barrage," Anthony said.

Left unsaid was that only a fool would run through an artillery barrage. "When I was almost to the enemy trench, one of our shells exploded so close it blew me off my feet. I must have looked like a ragdoll as I flew through the air in a shower of dirt, rocks, and shrapnel. I landed on my back, half in, half out of a crumbling shell crater. I was bloodied and in excruciating pain, but by some miracle, not incapacitated.

My men saw the whole thing from our trench line. They were sure I was dead."

Anthony's face turned white. "I've seen men thrown through the air by a shell burst. Or parts of a man. It was enough to turn me to jelly."

"That's when I came to my senses and recognized the predicament I'd put myself in. I couldn't stay where I was right under the enemy's nose. Yet if I continued my one-man assault, I'd almost certainly be killed, either by our artillery or an enemy bullet."

"You could have retreated."

Jamie shook his head. "In the heat of the moment, that never occurred to me."

"Just like shootin' my prisoner and leavin' my wounded man to die alone never occurred to me," Anthony said.

"All I could think of was that I could very well have thrown my life away for nothing." Jamie crouched on the edge of his chair like he was getting ready to pounce on someone. "That awoke a raging beast in me I couldn't control. Though I was bleeding from more places than I could count, the pain didn't stop me from scrambling to my feet with one goal in mind. To kill every last German soldier on the face of the earth."

"Shootin' myself was a momentary act of madness," Anthony said. "Stagin' a one-man assault against a dug-in enemy was complete madness."

"Madness," Jamie repeated. "That's what it was. I'd lost the ability to reason. I didn't care what happened to me. No matter what, I was going to do everything I could to destroy those German machine guns before they slaughtered my men." Jamie gave a half-laugh. "As an example of how deranged I'd become, I frantically searched around for my helmet and jammed it back on my head before carrying on. After haranguing my men about wearing theirs, I didn't want them to see me charge the enemy without my helmet."

"I wouldn't have bothered," Anthony said. "Those helmets were no better than overturned metal soup bowls. Practically useless. And that damn chinstrap. If your helmet ever got caught up in somethin', say barbed wire, bein' so hard to release, the chinstrap could get you killed."

"That's why I never used the chinstrap. But I like to think I have something worth protecting inside my skull."

"If you ask me, that puts you in the minority among officers."

Unfortunately, Jamie sometimes felt the same. "Despite everything, I managed to reach the edge of the nearest machine gun nest, unseen by the enemy. I threw a grenade in amongst its crew. Half a dozen tried to levitate as my grenade rolled around at their feet. It exploded, throwing bits of metal and pieces of flesh my way, leaving behind a broken machine gun and a scattering of broken bodies."

Jamie rubbed his temples. "Eliminating one machine gun wasn't enough to satisfy the beast in me. Not when the remaining guns could still have torn my men to shreds."

"Some higher power had to have been lookin' out for you to get that far," Anthony said.

"I agree." Jamie rubbed his eyes. "Though I'd never hurt so bad in so many places, that didn't stop the beast from driving me on. I'd almost reached the next gun emplacement when our artillery knocked me off my feet again. I lay there in so much pain I wished I was dead. It wasn't to be. There were still three guns to deal with."

Such clear memories were torture for Jamie. He could only imagine the hell Anthony's indelible memory caused him. "I rose to my feet, not bothering with my helmet this time. More as a robot than a man, I came at the next gunners from their flank and caught them by surprise. I tossed in a grenade and ducked. After the explosion, there was still movement in the bottom of their nest. I tossed in another grenade for good measure."

Jamie began to pace. "I'd taken out two machine guns. Nobody would have faulted me if I'd stopped there. Nobody except me." Jamie shuddered. "Every part of my body was burning with pain. Still, the beast drove me on. Another pair of grenades and only one gun remained." Jamie wiped his sweaty palms on his thighs. "Our artillery was still falling all around me. Another explosion tossed me into an empty section of their trench. I lay there for a few seconds, thinking I should be dead. Yet the beast lived on. I became like the unstoppable man of the tombs possessed by a legion of demons. I rose to my feet and moved on to the last machine gun. Somehow, I was able to climb their parapet and toss in my last two grenades."

"I don't understand," Anthony said. "You came out of all this paralyzed from the waist down, didn't you? Yet you could move from one machine gun nest to another and climb their parapets?"

"That's one of the most amazing parts of my story. Any one of the explosions that knocked me off my feet could have delivered the shrapnel that eventually paralyzed me. The key word there is eventually. I would have been paralyzed instantly if the shrapnel had severed my spinal cord. As it was, a jagged piece of metal was only impinging on my spinal cord, and my paralysis came on over the next day or two."

Anthony shook his head. "You were one lucky son of a—

no, not lucky. You had to be under the protection of a higher power."

"Again, my thoughts exactly." The memories of that day had drenched Jamie in sweat. He tugged at his shirt collar to let in some air. "Our artillery barrage ended just as I reduced the last machine gun nest to a smoking ruin. And in that instant, all my rage evaporated. Then, as though out of nowhere, a German officer appeared not more than three paces from me. He had his revolver drawn." Jamie's mind drifted. "It's funny the things we notice. His collar devices indicated he was a supply officer. And he had a birthmark high up on his right cheek."

Jamie slouched onto Anthony's chair. "With the machine guns destroyed, the beast that had driven me so far was nowhere to be found. After all I'd been through, I didn't have the strength to defend myself. I was in so much pain I thought it would be a mercy if that German officer shot me and put me out of my misery."

Jamie rose again and stretched out his arms like Christ on the cross. "I stood before him as still as a target on the practice range." Jamie closed his eyes. "I can see him now with his pistol leveled at my head." Jamie scrunched his head into his shoulders as though to avoid the shot. "I was staring into the barrel of his Luger as he began to squeeze off his round. In another twist of fate, being a supply officer rather than a front-line soldier, he must not have had the stomach for a cold-blooded execution. He turned his head away slightly, which threw his aim off a critical degree or two." Jamie opened his eyes wide. "I swear I saw his bullet coming at me in slow motion. It grazed the side of my head and spun me around. I went down like a sack of coal."

Anthony propped himself up on his elbows. "If the fact that you're still alive isn't proof of miracles, nothin' is."

Jamie felt the scar on his temple. "I remember only bits and pieces of what happened after that. I know my first sergeant carried me to a battalion aid station even though he thought I was dead. Records show that the ground they placed me on was uneven. My feet were above my head. As with any unconscious soldier, a corpsman immediately started a saline IV drip in my arm." Jamie looked at the inside of his elbow. In his mind, he could still see the puncture mark. "One thing I remember haunts me to this day. The triage doctor, with his face a few inches from mine, saying, 'This one's dead. We need to move on,' and me being too weak to move a muscle or make a sound." Jamie flicked a bead of sweat from his chin.

"What kind of dumb-ass doctor couldn't tell you were alive?"

"I was most likely in hypovolemic shock when that doctor took a quick look at me."

"Shock due to severe loss of blood," Anthony said. "I learned about that firsthand in the trenches. Your pulse would have been very rapid and weak."

"In the heat of battle, a doctor under stress *could* have missed it altogether." Jamie took a deep breath. "I don't believe he did."

"Wait," Anthony said. "It sounds like you're sayin' you really were dead."

"That's exactly what I'm saying. And I know because my spirit had left my body, and *I* was watching over the doctor's shoulder as he pronounced me dead, and he and his corpsman moved on."

From the look on Anthony's face, he clearly thought he

was listening to a madman. That wasn't going to stop Jamie from telling the rest of his story. "I remember thinking how small and insignificant my inert body looked. A soldier from Graves Registration soon arrived to remove what was left of me." Jamie opened his eyes wide. "At that moment, I remembered someone back in the States was praying for me, and that she'd dreamt I was so badly wounded I was declared dead, but I made a complete recovery."

Anthony squinted at Jamie. "What was she, some kind of psychic?"

"Call her what you will, when that private from Graves Registration jerked the IV from my arm, my spirit was suddenly back inside my shattered body, and I found the strength to moan." Jamie leaned back in his chair. "It was in a field hospital that I realized the beast that had destroyed all those German machine guns and their crews hadn't destroyed me." Jamie looked into Anthony's eyes. "Having survived all that, what scares me now is the thought that the beast that drove me to kill so many Germans wasn't just a part of me. It's who I am."

Anthony was silent for an uncomfortable moment. Then he leaned on his elbow and looked directly at Jamie. "I believe we each have a part of us that acts without a thought and can do amazin' things—good and bad. In my case, it led me to shoot myself. In your case, it led you to spare your men from bein' cut down by a battery of machine guns. That beast of yours served you well in France. Don't deny it. Accept it. You might need it again someday."

One never knows when or from whom wisdom will come. "You're right. And maybe I needn't be so afraid of who I really am. A very special woman recently told me I hadn't let the war take the kindness out of me. When I hold onto that thought, I can accept that I'm the person who killed all those men, and yet I'm still a decent human being."

Anthony shook his head. "Forget holdin' onto a thought. You should hold onto that very special woman."

Jamie smiled. "That may be the best advice I've ever received."

Jamie moved to the window. "My story would be so much hot air if it didn't speak to me. And here's what I think it's trying to say: I really was dead, and the Lord raised me for a purpose."

Anthony drew back from Jamie. "What purpose?"

"I'm still trying to figure that out. I'm sure it's nothing earth-shattering." Jamie smiled. "It might be something as simple as reestablishing an old friendship."

Anthony struggled to find his voice. "Major Collins, sir, will you do me a favor?"

Anthony had never called Jamie "sir" before. "Sure. Just name it."

"From now on, will you call me Butch, like you used to when we were friends?"

Jamie had been staring out the window. He slowly turned and faced his old nemesis. "Butch ... we are friends."

Chapter 23

Dealing with the Devil

Thursday, 15 May 1919

Jamie awoke to find Nurse Eliot studying the paperwork attached to the clipboard hanging from the foot of his bed. He allowed himself a moment to fantasize about how nice it would be if she were always nearby when he awoke.

"Excuse me, Nurse Eliot," he said. She smiled at him, and he forgot what he wanted to say.

She moved closer. "Sir?"

His head cleared. "Can you tell me how Butch's surgery went—I mean, Private Lightner?"

"Yes, sir, I'm happy to say it went well."

"He had trouble with the anesthesia during his previous surgery. He was afraid he might not wake up this time."

"He came through just fine, sir."

Jamie breathed a sigh of relief. "I'm so glad. And his leg ... do the doctors think he'll need any more surgeries?"

"No, sir. Our biggest concern now is ensuring he doesn't

317

put too much stress on his sutures. The surgeon had to do some delicate work around his amputation site. It's imperative that he remain on his back and as still as possible for the next week, or his sutures could tear out."

"Thank you, Nurse Eliot. I'll remind him of that."

Armed with that information, Jamie got out of bed, took care of necessities, put on his uniform, and paid Butch a visit. "I'm glad to see you're still among the living."

"Thanks," Butch said. "I can tell you, though, that anesthesia is strange stuff. It's not like bein' asleep. I'm sure you know as well as anyone what with all the surgeries you've been through. One second, you're in the operatin' room surrounded by medical staff. The next thing you know, you're in a surgery recovery room, and it's like no time has passed at all. I don't believe all that heaven and hell stuff, so I wonder if that's what it's like bein' dead: You lose consciousness, and time stands still, forever."

"I do believe all that heaven and hell stuff," Jamie said. "And I'm afraid we can't both be right." He was about to remove his jacket and sit when a lieutenant colonel appeared in Butch's doorway. A stylishly dressed civilian was by his side.

"Pardon us for interrupting," the civilian said.

Jamie found the man's slight Irish accent pleasing. Though the visitor's manner was amiable, he spoke with such authority no one would dare *not* pardon him.

Butch straightened his collar. His smile couldn't mask the haunted look in his eyes.

It was clear to Jamie who the stylish man was. "Please, come in," Jamie said when Butch couldn't find his voice.

"I'm Matt Kavanaugh," the gentleman said. He indicated

his escort. "This is Colonel Hunt, the deputy base commander."

Showing little more life than a ventriloquist's dummy, Lieutenant Colonel Hunt offered a weak, "Morning."

Jamie glanced beyond the visitors, expecting a man with Kavanaugh's reputation to be surrounded by bodyguards. To Jamie's surprise, every indication was that Kavanaugh and Colonel Hunt were alone.

An even greater surprise was Jamie's first impression of Kavanaugh. Yes, he was authoritative. But far less arrogant or domineering than Jamie would have expected. In fact, he didn't strike Jamie as a bad man at all. There was something about him, though, something Jamie couldn't quite put his finger on, that said only a fool would cross him.

"I've come to see how my man Lightner is doing," Kavanaugh said.

Jamie couldn't help staring at the man's crooked nose. Few prizefighters had a proboscis that could compare. Considering Kavanaugh's bearing and physique, Jamie suspected whoever broke it paid a heavy price.

Jamie turned toward the door. "I'll excuse myself and let you gentlemen talk."

Kavanaugh held up his hand. "A minute, please, major." He pointed to the rows of ribbons above Jamie's left breast pocket. "Does that top ribbon represent the Medal of Honor?"

"Yes, sir." Jamie surprised himself by calling a man with Matt Kavanaugh's reputation "sir." Such was his presence.

Kavanaugh stood at attention and held a salute. From the corner to which he'd been relegated, Lieutenant Colonel Hunt did likewise.

It was expected that Colonel Hunt would salute Jamie's

medal. He was surprised that a civilian would. And it was his medal they were saluting since they didn't know Jamie from Adam.

Jamie returned their salutes smartly.

"You must be Major Jamie Collins."

Why would Kavanaugh know his name?

"I hoped I'd get to meet you." Kavanaugh extended his hand.

Though Kavanaugh's reputation was sordid, that was no reason not to be polite to him. "I don't stand on formality. I go by Jamie."

Kavanaugh's grip was firm—unlike a man who spent his days idly ordering others around—although Jamie felt a slight tremor in his hand. And he presented well. Five nine or ten, muscular physique for a man around fifty, clean-shaven, not a single greying hair out of place. And his suit. Jamie couldn't imagine what it cost. He recalled an old saying. *Clothes don't make the man.* True, but they do make an impression.

"Right enough, Jamie." Kavanaugh tilted his head toward Butch. "I believe you've known my man Lightner for quite some time."

"Yes, sir." Had he really called such a man "sir" again? "Butch and I grew up together."

"Butch, is it?" Kavanaugh smiled. "More than fifteen years since you two first met, I believe."

Jamie wouldn't have expected a "big man" like Kavanaugh to clutter his mind with such trivia.

Kavanaugh turned to Lieutenant Colonel Hunt. "Thank you for showing me the way, Alan. I'll find my own way out."

Hunt silently slipped out the door.

Kavanaugh smiled at Jamie. "I read about you in the

newspapers, and I liked what I saw. I had my lawyers dig into your background, and they liked what they saw."

Jamie was immediately on his guard. What reason would a man like Kavanaugh have for looking into his background?

Like a hitchhiker flagging a ride, Kavanaugh pointed to Butch with his thumb. "My man here can tell you I'm one of the most generous philanthropists in the Bay Area."

"More like in the Western States," Butch said, having found his voice.

"I understand that you're to be discharged from the hospital soon, and you'll be returning to your university job," Kavanaugh said.

Jamie felt a chill run down his spine. Why would Kavanaugh know that, and why would he care?

"I'm wondering," Kavanaugh said, "in your spare time, how would you feel about working with me to establish a charity for disabled veterans?"

Butch cringed. Jamie was speechless.

"I'd be willing to provide the seed money." Kavanaugh crossed his arms. "Or would you be squeamish knowing the money came from me?" Kavanaugh raised his chin. "It's no secret that some of my wealth comes from giving people what they want when the law says they can't have it."

Jamie had to ask himself why he wasn't immediately repulsed by the idea of working with a racketeer. In his heart, Jamie knew the answer. Just as there's a beast in each of us, there's also a longing to live dangerously. God help him, Jamie was intrigued by the idea of working with Kavanaugh.

In Jamie's defense, if Kavanaugh was serious about helping disabled veterans, he was the answer to Jamie's prayers. He and Nurse Eliot had discussed the inadequacies of the Soldiers' Rehabilitation Act. They agreed it would take someone of means to establish a private charity to provide disabled veterans the training they'd need to find meaningful employment once they were discharged from the army. Surely, she'd understand if he worked toward that end with a man like Matt Kavanaugh. "Why disabled veterans?" Jamie said.

"Because they deserve better than what our government's doing for them."

Jamie's thoughts exactly. "Education," he said.

Kavanaugh cocked his head. "How's that?"

Jamie squared his shoulders. "A man needs to feel useful. A good job is a big step in that direction. A good job requires a good education."

Kavanaugh smiled. "I'd be happy to fund something along those lines."

Jamie offered *Mister* Kavanaugh his hand. "In that case, I won't ask where the money comes from."

Kavanaugh shook Jamie's hand and smiled triumphantly. "Work with me on this, and if there's ever anything I can do for you, you'll only have to ask."

"I'll be doing it to benefit disabled veterans, not myself." Jamie hadn't meant to sound so indignant.

"I'm glad to hear it. But think about it. Someday, you might want a favor for someone else—a relative, or maybe a friend."

Butch was emphatically shaking his head 'no' behind Kavanaugh's back.

Sergeant Binney and his dream of becoming a professional cake decorator popped into Jamie's mind. "I was initially thinking only of a college education. But, it occurs to me that some veterans might prefer vocational training. I'd consider it a favor if your charity provided training in whatever field a vet wants to explore."

"*Our* charity," Kavanaugh said. He straightened his tie. "Consider it done.

Kavanaugh stared off into space. "College wasn't in the cards for a kid like me. By the time I was twelve, I'd dropped out of school and was working morning 'til night trying to earn enough money to feed myself, my mother, and my worthless older brother."

Jamie had always wanted a brother, older or younger. If he'd been so blessed, he hoped he'd never come to think of him as worthless.

Kavanaugh inspected his diamond cufflinks. "Dropping out of school didn't stop me from educating myself. I believe I have a better command of the English language than most college graduates, and a larger vocabulary." He looked around the room as though daring someone to contradict him.

And a much bigger bank account, he might have added.

"Only in America could I have risen to the position I'm in," Kavanaugh said. "I love this country and want to give back to those who fought for it and paid a heavy price."

Jamie had some reassessing to do. This was not what he expected from a notorious racketeer.

Kavanaugh smiled. "We're going to do some good together," he said. "Now, if you'll excuse us, I'd like to talk some business with 'Butch.'"

As Jamie left Butch's room, the weight of what he'd just agreed to caused him to stagger a bit. He was genuinely thankful the war was over and looked forward to life as a physics professor. The problem was he missed the danger and excitement he experienced during the war.

* * *

Less than fifteen minutes passed before Kavanaugh emerged from Butch's room. "I'll be back to see you as soon as I've worked out the particulars of our charity," he said to Jamie. As he left the ward, his stride was that of a supremely confident man.

Nurse Eliot hadn't been on the ward when Kavanaugh and Lieutenant Colonel Hunt arrived, nor had she yet returned. Jamie knew her schedule. She'd have been in one of the seemingly interminable nursing staff meetings she had to endure every Thursday. Once Jamie learned the particulars of Kavanaugh's charity, if it looked like it really would help educate disabled veterans, he'd tell her all about it. She might want to get involved herself.

Jamie rejoined Butch. "You look like you've been force-fed a large dose of castor oil."

Butch grimaced. "That's how I feel."

"What did Mister Kavanaugh want, if you don't mind me asking?"

"First, I've got a question for you. Why would a straight shooter like you lower himself to work with a man like Mister Kavanaugh?"

Jamie walked to the window. "I don't care what kind of man he is." He turned to face his old friend. "He's offering to help our disabled veterans."

"I warn you. You're wrong if you think you can dance around the outskirts of his world. If you work with him, he'll find a way to draw you in deeper and deeper." Butch craned his neck toward Jamie. "If you value your freedom, you'll stay as far away from him as possible."

Jamie clenched his teeth. Butch was in no position to be

giving advice. "If it would help our disabled veterans, I'd make a deal with the devil."

Butch glared at him. "You just did when you shook hands with Mister Kavanaugh."

Jamie stood with his feet apart, hands on hips. "I can take care of myself."

Butch laughed. "Mister Kavanaugh feasts on people who think that." He turned deadly serious. "If you think he's gonna help veterans out of the kindness of his heart, you're wrong. I'd bet anythin' he wants somethin' from you. And knowin' him, he's gonna get it. Then, before you know it, he'll own your soul."

Jamie imagined David facing Goliath—without his sling. He unbuttoned his jacket and laid it over the back of Butch's guest chair. "Your warning is duly noted. Now, what did Mister Kavanaugh want."

"Didn't I warn you? You're already callin' him *Mister* Kavanaugh."

"A man who's going to establish a charity to help educate our disabled vets deserves to be called mister."

"Yeah, sure." Butch shook his head.

"Now, what did he want?"

"I told you he'd be in here askin' when I'd be back workin' for him."

"What did you tell him?"

Butch glanced at the doorway—as if he was afraid Kavanaugh might be lurking just outside. "I gave him the only answer I knew he'd accept. I told him I'd be back just as soon as the army releases me."

The irony of the situation didn't escape Jamie. This was one instance when it would be nice if a former employer didn't want a disabled veteran to return to work. "Didn't you tell him you're now a rich man and don't need to work?"

"I was afraid to. Now sit down, will ya? You're makin' me nervous."

Jamie sat. "We need to find a way for you to escape his clutches."

"We?" Butch raised himself up on an elbow. "It's always been me against the world."

"Not the best of odds. And don't try to sit up. Remember, you're supposed to lie flat and still to protect your sutures."

"Yeah, yeah." Butch laid back down. "You're right about the odds. And the situation's gonna get even worse soon. Mister Kavanaugh intends to retire before Prohibition goes into effect."

"Retire?" Jamie said. "Isn't he sitting on top of the world with all his money and power?"

"He's got to be tired of lookin' over his shoulder all the time, worryin' about the law and former business associates who want to settle a score." Butch's smirk said he didn't feel at all sorry for Kavanaugh. "With all the enemies he's made over the years, there's no way he's gonna enjoy a quiet retirement."

"There's an old saying: *You reap what you sow.*"

"Yeah, I've heard that." Butch frowned. "If it was up to me, he'd never retire."

"You'll have to explain that."

"It's a matter of the devil you know. Despite the hard feelin's between them, Mister Kavanaugh's brother, RK, was gonna be his successor."

"Was?"

"Didn't I tell you? RK drove his Dodge Roadster into a

tree last New Year's Eve. Died at the scene." Butch showed even less sympathy for RK than he had for Mister Kavanaugh. "Sonny's the next in line—and he's as evil as they come." Butch rubbed the stubble on his cheek. "I figured someday RK would push Mister Kavanaugh over the edge, and brother be damned, RK would end up in his fancy clothes floatin' face down in Monterey Bay—or with his chest caved in after crashin' his car into a tree." Butch seemed lost in thought for a moment. "The newspapers said there weren't any skid marks at the scene of RK's crash."

"You mean it wasn't an accident?"

"Hard to say. But knowin' he'd be next in line to take over Kavanaugh Enterprises, I wouldn't put it past Sonny to have tampered with RK's brakes."

"And kill his own father?" Whoops. That was insensitive.

Butch closed his eyes. "Patricide. That's the word for someone like me who kills his father."

"Your circumstances were completely different. You were protecting your mother. If Sonny tampered with his father's brakes, it would be murder."

Butch looked at Jamie. "Which is why I'd rather spend the rest of my days in the trenches than work for Sonny. He'll stop at nothin' to make a buck, and it's fine with him if somebody gets hurt along the way."

"But if Mister Kavanaugh retires, wouldn't that mean you'd be free?"

"Kavanaugh Enterprises would still have a lot to lose if I talked too much. Sonny's gonna want to keep me under his thumb."

"If you don't want to work for Sonny or Mister

Kavanaugh, you need to figure out how you do want your life to play out."

Butch seemed to enter a world long past. "You remember as kids how we used to explore the tidepools on the rocky beach in front of my grandma's house?"

"Sure. About all you ever wanted to do was poke around and see what kind of marine life you could turn up."

Butch sighed. "If I could start all over again, I'd be a marine biologist and spend the rest of my life studyin' the creatures that live at the border between sea and land."

Jamie thought about it for a moment. "With your inheritance, you can afford to go back to school and study marine biology."

"I don't know. First, I'd have to come to terms with everybody thinkin' I'm a coward. Otherwise, I'd be tempted to creep too close to the water's edge, let a wave wash me out to sea, and end all my shame."

"You're no coward. No matter how strong he is, any man can fall victim to shellshock."

"That's what I keep tellin' myself. I just wish I could believe it." Butch shrugged. "Besides, I was so bored in high school I pretty much blew off all my classes. Biology was the only one I didn't sleep through. With my grades, no decent college would admit me."

"You never know. Lots of fine universities are opening their doors to veterans whose attitudes toward education were transformed by the war. And you'll love this: Stanford has the oldest marine laboratory on the West Coast. Hopkins Marine Station. And it's right there in Pacific Grove. Less than a mile from that mansion your grandmother left you. As a Stanford associate professor, maybe I can pull some strings and help get you admitted to their marine biology program."

"With my war record? They wouldn't give me a minute's consideration. Unless ...."

"Unless what?"

Butch stared at the ceiling for a moment. "Say you weigh a man's acts of bravery against his acts of cowardice, and they come out even. Will he be seen as a hero or a coward?"

Obviously, the question wasn't hypothetical. "Would we be talking about a man who would have received a Silver Star Medal if he hadn't gone on to shoot himself?"

"We would. A Silver Star you say I deserve. But here's the catch: how a man is seen depends on which act occurs last. Heroic followed by cowardly, and he'll be seen as a coward. Cowardly followed by heroic, and people will think he's even more heroic."

"Is that just you theorizing, or do you know that to be true?"

"We both know it's true," Butch said. "It's human nature. Think about it. Even a minor act of cowardice by someone people see as a hero will ruin his image. On the other hand, a simple act of bravery by someone people think is a coward will strike them as even braver than it is—*and he will be redeemed.*"

"Okay," Jamie said. "Now I understand. So what heroic act do you intend to perform?"

Butch locked eyes with Jamie. "I don't know. But if there's any justice in this world, I'll get my chance." He settled back onto his pillow. "I don't care what it costs me. Someday, somehow, I *will* be redeemed."

* * *

Saturday, 17 May 1919

Jamie was deep into Jack London's *The Call of the Wild*, one of the books Nurse Hobbes got for him from the base library, when Hendricks materialized next to the brotherhood table. "Sir, a visitor is waiting to see you in the chapel."

Jamie tossed his book aside. "A visitor? In the chapel?" His heart began to race. He couldn't help picturing his bride waiting for him at the altar—but as her face came into focus, he was stunned to see it was Nurse Eliot's, not Rachel's.

"It's the gentleman the deputy base commander escorted in for a visit with Private Lightner the other day."

Despite his disappointment, Jamie sprang to his feet—as best he could. He certainly didn't expect to see Matt Kavanaugh again this soon.

With cane in hand, Jamie negotiated Letterman's maze of corridors and pushed open the chapel's double doors. In the front pew of the otherwise deserted chamber sat Mister Matt Kavanaugh.

The Western States' leading racketeer stood as Jamie entered. "Thank you for coming, Jamie." His lilting Irish-accented tone was warm yet unmistakably authoritative. Kavanaugh extended his hand.

"It's not every day I'm summoned to the chapel." Jamie gripped Kavanaugh's hand—and again noticed a tremor.

Jamie made a sweeping gesture that took in the empty chapel. "By yourself today?"

"Lieutenant Colonel Hunt escorted me here and then hurried off to take care of other business. My limousine driver is waiting for me out front." Kavanaugh sat. He gestured for Jamie to join him.

Jamie unbuttoned his jacket and sat. "I've only seen Colonel Hunt once. That was when he escorted you in to visit Butch. He didn't strike me as a very happy man."

"He was having a particularly bad day."

"Oh?"

"The San Francisco Chronicle had just run an article criticizing him for signing a contract that gave Kavanaugh Enterprises the exclusive right to provide *all* the Presidio's services and supplies."

"What is there to criticize about that?"

"Kavanaugh Enterprises wasn't the lowest bidder."

"I see."

"No, you don't. And neither would the Chronicle's readers. The article failed to mention that the lowest bidder, Salinger Services and Supply, had been providing the base unreliable services and notably substandard supplies over the past several years. Nor did it mention that Kavanaugh Enterprises now provides top-quality supplies and services on time every time—for only a few pennies more than Salinger had been charging."

Jamie shrugged. "In that case, it sounds like Colonel Hunt made a good decision."

"I agree. And so would the reading public if the article had given them all the facts. What especially irritated me were the Chronicle's allegations that Salinger had no choice in the quality of supplies they provided because Kavanaugh Enterprises controlled the market and refused to sell to Salinger. Worse, the article said Salinger's services were unreliable only because my men routinely waylaid theirs. Allegations for which the Chronicle did not, nor could they, offer any proof."

Now Colonel Hunt's dark mood was understandable. "And you're saying the Chronicle's allegations are untrue?"

"The part about controlling the market is true. For which

I offer no apology. Tennyson's description of nature applies equally well to business. Red in tooth and claw."

A racketeer familiar with Tennyson? What a world. "What about waylaying Salinger's men?"

"We didn't have to. We just hired their best men away from them. A perfectly legal business practice."

"And a good way to make enemies," Jamie said. "Which is why I expected the Matt Kavanaugh I've read about in the newspapers to be surrounded by bodyguards."

"As I've just illustrated, you can't always believe what you read in the papers." Kavanaugh put his hand over a bulge under his suit coat. "Letterman is an army hospital. This is all the protection I need within these walls." He opened his jacket to reveal the butt-end of a handgun.

Jamie's eyes opened wide. "That's a step up from the Colt .45 the army issued me. Mine didn't have a pearl handle."

Kavanaugh smiled. "I think it compliments my diamond cufflinks, don't you?"

Jamie didn't answer.

Kavanaugh gave Jamie a cold stare. "I'm here by myself because I prefer to keep business matters private. I suggest you do the same."

Jamie shrugged. "I don't have anything to hide."

"You will by the time we're finished—if you're serious about helping disabled veterans."

This was a decision point. If Jamie was going to heed Butch's warning and not get entangled in Kavanaugh's world, he had to leave now. If he stayed, there'd be no turning back.

Jamie exhaled deeply and leaned back in the pew.

Like the victor he was, Kavanaugh smiled. "How does 'the Disabled Veterans' Education Trust,' or DVET, sound?"

It sounded good. Real good. But was it just a nice name for a scam? "Hmm. Not bad. Did you think of it yourself?"

"I did." Kavanaugh sat a little taller. "I've also worked out the particulars of our charity."

"That was fast," Jamie said. "I'm going to have to stay on my toes to keep up with you."

"Don't bother. All I'm going to ask of you is that you show up in uniform when needed and say the right things."

"I should be able to manage that."

"Here's the way we're going to work it. First, we're going to have a reception at an art gallery in town—"

"Hutchins?"

Kavanaugh's eyes narrowed. "There are plenty of galleries in the city. How could you know it was going to be Hutchins?"

"Fate. That gallery's already played a big part in my life." Jamie leaned back and rested his arm on the back of the pew, mirroring Kavanaugh.

His visitor raised his chin. "We're going to have a reception—at Hutchins Fine Art. Invitations will go out to several dozen of my closest business associates. You'll be there with a beautiful young woman on your arm."

Jamie went into a near-trance as again he pictured not Rachel but Nurse Eliot by his side.

"If it's going to be a problem coming up with someone who fits the bill," Kavanaugh said, "I'll provide you with one of my young ladies."

Young ladies—or call girls? Jamie could feel the beast in him begin to stir. He didn't want Kavanaugh's offer to tarnish the image of himself in the company of Nurse Eliot. "That won't be necessary. I have the perfect person in mind. She's just as determined to help disabled veterans as we are. And she'll make a great impression on your guests." Jamie glanced at the altar. "I'll just have to find the courage to ask her to accompany me and hope she'll say yes."

This was met by another cold stare. "Don't think you're too good to be seen with one of my young ladies."

Jamie was unnerved by Kavanaugh's tone. He retrieved his cane. It would provide a measure of protection if Kavanaugh became really angry.

"I've trained my young ladies how to act when out in public on the arm of a prominent citizen. I've even arranged a goodly number of successful marriages between so-called pillars of society and beautiful young women half their age," Kavanaugh said.

Butch mentioned that Kavanaugh had a host of prominent men in his pocket. How better to control them than through their wives? "I'm sorry if I gave the impression that I think too highly of myself," Jamie said. "But for the grace of God, I know I could be looking up at the rest of humanity from a hole deeper than the Marianas Trench."

Kavanaugh chuckled. "You can't get any lower than that." His tone softened. "The men I'll be inviting to our reception each make $50,000 a year or more."

Jamie just about choked. "Are there really people who make that much money?"

"Sure. And a few of them are even honest."

There wasn't much Jamie could say to that. "I saw in the newspaper recently that the average salary in this country is about $1,200 a year. Fifty thousand, and you're talking about more than 40 times what the average man makes."

"That's why they'll be on our guest list. People who

make that kind of money can afford to donate to a worthy cause." Kavanaugh straightened his already straight tie. "After we stuff our guests with hors d'oeuvres and ply them with champagne, I'll ask for everyone's attention. I'll explain that our country owes a debt of gratitude to our disabled veterans and that patriots can help settle it by contributing toward their education."

On occasion, Kavanaugh slurred his words. Surely, he hadn't been drinking this early in the day. Jamie detected not the slightest smell of alcohol about the man.

He looked Jamie up and down. "I'll introduce you. You'll make a nice little speech telling our guests how important the DVET is to you." He folded his arms. "Then I'll announce that I've made a seed donation of ten thousand dollars."

"Ten thousand dollars? That's a lot of money!" Jamie raised an eyebrow. "Why that particular amount?"

Kavanaugh steepled his fingers. "It's twenty percent of the $50,000 income we'll be targeting. Which will make the five percent we're going to suggest my associates donate look small by comparison."

"Suggest they donate? Or pressure them into donating?"

"I wouldn't use the word pressure," Kavanaugh said. "Incentive would be more accurate. Even the dimmest of our guests will realize they'll fare better with Kavanaugh Enterprises if they donate."

Jamie was beginning to see why Kavanaugh was so successful.

"Here's something else you should like," Kavanaugh said. "Donations to a lot of charities, perhaps most, end up in the pockets of the charity's executives—disguised as so-called administrative fees. That's not the case with any of my charities. And it won't be the case with the DVET. I'm going to have Kavanaugh Enterprises' accountants do all the administrative work as part of their normal bookkeeping duties."

Kavanaugh smiled. "The government will also give them an incentive to donate. A clause in the War Revenue Act of 1917 authorized individuals to claim a tax deduction for charitable contributions. Even though the war's over, that clause still stands, and the way things get entrenched in our tax code, it's likely to remain in effect forever."

Jamie shrugged. "I don't know the first thing about our tax code. How does this deduction work?"

"I'll give you a simplified example. Consider a man earning $50,000 a year. Without any deductions, at the end of the year, he'd owe the government $15,000 in personal income tax."

Jamie sat up straight. "Fifteen thousand dollars! That's—he did a quick mental calculation—twelve times the average annual salary of a working man in this country."

"Which plays right into our hands. Nobody wants to pay that much in taxes. So let's say our man donates five percent of his income, or $2,500, to a worthwhile charity like the DVET. The War Revenue Act would allow him to deduct that amount from his gross income. Then, since it's net income that gets taxed, his donation would effectively reduce his five percent donation to only three and a half percent of his gross."

"I imagine that would sound good to a rich man."

"Absolutely. And we're not going to stop there." Kavanaugh leaned back and smiled. "To persuade my associates to donate even more, I'll drop a bombshell on them. I'll announce that I'll make an additional donation of fifty cents for every dollar over $2,500 any single donor makes."

Jamie was impressed. "That's mighty generous of you."

"I'm a generous man."

It was hard for Jamie to hold his tongue. A man can afford to be generous when he has money pouring in from multiple illegal businesses.

"Some of my associates are equally generous. One, in particular, can always be relied on to donate to a worthy cause. He owns a big maritime insurance company. And you'll like this. He's as honest as any man you'll ever meet."

"It's good to know there are some honest businessmen."

"Others will need a little more incentive to donate." Kavanaugh leaned toward Jamie. "So, here's what we're going to do."

Uh-oh. Here comes trouble.

"As you and your lady circulate among our guests, I'll take those sitting on the fence aside one by one—men whose businesses will benefit from keeping me happy. If I can't nudge them off the fence with an appeal to their better nature, I'll make them an offer that will draw them to our charity like bears to honey."

The devious look on Kavanaugh's face reminded Jamie of Butch's warning about dealing with the devil. The thought that he'd be helping disabled veterans was the only thing that kept Jamie from running out of the chapel.

Kavanaugh adjusted his diamond cufflinks. "If they'll donate $2,500 or more, I'll offer to give them a receipt stating that they've donated fifty percent more than they actually have."

Jamie's beast began rattling its cage. "Why bring tax fraud into an otherwise legitimate charity?"

"You want to educate as many disabled veterans as possible, don't you?"

"Not so badly that I'm willing to go to prison—or hell."

"Don't worry about prison. The government would have a hard time prosecuting us for what I have in mind." Kavanaugh smiled. "As for hell, that will be between you and God."

Back out now, Jamie's conscience insisted, only to be shouted down by the thought that he'd be helping disabled veterans.

"Before you get on your high horse," Kavanaugh said, "let me tell you how this is going to work."

Jamie sat paralyzed by indecision. He had to make a choice. Turn his back on disabled veterans and run, or stay and compromise his ethics.

When it was clear that Jamie wasn't going anywhere, Kavanaugh pressed on. "Say a man making $50,000 a year makes the five percent donation we'll be asking for, but I give him a receipt stating that he donated fifty percent more than he actually has. Then, since it's net income that gets taxed, his donation would effectively be reduced to only two and three-quarters percent of his gross."

Jamie swallowed hard. "That's like getting paid to claim a bigger donation!"

"Not a bad hook, is it?" Kavanaugh smiled that conniving smile of his. "In which case, I don't think my business associates will mind helping to fill the DVET's coffers, especially knowing it will strengthen their relationship with Kavanaugh Enterprises."

"But if the Bureau of Internal Revenue audits them, they could go to jail. We could go to jail!"

"Not us," Kavanaugh said. "Not the way we're going to

play it. Say our offer induces one of my associates to donate to the DVET when he otherwise wouldn't have. That would mean a bit less money would go into the US Treasury—and more than three times the government's loss would go into the DVET."

"Wait a minute," Jamie said. "The DVET's books wouldn't balance if you gave out an inflated receipt."

Kavanaugh looked supremely pleased with himself. "That's a part of our scheme you should like. I'll happily make up the difference—by making an additional donation to the DVET *in honor of* our previously fence-sitting donor."

"In honor of?"

"His inflated receipt will say something to the effect of, 'Thanks to your generous donation, the DVET has X dollars more to use in educating disabled veterans.' And it will be true. Their receipt just won't mention that about a third of that amount will have come out of my pocket. But the DVET's books will state unequivocally where every dollar comes from."

"So, in essence," Jamie said, "we'd be saying we know better than our government how to allocate limited tax dollars."

"Don't we?"

Jamie was slow to answer. "In the case of the DVET, I believe we do. But what if the Bureau of Internal Revenue accuses the DVET of abetting tax evasion?"

"By not providing a donor with an itemized receipt?" Kavanaugh rubbed his hands together. "We'll just say it was a simple oversight and rest easy knowing that since the DVET's books balance, such a minor administrative deficiency won't rise to the level of a crime."

"It would be a crime if a donor uses his receipt to get an unauthorized reduction of his taxes."

Kavanaugh seemed to be losing his patience. "Instead of the government getting the true amount my associates will owe, the government will get a paltry amount less that they would have spent on God knows what. As a result, the DVET will receive a significant donation, every penny of which will go to educating veterans whose bodies and lives were torn apart while serving our country. Tell me, where's the crime in that?" Kavanaugh gave a little laugh. "And I'll be able to deduct what I put in the DVET's coffers in honor of our donors from my taxes."

If this was how all successful businessmen thought, Jamie was glad he was a physicist.

Kavanaugh again put his arm over the back of the pew. "Think of the good the DVET will do. I guarantee at least a dozen of my associates will donate—either out of patriotic duty or the incentives we'll offer them. Which means the DVET's initial funding will be no less than $60,000—with less than half coming out of my pocket."

Jamie looked at Mister Kavanaugh with a measure of genuine respect. Though a substantial portion of his wealth may have been ill-gotten, it was still impressive that he was willing to part with so much of it. "Whoever devised this scheme must be pretty bright."

Kavanaugh smiled. "That would be me."

"I'm impressed." Although not altogether favorably.

"I'm good with numbers," Kavanaugh said. "Always have been."

"I can tell you've given this a lot of thought. For our sakes, I hope you haven't overlooked anything."

"Look at it this way," Kavanaugh said. "With the

DVET's initial funding alone, we'll be able to provide room, board, tuition, and books for around twenty disabled veterans to earn four-year college degrees." He sat back. "Don't you think that's worth the small risk we'll be taking?"

Despite the eerie feeling that the backlit stained-glass rendering of Jesus that stood in the front of the chapel was frowning at him, Jamie made a quick decision. "I've taken bigger risks. Let's do it."

As they shook on the deal, Kavanaugh's tremor was still noticeable—but not quite as pronounced.

Kavanaugh stared off into space. "It's only because I educated myself that I have the confidence to meet one-on-one with someone like you—a professor at a fine university."

Jamie was sure Kavanaugh wasn't just bragging. The man had to be working up to something.

Kavanaugh smiled. "But I get the feeling you don't sit in judgment of others. When we first met, you called me 'sir' and shook my hand like you would any other successful businessman. And you're willing to work with me on our charity."

How honest did Jamie want to be? What was the old saying? *Honesty's the best policy.* "I *need* to work with you," he blurted out.

For once, it was Kavanaugh who was surprised. "I ... I don't understand."

"As bad as the war was, I've never felt more alive. It was my men and me against the Germans. To survive, we had to band together. We came to think of ourselves as family. I miss that sense of purpose and belonging. I hope working with you will give me a similar sense. You and me against a country indifferent to the needs of our veterans."

"I like your thinking."

Jamie lowered his eyes. "There's more. As much as I'm looking forward to life as an academic, I'll miss the excitement and danger I experienced during the war."

Kavanaugh smiled. "I'm hoping to disappoint you in that respect. If our scheme to fund the DVET works as planned, you'll find it about as exciting and dangerous as watching paint dry." He leaned back and crossed his arms. "But I might be able to accommodate you in another way. There's another group of deserving individuals who need my help. I have a plan to rescue them. You might find you'd like to get involved yourself."

Jamie was intrigued—but wary. Butch warned him there'd be strings attached if Kavanaugh helped disabled veterans. Jamie had to be careful those strings didn't turn into a noose.

Kavanaugh covered a dramatic yawn with his hand. "Excuse me. To meet an absolute deadline, I've been working extra hard lately, staying up late and getting up early. Thankfully, tomorrow will be Sunday, a day of rest." He took a moment to straighten his tie and then his cufflinks. "I've given you a lot to think about. I'll tell you what. I'll be here again Monday afternoon, let's say at 3:30. If you want to know how I plan to help another deserving group of individuals, this is where you'll find me."

It was disappointing that he'd have to wait to find out what other surprises Kavanaugh might have in store for him. But it was true. Jamie had a lot to think about.

As Butch said, he'd always been a "straight shooter." And now he was conspiring with a notorious racketeer to defraud the US Government. Jamie was sometimes appalled by the person he was becoming. He was willing to work with a man he shouldn't trust while becoming increasingly distrustful of those he should. Shell shock, he told himself. But that excuse was wearing thin.

It would be best to mull over what he'd gotten himself into before venturing further with a man as calculating and persuasive as Matt Kavanaugh.

* * *

Soon after leaving the chapel, Jamie was telling Butch all about Kavanaugh's plans for the DVET.

"It sounds good," Butch said. "And it would be if we were talkin' about someone other than Mister Kavanaugh. Especially concerning is that bit about tax fraud. From the tiniest seed ...."

"I'll be careful," Jamie said. He wasn't going to tell Butch that Kavanaugh had offered to meet with him again in a few days.

Later that evening, Jamie was able to have a quick word with Nurse Eliot. "Good news," he said. "As we were hoping, someone of means has come forward and offered to fund a private charity to help educate disabled veterans."

Her face lit up. "That's wonderful news."

That he didn't tell her about Kavanaugh's tax scheme was as good as an admission that Jamie knew it was wrong. Nevertheless, Nurse Eliot's enthusiasm removed Jamie's last misgivings about meeting with Kavanaugh again.

Chapter 24

Redemption and Rejection

Sunday, 18 May 1919

Jamie attended church services with Toby and Carl again and spent the rest of the day immersed in another of the books Nurse Hobbes got for him from the base library. Ten minutes until lights out, he was sitting immobile at the brotherhood table, his mind in a different world. How would Sherlock Holmes save Sir Henry Baskerville from the fangs of the monstrous hound snapping at his heels? Jamie wouldn't be able to sleep until he read the ending of Sir Arthur Conan Doyle's *The Hound of the Baskervilles*."

At that critical moment, Nurse Eliot came through the ward's double doors. She and Jamie exchanged smiles as she headed toward the nurses' station. Hendricks was a few seconds behind her.

"Hendricks," Nurse Eliot shouted, "come quickly."

Hendricks took off running. Jamie stood as Nurse Eliot approached Lieutenant Walberg's door. Other heads turned her way. Jamie hurried toward her. From thirty feet away, he saw a heavy blood trail on the floor between Butch's room and Lieutenant Walberg's.

Jamie rushed to Walberg's door and stopped dead. Butch's body was draped over the side of Tom's bed—as still as a corpse. A shockingly large pool of blood had formed beneath Butch's stump. Tom's nebulizer mask was clutched in Butch's blanched hand. The mask was pulled down below Tom's chin. Pulses of yellowish liquid were shooting from the mask across Tom's chest.

"Nebulizer malfunction," Hendricks shouted. He dashed across the room and violently jerked the machine's power cord out of the wall socket. The mask stopped hissing.

Nurse Eliot placed her fingertips on Walberg's neck. After a moment, she exhaled deeply and closed Tom's eyes forever. Jamie noticed the white king on Tom's chessboard had fallen over.

Hendricks wrenched Tom's mask from Butch's hand. He pressed on Butch's carotid artery. The look on Hendricks' face confirmed Jamie's fears. "He's dead," Hendricks said. He lifted Butch's body and placed it flat on the floor, away from the pool of his blood.

Jamie stood as though rooted to the ground. Two friends dead. Friends who had survived the war, however broken, but hadn't survived the peace. It didn't seem fair. It *wasn't* fair.

Hendricks covered Butch's head and torso with Tom's spare blanket. Nurse Eliot pulled Walberg's sheet up over his waxen face.

It looks like a slaughterhouse in here. The ugly thought had popped into Jamie's head uninvited and wouldn't leave. He followed the blood trail to Butch's door, where it began as a light spattering near the edge of his bed. From there, the pattern alternated between a concentration and a trickle at intervals about a foot apart. Each concentration was wider and deeper than the last until the pattern ended in a large smear, and the heavy, continuous trail began.

Nurse Eliot and Hendricks stood in the hallway. Nurse Wolenski appeared behind Hendricks and peered around his shoulder. Her face turned whiter than Butch's as she stared at the smear of blood at her feet. "My God, what happened here?" she said.

"We can only guess," Jamie said. He followed the trail back to Tom's room, knelt, and put his hand on Butch's shoulder. "I told Butch that Tom's nebulizer tended to malfunction, and if it did, it could kill him. I asked Butch to keep an ear tuned to it and, if it ever started to sound funny, to alert the staff."

"Then why didn't he alert us?" Nurse Eliot said.

Jamie stood. "Maybe he thought the staff's response was too slow." He looked for a reaction. Only Nurse Wolenski lowered her head. "From the blood pattern, I'd say Butch got out of bed, hopped to his doorway, fell, and then dragged himself into Tom's room."

"Tearing out his fresh sutures in the process," Nurse Eliot said.

"Once he got to Lieutenant Walberg's room," Hendricks said, "he must have climbed onto the side of the lieutenant's bed and snatched the nebulizer mask away from his face."

"Then passed out from loss of blood." Nurse Eliot squeezed her eyes shut as though she was trying not to picture the scene. "Lightner must have been in terrible pain the whole time."

"For Butch's sake," Jamie said, "I hope he died believing he saved Tom's life."

Nurse Eliot clasped her hands below her chin and closed her eyes. Jamie assumed she was praying. When her lips stopped moving, she opened her eyes. Her stoic "Nurse Eliot" expression had returned. "If no one else is going to say it, I will. I'm glad Lieutenant Walberg's suffering has ended."

"Me too," Jamie said. "It was heartbreaking listening to him struggle for every breath."

"And yet he could still laugh," Hendricks said.

"A lesser man's spirit would have been crushed knowing he'd never get better." Jamie came to attention and saluted Tom's corpse. "May your soul rest with the Lord, my noble friend."

Jamie turned to Butch's shrouded body—and what a pitiful sight it was. A large inanimate lump covered by a blanket with one leg and a stump protruding from beneath it. "And may your soul also reside with the Lord, my troubled old friend." Jamie saluted Butch's corpse as he had Tom's.

"None of this makes sense," Nurse Eliot said. "Why didn't Lightner keep pressing his call button until someone answered?"

Nurse Wolenski let out a choked sob. "This is all my fault."

"Explain." Nurse Eliot's command tone would have put General Pershing to shame.

Nurse Wolenski shied away from the trail of blood at her feet. "I've been ignoring Private Lightner's call button, and I encouraged others to do the same."

Nurse Eliot grabbed her assistant by the arm and dug in her nails. "Why would you do such a thing?"

Wolenski stopped crying and stood up straight. "When

Lightner shot himself to get out of combat, some other boy had to take his place. It would have been Lightner's fault if that boy had been killed or injured. I saw no reason for us to wait hand and foot on such a man."

Angry red streaks appeared on Nurse Eliot's neck. "Leave this ward this instant, nurse. I'll deal with you later." A violent outburst would have been less intimidating than her measured tone.

Wolenski's shoulders sagged as she headed down the boulevard. She tripped slightly after a few steps as if weighed down by the burden of guilt she was carrying.

She wasn't alone in her guilt. Jamie had promised to do something about the staff ignoring Butch's calls. He hadn't. Yes, he had forgiven Butch for the bullying so many years earlier, but the resentment still festered in the darkest recesses of Jamie's heart. He couldn't help feeling that Butch deserved this little bit of punishment—this little bit that had such tragic consequences. It stung to know he'd broken his promise to his friend, and now it was too late to do anything about it.

Nurse Eliot put her hands on her hips. "Wolenski's little conspiracy doesn't explain why Lightner didn't call out for help from the hallway."

"Butch hated being known as a coward," Jamie said. "He was hoping for a chance to redeem himself. How better than to arrive just in time to save Tom's life? The most charitable assumption we can make is that his efforts robbed him of the strength to call out."

Nurse Eliot sighed. "The sad truth is that if he had called out, he would have ruined a dramatic exit from this life and his best chance to be remembered as a savior rather than a coward."

Hendricks repositioned Butch's shroud to cover his stump. "As far as I'm concerned, what Lightner did here makes him a hero."

"I agree," Jamie said. "I've known Butch since we were kids, and I can tell you the things he had to deal with throughout his life would have destroyed the soul of most men. And the events that led to him shooting himself were so gruesome they traumatized me just hearing about them." Jamie looked from Nurse Eliot to Hendricks and back. "It would be heartless of us to remember him by anything other than his last act."

* * *

Monday morning, 19 May 1919

The day after Butch's death, Jamie found Carl and Toby with their heads together, deep in conversation. Jamie pulled out a chair from the brotherhood table and slumped down across from them. "Have you guys come up with a solution for all the world's problems?"

"Major Collins, sir, we were—"

Jamie sat up straight. "*Major Collins?*"

Toby and Carl looked at each other. "Sir, Professor, Doctor. We're not sure what to call you."

"What's wrong with 'Jamie'? "

Carl elbowed Toby.

"Well, sir," Toby said, "it was fine when we were all part of a brotherhood."

Jamie put his palms flat on the table. "And now we're not?"

"Sir," Toby said, "what made us brothers was that we

had all lost a part of ourselves. What separates us now is that you're whole again."

"And you'll be getting out of here soon and going back to a normal life," Carl said.

Toby pushed his chair back from the table. "Sir, you should be happy you're no longer one of us."

The last time Jamie felt such pain, he was lying on the ground after being thrown through the air by an exploding artillery shell. Being shut out from the Brotherhood of Loss was like having a piece torn from his heart.

Nevertheless, Jamie *was* happy. Beyond happy. And not just because he could walk again. The men on the ward—the brethren—were now so close they were blind to race, religion, and ethnic origin. All they saw in each other was their shared losses. In Jamie's mind, their closeness was an indisputable declaration that he had won the war against their isolation, depression, apathy, and every other psychologically crippling state of mind that stood in the way of their independence.

But victory always comes at a cost.

Jamie got up from the table. "Maybe we'd all be more comfortable if I moved back into my old room."

Neither Toby nor Carl offered any objection.

With all the dignity he could muster, Jamie headed toward his newly vacated private room. Nurse Eliot was nearby. She had to have heard every word. When he came even with her, she grasped his upper arm and gave it a squeeze. Without saying a word, she turned her attention back to the patient she'd been helping.

Jamie walked on with his head held high. Only Nurse Eliot could have eased his pain with merely a passing touch.

Chapter 25

Reforming Kavanaugh Enterprises

Monday afternoon, 19 May 1919

The chapel was deserted when Jamie arrived. He sat in the front pew and waited. Kavanaugh pushed open the chapel's double doors at exactly 3:30. As Kavanaugh moved toward the front of the chapel, he staggered. He leaned against the end of a pew to keep from falling, then pretended it hadn't happened.

Jamie rose. They shook hands. Kavanaugh's tremor was even more noticeable.

"I heard that Butch died trying to save another patient," Kavanaugh said without any preamble.

Did Kavanaugh have a spy on Jamie's ward? "How'd you hear about that so soon?"

"It doesn't matter how. What matters is that it was an honorable death, and now a troubled soul can find some rest."

Jamie was sure he heard compassion in Kavanaugh's

voice. "Did you actually know Butch, or was he just another of your many employees?"

"I wasn't going to let someone work closely with me without first getting to know him. So yes, I knew Butch well."

"Then you must know the tragic story of his parents' passing."

Kavanaugh turned and faced Jamie. "I never believed his mother killed his father. I always suspected Butch. Otherwise, why would she refuse to take the stand and defend herself? Oddly, that's one reason I hired Butch. I reasoned that she wouldn't have taken the blame unless she believed Butch was worth protecting."

Apparently, Butch was right when he said Kavanaugh understood people.

To Jamie's amazement, Kavanaugh knelt and bowed his head toward the cross at the front of the chapel. After a moment, he crossed himself and then sat. "I've said a prayer for Butch," Kavanaugh said. "I hope you have too."

"I have," Jamie said. "More than one." He sat next to Kavanaugh and rested his hands on top of his cane. Jamie felt he was dealing with a living contradiction: a prayerful racketeer.

"Yesterday," Kavanaugh said, "I laid out a plan for how you and I can help disabled veterans. Today, I'd like to tell you about a plan I have for saving the jobs of more than a thousand of my hardworking, honest employees and continuing my charities."

So that was it? Kavanaugh had "laid Butch to rest," and now it was on to other business? "Why tell me?"

"You're an intelligent man," Kavanaugh said. "And

compassionate. I want to know what you think of my plan. If you like it, I hope you'll want to play a part yourself."

Butch said Kavanaugh would try to draw Jamie deeper into his world. Was it a weakness that Jamie could never turn his back on those in need? Or a character strength? "If your plan doesn't involve anything illegal, I'll listen."

"Illegal? Just the opposite. I'm going to retire, and when I'm gone, I want to be remembered for the good I've done."

"How are you going to manage that?"

"I told you big changes were in store for Kavanaugh Enterprises. Now that it's well established, I want Kavanaugh Enterprises to carry on as a model of ethical business practices."

That was the biggest surprise yet from a man full of surprises. "From the rumors that swirl around Kavanaugh Enterprises, that will be a big change."

Kavanaugh smiled. "Not as big as I've led people to believe." His smile disappeared. "Let me tell you about Kavanaugh Enterprises, so you'll know what's at stake."

Jamie searched Kavanaugh's face. "Are you sure you want to do that?"

"You should know all there is to know about Kavanaugh Enterprises before you decide whether you want to play a part in my plan—a plan which I assure you is entirely legal."

Jamie imagined himself a trout being played by a master angler. So be it. If Kavanaugh's plan to protect hundreds of jobs and maintain his charities didn't include anything illegal, what would be the harm in listening?

"When I was a boy," Kavanaugh said, "I dreamed of becoming a priest. That dream went down the drain when a storm took my father, his fishing boat, and his crew to the bottom of the sea."

Hence the genuflection and prayer, Jamie thought.

"To keep my mother, older brother, and myself from starving, I took the only job a kid like me could find. Selling newspapers on the street. That's where I learned how brutal the business world can be."

Jamie had seen enough brutality for a lifetime. Another reason he was glad to be a scientist and not a businessman.

"I had to fight some pretty tough kids for the right to sell my newspapers on the busiest street corner by the train station." He touched his crooked nose. "One of those kids came up from behind me and shoved my face into a telephone pole. Gave me this." There was malice in Kavanaugh's eyes. "I whipped around with blood pouring from my nose and lit into him like a tornado. By the time I was done with him, that kid had to spend a week in the hospital."

Jamie could imagine that. Kavanaugh was only about Jamie's five-nine, but he was built like one of those British Mark V heavy tanks that used to scare the hell out of the Germans.

"I thought I was pretty tough, taking over that corner and keeping it. So when I turned seventeen, I decided to try making a little money as a prizefighter. I lied about my age since you had to be eighteen to get a license. I went about it scientifically. I studied my opponents as they fought other boxers, looking for their weaknesses—we all have weaknesses, you know."

"Only a fool would deny that," Jamie said.

"I'd step into the ring, duck the other guy's punches the best I could, wait until his weakness showed up, then floor him. It worked well enough to earn a twelve-and-oh record. The trouble was I was taking a lot of punishment waiting for my opening. Those twelve wins cost me far too many concussions."

He rubbed his forehead. "I quickly realized I was going nowhere in the fight game. I might as well have beat my head against a brick wall as trade another concussion for the few dollars I was earning." Kavanaugh smiled his wicked smile. "I did get something out of it, though. You beat the hell out of a kid, you tally an undefeated record in the ring, you get a reputation. So when the 'Elders' who ran the local numbers game needed a new runner, they picked me, figuring I was tough enough to handle the job."

"Butch mentioned that he was a runner for your brother before coming to work for you."

"That's right. He worked the Golden Gate game. The game I worked as a kid, and that I eventually owned."

Jamie lost his grip on his cane. It bounced off the floor and slid up against Kavanaugh's foot. "Sorry," Jamie said. He hadn't expected Kavanaugh to admit so freely that he owned an illegal operation.

The sound of his cane hitting the floor was still reverberating throughout the chapel when Kavanaugh picked it up and offered it to Jamie. He didn't let go when Jamie took hold. "You don't really need this thing, do you?"

Jamie sensed his face reddening. "No. I've just gotten used to carrying it."

"Not a bad thing to carry." Kavanaugh let go. "It would make a good weapon in a pinch."

Jamie held the shaft in one hand and tapped the head against the open palm of his other. It was true. One blow could easily kill a man.

"I wonder," Jamie said. "The Golden Gate game is so

heavily stacked in your favor do you ever feel guilty about profiting off players' shattered dreams?"

Kavanaugh's back stiffened. "Not when I'm the one who makes it possible for them *to* dream." He smoothed his ruffled feathers. "Is it so bad to give people a ray of hope in their otherwise dreary lives? Besides, it's not like I have to twist anybody's arm to get them to play."

Kavanaugh straightened his tie. "I've never understood why numbers games are illegal. Men have been gambling since the dawn of history, and civilization hasn't collapsed yet. Even the disciples drew lots to decide who would replace Judas. My bet is, if you'll excuse the pun, if the government ever stops intruding in people's lives, there'll be state-run lotteries all across the nation."

Legalize, regulate, and tax. That's how Jamie would address gambling and every other so-called victimless crime.

Kavanaugh put his arm over the back of the pew. "Gambling provided only a small portion of my income."

Had Jamie heard correctly? "Provided? Past tense?"

"I told you I was making some big changes to Kavanaugh Enterprises."

"Changes your honest employees are going to like?"

"They would if they knew the changes would matter to them."

"You've lost me," Jamie said.

"The way I've structured Kavanaugh Enterprises, most of my employees don't even know they work for me. Kavanaugh Enterprises is a privately owned holding company consisting of an assortment of separate corporations. For instance, Pacific Culinary Arts Corporation owns dozens of restaurants. Few people realize I, or as I prefer the public to think, Pacific Culinary Arts owns such dining hallmarks as Dante's Seafood or Biaggi's Steakhouse." He gave a little laugh. "Just last month, I had a great meal in Ludwig's German Restaurant. I was so impressed I went to the manager who runs Pacific Culinary Arts for me and told him to look into buying Ludwig's. My man smiled and said I already owned it. And then there's Pacific Hardware Corporation. It owns Hardy's Hardware and a bunch of other well-known hardware stores."

"Do the names of all Kavanaugh Enterprises' corporations start with 'Pacific?' "

"They do. It's symbolic." He smiled. "I'll explain shortly."

"I assume there are advantages to Kavanaugh Enterprises holding a bunch of separate corporations," Jamie said.

"There are. If one of Kavanaugh Enterprises' corporations were to go bankrupt, its creditors couldn't touch the assets of any other corporation."

Kavanaugh settled back. "Not all my corporations are equally profitable. Pacific Transportation is the jewel in the crown of Kavanaugh Enterprises, primarily due to trucking."

"Trucking?" Jamie wouldn't have thought a man could gain Kavanaugh's apparent wealth through something as commonplace as trucking.

"I, or again, as I prefer the public to think, Pacific Transportation owns a piece of every trucking firm west of the Rockies. If someone's going to ship or receive goods from a port, railhead, or shipping dock anywhere in the Western States, they have to deal with me. Which means I set the price of transit. Consumables are my biggest money-maker."

"Excuse me. Did you say 'consumables?' "

"That's right. Things most people grossly undervalue: flour, sugar, milk, butter, coffee, meat ...."

Jamie tilted his head. "What's so special about consumables?"

"Think about it. Say a family is moving to a new house in another state, and I transport their household goods. That family may never move again, so I can't count on them becoming regular customers. Consumables are another story. They get used up. Then I get paid to transport another shipment, and then another, and another. In business terms, it's the difference between recurring income and non-recurring. And since most people fail to recognize the profit in consumables, potential competitors seldom try to horn in on my business."

"And there's nothing illegal about transporting consumables," Jamie said.

"That's the beauty of it. It's how I secure and maintain monopolies that can get ugly. That takes an army of enforcers and a large payroll." Kavanaugh's eyes bore into Jamie. "And a willingness to play rough."

Enforcers. What if someday Jamie stepped on Kavanaugh's toes?

"Don't worry," Kavanaugh said. "It's not as bad as it sounds. I use incentives, rarely coercion, to persuade business owners to become part of Kavanaugh Enterprises. Only when someone tries to take what's mine do I allow my men to use reasonable force—or if someone hurts one of my people."

Jamie shuddered—that from a man who seemed to think the whole world belonged to him.

"I only charge a tenth of a cent more than the free market would to ship a five-pound bag of flour. You might ask why, if I have a monopoly on transportation, don't I charge an arm and a leg ...." He took in a sharp breath.

"Sorry. That was insensitive, considering the ward you're on. Let me start over. Why don't I charge more? Because the government won't waste its limited resources trying to rein me in over a mere tenth of a cent. So, with relative impunity, I become a little richer every time a baker, restauranteur, or housewife uses a measure of flour. Same with sugar. And coffee. And the consumer barely feels the pinch."

"Yeah? What about those living on the edge of poverty?"

"I don't let anybody starve. I'm famous for the open cafeterias I operate throughout the West. Customers there are only asked to pay what they can afford—anywhere from what their meal would cost in the best cafeteria all the way down to nothing at all."

It was true. Kavanaugh's cafeterias were legendary for the quality and quantity of food they provided to those who were down and out. And the working classes loved him for it.

"I've often wondered how you can afford to feed so many people."

"It's simple arithmetic. The number of people who can afford to feed themselves far exceeds the number of those who can't. So, in effect, those who can end up feeding those who can't, and I look like Father Christmas."

Kavanaugh leaned forward. "How many people in the Western States do you think start every day with a slice of buttered toast and a spoonful of sugar in their coffee?" Kavanaugh smiled. "A tenth of a cent here, a tenth of a cent there may not sound like much. I'm sure a man with your mathematical training can appreciate that it adds up fast when you multiply each tenth of a cent by maybe twenty thousand a day."

"Clever," Jamie said. "Very clever. But what about your liquor interests? I seem to recall that Prohibition will make the production, *transport*, and sale of intoxicating liquors illegal. Won't that dry up—if you'll excuse *my* pun—your liquor business altogether?"

Kavanaugh laughed. "Hardly. What Prohibition's going to do is create a black market with soaring profits. And that will draw competitors out from under every rock."

Rachel had said almost the same thing.

"I have enough sense not to compete with those well-entrenched 'businessmen' on the East Coast. They've had generations to secure monopolies. And I leave the Midwest to those crazy Chicago gangsters." He raised his chin. "I told you including *Pacific* in the name of Kavanaugh Enterprises' corporations was symbolic. It's my way of putting potential competitors on notice that everything west of the Rockies is my territory."

A racketeer who knows his place. The man was smart. Real smart.

"And *Pacific* means peaceful," Kavanaugh added. "Which is the way I like things. Nice and peaceful. My business philosophy is that there's enough profit to go around, provided everybody sticks to their own territory. When they do, peace reigns. When they don't, I make it painfully clear to anyone who crosses the line that I'll go to war to keep the peace."

No course at Stanford could have given Jamie a better education in the brutality of the business world. Why hadn't he listened to Butch's warnings? *Leave now*, a voice was shouting in the back of Jamie's head. Then he remembered why he was in this conversation. Kavanaugh had a plan to protect the jobs of hundreds of his honest employees.

"Unfortunately," Kavanaugh said, "it will be war when Prohibition goes into effect. People aren't going to stop drinking. They'll just buy their alcohol on the black market and drive prices through the roof. Then, every two-bit punk will crawl out from under his rock and try to infest territory that belongs to someone else. There'll be turf wars, killings, you name it." Kavanaugh shook his head. "That's one reason I'm going to retire. I'll leave it to my nephew, Sonny, to fight those battles."

How likely was retirement for a man in Kavanaugh's position? "Can you really retire from the business empire you've built?"

"Sure. It's staying alive long enough to enjoy it that's the challenge."

You reap what you sow, Jamie might have said if Kavanaugh wasn't going to be a major contributor to the DVET.

"I'm sure even Sonny will want to settle a score with me when he learns how my retirement plans will affect his dreams."

"I knew Sonny when we were kids," Jamie said. "Or, more accurately, I knew of him. He was the stuff of nightmares for kids like me."

"Sonny was an only child who grew up around money and power," Kavanaugh said. "That does something to a kid. Seeing the kind of man he became, I wasn't nearly as sorry my son died along with his mother in the delivery room."

To hear Kavanaugh speak so dispassionately about the death of his wife and child scared Jamie.

Kavanaugh sighed. "Don't get me wrong. I loved my wife. Nieve was a wonderful woman. And I wanted a son more than I can tell you. I've never gotten over losing Nieve. But at least I didn't have to suffer the heartbreak of seeing Liam—that's the name I put on his birth and death certificates." He blinked several times. "I didn't have to suffer the heartbreak of seeing Liam grow up to be such a sorry excuse for a human being as Sonny has become."

That was harsh. Granted, Sonny was a jackass, but would any son be able to live up to Kavanaugh's standards?

"Perhaps the biggest mistake of my career," Kavanaugh said, "was letting it be known soon after RK died that Sonny would take the reins of Kavanaugh Enterprises when I retire. Believing he'll someday be in charge has gone to Sonny's head. He thinks he'll be able to do things his way. That would be a disaster for my employees. I've tried to teach Sonny to get what he wants through negotiation and mediation and to resort to violence—controlled and strategic—only when reason fails. It's been impossible to get through to him. To this day, his first reaction in any situation is to resort to violence, which he seems to enjoy applying himself."

Kavanaugh stared at the floor. "I hate to say it, but I believe Sonny is what psychologists call a psychopath." He raised his chin and looked down at Jamie. "If you don't know what that is, I'll tell you: it's someone like Sonny who thinks he's the center of the universe. Someone who totally disregards and freely violates the rights, feelings, and safety of others." Kavanaugh's face was turning red. "That definition has described Sonny since he was a kid, and he's only gotten worse. He never shows remorse for any of the cruel things he does or empathy for his victims. On top of that, he has a remarkable disregard for the law."

That was the harshest assessment of anyone Jamie had ever heard. But probably warranted. "You've pretty much described Sonny as I knew him," Jamie said.

Kavanaugh stared at the cross at the front of the chapel. "One of the big changes to Kavanaugh Enterprises is that

I've transferred all my liquor distribution and gambling interests to Sonny."

Another startling revelation. Jamie gave it a moment's thought. "On the surface, that seems generous, but won't *both* those lines of business be illegal once Prohibition goes into effect?"

Kavanaugh leaned back and nodded. "Sonny won't mind. Profits will be unlimited for those willing to take risks."

All these revelations were interesting, but .... "I'm not sure why you're telling me all this. How is it related to saving the jobs of your *honest* employees?"

"That's the point. Having disposed of my liquor and gambling interest, *all* my remaining employees are honest."

"Really." There was another part of Kavanaugh Enterprises that greatly troubled Jamie. "What about your 'Pacific Businessmen's Club?' "

"PBC? What about it?"

"Rumors say it's a front for half a dozen high-class whorehouses." Normally, Jamie wouldn't have used the term 'whore' because it unfairly put women with diverse stories into one group 'polite' society condemned unquestioningly. He used it in this instance because he wanted to see Kavanaugh's reaction.

His reaction was immediate. And adamant. "That's not true."

It would take more than a simple denial to convince Jamie otherwise.

Kavanaugh closed his eyes and rubbed his temples.

"Are you all right," Jamie said.

"Not really. I've been getting these damn headaches for months now. They used to come only in the morning. Lately

...." He leaned back and looked at Jamie. "Would you mind if we take a break? I can't concentrate right now, and there's more you should know about Kavanaugh Enterprises. If I sit here quietly by myself for fifteen or twenty minutes, I should be able to set your mind at ease concerning my Pacific Businessman's Club."

Jamie shrugged. "I could use a break myself. How about I get some air and then come back in half an hour?"

Jamie found a sun-drenched bench outside the chapel that provided a great view of the bay. He was relieved to have a break. It would give him time to process all Kavanaugh's revelations.

Jamie found it surprising that Kavanaugh had wanted to be a priest. And sad that his father's death necessitated leaving school early to help support his remaining family. It was mildly interesting that Kavanaugh had been a boxer in his late teens and had taken a beating tallying a twelve-and-oh record. It was a pleasant surprise that soon, Kavanaugh Enterprises would no longer have any liquor or gambling interests. But so what? As far as Jamie could see, none of that was relevant to saving the jobs of hundreds of Kavanaugh's honest, hardworking men and women or furthering his charities.

Nevertheless, Jamie wanted to know more. And that worried him. Was it a prurient interest, or was he really hoping for good news about the Pacific Businessman's Club? Perhaps he'd learn something that would ease his conscience about working with Kavanaugh on the DVET. Kavanaugh wasn't a fool, so maybe PBC wasn't the sordid kind of establishment rumors said it was.

* * *

As though no time had passed, Mr. Kavanaugh picked up their conversation where it left off. "Let me tell you about my Pacific Businessman's Club, its origin, what it's become, and its future."

Jamie sat. "I'm listening."

"I've shown you I'm good with numbers. The 'Elders' I ran numbers for noticed." He looked at Jamie. "I'm talking ancient history now, a quarter-century ago, okay?"

Jamie nodded.

"The Elders drafted me to keep books for a saloon they owned. Gallagher's, it was called. I'd never been to the place and knew practically nothing about it. That didn't matter. Numbers are numbers. Plain and simple. I did such a good job keeping their books that the Elders wanted to promote me to manager. That sounded good, but when I went to the place, it only took a minute to realize I'd been keeping books for a sleazy knocking shop. I told the Elders there was no way I would lower myself to managing a whorehouse."

"Good for you," Jamie said.

"No, bad for me. The Elders weren't the kind of men to take no for an answer."

"Are you saying you were forced into managing their brothel?"

"That's exactly what I'm saying. Fortunately, I wasn't a complete fool. I did what I've been doing in every tight situation since I was a kid. I negotiated—a skill that's gotten me to where I am today. Even though I had no leverage, the Elders agreed that I could do whatever I wanted with Gallagher's so long as the place made a profit."

Jamie hoped that somehow this would lead to Kavanaugh's involvement in the brothel business being, as he claimed, ancient history.

"I changed everything once I was in charge," Kavanaugh said. "The Elders treated their girls like cattle. I treated them as ladies and customers as gentlemen—so long as they followed my rules. And I made sure they followed my rules by hiring the biggest, most intimidating enforcers I could find and paying them well."

Kavanaugh adjusted his diamond cufflinks. "My management style practically guaranteed my house made a profit. The Elders were so pleased they gave me raise after raise. And every time I got a raise, I made sure my men knew it by giving them one as well. That earned their loyalty."

"I'm confused," Jamie said. "You told me you weren't in the brothel business. But all I've heard so far is how you got into that wretched business."

"And now you're going to hear how I got out. As the manager of Gallagher's, it wasn't long before I realized prostitution is a poor way to make money. I'd bet less than fifteen percent of American males have paid for sex, ever. On the other hand, I'd bet more than eighty-five percent would be happy to pay for an opportunity to spend time with an attractive woman in a pleasant social setting. So, I set about transforming Gallagher's. I used the Elder's money to buy the warehouse next door, knocked down the wall that separated us, installed a dance floor, and filled the place with comfortable furniture. I eliminated the sale of hard liquor and made only weak beer available—for a considerable markup. And before the Elders knew it, I was managing a legitimate workingmen's club, and I put whoremongering behind me, *forever*." He straightened his tie, a habit that was getting on Jamie's nerves. "Only then could I hold my head up in society again."

What an amazing story. And just as amazing? Jamie believed it.

Kavanaugh smiled, displaying teeth almost too perfect to be real. "After a while, I asked myself, why manage when you can own?"

It was hard to imagine Kavanaugh as anything other than the boss.

"I had enough muscle working for me by then that I was able to persuade the Elders to sell out to me—at a very reasonable price. Then, I used the profits from my working-men's club to branch out. I opened my first trucking company. Quickly followed by my first laundry, my first building contractor, my first secretarial service—and eventually the first of half a dozen chapters of the Pacific Business-men's Club, each in a different major west coast city and each having its own clubhouse."

Jamie stopped diddling with his cane. "What exactly is this club of yours if not what the rumors say?"

"Rumors be damned. PBC's clubhouses are places where well-to-do men of social standing can get away for a while. Quiet environments where men of substance associate with others of their kind. Places where business deals are made that could only be made between members of the same club. Retreats where the well-heeled are attended to by lovely young ladies I've trained to be as cultured as debutantes."

"That all sounded fine," Jamie said, "until you mentioned being attended to by 'lovely young ladies.' That's what the rumors are about. The young ladies and their attendance. And yet, your club is popular among the rich." Jamie crossed his arms. "Why would a man of social standing want to join the Pacific Businessman's Club and put his reputation at risk."

"There's not a successful businessman west of the Rockies who doesn't know that if he wants to get ahead and stay ahead, he'd be well served to join. And there wouldn't be a prosperous man left standing if membership was damaging to a businessman's reputation."

"So, you're saying the rumors about the 'extraordinary services' your women provide aren't true?"

Kavanaugh set his jaw. "I didn't say that. But you should know by now I'm not stupid. I do not allow anything of a sexual nature to take place on the premises of one of PBC's clubhouses."

Kavanaugh assumed a fatherly tone. "Most rumors are the product of jealousy, wouldn't you agree? I'm sure the rumors you've heard were started by someone who wanted to be a member but who wouldn't fit in."

"Okay. Forget the rumors. But there has to be more to your club than simply a pleasant gathering place where deals are made."

"There is. There's one benefit I especially enjoy myself— at no cost to me, of course—but for which members pay a considerable additional fee. That's the privilege of having one or more of my young ladies accompany them on an outing to a concert, the theater, the best restaurant, or the like. Essentially, on a date."

Now, they were getting somewhere. "A date with a guaranteed happy ending?"

Kavanaugh's eyes narrowed. "There are no guarantees in

life. Only probabilities. If extraordinary services are requested, the answer might be yes. But, like any date, that's completely up to the lady. If she says no, the answer's no."

"And if the lady says yes?"

Kavanaugh raised his chin. "That would be none of my business—so long as she's happy with the gift she receives for her efforts. A gift, mind you. Not payment."

Who was Kavanaugh trying to fool, himself or Jamie? One "no" too many from a particular young lady, and Jamie would bet she'd be looking for another job. If there was a distinction between Kavanaugh's "young ladies" and prostitutes, it wasn't apparent to Jamie.

Kavanaugh assumed his fatherly tone again. "Let me tell you about my young ladies. I only hire women who come to me by referral from either club members or employees. I never recruit, ever. And before I place a woman into one of PBC's clubhouses, I offer her a job in one of Kavanaugh Enterprises' more conventional businesses."

Kavanaugh drummed his fingers on the back of the pew. "I don't claim to be a saint or a social worker. My job offers are decidedly lopsided. Hard work in difficult circumstances versus easy work in pleasant surroundings for three times the pay. Easily ninety percent of my referees opt to work in one of PBC's clubhouses rather than in, say, one of Kavanaugh Enterprises' laundries. And a young lady can leave at any time, for any reason—no questions asked. Or if a young lady wants a change after a while, I'll accommodate her in one of Kavanaugh Enterprises' other lines of business."

Jamie's assumption still stood that only a woman with no real choice would work in one of PBC's clubhouses.

"Some say I exploit my young ladies. I say ask one how she likes working for me. Or you could have asked your friend Butch how I treat them. Some of my young ladies have chosen to stay with me for years."

"What happens when a woman's no longer young and pretty enough to appeal to your club members?"

"If she stays with me and follows my rules long enough, she doesn't have to worry about her future. When the time comes, she can have an easy job in one of Kavanaugh Enterprises' other businesses. And there are more subtle advantages to working for me. If, after a while, a young lady prefers to set off on her own, with the cultural training I give her, she can re-emerge in society as a new person at a much higher social level than when she came to me."

Jamie's mind was reeling. Could all this be true? He wished he could ask Butch.

"Obviously, it's not all wine and roses for my young ladies. But in return for their best efforts, I give them unsurpassed benefits. Excellent room and board, fine clothes, lots of money—and protection." He put his hand over the bulge under his jacket. "No one would dare raise a hand to one of my young ladies."

And all these pretty young women have to do is occasionally have sex with random, rich, pitiful old men. Such an arrangement trampled all over the respect Jamie believed women deserved. If he implicitly condoned it by working with Kavanaugh, how could he face his sister, or Rachel, or Nurse Eliot?

"You mentioned that you've arranged a goodly number of successful marriages between pillars of society and beautiful young women half their age," Jamie said. "I assume you mean marriages to one of your young ladies."

"No. I mean marriages to 'special' referees to PBC. And matchmaking is nothing to be ashamed of. Plus, it's something I enjoy. It's more or less a hobby of mine—a profitable one, I'll admit."

"What do you mean, 'special' referees?"

"Referees to the Club who possess a certain level of sophistication, orphans with no siblings and not yet jaded by this cynical world of ours. I offer them special training. A young woman who accepts doesn't have to work in one of PBC's clubhouses. Instead, I groom her with a private tutor, and when the time is right, I introduce her to a select club member." Kavanaugh leaned back and smiled. "I'm happy to say, for a price only the wealthiest can afford, I've arranged almost two dozen successful marriages between one of my special young ladies and a prosperous gentleman who's at least twice her age. And I make sure it remains an amicable marriage."

"How's that possible?"

"I selected my gentleman very carefully, and I make sure husband and wife know I'm watching them." Kavanaugh's menacing expression said the rest.

"I hate to think of a young woman being tied to some old man while her life slips away," Jamie said.

Kavanaugh smiled his conniving smile. "Why do you think I match my special young ladies with men at least twice their age? They just have to be dutiful wives while waiting in luxury for their husbands to succumb to old age. Then they become rich widows free to do as they please."

"How cold-hearted."

"I don't know. Most of my special young ladies developed a real affection for their husbands. And arranged marriages are nothing new. Queen Victoria's marriage to Prince Albert worked out just fine."

One thing Jamie knew for sure. He'd sooner die an

elderly bachelor than be a party to one of Kavanaugh's arranged marriages.

Kavanaugh pasted on a smile he seemed capable of displaying at will. "Now that I've set the record straight, I want you to know I'm in the process of selling my Pacific Businessman's Clubs."

Another surprise from a man full of surprises. "Mind telling me why?"

"I don't want to take the chance of some future director of Kavanaugh Enterprises turning one of its assets into what you so indelicately referred to as a whorehouse."

Would the man never run out of surprises?

"Of course," Kavanaugh said, "now that I'm selling PBC, I won't be able to continue matchmaking, so I'll need to find a new hobby. I'm thinking of gardening."

Jamie laughed. "Come on. I can't imagine a man like you puttering around in a garden."

Kavanaugh shrugged. "You never know what interests others might have."

That was true. Nobody ever guessed that Jamie's hobby was building model sailing ships—something he hadn't had time for in years.

"As for the major corporations that belong to Kavanaugh Enterprises, I'm proud to say Pacific Building Supply is the biggest construction supplier on the West Coast."

"You're not a builder yourself?"

"No. A builder's income is too inconsistent. Most work only one project at a time. Then, they have to look for another project. As a supplier, my income is much more steady. There's always a builder somewhere in my territory who needs supplies."

"That makes sense," Jamie said.

"Kavanaugh Enterprises also holds major plumbing, heating, and electrical contractors, a chain of laundries, a secretarial service, a taxi company—and more. I'm sure you get the picture. The people who work for those companies are honest, hardworking men and women, many with families. Oh, and I also own a handful of bakeries." He patted his stomach. "My bakeries are my greatest weakness since I don't drink, gamble, or smoke."

Jamie was momentarily dumbfounded. Next, Kavanaugh would claim he could walk on water. "What about the companionship of your young ladies?"

"I said my bakeries were my greatest weakness. I didn't say they were my only one."

No drinking. No gambling. No smoking. He was making himself out to be a model citizen. But what explained Kavanaugh's occasional slurred speech and unsteady steps if he didn't drink?

As he often did after making a point, Kavanaugh straightened his tie. "Any questions?"

The man had gone to great lengths trying to justify himself. As far as Jamie was concerned, his efforts fell woefully short. "Do I have any questions? I have a thousand. The most pressing being, why have you *really* told me all of this?"

"Until recently, Sonny thought he'd take over Kavanaugh Enterprises when I'm gone. I can't let that happen. He'd be my employees' worst nightmare. He'd liquidate the majority of my businesses in a heartbeat and turn the remainder into a cesspool of crime. And I'd be shocked if he ever gave a penny to charity." Kavanaugh shook his head. "Instead, I'm in the process of placing Kavanaugh Enterprises in a business trust."

Jamie didn't know the first thing about business and certainly not business trusts. "To what end?"

"First of all, to keep Kavanaugh Enterprises out of Sonny's hands. Once everything's in a trust, control will be in the hands of a trustee who will have a fiduciary duty to act in the best interests of the trust's beneficiaries."

"And they are?"

"My employees and charities"

That brought a smile to Jamie's face. "I'd hate to be around when Sonny finds out it's not going to be him."

"He's already found out. With all the lawyers, bankers, and accountants involved in such a complex transaction, Sonny didn't have to look far to find someone he could bribe into breaching his duty of confidentiality and telling Sonny everything he wanted to know."

Kavanagh leaned back and crossed his arms. "Of course, I have informants of my own. I know Sonny's plans. He intends to pressure my trustee into embezzling profits and sharing the proceeds with him."

"Then you'll have to find a trustee Sonny can't intimidate."

"I believe I have." Kavanaugh looked Jamie up and down. "Someone of exceptional intelligence and bravery who's distinguished himself in peace and in war."

Jamie still didn't understand why .... His jaw dropped so far he was surprised it didn't bounce off the floor. "You can't possibly have me in mind!"

Kavanaugh smiled. "I'll just say you're in the running, and the competition has yet to leave the starting blocks."

"That's insane! You hardly know me!"

"Nothing in the law says a trustor has to know his trustee." Kavanaugh leaned toward Jamie. "I've had someone like you in mind since one of my contacts told me about you several months ago. When my man Butch was placed on your ward, I realized I didn't have to settle for someone *like* you. I could have the genuine article. Now that we've met, I'm convinced you're the man for the job."

Jamie would have laughed if Kavanaugh hadn't seemed so sincere. "The whole idea is absurd. I'm a scientist. I don't know the first thing about running a business."

Kavanaugh did laugh. "Lord have mercy. I don't want you to run my businesses. That's what general managers are for."

"Then hire a competent general manager and forget about me."

"General managers have too much freedom. Trustees are legally obligated to manage the trust's assets in the best interests of the beneficiaries."

"That leaves me out. I couldn't manage a lemonade stand."

"Your GM will handle day-to-day operations. Your job will be to direct the trust's long-term course."

Jamie sat back and stared at Kavanaugh. "That's all?"

"That's a lot. You'll advise and consent on all manner of things: acquisitions, investments, divestments, you name it. Think of yourself as the trust's navigator, or more in keeping with my intentions, the trust's moral compass."

Jamie almost choked. "Moral compass? Yesterday, I agreed to join you in a scheme to defraud the Bureau of Internal Revenue. What kind of moral compass could I be?"

"You merely agreed not to stand in the way of my plan to increase the funding of a worthwhile charity. When you're in charge, do things your way. As trustee, you'll have as much say as you want about business matters and which charities the Trust supports, and by what means. And you'll like this. My declaration of trust specifically states that all future Kavanaugh Trust transactions must be carried out in strict accord with the letter and spirit of the law."

Jamie stared at Kavanaugh. Was this a scam? "That's quite a turnaround for you, isn't it?"

"Regardless, don't you think you'd be doing society a notable service by reforming Kavanaugh Enterprises?"

Jamie didn't have to think for very long. "Someone would be. But me? I don't think so."

Kavanaugh put his arm over the back of the pew. "You could help a lot of people. Not just my employees and those who depend on my charities, but innumerable others who interact with them."

Kavanaugh scooted forward. "To be clear, I'm not offering you a gift. You'll be compensated well, but you'll earn every cent. The business world is brutal. It will take someone with guts and determination to steer the trust on the right course regardless of the consequences. And when I'm gone, no doubt Sonny will try to intimidate you into cutting him in on the profits. And as you know, Sonny doesn't play fair. It will take courage to stand up to him— which you demonstrated you have in abundance by what you did France."

"I wasn't all that brave. I just did what had to be done."

Kavanaugh smiled. "Exactly. And now someone has to stand up to Sonny."

"If your trustee—whoever he might be—refuses to cooperate with Sonny, wouldn't that be a good way to get hurt?"

"I've thought of that. My declaration of trust makes it crystal clear that if anything bad happens to you, your family, your friends, your household, or any of the trust's officers over the next five years, and there's even a hint that Sonny was involved, the trust will be dissolved, and all its assets will immediately become yours, free and clear." Kavanaugh smiled. "That will have Sonny praying that you or anyone else in your world won't catch so much as a cold over the next five years."

"Hang on. I haven't agreed to serve as your trustee. And what's this about five years?"

"I'll clarify that once I have your word you'll faithfully serve as my trustee. For now, I'll just say you'll like it."

"Your audacity astounds me. Do you really expect me to accept a job I'm not qualified for, knowing I'll make an enemy of a dangerous man like Sonny?"

Kavanaugh shrugged. "Didn't you say you missed the danger and excitement of the war? Sonny will give you a taste of that." Kavanaugh crossed his arms. "Think of it as banding together with my employees and those who can't feed themselves against Sonny and his men. That should give you a similar sense of family to what you had with your infantry company."

Kavanaugh was right. In some ways, reforming Kavanaugh Enterprises would be like the war. But a different war. A war that made sense to Jamie.

And someone had to stand up to the likes of Sonny. Damn it, Jamie *needed* to stand up to Sonny to prove to himself that he was no longer afraid of bullies. In fact, Sonny should be afraid of him. Odds were, he'd never faced a man who'd been raised from the dead.

"I'm not asking for a commitment today," Kavanaugh said. "Think about it for a week or two. But bear in mind that I'm up against a deadline. It's imperative that I know your decision before mid-June."

Jamie folded his arms. "It occurs to me that there might be a deeper motive behind the Kavanaugh Trust. A man about to retire knows he's closer to the end of his life than the beginning. You wouldn't be trying to earn your way into heaven, would you?"

Kavanaugh looked to the cross. "I know that's not possible. I just want to do the right thing. And I'm asking you to help."

Jamie studied Kavanaugh for a moment or two. His instincts told him the man really did want to make things right. And after all he'd been through, Jamie was confident he could handle the job of trustee—and Sonny.

Something Butch said popped into Jamie's mind. *Mister Kavanaugh feasts on people who claim they can take care of themselves.* If Jamie agreed to serve as Kavanaugh's trustee, he was afraid he'd be offering himself up as an appetizer.

Chapter 26

Blessings

Friday, 23 May 1919

Jamie was back in his private room, reclining on his bed with his hands behind his head, fingers interleaved. He'd played his part in the war against the obstacles that stood in the way of the men's rehabilitation so well that the Brotherhood he created could now continue the fight without him. That meant Jamie needed a different war to fight if his life was to have purpose. Could reforming Kavanaugh Enterprises fit the bill?

He wished he could discuss the question with someone. No, not someone. Nurse Eliot. But in her mind, he might be just another patient, whereas she was becoming everything to him.

He had better find the courage to tell her how he felt about her, and soon. He couldn't stay in the hospital forever. He had a life to live with or without her. And inevitably, she'd be moving on to her next duty assignment.

The Army had little reason to keep him at Letterman

much longer. He could walk again, and he'd convinced his doctors that he'd fully recovered from his shell shock. Sadly, he hadn't. A sight, a sound, a taste, a touch, a smell—little things most people wouldn't even notice still triggered paralyzing memories of the battles he fought. He could cope while in the company of his fellow patients and the caring medical staff. Beyond his hospital ward, the world would be a dangerous place.

A knock on his door interrupted Jamie's thoughts.

"Good afternoon, Major Collins," his visitor said. His voice was loud and cheerful. He held a salute.

Jamie stood and returned his salute. "Please, come in. What can I do for you?"

The man was so tall he practically had to duck under the header of Jamie's doorframe. His standard-issue army glasses looked tiny on his broad face.

"I'm Captain Christianson of the Judge Advocate General's Corps. I believe I have some good news for you."

"I could use some good news." Jamie indicated his straight-backed, armless guest chair. "Have a seat." Jamie sat on the edge of his bed.

Christianson sat. He opened the flap of his soft-sided briefcase and removed a sheaf of paper. He balanced his briefcase on his lap, turning it into a makeshift desk. "Sir, this is the last will and testament of Private Anthony Lightner, recently deceased."

"Really. He's only been dead five days."

"Sir, I'm sure you can appreciate that in a hospital, a will often becomes effective soon after it's written."

"What's Lightner's will have to do with me?"

"Sir, Private Lightner named you the sole beneficiary of his estate, which is considerable."

Jamie sat up straight. "Are you serious?"

"Yes, sir."

"Butch left everything to me?"

"Butch, sir?"

"That's what we called Lightner when we were kids."

"Sounds like you've known him for some time, sir."

"Since grade school." Jamie thought back to the fun they used to have before Butch's family crisis, and the many times he hid from the bully Butch became. "This has to be a mistake. What about his relatives?"

Captain Christianson centered the will on his improvised lap desk. "Sir, Lightner had no living relatives."

"I'm amazed Butch would honor me in this way." Jamie wiped his forehead. "You say he left me his entire estate?"

"Yes, sir." Christianson offered a copy of the will to Jamie. "If you don't want to wade through all the legalese, sir, I'll be happy to point out the highlights for you."

"Please do." The archaic legal language on the front page was about as easy to follow as hieroglyphics scrawled across a sheet of papyrus.

"Private Lightner—"

"Butch," Jamie said.

"Right you are, sir. Butch." Christianson turned to the will's second page. "Sir, I direct your attention to Page Two, where 'Butch' says, 'Major Jamie Collins, Medal of Honor recipient, is the only true friend I've ever had. He stuck by me through the worst of times, even when I tried to push him away. Jamie gave me something far more valuable than material goods. He gave me hope that someday, my past will be forgotten, and I can be remembered as a man of honor. I'm therefore happy to leave all my earthly possessions to my friend Jamie Collins.'"

It took Jamie a moment to find his voice. "I'm over-whelmed," he said. "You never know the impact you have on someone."

Christianson smiled. "True, sir. Very true."

"I'm surprised by the language in this part of Butch's will. It's so personal and informal. Is that normal?"

Christianson covered the will with his gigantic hand. "Sir, this document was prepared with the help of a lawyer in my detachment. It's standard procedure for us to visit a soldier before a serious operation and review or create his will. My colleague told me Butch was more than eager to do so. I assure you this will is completely valid and would with-stand any challenge."

Jamie stood and walked to his window. He hadn't both-ered to look outside since moving back into his old room. The colors of the ornamental shrubs and flowers he could see outside his window were more vibrant than he remembered. The dancing shadows cast by the afternoon sun as it filtered through the branches of the cypress trees were more dynamic. The entire world was a brighter place. He turned back to the captain. "I'm humbled to learn that Butch thought so highly of me."

Captain Christianson leaned forward. "Let me read you another provision that can be found further on." There was the rustling of paper. "Ah, here it is. 'With respect to BayView, the house in Pacific Grove I bequeath to Jamie Collins, it's my desire that he fill it with happiness, as my grandparents would have wished.'"

Captain Christianson removed his glasses and massaged the bridge of his nose. "Sir, I'm sorry I never got to meet Butch. He sounds like quite a guy."

Jamie glanced toward Lieutenant Walberg's old room.

"Butch lived a lonely, tragic life. Few people ever got to see the good in him. But in the end, I'm happy to say the world got to see who Anthony Lightner really was."

Captain Christianson was silent for a moment. "A good ending to a sad story, sir?"

"I assume you know Butch would have received a dishonorable discharge once he was well enough to leave the hospital."

"Yes, sir. And I believe I have good news for you in that regard as well." Captain Christianson extracted a sheet of paper from his briefcase and read it to Jamie. "A service member who was adjudged a punitive discharge at a court-martial and then dies before the appellate review process is complete is considered to have died on active duty under honorable conditions."

Jamie stared at Christianson. "You mean Butch's records won't show that he was dishonorably discharged?"

"That's right, sir."

"That's *great* news." Jamie reached out. "May I have that sheet of paper?"

"Certainly, sir. I have the original in my office."

"Thank you very much. This should make a big difference in the way Butch is remembered."

An hour after Captain Christianson left, big Charlie Gowan, Letterman's master prosthetics craftsman, knocked on Jamie's door. "Can you spare me a few minutes of your time, Jamie, sir?"

Jamie smiled at Charlie's slow, melodic, southern drawl. It took President Lincoln two to three minutes to deliver the

Gettysburg Address. Jamie figured it would have taken Charlie twice as long. "I'll be happy to." Jamie always enjoyed spending time with Charlie.

"I promised to see Sergeant Binney first. He's a changed man since the flu almost killed him. Nurse Hobbes said he wants to know if there's anythin' I can make that will enable him to stand."

"Is there?"

"Certainly. He should even be able to walk short distances. And with the aid of crutches, there's no telling how far he'll be able to go. I offered to help him the day he arrived. You knows how he was. He told me where to stick my prosthetics—which I'm sure would have been a very uncomfortable experience, if not anatomically impossible."

Jamie laughed. "I can only imagine."

Charlie looked at his watch. "Say we meet in my workshop in fifteen minutes? I got something I'd like to show you."

"I have a feeling I'm going to like it."

Charlie ran the back of his hand across his forehead. "I sure hope so."

After Charlie left, Jamie self-consciously moved down the boulevard and headed for Charlie's workshop. He felt out of place now that he was no longer one of the brethren.

Charlie hadn't arrived yet. Like a kid secretly playing with another kid's toys, Jamie picked up a power hand drill. The thing was so new on the market Jamie had never held one before. He put a bit in the chuck and bore several holes in a piece of pine he found in Charlie's scrap bin. The door opened. Charlie lumbered in.

Caught in the act! With a guilty grin, Jamie held up the

drill and the scrap wood. "Goes through pine like ...." Jamie tried to think of a good example.

"Like money through the hands of a drunken soldier?" Charlie said. They both laughed.

Jamie reverently set the drill down on Charlie's workbench. "What's up, Charlie?"

Charlie absentmindedly picked up the drill and knocked the sawdust out of the twists in the bit. "Remember the other day I told you I'd be leaving the army soon and settin' up my own shop?"

"Sure. I'm happy for you."

"I was only gonna do furniture and guns. But a couple of doctors been encouragin' me to carry on makin' prosthetics."

Jamie smiled. "I think you should. It's an important job, and you're good at it." From his grin, Jamie guessed Charlie wasn't used to being complimented.

Charlie picked up a brush and dustpan and swept up the sawdust Jamie had left on his otherwise immaculate workbench. "I heard through the grapevine that you is a professor of physics."

"Word travels fast."

"Here's the deal." Charlie laid a notebook on his workbench. "Durin' my time at Letterman, I been asked to make all kinds of medical devices." He opened his notebook at random and flipped through several pages. "These is sketches of just a few of 'em."

Jamie was impressed. "They aren't just sketches. They're more like detailed schematics."

Charlie smiled. "I've decided to carry on makin' medical devices. I'm gonna call that part of my business 'Advanced Medical Devices.' " Charlie's eye began to twitch. "The work we done on Toby's foot and Carl's typewriter proves that we works well together. I'd like you to be AMD's technical advisor—and before you says no, let me tell you what I have in mind." He pointed to his notebook. "I thought of a dozen ways to make each of these devices. My problem was I wasted a lot of time and effort decidin' which way would be best. In the future, I'd like to run my ideas past you before gettin' too deep into a project and hear what approach you think I should take." Charlie's other eye began twitching in unison with its neighbor. "Together, we could make some really useful devices and maybe improve a few lives along the way."

The idea appealed to Jamie. Applying his scientific expertise to something as important as medical devices would be great. "You do realize I'm a physicist and not an engineer, don't you?"

"You is trained in science, ain't you?"

"Absolutely."

"I'll take care of the engineering if you'll just tell me whether you thinks my ideas are scientifically sound."

Jamie thought about it for a moment. "That actually makes sense."

"I hoped you'd see things my way," Charlie said. "On AMD's letterhead, I'd list me as owner and you as technical adviser with all your academic credentials. Your name and stature would give AMD instant credibility." Charlie took a deep breath. "I wouldn't be askin' for anythin' more than a bit of your time." He closed his notebook. "What do you think? Will you at least consider my proposal?"

Jamie put his hands in his pockets. "Would you, by any chance, be thinking of compensating me?"

Charlie laughed nervously. "I forgot to mention that." His hand began to shake in time with his twitching eyes.

Jamie was concerned to see Charlie turning into a nervous wreck right in front of him. "Relax, Charlie. I'm with you so far."

"I'll p ... pay you a monthly retainer, plus a fair percentage of the profits from anythin' you helps me with, proportional to your efforts."

"And who decides the proportion?"

"We do." Charlie canted his head. "If you don't trust me to be fair, we probably shouldn't do business together."

Jamie smiled. "I trust you, and I'm honored that you trust me."

"Never a doubt, Jamie, sir. Never a doubt." Charlie looked past his twitch and locked eyes with Jamie. "There's one thing I needs to tell you straight up, somethin' I won't budge on. Before divvyin' up any profits, I'll be givin' one-tenth to charity. And if we ever gets to the point where we is manufacturin' one of our devices, I'll be givin' every tenth one to a clinic somewhere in the US that provides free care to folks who can't afford to pay for it."

It would have been cruel to keep Charlie in suspense any longer. Jamie stuck out his hand. "Sign me up."

Charlie hesitated. "Just like that?"

"I was tempted to come on board even before you mentioned tithing. Your spirit of generosity sealed the deal."

Charlie's nervous symptoms disappeared in a flash. He pumped Jamie's hand so vigorously Jamie was afraid he might have to ice it later—if Charlie ever let go.

* * *

Monday, 26 May 1919

The rumor that Jamie would soon be discharged from the hospital spread like wildfire. If true, it would be the height of ingratitude if he left without first thanking Colonel Thornburgh for the excellent care he'd received.

The instant the colonel's civil service secretary ushered him into Thornburgh's office, Jamie became mesmerized by the view through the bank of bowed windows behind the colonel's desk. "What an incredible view of the bay you have, sir. The Golden Gate, Sausalito, Alcatraz, and all those colorful sailboats."

Thornburgh followed Jamie's gaze. "If I hadn't arranged my desk so my back was to it, I'd never get any work done." He got up and moved to the front of his desk.

Jamie snapped out of his trance and shook the colonel's extended hand.

"Doctor Crandall tells me you'll be leaving us soon," Colonel Thornburgh said.

"Then it must be true. Did he happen to say when?"

" 'Fraid not."

"You and your staff pulled off a miracle to get me back on my feet and walking again. I just had to come thank you for all you've done for me."

The colonel smiled. "You're one of our greatest success stories, and we couldn't be happier for you."

Jamie sighed. "I only wish every orthopedic patient could walk away whole."

Colonel Thornburgh indicated one of the chairs in front of his desk. "Please, sit." Jamie obeyed. The CO sat in a twin chair next to him. "What are your plans now that you'll soon be leaving us?"

"Sir, I'll be on terminal leave for the next month. Then, the army will automatically transfer me to the retired rolls, and I'll be a civilian again. In the fall, I'll return to Stanford and resume teaching and working toward tenure."

Colonel Thornburgh interleaved his fingers across his ample belly. "That will give you what—a nice four-month vacation before facing your students again?"

"Yes, sir. And I plan to enjoy it." Jamie cast his gaze over the bay and smiled. "I'm hoping to spend some time in the city with a young lady I've met. And I'll take the train down the coast to Pacific Grove to see the house Private Lightner left me."

"Wait." Colonel Thornburgh squinted at Jamie. "Lightner left you a house?"

"Not only a house, his entire estate, which is worth more than I could earn in a lifetime."

Thornburgh sat back and gripped the arms of his chair. "Then why are you going back to teaching?"

It was a fair question. "It's what I love to do."

For a moment, the CO seemed lost in thought. "Lightner's attempt to save that other patient tells me he was no coward."

"I'm sure you're right, sir. He told me about the circumstances that led to him shooting himself, and I can tell you, despite all I've seen and been through, they traumatized me just hearing about them."

Thornburgh nodded. "I have no doubt he was firmly in the grip of shell shock when he shot himself. And it would be almost impossible to fake a catatonic state of any length of time, let alone for a month."

Jamie took a deep breath. "Sir, is there any way we could re-submit his lieutenant's recommendation for the Silver Star Medal?"

"I don't know." Colonel Thornburgh stood and walked

to the bank of windows behind his desk. "I'd be surprised if the army would even consider giving a man who was to receive a dishonorable discharge a medal for valor."

"Sir, a lawyer from the Judge Advocate General Corps gave me this." Jamie reached into his jacket pocket and pulled out the sheet of paper Captain Christianson gave him. He read the regulation out loud.

"Does that mean Lightner's records won't show that he would have received a dishonorable discharge?" Colonel Thornburgh said.

"That right, sir. And the actions that led to Lightner's Silver Star recommendation occurred well before he shot himself. I'm sure you agree that his attempt to save Lieutenant Walberg was above and beyond the call of duty." Jamie sat up straight. "Don't you think a posthumous award of the Silver Star is justified?"

Colonel Thornburgh stopped pacing. "I've been trying to get the army to recognize shell shock as a legitimate ailment. Lightner's case strengthens my argument." The colonel slammed his palm down on a stack of reference books perched on his desk. "Hell, I'll re-submit the recommendation myself."

Jamie jumped to his feet. "Thank you, sir. Thank you very much."

Thornburgh waved his hand dismissively. "There's something you can do for me if you don't mind me asking."

"Just name it, sir."

"My wife's old college roommate is married to a man named Samuel Finley Brown Morse, a distant relative of the inventor of the telegraph. Sam's an engineer down near your hometown."

Jamie had no idea where this was heading.

"The thing is, the four of us were having dinner together last weekend, and your story came up, you being one of Letterman's greatest success stories. Sam was especially interested in you being a scientist. He'd like to talk to you about doing some consulting work for him."

That was unexpected. "That's nice, sir, but why me? I'm a physicist, not an engineer. And the war's kept me away from science for the last several years. I'm sure to be a bit rusty."

"Sam is a fascinating individual and quite a character. And a real leader. Among his many accomplishments, he was captain of the undefeated 1906 Yale University football team. I told him how you drew the men on your ward together and got them to support each other."

"You knew about that, sir?"

Colonel Thornburgh smiled. "I try to keep my finger on the pulse of all the wards in my hospital. After hearing me sing your praises, Sam figured you two would work well together. He believes he would benefit from having a scientist bring a fresh set of eyes to the projects he takes on."

Jamie combed his hair back with his fingers. "What kind of work does he do, sir?"

"He's a land developer and a conservationist."

Jamie did a double take. "A land developer *and* a conservationist? Aren't those mutually exclusive?"

"I couldn't say. All I know is it will help maintain domestic tranquility in my household if you get in touch with him."

"I'll be happy to, sir."

"Good." Colonel Thornburgh rummaged through the top side drawer of his desk. "Here's Sam's card. He's looking forward to hearing from you."

Jamie stuffed the card into his jacket pocket and came to attention. "Thank you again, sir—for everything."

* * *

Jamie's next stop was Ward 321. He entered through one of the double doors and walked down the boulevard with only a trace of a limp. Nurse Hobbes was at the nurses' station with her back to him. He silently walked up behind her. "Sarah," he said softly. She spun around.

"You don't expect to hear your first name on the ward, do you?"

She lowered her head shyly. "No, sir."

"Rumor has it that I'll be discharged soon. I wouldn't be able to live with myself if I didn't first thank you for all you've done for me."

She studied the floor at her feet, the picture of humility. "It was truly my pleasure, sir."

He took her hand and kissed it. "Such caring hands. You're becoming a great nurse, Sarah Hobbes."

"Oh, sir." She clasped her hands below her chin.

Toby and Carl were standing near the foot of Toby's bed. Jamie walked back to them and put his hand on Toby's shoulder. "Being on the faculty at Stanford gave me access to the right people. They have an opening for you in the School of Education. If you're interested, you'd be welcome to complete your Ph.D. there."

Toby was speechless. He plopped down on the edge of his bed and stared up at Jamie open-mouthed.

"Tuition-free, room and board included." Jamie smiled. "Of course, there's a catch." Toby deflated like a balloon that was slowly losing its air. "Stanford's School of Education is very progressive. You'll be required to 'volunteer' in their experimental reading labs and remedial education programs. Basically, doing what you've done here for Doug Jankowski. Helping adults bring their reading skills up to par."

Toby shook his head. "You never pass up a chance to tease, do you? It will be a pleasure to volunteer." He canted his head. "I never imagined Stanford would let someone like me into their Ph.D. program."

"Why not? They tell me you had a fine academic record in your previous program, which you left only because you were called to serve our country."

Toby's eyes widened. "They've seen my transcripts?"

"Of course."

"Then they know I'm colored?"

"Your transcripts came from Howard University, so they probably assume you are."

"Would I be Stanford's first colored student?"

"Hardly. A man named Ernest Huston Johnson was the first way back in 1891, the year the University was founded. He graduated with a bachelor's degree in economics and then attended Stanford Law School. By all accounts, he was popular among his classmates."

"Sounds like you looked into it. Are you worried the other students might not welcome me?"

"Not at all. Just be aware that you'll be greatly outnumbered. At times, you might think it's you and me against the world."

"You and me?" Toby smiled. "You've shown the world you're an army unto yourself. With you on my side, I like the odds."

"Then you'll do it?"

Toby jumped to his feet—or rather his foot and Charlie

Gowan's creation—and just about crushed Jamie in a bear hug. "I don't know how to thank you."

Jamie worked himself free. "Become a great teacher. That will be more than enough thanks."

Jamie turned to Carl. "I thought you should know the San Francisco Chronicle is about to make a job offer to someone they want to cover college sports for them."

Carl looked as deflated as Toby had. "Lucky guy."

Jamie kept a straight face. "Not lucky. Deserving. And I think you know him. He's some guy named Carlo Zanardi."

It took a full second for Carl to realize what Jamie was saying. "May the Lord bless you forever and ever!" he shouted. With his one arm, Carl unabashedly hugged Jamie.

Jamie was saddened to see Sergeant Binney sitting by himself at the table of discontent. He had hoped Binney's near-death experience would have motivated him to move to the brotherhood table. There was still hope. "A business associate of mine owns several bakeries," Jamie said to Binney.

The little mess sergeant responded with a blank stare.

"One of his managers is moving on, and my associate is looking for someone with supervisory experience to replace him. It occurred to me that as a Mess Sergeant First Class, you've had years of experience supervising all kinds of cooking staff, including bakers."

Binney's semi-permanent scowl disappeared.

"My associate could also use an accomplished cake decorator. Can you think of one man who meets both those requirements?"

Binney pressed down on the arms of his wheelchair and looked up at Jamie. "Sir, I'd jump at the chance—if I could."

"No worries, Reggie. You can do the job just fine sitting

in your wheelchair. In fact, my associate's already having business cards printed up listing you as manager and master cake decorator."

Binney shook his head and smiled. "Major Collins, sir, ... you're making it damned hard for me to keep feeling sorry for myself."

* * *

Jamie returned to his room. Someone, probably Hendricks, had retrieved his footlocker from the general ward and placed it against a wall. "What am I going to do with you?" Jamie asked the thing. The problem was he had yet to arrange for housing at Stanford.

"Oh well." He wrote the address of Butch's house on a shipping label Hendricks had provided and slapped it on the side of his footlocker. He smiled as he envisioned his inherited housekeeper wondering what to do with it. He wrapped the cardboard box containing his medals in butcher paper that Hendricks, always thoughtful, had also provided and bound it with enough string to reach halfway to the next county. He'd send it to Butch's address via Registered Mail.

A wave of melancholy swept over him. He sat down on his footlocker. He'd never felt as useful and appreciated as he did on Ward 321. "I'm going to miss this place," he said aloud.

There was a knock on his door. Jamie looked up to find Carl standing at attention with the dreaded neutral look enlisted men adopt when they think they're dealing with an officer who's a fool. "Sir, would you mind accompanying me to the brotherhood table?"

Jamie searched Carl's face for any clue as to what he had in mind. "Am I going to like this?"

The corners of Carl's mouth twitched into a smile that quickly disappeared. "I couldn't say, sir."

"Lead on, sergeant. The Articles of War say you can't torture me."

As the two approached the brotherhood table, the other men converged around him, as did the staff. No one was smiling.

Sergeant Zanardi called everyone to attention. Toby stepped forward.

"Major Collins," Toby said in his deep, powerful voice. He scanned the room. "We're sure going to miss you." The room was suddenly filled with laughter and shouts of "good luck, best wishes, and thanks for everything" until Toby called for silence.

"Sir, you've given every man here reason to be optimistic about his future. That's a gift we can't possibly match." Toby signaled to Carl, who produced a three-foot-long, inch and a half in diameter, cylindrical package that was remarkably poorly wrapped in bandages and tied off with a gauze bow.

Carl held it out to Jamie. "Sir, as a small token of our appreciation, we'd like to present you with this going-away present." Carl looked around the room. "It's from all of us, sir."

Jamie tried to speak. Words failed him.

"Go ahead," Harvey Shipman shouted. "It won't bite. Unwrap it,"

Jamie untied the gauze bow and removed the bandages, revealing a mahogany-shafted walking stick topped with an ornate silver handle. Jamie's throat constricted, and his eyes watered.

"There's an inscription," Toby said.

Doug Jankowski, the man Toby had been helping improve his reading skills, stepped forward. "Please, sir, let me read it for you."

Jamie handed him the stick. "To Major Jamie Collins," Doug read aloud, "the one officer we'd gladly follow to hell and back."

Jamie closed his eyes and fought back tears.

Doug continued. "From the patients and staff, Ward 321, Letterman Army Hospital, 1919."

"Well read, Doug," Jamie said as he struggled to maintain his composure.

Doug smiled. "Toby's a great tutor."

It was taking a monumental effort for Jamie not to break down in front of the men. "Thank you, men." He glanced at Nurses Eliot and Hobbes, "And ladies."

He grasped his gift with both hands like a baseball bat and took a slow-motion swing. "This should keep my students in line."

Hendricks stepped forward. "Sir, Charlie Gowan's put together another little something we hope you'll like."

Charlie held out a finely detailed wooden box about the size of a shoebox. "Sir, Sergeant Hendricks told me you keeps all your medals in a beat-up cardboard box. We hope you'll use this instead."

Charlie's work of art was so highly polished Jamie could see his reflection in it.

"Thank you, Charlie. I'll cherish this for the rest of my life."

Jamie moved to the head of the brotherhood table and climbed onto a chair where he could see everyone, and they could see him. He held up his hand for silence. "Men, when

I arrived at Letterman, all I wanted to do was hole up in my room and feel sorry for myself."

He smiled at Nurse Eliot and Doctor Crandall, who were standing together. "Nurse Eliot and Doctor Crandall reminded me that as a field-grade officer, it was my duty to bring you men together as a fighting unit and lead you into battle against your disabilities. I also saw it as my duty to help each of you find a purpose in life and help you develop a plan toward that end." Jamie surveyed the men. "In return, you made me feel useful again. For that, I owe each of you an extreme debt of gratitude." Jamie came to attention and held a salute.

An uncomfortable silence was shattered when Sergeant First Class Binney bellowed, "Attention." The men responded as they would on a parade field. Following Binney's lead, they held a return salute until Major Jamie Collins, Medal of Honor recipient, stood them down.

When Jamie returned to the solitude of his room, he tore open the cardboard box his medals were in and placed them in Charlie's wooden box. He'd send that via Registered Mail to Pacific Grove. Then he broke down in tears. His newfound wealth, the respect of his men, so many other blessings—they were all wonderful. The problem was they weren't going to cage the beast in him—or fill the void in his heart. That, he feared, could only be done by a certain green-eyed nurse. And she might have other plans for her life.

Chapter 27

A Sacred Duty

Tuesday, 27 May 1919

Jamie was alone in his room, staring at his reflection in the window, wondering how it could be that he had charged a battery of enemy machine guns single-handedly, yet he couldn't find the courage to tell Nurse Eliot how he felt about her.

As if on cue, she appeared in his doorway. "Good news, Major Collins. You're to be discharged from the hospital at the end of the week."

"Really? This isn't just another rumor?"

"Really, sir. By mid-afternoon Friday, if not earlier."

That was good news. So why didn't she sound happier for him? "Thank you, Nurse Eliot. That's what I've been dying to hear—or perhaps, in consideration of departed friends, I should say *longing* to hear."

"We'll miss you, sir." Her voice sounded far away. And sad.

"We?"

"*I'll* miss you."

That was even better news. He looked deep into her emerald eyes. "I'll miss you too." He swallowed hard. "You brighten my day anytime you're near." There. He'd finally stuck his toe in the water.

Nurse Eliot didn't say anything, but she hadn't laughed or run away. It was now or never. "I've been trying to find the courage to ask, will you do me the honor of dining with me once I'm discharged?"

"Do *you* the honor?" She laughed. "I've been praying that you'd ask me out."

Toe in the water? It was time to dive into the deep end. "Am I being too forward in saying I hope our first date will be followed by many others?"

When she didn't answer immediately, Jamie broke into a cold sweat. Maybe he'd jumped in too quickly.

A smile slowly spread across her face. "I'd be disappointed if that weren't the case."

Jamie was afraid his smile was going to tear his face apart. He boldly took her hand. "I know *Nurse* Eliot well. I look forward to knowing *Miss* Eliot even better."

"I'm not sure there's much more to know."

"Oh, but there is. I want to know your deepest, darkest secret."

Nurse Eliot angled her body toward the door. "What secret?"

"Please tell me your full name."

She laughed, that musical laugh that always made him want to laugh with her. "It's Andrea Jean Eliot, sir."

"Andrea Jean—that's a beautiful name."

"My family and friends call me Andi, sir."

"Andi Eliot—I love the sound of that." Jamie let go of her

hand and took half a step back. "At the risk of asking too much, will you do me a huge favor?"

Nurse Eliot stood tall. "Anything, sir."

"Please allow me to call you Andi—*and stop calling me sir!*"

"Certainly, Major Collins." She maintained a straight face for a few seconds, then laughed, putting him on notice that, like her bluebirds, if she was going to be teased, she was going to give as good as she got.

"We're going to have fun together, Andi Eliot. Now, please tell me a little about yourself. Do you come from a large family?"

"I have two younger sisters. We grew up in Denver, where my father's a Presbyterian minister."

"And your mother?"

It was a moment before Andi answered. "She died shortly after giving birth to my youngest sister."

"I'm sorry." Jamie thought of his parents, both deceased, and hurried to change the subject. "Have you always wanted to be an army nurse?"

"You could almost say I was born to it. My father's first ministry after divinity school was as an army chaplain. I was born at Fort Leavenworth, Kansas. Forgive me if I sound like a recruiting pamphlet, but I can't think of a higher calling for a nurse than to care for those willing to place themselves in harm's way to protect the country and way of life I love— those and their families."

She seemed lost in the past for a moment. "My father loved being an army chaplain. Sadly, he suffered a severe injury to his right leg in a training accident soon after I was born. To this day, although he's very independent, if not stubborn, he walks with a cane."

Hendricks said she'd asked to be assigned to an orthopedic ward at Letterman. Perhaps this was one reason. And perhaps it was also part of the reason she had been so supportive of Jamie from day one.

Jamie wiped the perspiration from his forehead. This was going far better than he ever imagined.

Perceptive as always, Andi stepped to his window. "Would you mind ... Jamie ... if I open this?" She went ahead without waiting for permission and inhaled deeply. "I love the smell of the sea. Don't you?"

Maybe he'd keep the house in Pacific Grove that Butch left him. "I've heard that acceptance into the Army Nurse Corps is very competitive."

"That's true. Graduating from high school at the top of my class helped." She turned to face him. "And my father encouraged me to apply to the best nursing schools in the nation." She smiled wistfully. "I was worried about the cost. He wasn't. He was confident God would provide."

"I can tell how much you love your dad just from your tone. Did he bring you and your sisters up by himself?"

"That was mainly left to a series of housekeepers."

Jamie canted his head. "Not an ideal situation, I'm sure."

Andi crossed her arms as though hugging herself for support. "We missed out on the motherly love most children take for granted. And every time I started to get close to one of Daddy's housekeepers, circumstances took her away. She'd marry and leave to start her own family, a parent or sibling would need her full-time care, ..."

Jamie vowed to himself that he'd never allow circumstances to remove him from Andi's life.

"As the eldest daughter, I did what I could to help raise my sisters even though I was still a child myself. When I was accepted into the University of Minnesota School for Nursing, the first university-based nursing program in the nation, I had to make a hard choice. Enroll or stay home and continue to help raise my sisters."

"I'm glad you chose to enroll."

"Daddy convinced me to follow my dream. And I needn't have worried. My sisters have grown up to be fine women. Daddy was also right about the cost of nursing school. God did provide. The elders of the church where he's still pastor established a scholarship. I was its first recipient."

"I'm sure you deserved it."

Andi shrugged. "To show my appreciation, I worked harder than I'd ever worked in my life and again graduated at the top of my class. I breezed through Colorado's Registered Nurse Exam and was accepted into the Army Nurse Corps —a dream come true."

He watched as she stood before the window and tracked the flight of a lone seagull as it beat against the wind. He imagined her overcoming the obstacles she faced in becoming a head nurse at such a young age with equal grace and determination. "You'd have to really want to be an army nurse to accept the unique demands they place on their RNs," Jamie said.

"Unique demands?"

"The army can send you anywhere in the world at a moment's notice. You have no choice about who you work with. And like a nun, if you want to marry you have to leave the order."

He needed to slow down. One minute, he was asking her out on their first date, the next, he was bringing up marriage.

"A woman who doesn't want to go where she's needed or work with certain others is free to leave the Army Nurse

Corps at any time. In fact, she should." Andi looked directly at Jamie. "As to marriage, it's no secret that I've been engaged twice, which means I was prepared to leave the Corps."

Uh oh. He'd promised Hendricks he wouldn't let on that he knew about her tragic engagements or that Hendricks was the one who told him. "I'm sorry," Jamie said. "I shouldn't get so personal."

"I don't mind." She glanced at her watch. "I'm entitled to a break now and then." She raised her chin. "If you want to know me better, my engagements are a good place to start."

Did he really want to hear about other men she'd loved—and lost?

She got a faraway look. "My first year in the ANC flew by as I became more and more engrossed in my work. Then, an idealistic young army doctor came into my life. Norton—a rather pretentious-sounding first name for a man who was anything but pretentious."

She paused. Was she picturing him in her mind?

"Norton asked me out. I declined. He asked again. I accepted. Eventually, he proposed. After much prayer and soul searching, I said yes, knowing marriage meant I'd have to leave the Nurse Corps." She smiled reflectively. "The choice wasn't difficult. We were in love. We planned to marry when he returned from a six-month tour of duty in Panama." Andi sagged against the window frame. "He never returned." Her voice wavered. "Malaria claimed him the joyous day the canal opened." She seemed to remember herself and stood up straight. "After that, I put all thoughts of leaving the ANC behind me. I began telling friends I'd never consider marriage again."

Jamie took her hand to comfort her, more as a friend than

a suitor. His heart just about melted when she intertwined their fingers.

"Two years later, acquaintances at church introduced me to a captain from the Air Corps." She smiled. "Cameron—another grand name for a fine man who, if you'll excuse the pun, was well-grounded."

Thank God she could still joke about her past. Hmm. Had it occurred to her that the name "Jamie" was anything but grand or pretentious?

"Cameron and I had much in common, and he was fun to be with. He spoke of finding a nice young lady, marrying, and starting a family. My claim that I'd never consider marriage again was soon forgotten. We became engaged." She stopped.

Perhaps it was too painful to go on. "Another tragic ending?" Jamie said.

"A collapsed landing gear put an end to Cameron and our wedding plans."

Hendricks said she'd built a wall around her heart. No wonder. She'd lost her mother. The housekeepers who brought her up kept disappearing. Two fiancés had died. Jamie knew the pain of abandonment. *Please, God, see to it that I never abandon Andi.*

"In the weeks and months after my second fiancé's death, I became blind to many of the things that used to give me joy. 'Jokes' about me began circulating the wards: 'Putting a ring on Nurse Eliot's finger is like putting a noose around your neck.'"

Jamie shook his head. "People can be so heartless."

"I cried and cried when I overheard several orderlies joking that my fiancés had succumbed to 'The Hangman's Curse.'"

Andi was silent for a moment. "Those in the trenches aren't the only ones who suffer from shell shock. I doubt there's a doctor, nurse, or orderly who isn't still haunted by the unrelenting trauma we witnessed during the war. In my case, it's gotten to where sometimes I hardly recognize myself. I've become less rational and more fearful—to the point that despite my supposed sophistication, I believe in The Hangman's Curse."

"It can't possibly—"

She cut him off. "I know it's silly for a modern woman to believe in a curse. But knowledge can't overcome a damaged psyche."

Jamie closed his eyes for a moment. "I made it my mission to help the men on our ward put the war behind them. I'd consider it an honor if you'd let me help you."

She stared at him in silence. A wave of relief slowly seemed to wash over her. "That would be a wonderful way to get to know each other better."

Jamie lowered his head. "I know what it's like to be afraid of something others laugh off."

"Your fear of being left alone in the dark?"

"I had hoped to keep that between Hendricks and myself."

"To effectively address all our patients' needs Hendricks and I need to share information." She placed her hand on Jamie's forearm. "And I'm not laughing."

If he hadn't already fallen in love with Andi, her empathy would have pushed him over the edge.

Someone knocked on Jamie's door. Andi instantly became *Nurse* Eliot again.

"Please pardon the interruption," Hendricks said. He didn't acknowledge their closeness, though he looked uncommonly pleased. "Ma'am, Doctor Crandall is here to discuss Private Jankowski's treatment plan."

"Thank you, Hendricks. I'll be right with you."

They heard Hendricks' footsteps fade away.

Andi gave Jamie a quick kiss on the cheek and hurried after the big corpsman.

She had kissed him once before, on the top of his head, when he told Binney why he'd nursed him through his fever and delirium. As heartwarming as that kiss had been, this one was different. This kiss was one soul touching another.

* * *

Jamie spent the entire time Andi was away worrying about how she would react to what he was about to tell her—what he *had* to tell her.

An hour passed before she returned. "I'm so glad you're back," Jamie said as soon as she entered his room. "There's something I need to tell you."

"Yes?"

"The war taught me how fleeting life can be and how important it is to tell the people in our lives how much they mean to us."

"An important lesson for us all."

Come on, Jamie told himself. Stop beating around the bush. "My parents, my best friend, I never told them what they meant to me. Now it's too late."

"I'm sorry," Andi said. She clearly had no idea where Jamie was heading.

"I'm not going to make that mistake again. So I'm going to tell you something now that before the war, it might have taken months for me to find the courage to say. Something from deep within my heart."

Andi canted her head and waited.

He had to quit stalling before his courage failed him completely. "Andrea Jean Eliot, ... I love you."

She staggered backward. "You what?"

Jamie spread his arms wide and repeated loud and clear, "I love you."

Tears welled up in Andi's eyes. She practically leapt into his embrace. Jamie held her tight—once he regained his balance.

They found each other's lips. Their first kiss was so passionate Jamie's once-dead toes tingled.

She took half a step back so they could look into each other's eyes. "You are a brave man to make such a bold statement before we've even gone on our first date."

She took both his hands in hers. "It's my turn to tell you what's on my heart." She took a deep breath. "When rumors began to circulate that a hero from the Western Front was to be placed on my ward, I paid little attention. Any soldier will tell you that rumors are the lifeblood of every army—but they're seldom true. In this instance, contrary to the most cherished traditions of the army, Hendricks was soon rolling you onto my ward."

"The most pivotal day of my life," Jamie said.

"Everyone knew the legend of Captain Jamie Collins, the hero who was raised from the dead. And now you were to be my patient. I had pictured you as a big, loud man and none too bright. I imagined you demanding everyone's attention, arrogant and overbearing."

"I hope I proved you wrong."

"Wonderfully wrong. Despite your many accomplishments, I was pleased to learn you're a modest man. Bright enough to be a physics professor at a major university. Considerate and caring. And when it comes to caring for your men, as brave as your medal says you are."

Jamie could hardly believe so many nice things were being said about him by someone he was desperate to please.

"Do you remember the day you included me in your conspiracy to bypass Sergeant Binney and enlist Carl Zanardi in your plan to bring the men on our ward together?"

Jamie nodded. "It's a day I'll never forget."

"Your trust helped me realize all my posturing about being married to the ANC was a lie I'd made up to protect my heart from being broken again."

"We never know the effects we have on others," Jamie said.

"All my defenses began to crumble when you left your private room and moved out onto the general ward—something almost unimaginable for a field-grade officer."

Nor would Jamie have imagined it himself if he hadn't wanted to impress this nurse who impressed him in every way.

"By the sheer power of your personality, you gave the men on our ward what they desperately needed: hope for the future and encouragement to dream big."

"A man has to dream big if he's going to accomplish big things," Jamie said.

"I was beginning to dream of a life with you."

Jamie was stunned. "But I was confined to a wheelchair!"

"Your spirit wasn't."

Jamie was speechless.

Andi smiled that radiant smile of hers that lit up Jamie's world. "When you risked your life to nurse Sergeant Binney back to health, it would have been impossible for me not to fall madly in love with you."

Jamie closed his eyes for a second or two and savored the moment. "I am the most fortunate of men." He looked deep into her emerald green eyes. "I can't imagine my life without you."

She smiled. "Nor I you."

He encircled her tiny waist with his hands and twirled her around the room to a waltz only he could hear. After a few circuits, Andi brought their dance to a halt. Her smile disappeared.

"What's the matter?"

"I so wish we had been open with each other sooner." Her chin began to tremble. "Just yesterday, I made a commitment that will soon separate us."

Fear coursed through Jamie's veins. "Please tell me there's not another man."

"No. It's nothing like that. I've been selected as the next Assistant Dean of the Army School of Nursing. It's a three-year tour of duty in Washington, DC."

Just yesterday! That's what Jamie got for his cowardice in putting off telling Andi how he felt about her. Three more years. The same sentence he'd imposed upon himself when he told Rachel he'd wait before committing to anyone.

There were tears in Andi's eyes. "It would be the height of ingratitude if I backed out now after Dean Stimson and others worked so hard to secure the assignment for me. And I'd pass up the opportunity to shape the school's entire curriculum." Andi lowered her eyes. "I'll be leaving Letterman at the end of June."

Jamie's mind was racing. "How important is this assignment to you?"

"It would be the highlight of my career."

Although he was sure Andi was the woman for him, he didn't want to possess her. "I'll tell you what. Why don't we take up our respective posts for a year, you in DC, me at Stanford, write often, and see each other when we can? By then, we'll have a far better idea of how we want our relationship to play out."

Andi clutched Jamie's upper arm. "You'll wait for me?"

He'd promised Rachel, a woman he hardly knew, that he'd wait three years for her. One year would be no time at all to wait for Andi. "For as long as it takes."

Jamie was afraid he might end up in traction she hugged him so tight.

Then his conscience—that most inconvenient irritant—kicked in. "I wouldn't have been free to commit to you anyway until after mid-April," he blurted out.

Andi's shoulders sagged. "I ... I don't understand. Are you saying there's someone else?"

"No. I'm saying there was the *possibility* of someone else."

That only seemed to confuse her.

"I met a girl just before I was called up. We were together for less than 24 hours, but with the war looming over us, we let our fear of the unknown rush us into a relationship neither of us was ready for."

Andi crossed her arms. He needed to explain before her imagination ran away with her.

"We were just starting to establish ourselves in our respective careers. And I would soon be off to war—for how long, nobody could say. Under those circumstances, trying to grow a relationship would have been difficult, if not impossible. But she wasn't ready to give up on me. She promised not to commit to anyone before we meet again next April."

"Next April?" Andi seemed incredulous. "That would make it three years—an eternity as far as a relationship is concerned."

"Hard to believe, I know. I guess she thought I was worth waiting for. And since I never imagined I'd meet anyone as wonderful as you, I promised her in return that I wouldn't commit to anyone either until after we meet again."

"You must have thought she was worth waiting for."

At the time, yes. But now? "Rachel is a remarkable person. Under other circumstances, I'm sure you'd like her."

Much to Jamie's relief, Andi smiled. "I might like her under these circumstances. She's part of the history that made you who you are today, isn't she?"

"More than you realize. She promised to pray for me every day until she knew I was back in the States and safe. And here's something you'll find hard to believe. Before we parted, she dreamt that I was so gravely wounded I was pronounced dead, but I made a full recovery."

Andi stared at Jamie. "That sounds more like a vision than a dream."

"Whatever it was, it gave me the will to keep fighting for my life after I was pronounced dead."

Andi was silent for a moment. "Then you must keep your promise to her."

What a remarkable woman *Andi* was. "You don't mind?"

Andi put her hands on her hips. "Of course, I mind!" She smiled. "But there's a silver lining in your promise. It gives me almost a year to get over my Hangman's Curse madness."

She gave him a penetrating look. "I'm curious. Why hasn't this former possibility come to visit you?"

In retrospect, Rachel's reason struck Jamie as so weak he was embarrassed to have accepted it. "To put our relationship in the proper perspective, she thought we should take a complete break from each other. No visits, no letters, no contact at all." He wasn't going to mention Rachel's secondary reason. That she wanted time to convince herself she wasn't a sexual predator. "She also thought we should date other people. Otherwise, how would we know whether there was anything special between us?"

Andi raised her chin. "A rather cold and calculating approach to matters of the heart."

Jamie knew it would be unwise to try to defend Rachel. "Being a complete novice in matters of the heart, I didn't know any better. But there's more. She said if I found someone else, she'd understand."

Andi couldn't have looked more skeptical. "And you believed her?"

"Shouldn't I have?"

"If she's that understanding, she's unlike any woman I've ever met." Andi took a deep breath and let it out slowly. "But let's take this Rachel at her word. Let's assume we have her blessing to be together."

"Let's." Jamie reached for Andi.

She kept him at arms-length. "I still can't help seeing this former possibility as a threat."

"She isn't. Really." Jamie was desperate. "What can I do to convince you?"

Andi didn't answer for what felt to Jamie like half of eternity. "What if I ask you to do something totally outrageous?"

"I'll do it," Jamie said without hesitation.

Andi stood as ridged as a sculpture, like she was afraid she'd be struck down by a bolt of lightning if she told him what was on her mind. "Like so many of us who served at the front, I suffer from the most dreadful nightmares."

Jamie couldn't count the number of times he'd been awakened on their ward by patients crying out in their sleep. "Tell me how I can help."

She stared into his eyes. "I should know better, but my pride and standing in the medical community won't allow me to seek professional help. I didn't know what to do—until I met you. You're special in every way. You were pronounced dead, and yet here you are. You've been to hell and back. But even that couldn't take the kindness out of you." She lowered her eyes.

"Go on," Jamie gently encouraged her.

"When my nightmares scare me awake, I'm convinced that if someone tenderhearted and kind were there to hold me, the ghosts of the men I couldn't save would stop tormenting me." She pressed her arms to her sides. "I'm going to take some time off before I leave for DC. I've wanted to ask you this for weeks, but I couldn't find the courage." Her cheeks turned crimson.

"Ask me anything," Jamie said.

"You've said you want to help me put the war behind me. I wouldn't dream of asking this of anyone else." She looked deep into his eyes. "Will you spend a few nights with me and be the one to chase away my nightmares?"

Jamie's field of vision collapsed so completely all he could see were Andi's pleading eyes. To say he was shocked by her request would be the grossest understatement. A thought slammed into his consciousness: Could this be the purpose for which I was raised from the dead?

It seemed unlikely. He wasn't qualified to deal with anyone's nightmares. That was a job for a doctor, not a physicist. In his ignorance, he could easily do more harm than good. Yet he couldn't say no. If he didn't help her, who would? She said she wouldn't dream of asking anyone else.

The fear in her eyes said she was afraid she'd asked for too much. She hadn't. There wasn't anything he wouldn't do for her. But he wasn't going to jump into bed with Andi the way he had with Rachel. Not after developing such respect for her. Andi deserved better than that. Far better.

"I want to have a clear understanding of this," Jamie said. "You're asking me to hold you when your nightmares wake you. You're *not* suggesting anything sexual. Is that correct?"

"I'm sorry. I'm asking too much." She angled herself toward the door. "It's just that I've seen how far you're willing to go to help other troubled veterans. I'm simply asking you to be there for me."

Jamie took her hand. "We'd be going from wading in the shallows of the relational pool to diving into the deep end. Are you sure you're ready for that?"

"I'm sure."

"In that case," Jamie put his hands on her shoulders, "Andrea Jean Eliot, I'll make it my sacred duty to chase away your nightmares."

Andi threw her arms around him. "Thank you. For understanding. And for loving me."

At the sound of approaching footsteps, Andi resumed her regal bearing. Nurse Hobbes appeared in Jamie's doorway. He guiltily stepped back from Andi.

Seeing them so close together must have been quite a shock for Nurse Hobbes.

"Excuse me, ma'am," Nurse Hobbes said after composing herself. "Corpsman Gowan has a question for you when you have a moment."

"Thank you, Nurse Hobbes. Please tell him I'll see him in his workshop within the next fifteen minutes."

"Yes, ma'am." Hobbes stole a peek at Jamie. "Sir." She backed out of the room.

"That was strange," Jamie said. "It was as though she was afraid to look at me."

Andi glanced at the watch suspended upside down from her blouse. "Fifteen minutes," she said to herself. She looked at Jamie. "Nurse Hobbes came to me for advice yesterday. She's become infatuated with one of our patients and didn't know how to deal with the situation."

"Did she say who the lucky man was?"

"She didn't have to. It could only have been you."

Jamie held up his hand like he was in court, swearing to tell the truth. "On my honor, I didn't encourage her."

Andi smiled. "Don't worry. I'm sure you haven't done anything wrong."

Jamie relaxed. "What did you tell her?"

"I told her not to worry. Long-term patients and their caregivers can easily delude themselves into thinking they've fallen in love. That usually, when the patient leaves the hospital, both parties realize what they had was a relationship built only on proximity and dependence."

Jamie's chest tightened. "Should we be concerned about our relationship?"

Andi smiled. "Not at all." She put her hand on his forearm. "I'm not some giddy student nurse. I'm a fully mature woman who knows her heart." Her smile disappeared. "Are you concerned?"

"Not in the least. I love you. Plain and simple."

"And I love you," Andi said.

They kissed, and she was gone.

* * *

Wednesday, 28 May 1919

Jamie didn't see Andi until late the next morning. She looked tired. Had her nightmares tormented her throughout the night?

She moved to his side. "I was tied up in emergencies for hours yesterday and again this morning. I looked in on you late last night, but you were asleep, and I didn't want to wake you."

"I've been going crazy with worry," Jamie said. "Please tell me I wasn't dreaming. Tell me you love me as much as I love you."

Andi pressed her body against his. A passionate kiss was her answer.

"I'll take that as a yes," he said once he caught his breath.

She suddenly stood up straight. "Have you heard of the Palace Hotel?"

"Sure. It's a San Francisco landmark. Those who know about such things say it's one of the most luxurious hotels on the West Coast."

"I've been there for high tea. I can attest to that."

Thanks to Butch's bequest, Jamie could easily afford a room at the Palace. He took Andi's hand. "I think it would be the perfect place to chase away nightmares."

"I agree. Let's stay there—since it won't cost us a penny."

"What?!"

"I telephoned my cousin Leslie last night. We're best friends. She knows about my nightmares. She also knows about you."

"Nothing bad, I hope."

"I'd have to make up anything bad." Andi turned slightly. "I told her you were going to chase away my nightmares."

"You didn't!"

"I did. She called me back an hour later. Her husband is the assistant manager of the Palace. For the next month, Howard's going to be acting manager. He's offered us a suite, free of charge."

"Seriously!? Your cousin and her husband won't be scandalized if we share a bed!?"

Andi met Jamie's eyes. "Leslie knows this isn't about sex. And Howard served in France. He understands about nightmares. Besides, they know we love each other."

Jamie hugged Andi tight. "Life can't get much sweeter than this."

"It will once we're able to spend uninterrupted time alone together. Now, I really must run."

She almost collided with Kavanaugh on her way out. They gave each other looks Jamie couldn't decipher. God forbid that they knew each other.

"May I come in?" Kavanaugh said. He entered without waiting for Jamie's consent. "I hope I didn't scare away that pretty nurse."

"She was just leaving." Jamie crossed his arms. "What can I do for you?"

"I understand you'll be leaving here Friday."

Another shock to Jamie's system. "How'd you find out so fast?"

"Let's just say a little bird told me."

Could he mean one of Nurse Eliot's bluebirds? Please, not Andi herself.

"I have two questions," Kavanaugh said. "First, are you still going to front our Disabled Veterans' Education Trust?"

"I told you I would." Jamie hadn't meant to be so curt. It was just that things had been going so well with Andi he hated to think there might be something behind the looks that passed between her and Kavanaugh.

His visitor clearly wasn't used to being spoken to so harshly. And Kavanaugh was right to be offended. He hadn't implied that Andi was the source of his inside knowledge. That was all in Jamie's imagination.

"I'm sorry," Jamie said. "I've had a stressful morning. And no, I haven't changed my mind. There's not much I wouldn't do for our disabled vets."

"Good." Kavanaugh's hands shook as he straightened his tie. "Second, have you given any thought to becoming trustee of the Kavanaugh Trust?"

"I've given it a lot of thought."

"And?"

"I'd be crazy to do it and make an enemy of Sonny. You said yourself he likes to hurt people." And even crazier to increase the chances that The Hangman's Curse might someday steal another fiancé from Andi.

Kavanaugh couldn't hide his disappointment. "So, the answer's no?"

"I didn't say that. I wouldn't be in this hospital if I hadn't done crazier things. And somebody has to stand up to the likes of Sonny Kavanaugh."

"Then you'll do it?"

If Jamie really had been raised from the dead for a purpose, if not to chase away Andi's nightmare, perhaps it was to reform Kavanaugh Enterprises. But any one of a thousand men could do that. Jamie felt the purpose for which he'd been raised had to be something only he could do. "I'm still thinking about it."

"You'd become a rich man."

Jamie wasn't going to mention that he was already a rich man. "If I serve as your trustee, I won't be doing it to make myself rich."

"Which is why I believe you're the right man for the job. But don't discount being rich. So long as you don't let money possess you, it can do a lot of good. Especially during a recession like our country's struggling through. Wouldn't you want to know your family would never go hungry?"

"I don't have a family."

"You might someday. Then you'd be so glad you could provide for them you'd want to name your first-born son after me. Matthew Collins has a nice ring to it, don't you think?"

Jamie laughed. "I'd need a wife first."

"I saw the way you looked at that nurse who just left. If you were rich, maybe she'd be interested in you. I could talk to her for you."

Jamie bristled. He didn't want Kavanaugh anywhere near Andi. "You do, and I'll never serve as your trustee."

A devilish grin spread across Kavanaugh's face. "How do you know I haven't already?"

The question hit Jamie like an exploding artillery shell.

Kavanaugh laughed. "Don't worry. I'm only teasing. I've never exchanged a word with that young lady."

Too late. The damage was done. In Jamie's fragile state

of mind, Kavanaugh's simple question was all it took to ignite a suspicion, however unlikely, that Andi was conspiring with Kavanaugh to snag a rich husband.

"I'll leave you alone with your thoughts," Jamie heard Kavanaugh say as though from a million miles away, "but I'll need to know soon what you decide to do about my trust."

The Kavanaugh Trust was the furthest thing from Jamie's mind. What if it wasn't the real Andrea Jean Eliot he loved but a manufactured image of her he'd created in his mind?

Kavanaugh took a step toward the door, stopped, and turned around. "I almost forgot." He reached into his inside coat pocket and pulled out an envelope. "Lieutenant Colonel Hunt asked me to give you this."

"The deputy base commander?"

"He's the one." Kavanaugh dropped the envelope on the foot of Jamie's bed and slipped out the door.

Jamie's mind was on fire. The look that passed between Kavanaugh and Andi was seared into his brain. Was there something between them?

No, no, no. That was crazy. There could be any number of explanations for the looks they gave each other. Most likely, Kavanaugh was stunned by Andi's beauty. Perhaps she recognized him from pictures in the newspaper.

Jamie suddenly remembered Andi saying she loved a good conspiracy. If she'd learned from Kavanaugh that whoever served as trustee of the Kavanaugh Trust would become a rich man, might she try to persuade Jamie to accept the job and then entice him to marry her?

A thought popped into Jamie's mind, uninvited, unwelcome. *Better keep your options open with Rachel.*

A welcome thought pushed it aside. Suspicions are the enemy of rationality. Healthy skepticism is its ally.

Andi had advised Jamie not to accept or reject anything without sufficient evidence. That advice worked in her favor. The only evidence that she and Kavanaugh were in a conspiracy was the look that passed between them. The overwhelming evidence against it was that Andi would soon leave for DC to take up a post requiring her to be single for the next three years.

Follow the evidence, Jamie. Follow the evidence.

As for Kavanaugh, the man was merely playing with him. Having a little fun with an unworldly academic. Jamie couldn't fault the man for that. Jamie was something of a tease himself—just ask Toby, or Carl, or even Andi. Kavanaugh said he'd never exchanged a word with Andi, and there was no evidence to the contrary.

Why not turn the tables on Kavanaugh? Have a little fun at his expense? Let him know what it's like to live with uncertainty.

Considering all that was at stake for Kavanaugh's employees and his charities, anyone who knew Jamie well would have no doubt that he was going to serve as Kavanaugh's trustee. But Jamie wasn't going to let Kavanaugh off the hook yet. He'd let him sweat it out until his mid-June deadline.

Jamie absentmindedly picked up the envelope Kavanaugh had dropped on the foot of his bed. He extracted a handwritten letter.

Tuesday, 27 May 1919

Dear Major Collins,

Matt Kavanaugh told me about the many things you've done for the men on your ward. I'm writing to thank you.

During the war, I commanded an infantry battalion in France. Far too many of my men lost a limb or were left paralyzed. That sent many of them into a deep depression from which I was afraid they'd never emerge. To keep that from happening to the men on your ward, Matt told me you made it your mission to form them into a fighting unit and lead them into battle against the constraint their disabilities threatened to impose upon them. More than that, you helped them find a purpose in their shattered lives and inspired them to dream big.

Thanks to your leadership, I understand many will be enrolling in college and earning degrees once they're released from the army. Others will be going to vocational school and then taking good jobs in the trades. Still others plan to rejoin and expand a family business.

I say to you, sir, mission accomplished and well done!

Respectfully yours, Alan Hunt, Lieutenant Colonel

Deputy Commander

The Presidio of San Francisco

Colonel Hunt's letter couldn't have arrived at a better time. It was longed-for acknowledgment from someone who'd been to hell and back that despite all Jamie had been through, he never stopped fighting for his men.

But Colonel Hunt was wrong. Jamie's mission hadn't been accomplished. There was one brave soldier from Ward 321 who still needed his help. A decorated combat veteran who hadn't stopped caring for others long enough to care for herself.

Like every disabled veteran on their ward, despite any conspiracy she might be in, by her service in France, Andi had earned and deserved all the support Jamie could give her. And holding her when her nightmares scared her awake would be a wonderful way to get to know the real Andi Eliot.

As for his suspicions, they were yet a different war he had to fight. A war in which surrender was not an option if he didn't want to risk building a wall between himself and Andi.

In his more rational moments, Jamie assessed the odds as overwhelming that Andi was exactly who she appeared to be: brave, dedicated, compassionate, honest, loving. And she was the only one who could tame the beast in him.

Jamie said he never bet unless the odds were in his favor. But regardless of the odds, he was going to bet everything good he'd ever hoped for or dreamed of that Andi would also be the one to fill the void in his heart.

Author's Note

Historical Notes for *A Different War*

I've made this novel as historically and medically accurate as I could. While my characters are fictional, many were inspired by real people, some I have known, others I have only read about. I have done my best to describe the settings in which my characters appear just as the history books say they were over one hundred years ago.

I hope the following notes add to your enjoyment of *A Different War*.

William R. DeHay

Chapter One – The Beast

In case readers think Jamie's bravery is unbelievable, see the website: List of Medal of Honor recipients for World War I.

One hundred and twenty-one Medals of Honor were awarded to US military personnel for their actions in the Great War. The actions that led to those awards were truly above and beyond the call of duty. Those of First Lieutenant Harold Arthur Furlong are representative. The citation to his medal reads:

Immediately after the opening of the attack in the Bois-de-Bantheville, when his company was held up by severe machine gun fire from the front, which killed his company commander and several soldiers, 1st. Lt. Furlong moved out in advance of the line with great courage and coolness, crossing an open space several hundred yards wide. Taking up a position behind the line of the machine guns, he closed in on them, one at a time, killing a number of the enemy with his rifle, putting 4 machine gun nests out of action, and driving 20 German prisoners into our lines.

Lieutenant Furlong also received the Croix de Guerre with Palms and was made a Chevalier of the Legion of Honor by the French Republic.

The actions of British infantry lieutenant Siegfried Sassoon are also incredible but true. Enraged when a German sniper killed one of his friends, Sassoon grabbed a bag of hand grenades and staged a one-man assault on the enemy trench from where the sniper fire had come. Upon reaching the enemy trench—a remarkable feat in itself—Sassoon, with a grenade in each hand, pulled the arming pins with his teeth and routed the occupying Germans. It is estimated that Sassoon caused between 50 and 60 Germans to abandon their posts.

Would an academic such as Jamie voluntarily join the military? Consider William Lawrence Bragg. While a graduate student at Cambridge University, Bragg joined a university cavalry troop and spent many summers at camp, training in marksmanship and horsemanship. Within two weeks of Great Britain's declaration of war on Germany, Bragg voluntarily joined the Royal Horse Artillery. How serious an academic was he? For his X-ray analysis of crystal structure, Professor Sir Lawrence Bragg became the youngest person ever to be honored with a Nobel Prize in Physics.

During the Great War, the US Army Medical Department provided continuous care through a hierarchy of specific units. Wounded, non-ambulatory frontline soldiers were carried by stretcher from where they fell to a battalion aid station. From there, depending upon the severity of their wounds, if necessary, they were taken to a dressing station. The more serious cases were taken from a dressing station by ambulance to a field hospital. When it was determined that a man needed an even higher level of care, he was moved by ambulance from the field hospital to an evacuation hospital. Finally, he was taken by rail from the evacuation hospital to a base hospital.

The staffing at each successive facility varied. Field hospitals were the first level at which female nurses served. Field hospitals were placed between two and four miles behind the front lines, well within range of enemy artillery and air attack.

American Expeditionary Force (AEF) Base Hospital No. 15 was the first base hospital to arrive overseas. (As with "church," "hospital" refers to a group of people, not the building they occupy.) AEF Base Hospital No. 15 was stationed at Chaumont, Haute Marne, France, where it arrived on 16 July 1917. It closed on 15 January 1919. The last AEF Base Hospital to close was No. 57, which was in Paris. It closed on 13 August 1919.

By far, the greatest number of wounds in the Great War were from shell fragments, known as shrapnel.

The Distinguished Service Cross, the country's second-highest gallantry award, was presented to three women, all nurses, for their actions during the Great War. The Distinguished Service Medal, the highest non-combat decoration, was awarded to twenty-three women. See the US Department of Defense website https://valor.defense.gov/Recipients/Army-Distinguished-Service-Cross-Recipients/ .

I have said that the DSC was awarded to *four* women because I didn't want Nurse Eliot's fictional award to detract in any way from the awards three real Army nurses received.

Chapter Two – Letterman Army Hospital

Only about two percent of the world's human population has green eyes.

Chapter Three – A Ray of Hope

Blood transfusions were not performed at front-line medical facilities because it was not known how to store blood supplies for any useful length of time, especially without refrigeration.

Chapter Four – Captivated

For an interesting essay concerning the model for "Miss Republic," the Robert Ingersoll Aitken sculpture of the Goddess Victory that stands atop the Dewey Monument in Union Square, see https://www.foundsf.org/index.php?title=Alma_Spreckels.

Jamie's all-day cable car pass cost five cents in April

1917. Five cents then would be worth approximately $1.22 in January 2024 dollars.

In general, what cost a dollar in April 1917 would cost about $24.48 in January 2024 dollars. See https://goodcalcu lators.com/inflation-calculator/.

Chapter Eight – The Point of No Return

The term "bra" did not come into use until the 1930s. The German Christine Hardt patented the first modern brassiere in 1889. In 1912, Sigmund Lindauer from Stuttgart-Bad Cannstatt, Germany, developed a brassiere for mass production and patented it in 1913. Most fashion-conscious women in the US and Europe were regularly wearing brassieres by 1917.

Chapter Twelve – A Promise to Keep

Ainsley's stash of fifteen dollars was a significant sum in April 1917. It would be worth about $367.16 in January 2024 dollars.

Chapter 13 - Neighbors

The Scottish scientist Alexander Fleming discovered penicillin in 1928. It wasn't until 1942 that it came into common use to combat bacterial infections.

Chapter Fourteen – An Officer's Duty

Julia Stimson (May 26, 1881 – September 30, 1948) was an American nurse credited as one of several persons who brought nursing to the status of a profession. After volunteering for military service in April 1917, she served as the chief nurse at AEF Base Hospital 21, Rouen. For her service in France during the war, the United States government awarded Stimson the Distinguished Service Medal, presented by General John J. Pershing. Other nations bestowed the British Royal Red Cross, 1st Class; the French Medaille de la Reconnaissance Françoise; the Medaille d'Honneur de l'Hygiene Publique; and the International Red Cross Florence Nightingale Medal on Stimson. In July 1919, Stimson returned to the United States and was named acting superintendent, and later permanent superintendent, of the Army Nurse Corps and dean of the Army School of Nursing. In 1920, she received the relative rank of major, the first woman in the U.S. Army to obtain that rank. (It wasn't until 1947 that nurses were granted fully commissioned rank.) Though Stimson retired from the Army in 1937, she returned after the outbreak of World War II as chief of the Nursing Council on National Defense and recruited a new generation of women to serve as nurses. She was promoted to full colonel in 1948, shortly before her death. Stimson served as President of the American Nursing Association from 1938 to 1944 and was inducted into that association's Hall of Fame in 1976.

Chapter Fifteen – Introductions

Olive drab had been the standard US Army uniform color before the war, but olive drab was produced by German dye, which American manufacturers were unable to reproduce. By necessity, khaki became the new standard during America's involvement in the Great War.

Chapter Sixteen – The Great Migration

The majority of African Americans did not identify with the term "black" until well after the Great War.

"The Great Migration" usually refers to either immigrants to the colonies after the Mayflower arrived in 1620 or, more to the point of this story, to the movement of six million African Americans out of the rural Southern United States to the urban Northeast, Midwest, and West that occurred between 1916 and 1970. I have used "The Great Migration" as a counter-example, where white men move from one end of Ward 321 to the other end because they want to be near an African American.

Early in the war, anesthetics were in desperately short supply. Eventually, scientists at St. Andrew's University found ways to synthesize a range of anesthetics, which lessened but did not eliminate the shortage.

Chapter Seventeen – Unification

The first trigger-switch, pistol-grip, corded, portable drill was patented in 1917 by Black & Decker.

Chapter Eighteen – The Brotherhood of Loss

The baseball players and manager who were part of the first unassisted triple play in major league history were as follows:

Cornelius "Neal" Ball (April 22, 1881 – October 15, 1957)

Denton True "Cy" Young (March 29, 1867 – November 4, 1955).

Charles Francis "Heinie" Wagner (September 23, 1880 – March 20, 1943).

Garland "Jake" Stahl (April 13, 1879 – September 18, 1922). Alumnus of the University of Illinois. One of the few college graduates in the majors.

Ambrose Moses McConnell (April 29, 1883 – May 20, 1942).

Manager Frederick Lovett Lake (October 16, 1866 – November 24, 1931). A Canadian.

Chapter Nineteen – A Prayer Granted

For headlines throughout the years, see the historical website Newspapers.com.

Chapter Twenty – A Life Taken

For information about the Spanish Influenza pandemic, see_http://virus.stanford.edu/uda/fluscimed.html : "The Medical and Scientific Conceptions of Influenza."

Chapter Twenty - Butch

The U.S. Army Male Officer Class A Green Uniform was the Army's primary Service uniform for over sixty years, from its approval in 1954 until its mandatory wear-out date of 30 September 2015. Obviously, that was not the uniform Jamie wore. It is, however, the uniform with which most readers who have not served in the army are familiar. In the era of WW1, officers' uniforms were khaki since that color of dye was readily available at the time.

It wasn't until 1944 that the now-familiar neck ribbon replaced the suspension ribbon for both the Army and Navy versions of the Medal of Honor.

Award of the Purple Heart, which features George Washington's silhouette, was suspended between the end of the Revolutionary War and when it was revived on 22 February 1932 by Executive Order on the 200th Anniversary of George Washington's birth (War Department General Order No. 3, dated 22 February 1932).

Shell shock/Combat Stress Reaction (Battle Fatigue)/Post-traumatic Stress Disorder. Although these conditions are not identical, they are strongly related.

With respect to shell shock, see https://en.wikipedia.org/wiki/Shell_shock

Concerning combat stress reaction, sometimes a precursor to PTSD, see https://en.wikipedia.org/wiki/Combat_stress_reaction

For battle fatigue, see: https://en.wikipedia.org/wiki/Battle_fatigue

Concerning post-traumatic stress disorder, see

https://www.nimh.nih.gov/health/topics/post-traumatic-stress-disorder-ptsd

General George Washington established the US Army's Judge Advocate General's (JAG) Corps on 29 July 1775.

For a brief history of the Pennsylvania Hospital School of Nursing for Men, see http://www.uphs.upenn.edu/paharc/collections/exhibits/nursing/.

Trenches were dug in a zigzag pattern so the deadly effect of a shell impact would not propagate from end to end.

Chapter Twenty-Two – Horror Stories

In the Golden Gate numbers game, in May 1919, a ten-cent buy-in would be worth about $2.45 in January 2024 dollars. The $60 payout for a match would be worth about $1468.65 in January 2024 dollars.

Initially, San Quentin Prison housed both men and women.

Chapter Twenty-Three – Dealing with the Devil

My character, Matt Kavanaugh, is loosely based on Johnny Torrio, a mobster who helped build the Chicago Outfit in the 1920s. Torrio's criminal empire was inherited by his protégé, Al Capone.

Torrio had several nicknames, primarily "The Fox" for his cunning and finesse. Torrio impressed authorities and chroniclers with his business acumen and diplomatic skills. It was said that as an organizer and administrator of underworld affairs, Johnny Torrio was unsurpassed in the annals of American crime; he was probably the nearest thing to a real criminal mastermind this country has ever suffered. Although Torrio ran legitimate businesses, his main concern in his earlier years was the numbers game, supplemented by incomes from bookmaking, loan sharking, hijacking, prostitution, and opium trafficking. Once Prohibition went into effect, Torrio's income from bootlegging skyrocketed.

Torrio was wary of being drawn into gang wars and tried to negotiate agreements over territory between rival crime groups. Torrio supported the creation of a national body that would prevent the sort of all-out turf wars between gangs that had broken out in Chicago and New York.

In January 1925, Torrio was shot several times. After recovering, he effectively retired and handed control of the Outfit to Capone. At age 26, Capone became the boss of an organization that included illegal breweries and a transportation network that reached into Canada and was under the protection of crooked politicians and law-enforcement officials.

With Torrio out of the picture, Capone used more

violent measures to increase revenue. An establishment that refused to purchase liquor from him often got blown up, and as many as 100 people were killed in such bombings during the 1920s. Rivals saw Capone as responsible for the proliferation of brothels in Chicago.

The criminal empire Torrio handed over to Capone in 1925 grossed about $70,000,000 yearly (over $1.7 billion in January 2024 dollars) from bootleg alcohol, gambling, and prostitution.

My character, Sonny Kavanaugh, Matt's nephew, is loosely based on Al Capone. Big Al—or Scarface, a name he hated and one no one would dare use in his presence—was much more violent and far less rational than his mentor, Johnny Torrio. Many volumes have been written about Al Capone. There's no need for me to add more here.

The Marianas Trench is in the western Pacific Ocean, about 124 miles east of the Mariana Islands. It is the deepest oceanic trench on Earth. It was first sounded using a weighted rope during the Challenger expedition in 1875. A depth of 26,850 feet was recorded.

The $50,000 annual earnings of the business associates Matt Kavanaugh planned to invite to the DVET reception would be worth about $1.2 million in January 2024 dollars.

$15,000 in personal income tax in 1920 would be worth about $367,163 in January 2024 dollars.

Kavanaugh's $10,000 seed donation to the DVET would be worth about $244,775 in January 2024 dollars.

The average salary in the US of about $1,200 a year in 1920 would be worth about $29,373.05 in January 2024 dollars.

The $2,500 donation Kavanaugh was going to ask his associates to make would be worth about $61,194 in January 2024 dollars.

In 1953, Treasury Decision 6038 authorized a name change from "the Bureau of Internal Revenue" to "the Internal Revenue Service."

In working out the details of Kavanaugh's tax scheme, I used the equivalent of today's IRS Form 1040 and tax tables from 1920.

The $875 it would cost Kavanaugh for each of his business associates who purchased an inflated donation receipt would be worth about $21,418 in January 2024 dollars.

The $58,750 initial funding of the DVET would be worth about $1.4 million in January 2024 dollars.

The $21,375 of the initial DVET funding that Kavanaugh would be donating would be worth around $523,207 in January 2024 dollars.

In 1920, at the University of Pennsylvania, room and board averaged around $400 annually. Textbooks, around $40. And general fees (whatever they were) were around $20. That's $460 a year (about $11,260 in January 2024 dollars), excluding tuition. See https://archives.upenn.edu/exhibits/penn-history/tuition/tuition-1920-1929.

Initially, tuition was free at the University of California. Starting in 1921, California residents were required to pay an 'incidental fee' of $25 per year. Tuition for non-California residents was $75 a year. Not to be outdone, around the same time, contrary to Leland Stanford's intentions, Stanford University began levying a tuition fee of $40 per quarter. In contrast, an Ivy League engineering degree cost $300 a year for tuition alone at the University of Pennsylvania. With room and board, textbooks, general fees, and tuition, the total was $750 a year, or about $18,358 in January 2024 dollars, whereas tuition alone for a year at UPenn cost about $66,104 in 2024. Clearly, inflation is only a small part of the soaring cost of higher education.

Acknowledgments

I thank the following for all their help. My wife, Mary, for more than I can ever say. My mentor, author Nancy Rue. My writing coach, author Tim Shoemaker. My medical advisor, Dr. Lawrence Lesnak. My business consultant, cover and interior designer, author Gordon Saunders.

I also thank all those who have read my writing and encouraged me, especially Greg Sunset, Tadd Woods, Brain Shuman, Dr. Tony Rollins, PhD., Graham Cliff, PGA, Detectives Eric White and Tyler Josifek, and artist William Wyman.

About the Author

William R. DeHay, 'Bill' to his friends and family, holds degrees in math, psychology, meteorology, and law. Before becoming a full-time writer, Bill was a naval intelligence officer, an aerospace engineer, and an attorney. He currently volunteers with the Aurora, Colorado, Police Department's homicide unit, reviewing cold cases, surveillance videos and cell phone data.

Bill's education in psychology and law and his military experience bring authenticity to this and follow-on novels. Bill lives in Colorado with his wife, Mary, and Bombay cat, Timmy.

Bill can't quite remember, but he thinks he won this particular game of chess with Timmy's predecessor, Forrest—who, evidently, didn't hold it against him.

www.ingramcontent.com/pod-product-compliance
Lightning Source LLC
Chambersburg PA
CBHW020858060726
47591CB00004B/990